The
SWORD

JEAN JOHNSON

BERKLEY SENSATION, NEW YORK

THE BERKLEY PUBLISHING GROUP
Published by the Penguin Group
Penguin Group (USA) Inc.
375 Hudson Street, New York, New York 10014, USA
Penguin Group (Canada), 90 Eglinton Avenue East, Suite 700, Toronto, Ontario M4P 2Y3, Canada
(a division of Pearson Penguin Canada Inc.)
Penguin Books Ltd., 80 Strand, London WC2R 0RL, England
Penguin Group Ireland, 25 St. Stephen's Green, Dublin 2, Ireland (a division of Penguin Books Ltd.)
Penguin Group (Australia), 250 Camberwell Road, Camberwell, Victoria 3124, Australia
(a division of Pearson Australia Group Pty. Ltd.)
Penguin Books India Pvt. Ltd., 11 Community Centre, Panchsheel Park, New Delhi—110 017, India
Penguin Group (NZ), Cnr. Airborne and Rosedale Roads, Albany, Auckland 1310, New Zealand
(a division of Pearson New Zealand Ltd.)
Penguin Books (South Africa) (Pty.) Ltd., 24 Sturdee Avenue, Rosebank, Johannesburg 2196,
South Africa

Penguin Books Ltd., Registered Offices: 80 Strand, London WC2R 0RL, England

This book is an original publication of The Berkley Publishing Group.

Copyright © 2007 by G. Jean Johnson
Cover art by Franco Accornero
Cover design by George Long
Text design by Kristin del Rosario

First edition: February 2007

Library of Congress Cataloging-in-Publication Data

Johnson, Jean, 1972–
     The sword / Jean Johnson.
       p. cm.
     ISBN-13 978-0-425-21440-4
     I. Title.

PS3610.O355S96 2007
813'.6—dc22   2006048371

PRINTED IN THE UNITED STATES OF AMERICA

10   9   8   7   6   5   4   3

ACKNOWLEDGMENTS

I must thank my parents, Deni and Tom, without whom I would not exist. They probably won't ever read this book (it's not their cuppa), but they have encouraged me to write through the years. I definitely need to thank Stormi, AlexandraLynch, and NotSoSaintly, for their talents as beta-editors; these ladies are jewels! And, of course, I would like to thank the Mob of Irate Torch-Wielding Fans, for waving their torches in my direction to encourage me to write faster (and for obeying the local fire safety codes while doing so); Iulia, Marius, and Tibi, for their encouragements from afar; Cindy, for asking me if I had anything original I wanted to submit for publication; and JustJeanette, Piper, Stellarluna, Liz, Nylima, Longtail, Alienator, Okonchristy, Qestral, Seth, HD, Poobah, and Pern, for being my sounding boards.

. . . If anyone is interested in joining the Mob of Irate Torch-Wielding Fans (and is eighteen years or older; sorry, but you have to be an adult to join), you can visit us at http://groups.yahoo.com/group/MoITWF.

Hugs,
Jean

ONE

The Eldest Son shall bear this weight:
If ever true love he should feel
Disaster shall come at her heel
And Katan will fail to aid
When Sword in sheath is claimed by Maid

W hat have you done?"

"Who is this woman?"

"There's a *woman* in here?"

"Why is she here?"

"Dammit, Morg, you *know* the Curse! I don't care if the rest of us have it better, you *know* what Saber's gonna say!"

"Hey, I'm not too eager for my own part of the Curse! But shouldn't we listen to the brat? He *is* the most powerful of us."

Morganen folded his arms across his chest and waited while the six of his seven brothers finished griping and grumbling. When they were all staring at him expectantly, silently, he finally spoke. The youngest of the eight, he was the most gifted of all their people, and they knew it; what they could do to him physically for this, he could do to them eight times over magically. It was simply his duty—his part of the Curse, after all—to see that, at the proper time and place, the whole thing was set in motion. *And so it begins . . .*

"Koranen, if you'd get your head out of your cinders, you'd notice this woman has been badly burned. Since fire is your expertise, I suggest you start using your powers to heal her. And be circumspect," he added as his twin eyed the lightly clad female sprawled unconscious at their feet. "She might be your sister-in-law soon. You don't want one of the rest of us beating the *trakk* out of you for impropriety if she turns out to be one of our Destined wives."

The second youngest, Morganen's older twin, rolled his eyes and knelt by the woman lying in the middle of Morg's workroom. Sparks flickered up from his hands as his fingers began to glow, hovering mere inches over her singed flesh and clothes. Morganen looked away from his twin, up at the others in his workroom.

"As for the rest of you, I suggest we do everything we can to avoid Saber for a little while."

"Why do you wish to avoid me?"

The remaining, unoccupied five brothers instantly clustered around the youngest two twins, in front of the body on the floor. Doing their best to shield it from their eldest brother's view, even Rydan moved, though he was the slowest to do so.

Saber fixed his eyes on his brothers. Each one was different in coloring, even though all eight had been born in four sets of twins. His steel grey eyes and honey blond hair were different from his twin's golden eyes and brown hair, though Wolfer had the same chest-length locks he bore. The next set of twins, Dominor and Evanor, were as different as night and day, for Dominor had blue eyes and dark brown hair, and Evanor had brown eyes and light blond hair.

The third set were also an unlikely pair: Trevan had coppery-strawberry hair and green eyes; Rydan had blue-black hair and eyes so dark he looked like the night personified . . . and it was odd that the light-shunning sixth son was there, given the midmorning hour, though he had probably come up through the basement passages linking all of the castle's outer towers to the main keep.

Koranen's rich auburn hair could barely be seen through the tangle of his brothers, his hazel eyes fixed on whatever the others were shielding. The youngest of all the twins, Morganen, stood on the far side of the group, arms folded defiantly across his chest, his light brown hair pulled back in a knot to keep it out of his way. The dark band of cloth keeping his hair out of his aquamarine eyes was visibly damp from whatever major magic working he had somehow managed to cast without Saber noticing. Reminding Saber for a moment that Morg was not a young man to tangle with, even if he was the youngest of the eight of them.

None of his seven brothers spoke, though Saber could sense Koranen doing something beyond that tangle of lower limbs. What it was, he couldn't tell . . . but something stuck out just a little beyond Evanor's calf. Something out of the ordinary. Saber glanced down and focused on it.

It was a foot. A small, bare foot. With a shapely, if soot-smeared, ankle. Not a bony one.

It was not a male foot.

His brothers were attempting to hide a woman from him, when women were strictly forbidden on Nightfall Isle.

It didn't take much effort to figure out how she had arrived on the island that the eight of them alone occupied. Since exiling the brothers to the isle, none of the mainlanders would even think of sending a woman, let alone allowing one to come here. Which left his youngest, sweat-sheened brother as the most likely culprit for her presence. If she couldn't arrive easily by physical means, then she had to have arrived by magical ones . . . and Morganen was the most powerful mage among them. He could easily cast some sort of transportational spell without Saber noticing.

And they were in Morganen's tower, after all.

"Morganen." Saber held the eyes of his youngest brother, kind-hearted but reckless, in his opinion. Dangerously reckless. "Send her back. *Now*."

"I cannot."

"I don't care what you think you can or cannot do—" Saber broke off in frustration.

Their siblings stood in the way, trapped awkwardly between the youngest and the eldest. Even the stoic, normally expressionless Rydan looked a little uncomfortable, as Morganen replied, "She will burn to death, if I do. Shall I send her back, only to hear her screams echoing through time and space for my effort? She has lost her home and her livelihood to her enemies, Saber. She has no family to go to, no one to turn to, no sanctuary to hide in but here."

Saber threw his hand at the brother-shrouded figure on the ground. "Her presence could threaten the end of Katani civilization! Isn't it enough that we have been condemned simply for being born the Eight Brothers? Do you want more? Should I kill myself so the Song cannot come true, just so you can have a woman living on this island?"

None of the others answered him. No one dared look at him, whose verse in the Song was the most threatening. Save Morganen, who dared quite a lot, sometimes.

"Would you condemn her out of your fears as surely as the others have condemned us out of theirs?" the youngest countered calmly, if pointedly.

"Send her back," Saber growled, disliking the comparison. "For her *own* safety."

"She will die."

"Send her elsewhere, then!"

"She has nowhere else to go, right now. Like us. At least, not until I can scry for a safe place to send her."

Saber wasn't a cruel man. He could smell the odor of soot and char in the air. He also knew his second youngest brother was finishing the healing of the damage that distant fire had done. And he knew his youngest sibling wouldn't have risked the Curse of the Eight for anything less than a life-or-death need for the woman in question. "Then keep her away from me. She may stay, *temporarily* . . . but *only* if you find a place for her to go. Quickly. And keep her out of view of the merchant ships!"

The others scattered, none wanting to claim responsibility. Even Koranen fled a few moments later, as soon as his work was done. Leaving Saber alone in the stone-lined workroom with the unmovable Morganen. And the woman.

He really didn't want to look at her, though he did anyway. It was his duty as the eldest to know all of the dangers to their family and do what he could to remove or to minimize them. Having a woman on the island wasn't exactly minimizing their difficulties. Dangerous though it was, Saber needed to know exactly what he and his brothers had to face, ever since they had been exiled to Nightfall three years ago . . . when the meddlesome Morganen's powers had come into full strength and sealed the interpretation of the Curse of the Eight on all of their heads, by the will of the High Council of Mages of Katan.

Reluctantly, warily, Saber glanced down again; this time, there was no one between him and the figure on the floor to block his view of her. The woman was breathing unsteadily, as if caught in a nightmare. Here and there, her skin was flushed pink from Koranen's healing efforts. One set of fingers was curled in a fist near her head, and her strawberry blond hair still looked a little singed in places.

She was clad in loose, striped trousers, light blue and white, with some kind of matching, buttoned tunic that covered her from throat to wrists. It, too, was singed and blackened, and bits of her skin showed through, mainly the reddish-pink patches that would fade back to freckled pale like the rest of her flesh in barely a week or two. Koranen had done his usual good job of healing her burns, from the look of things. Nothing indecent was exposed, but she was restless, and there was a patch of striped fabric missing on her ribs that threatened to shift higher with each twitch.

Against his will, Saber moved closer. He watched that brow furrow, that strawberry mouth tighten, could see those fingers whiten as her muscles twitched and tensed. She was lean, not overly curvaceous . . . and she was beautiful, despite the fading burns and soot and the odd clothes on her body.

Morganen watched his brother, careful to conceal any signs of satisfaction from his expression and posture; he was younger than the rest of them, but no fool. Any moment now, the temporary sleep spell he had placed on the hysterical woman—her screams had summoned his other brothers, and belatedly their eldest—would wear off. Any second now, she would wake up and start their Destined fates rolling.

Her brow pinched, her teeth sinking into her lower lip.

"Is she in pain?" Saber murmured, as she twitched and whimpered, unable to help himself.

"She was badly burned," Morganen confided, equally quiet. "Her home was collapsing around her; she was trapped in her bedroom, awakened too late in the fire to save herself. Part of the roof collapsed on her; that was what woke her up, I think. I do not think she has any broken bones, but my twin only had time to heal the damage done by the flames; not her bruises, nor her memories. Just the burns she has suffered, though that is more than enough, for now. His skill with burns is something all of us have been thankful for at one point or another, living with him."

"Why is she not awake now?" Saber demanded under his breath, looking up at his brother from where he had crouched near the woman. Careful to not speak too loud.

Morganen didn't let any of his satisfaction show. Three years without a woman, and his twenty-nine-year-old brother was drawn to her even more than any of the other siblings. Morganen had studied this woman long and carefully to make certain she would be perfect for Saber. "I think she is still caught up in the nightmare of her near-death. Such a trauma requires comforting, to ease its pain."

Saber snorted and rose. "She can comfort hersel—"

The woman jerked and screamed even as Saber moved, scrabbling to get herself at least somewhat upright. She ended up twisting onto her knees, slapping at her flesh, at her hair and clothes, screaming repeatedly . . . The harsh yells trailed off quickly, as her eyes finally registered the real world around her, not the nightmarish one she had apparently been reliving.

Her breath caught as she stared at the border of white marble and light, at the granite stone floor under her palms, the stone walls lined with glass-fronted stone shelves that were stuffed with books. She turned to look around her. At the sight of Morganen less than a body-length from her, she shrieked again, throwing herself back and away from the unexpected, too-close apparition, and scrambled to her feet.

That made her stagger right into Saber. He caught her to keep both of them from being knocked over. She yelled something and whirled on him, thumping and tugging and doing *something* as she hollered that yanked him right off his feet and flung him roughly over her hip and onto the floor, as if he weighed less than a sack of flour.

A different noise broke through her unintelligible yells. Morganen, shoulders quaking, cheeks reddening, laughed breathlessly hard at the sight of his brother sprawled and stunned on the floor. Flushing from something entirely other than laughter, Saber shoved himself upright, ignoring the woman as he stalked his brother.

A shouted demand cut through Saber's determination to make his brother pay for laughing at his unexpected humiliation. Both men turned toward the cause of the unwarranted mirth. She was yanking down her scorched tunic and rattling off a babble of completely foreign words.

Saber looked at his shorter brother, frowning in confusion. "She doesn't speak Katani?"

Letting out a sigh, mouth still tempted to twitch up at the corners, Morganen shook his head. "Nor any language I know of. I saw her peril while I was scrying in distant realms—Jinga! Quick, catch her!"

Saber spun around in time to see the woman edging toward the workroom door. She saw that her movement had been spotted and whirled for the hall beyond. "Catch her?"

"*Catch* her!" Morganen repeated. "I'll have to give her a translation potion, and I obviously can't do it with a moving target!"

Letting out a sound of disgust, Saber loped after the woman. Visions of chaining the woman in the dungeon of the ancient palace they resided in danced through his head, as he spotted a bare foot scrabbling up the staircase at the end of the hall. Racing up the stairs after her, he saw her dart off at the first landing and followed, pleased with her mistake.

The eight brothers' workrooms were placed in the outer wall towers, in case one of the magically gifted brothers did something that might do a lot of damage. The only doors out of each tower were the two letting out onto the curved walls that stretched between the towers and the hidden doors that led to underground passages. This particular level simply let out into a short hall that bisected the tower and gave access to four wedge-shaped storage rooms. All of which were locked, as some of the things Morganen created were too dangerous to come across casually, even by his well-trained brothers.

Saber watched her yank on the handles to the third and fourth doors at the other end of the hallway, then whip around and face him, aquamarine eyes wide in that panic-paled face. She rattled off something in her native tongue that was probably the equivalent to "Don't come any closer!" One hand was thrust out to ward him off. He flinched, expecting her to hurl magic, but she only hurled more foreign words and shook her finger at him, backing up.

There was nowhere to go, though. Even the window behind her in the far wall of the tower was only a narrow, recessed arrow-loop. Big enough to illuminate the hall and its doors with daylight, and to put one of her slender arms through, but not large enough for the rest of her body. Continuing his advance, Saber watched her warn him futilely again, then position her body and hands in a funny stance—like she was ready for a fistfight, sort of, but with her knees bent and her fingers flattened. A strange stance, but graceful. He tried not to notice the way it accented her hip and waist, or the curve of her nearest calf underneath her faded trousers.

He was tired of her incomprehensible shouting and irritated by her unwelcome presence. "Come. I will take you downstairs and have my brother deal with you." Thrusting out his hand, Saber waited for her to take it. She eyed it warily, only shifting her stance a little for better balance. He gestured with his hand, impatient with her very presence. "Come! Or I will throw you in the dungeon *regardless* of whether you can speak!"

His half-shouted demand made her flinch. And attack. She thrust his hand aside, kicked him in one knee, as he quickly shifted both together to protect his groin—and flipped him again! A preposterous idea, when she was a full half-foot shorter than him and couldn't weigh three-quarters of what he did . . . but Saber still found himself sprawled on the stone-lined floor. Twisting onto his side, he saw her running for the door back to the stairs, escaping again. He threw out his hand.

"*Sh'kadeth!*"

The door to the hallway slammed shut in her face and locked with an audible *snick* under his spell-wrought command. The woman gasped and jerked back before she ran into the aged wooden surface, then backed up slowly, whispering something with a tone of deep fear.

Shoving to his feet, Saber stalked up to her silently, swung her around, and threw her over his shoulder as she screeched in shock, anger, and fear. Her fists thumped on his back as he waved his hand past the door handle, disabling the spell and swinging the panel open again. When she hit him again—hard enough to make him wince, since she thumped her double-clasped hands right on his spine— Saber smacked her on her backside, where it stuck up by his chin, ignoring how thoroughly curved and feminine his target was.

Her hollering snapped into a gasp of outrage, and she yelled something else, hitting him harder. He smacked her again with the flat of his hand as he descended the steps, yelling back himself, "*Behave!*"

I can't believe Morganen has done this to me. This woman is going straight back t—

"—Yeoww!! By *Jinga!*"

Her teeth had somehow managed to sink into the muscles of his back, making him almost miss the last step. She let go long enough to draw in a breath and yell at him some more in her strange tongue as he stumbled. Saber yanked her off his shoulder the moment he had his balance back and was safe on the ground floor. Shoving the staggering woman against the far wall, he pinned her there, growling in a way that would make his twin, Wolfer, proud. She tried to knee him as she struggled; he fixed that problem by pinning her thighs and hips to the wall with his own. Drawing in a breath, Saber prepared to blast her with an angry invective.

The fear in those wide blue green eyes stopped him. Sure, she struggled and yelled at him, but she didn't dare move her lower body. Only her arms struggled where he had her wrists pinned to the stone wall. If she had moved anything lower, Saber realized he would have grown quite hard from the friction and given her a real reason to harbor the feminine fears he could read in her eyes.

It also made him realize that she was bone-thin, maybe even fragile, despite the tough way she had managed to fight. His knee was still throbbing from that strong, well-placed kick . . . but her wrists felt like too much pressure might make them snap. Holding her tightly enough to still her struggles made him feel like a bully. Just for going after her without trying to calm her down, snapping orders at her, and grabbing her like a thoughtless brute.

It wasn't a pleasant set of impressions. It was made even less pleasant by the way her eyes gleamed, then threatened to water with tears, how her struggles had more or less stopped and been replaced by trembling. Cursing—glad she didn't yet understand any of the less than gentlemanly words he used—Saber pulled back from her, uncomfortable with the remorse he felt.

She wasn't a complete waterpot, though; the woman immediately jerked on her wrists to get herself free. He lost one wrist and almost the other one, as she lunged to the side in her attempt to escape. Swearing again, he yanked her back by her fingertips and the edge of her tunic, which ripped by a whole fingerlength at the nearer armhole. Saber flung her over his shoulder again as soon as he had her jerked back within better reach. Making her yelp, then moan.

Now he felt like a heel, one with a major headache coming on. That headache was clearly labeled Meddling Youngest Brother. When the petite, strawberry-blond hellcat bit him again, Saber spanked her one more time. He did, however, duck slightly as he moved along the hall, to make sure, in her struggles to right herself with an indignant shout and more kicking of her legs, she didn't whack her head on the doorframe as they passed through.

"Put her in the octagram. And make sure she *stays* there!" his youngest sibling ordered, not even looking their way as Saber came back into his workroom with his uncooperative burden.

Grumbling under his breath—wincing as she bit him *again*, then thumped that spot with a fist for good measure—Saber strode over to the large expanse of white marble inlaid in the center of the light gray granite flagstones tiling the floor. The octagonal figure had nothing to hold her in place, though. "I'll put a confining spell on her."

His brother shook his head, not even bothering to look Saber's way as he flipped through several books, looking for the right spell. "Please don't; the energies would only get in the way. This is not a language in the lexicon, Saber; it is not a matter of casting a transposition spell between our language and hers as we can do with all of the other languages known by the Katani. Her language is not known by anyone in this world, as far as I have been able to ascertain.

"No . . ." Morganen mused as much to himself as to his eldest brother. "It will have to be a very complex piece of translational magic, so that she will be able to understand us, and we her. Ultra Tongue, I think. Most of the other spells in my library rely on the languages being a lot more native than hers."

"*Fine*. I'll pin her here with a spell just long enough to go get a table or a chair or something . . . and a bunch of chains," Saber added half under his breath.

"Jinga's sacred ass!" Morganen exclaimed harshly, whirling on his brother, slapping the book in his hands shut with a bang for emphasis. The sharp sound made the woman pinned over his brother's shoulder flinch. "Are you *really* that insensitive and cruel? She's *frightened*, Saber! Scared out of her wits, utterly alone in completely unfamiliar territory, unable to communicate, completely unaware of how she was rescued from a death worse than fate, and you're thinking of *chaining* her? Oh, that's *really* compassionate, Brother!

"Why don't you just grab your sword while you're at it and shove it through her gut, saving her the trouble of having a stroke or a heart attack!" Normally the Mage, as the youngest of the eight sons was nicknamed, was a kind-spoken soul. But when he was riled, his tongue could cut sharper than his eldest brother's sword. Morganen scowled at his flinching eldest kin. "She's a woman alone in a castle with eight men, with no idea how she got here, bruised and battered and in less than decent clothes by most cultural standards—and certainly with no idea of what we're going to do with her! If the others weren't all cowards and hadn't fled, I would rather have someone more sensitive hold her in place. But no, I have to deal with *you*!"

Saber bristled at that. "I am the eldest brother! You will not talk to me in that manner!"

"Then stand there, hold her, and *comfort* her; don't scare her!" his brother shot back. "It isn't going to kill you—or trigger your gods-be-damned Destiny—to show a little understanding and kindness for a few gods-be-damned moments!" Yanking his book open, he turned his back on the pair of them, muttering harshly under his breath in a less than arcane manner.

The woman, still slung over his shoulder, panting from fear and from her exertions, bit him again.

Swearing, Saber yanked her down from his shoulder. To keep her knees from going for his groin, he pinned her squirming legs in the curve of his arm. To keep her arms from thumping him, he confined them to her ribs with his other arm—but he was not actually cradling her to his chest, dammit! It was self-defense, that was all!

Of course, he didn't want to break her arms and legs, so he had to hold her somewhat gently, but still firmly enough to keep her from squirming free. She certainly tried. Pressing her face up against his shoulder to keep her from squirming out of his grasp got him an-other bite in the nearest piece of flesh. His chest. Growling from the pain and the aggravation he was suffering, Saber glared down at her. She shrank back in his arms, eyes on his bared teeth, her aquamarine eyes wide and wary, but the jut of her chin belligerent and defensive.

"Oh, *that* sounds reassuring," his brother drawled sarcastically, attention still buried in his spellbooks. "Stop growling at her!"

"What, do you want me to sing her a gods-be-damned *lullaby*? I could be holding the destruction of Katan in my hands, Morg! You think I'm happy about this? *No women!*" he enunciated. Then had to do his best to keep the woman who wasn't supposed to be there from getting away, struggling hard again at the raising of his voice. "As soon as you're done with this damned spell, you start looking for someplace—anyplace—for her to go!"

"I'll find the right place for her to go, have no fear. *After* I've cast the right translation spell, and after she's had a chance to get her bearings and rest."

"In the *dungeon*," Saber muttered, as she tried to pinch him with the hand wedged closest to his chest.

"Saber! Just hold her still," Morganen ordered him, giving his eldest sibling a dirty look. "It'll take a little while longer."

"If she draws my blood, I'll—ow!—bind her in chains and throw her into the sea myself, to watch her drown! Stop *biting* me!"

Morganen, his back to his brother, knew in exactly which book to look—not the one in his hands, of course—and carefully hid his smile. *About five more minutes should have both of them calm enough, five past that to continue to "look" for the spell, and five more to gather the nec-essary ingredients* . . . Half an hour or so of ensuring their proximity to each other, if he stretched things out a little during the brewing process. If he was careful not to smile where his clearly irritated brother could see it. He wasn't a fool, after all.

TWO

❧❧❧

She was tired, she was bruised, and she was thoroughly pinned to the large stranger's chest. Trapped in a madman's arms, trapped in a madman's house—trapped in a world gone mad—Kelly Doyle finally gave up trying to get free. Neither of the two men seemed to speak plain English, and she had given up trying to remember any of her old high school French, so she couldn't try to see if they spoke that language, either. Of course, they didn't sound like they were speaking French, or Spanish, or German, or any language she recognized. So she lay there, squeezed to borderline bruising, panting and trying desperately not to cry, in the arms of the unnervingly good-looking, overly muscular stranger who was holding her.

It wasn't easy. Some people had bad days. She was having a bad decade. First had come the death of her parents in a collision with a drunk driver, leaving her almost penniless three years before. Then had come the offer of a great job, which had forced her to move away from all of her friends and family, halfway across the country. Then the company employing her had gone bankrupt, and all the employees had been let go a year and a half ago.

So she had tried to profit from her hobbies. She could sew, embroider, and make lace, and had made pillows, framed wall hangings, quilts, rag dolls, and clothing, ranging in style from modern to medieval. The Middle Ages Society had been the one place in her new location and new life where she could make friends quickly through shared interests. Even if the local members started out as complete strangers, she had made a few friends. Such as her closest friend, Hope, who had made Kelly feel more than welcome in the local branch of re-creation enthusiasts.

Her association with the medieval society in the tiny Midwest town had meant being associated with paganism and witchcraft and all sorts of other completely erroneous, bigoted assumptions, even though the Middle Ages Society was actually designed for historical education only.

Anonymous hate mail had started arriving in Kelly's mailbox. And then those notes had been tacked to her door. Whispers around town had driven most of her trade down to what the tourists brought in. And, one evening, someone had shoved her into a wall, while she was walking home from the movie theater. She had whirled on her attacker and fought him off, glad that her parents had enrolled her in kung fu when she was younger. The man had worn a mask and had run away.

When she reported the incident to the police, they suggested she had deliberately done something to draw her attacker's attention. They had sided with the general attitude of the others in the town, preventing her from getting any real help against the persecution mounting against her, and had dismissed her claim to attend to "more important" crimes. In a town where the most excitement was the occasional drunk or shoplifter eating fruit without paying for it at the grocery store, they had dismissed and ignored her complaints.

For a little while, Kelly had hoped that her going to the police had warned off whomever was tormenting her. Then new notes had started coming. And along with them, photocopies of old textbook pages, reciting the history of women who had been accused of witchcraft—hung in England and the colonies, burned in Scotland and France.

She had stepped outside one morning to find a hangman's noose dangling from her porch roof. She had gone outside to sweep off the porch and open the living room-dining room section that she had converted into a shop for her business. The noose had a note pinned to it, demanding in cutout newspaper letters that "the Witch" leave, Or Else. Angry, she had taken the note to the police, but they hadn't done anything beyond eyeing it and pointing out that it neither mentioned her name specifically nor identified what "Or Else" actually meant.

"Or Else" turned out to be waking in bed to burning hot pain a week later, with her house in flames around her. And then, while her lungs had scorched, as her flesh had seared, as the pain had grown unbearable, the flames too high to see any way out of the inferno— something had shaken the world upside down, rattled it around, dumped it out with a jerk . . . and she had awakened and found herself *here*. She must have fainted the first time, because Kelly remembered herself screaming from pain, shock, and fear, until a blackness had swept through her, blanking out everything for a little while.

Something beyond her comprehension had happened while she had been unconscious, however. Because though her clothing was still singed, her skin was just barely pink rather than blistered and burning. Now she was in something that had the look and feel of a castle, in the arms of a man wearing breeches and a sleeveless tunic who was arguing with a similarly clad man, all in a room that was lit by glowing white balls caught in claw-tipped iron poles set around the perimeter of the room. Those lights were suspended in their claw-cages in such a way that she could not see the cords that could provide power for their translucent white light . . .

Maybe they were battery powered or had the power cables running up through the floor directly into one of the supporting iron feet. But that door upstairs had closed *and locked*, with no sign of a spring or a machine or anything, not even a remote control, to trigger it. *That* was creepy to contemplate.

Kelly bit down on her lower lip to keep from crying. She might be bruised half to death, pinned in an uncomfortable mockery of being cradled against a completely unintelligible and thoroughly unfriendly stranger's chest, but she would fry in h—*wrong analogy*, she told herself as her eyes stung again. Just a short while ago, if she hadn't gone completely mad, she *had* been frying in a living hell—along with everything she had owned, the house she had mortgaged herself to the hilt for, and the business she had struggled for a year to keep going, barely able to pay the bills and keep herself fed in a too-hostile world.

At least the man holding her wasn't shouting at her or the other man anymore, and he wasn't hitting her or doing anything else but holding her starved, bruised body. She could only hope that the lack of attention being paid to her was because he and his friend hadn't thought of doing something even worse to her than she had previously experienced. Like raping her. Kelly didn't have much energy left to fight either of them off. For breakfast, she had only eaten a potato and half of a cheap, homemade granola bar. She couldn't always afford lunch and dinner.

She was a pathetic, pajama-clad mess . . .

Oh, great. Self-pity, she thought as her eyes stung again and her vision blurred. Kelly shut her eyes, but that only squeezed the liquid out; any liquid out of the eye was a tear, which was bad enough. Two of them would mean she was crying. Which she didn't want to do.

Keeping her eyes shut, Kelly prayed that the man holding her wouldn't notice, or worse, and that her already unsteady breathing wouldn't start to hitch with a sob or two, making it irredeemably official. While she had cried at the death of her parents, she had struggled not to cry at the death of her lost office job. Employment could always be found. Or be made.

She had tried not to cry when the harassing had begun, because her tormentors would have loved to see her break down under their vicious, anonymous attacks. She had tried not to cry when the police had brushed off her account of the attack and her reports of harassment. She had tried very hard not to cry at the noose dangling from her porch, because she was determined to make none of these things worth crying over.

It didn't work. Her breath hitched. She bit her lower lip, then pressed them both tightly together. Her nose sniffled as she drew in a breath. The arms and chest bracing her shifted a little, making her humiliation even worse, because that surely meant he had noticed. Doubly worse, because, as a pale-skinned, freckled redhead, even if only a strawberry blond redhead, crying always made her face blotchy; Kelly was woman enough to hate being blotchy when cradled in the arms of a handsome man, even an unhappy stranger, however frightening her situation was.

The man holding her shifted again, then groaned and muttered. She couldn't understand a word, but the tone was clear, that universal male one used to say "oh, great, now she's crying!" or something vaguely like it. The other man murmured something back in a "don't pay any attention to it" tone—and then something crashed.

She shrieked, eyes flying open, limbs flailing to get her free and away from the frightening, unexpected sound. The man holding her grunted, snarled, and managed to pin her again, this time angled away from him instead of toward him, because of her struggling. She had a view of curved, broken glass that the other man was picking up gingerly from the floor. Something green, dried, and leafy was mixed in with the shards, apparently from a broken jar. The motions of his crouched body were reflected in a rather large, broad cheval mirror not far away.

The man holding her growled something to the other one in a "hurry up, or I'll drop her deliberately" tone, and the other one returned something in a tone so calmly level, so nonchalant and only half-attentive, she couldn't guess what the nature of his reply was. If she hadn't been pinned so effectively, her back against the bigger man's chest, she would have tried to squirm free. If she weren't exhausted—physically, mentally, and emotionally—from the turmoil of her life over the past few years and these incomprehensible last few minutes, she might have had the energy to struggle in earnest.

Not that Kelly knew where she could have run to. One simply didn't go from a bed in the middle of a burning, collapsing inferno of a house to a medieval castle chamber that looked like some kind of magician's lair. Not in a sane and sensible world. Not in *her* world, at any rate. She wasn't crying anymore—being held so awkwardly seemed to cure her of the urge—but she did have to sniff a couple of times, as the unshed tears in her eyes finished draining into her nose. No doubt her skin was awfully blotchy by now, too.

And why am I thinking about my skin tone, when I'm god knows where, with a pair of men doing god knows what?

The other man finished taking care of the mess made by the dropped jar or whatever, then carefully used the few leaves that hadn't touched the floor in the accident, throwing them with a pair of glass tweezers into a large ceramic goblet that he had been muttering over and filling with other odd things. That goblet was now full of something muddy colored; it puffed a funny, opalescent mushroom cloud when the leaves disappeared below the liquid that rested just under the brim. Kelly stared; she'd never seen that particular trick before.

Shifting away from the workbench he was standing at, the second man carried the goblet toward her, slowed, eyed the man holding her, and shook his head disgustedly. He glared pointedly at the larger, somewhat older man who was holding her and rattled off a string of instructions that got her more or less righted in the bigger man's arms. Into a drinking position.

Eyeing that cup very warily, Kelly had visions of assorted date-rape drugs dancing in her head. When he held it up to her mouth, she shook her head hard, sealing her lips tightly. The man holding the goblet, his light brown hair drawn back in an odd style for a man, in a bun-knot at the back of his head, sighed and muttered something to the man holding her, the one with chest-length, lighter, honey-golden hair.

They argued back and forth a few moments, not very long, then the man holding her allowed the younger one—his brother, Kelly realized, or at least his cousin, taking into account the similarities in their features—to tip the cup to his own lips. This close, cradled upright in his arms again, she could see that he really was drinking the liquid, not just pretending.

She also caught his grimace, as the cup was pulled away, before its milky white contents had been more than half drunk. The younger man holding the goblet nudged his brother's arm sharply, and the muscular one holding her approximated a smile and an "mmm!" sound, as if trying to convince her it tasted good.

"Yeah. *Right*," she muttered under her breath, then watched as the man holding her winced, tipping his head. He frowned down at her as the wince eased, and shocked her, by speaking in perfectly understandable English.

"What did you say?"

Her eyes flew wide, aquamarine staring up at still-frowning gray. Kelly eyed him. "What did *you* say?"

He didn't reply to her. Instead he looked over at the other man and shrugged, asserting sarcastically, "At least we know it works. Thanks for not poisoning me. *This* time."

The man holding the chased gold goblet shook his head and smiled, muttering something that, from his rueful expression, sounded like "I can't understand a word you just said, remember?" But *one* of the two men in the room knew what was going on, and that was good enough for her. In fact, she recovered enough of a burst of energy to demand that very fact.

"What the hell is going on? Where am I? How did I get here? Who the hell are you? And put me down this minute, buster!" She kicked her feet for emphasis, since her arms were still tightly pinned to her sides.

The other two exchanged words in that other, incomprehensible language, arguing a bit more, then the one holding her looked down at her as she kicked again. "He says you're supposed to drink the damned potion—and if you bite me again, I'll bite your whole gods-be-damned head off!"

"You attacked me, so you deserved it!" she shot back, struggling in his grip, though she was losing strength once again, as the momentary adrenaline caused by finally being understood faded out. "And I'm not drinking anything I don't know about!"

"It's a *translation* potion, you little idiot!" the man holding her all but roared, glaring down at her with steel-gray eyes. "How else would I be able to tell you you're an idiot?"

The other man asserted something as she struggled, energized by his roar. She still didn't understand a word. Or how the thick, now white "potion" could translate a damned thing. It had to be a trick!

"Put me down!"

"I'll put you down when you drink the gods-be-damned potion, woman!" he roared back. His younger brother, or cousin, or whatever, roared at him, too, a string of vituperative-sounding, liquid syllables. The bully holding her backed down. Scowled as he did so, but backed down. And muttered at her, "Just drink the damned potion, and then you can yell at *him* all you want. *He's* the one who brought you here."

She eyed him. She eyed the other, younger man holding the potion. She eyed the goblet. She eyed the man holding her again. Maybe it wasn't a drug of some kind—*he* didn't seem to have been changed or altered by it. Kelly was weakened by her ordeals, but her sense of humor asserted itself for a moment through her exhaustion.

If he's still grumpy and aggravating after drinking it, it has to be perfectly safe. I think I'd be more suspicious if it had suddenly turned him kitten-sweet. So, in a way the other one picked the right guy to serve it to, if his intent was reassuring me of its contents . . .

Mouth quirking up on one side just a little, she sighed. "*Fine.* I'll drink the damned potion. But if you do anything to me I don't want you to, I'll bite off parts of you no woman should ever have to threaten to destroy. And that's *not* a threat," she added as he frowned in confusion, blinked, and finally got her meaning with a bronzing flush on his lightly tanned cheeks. "That's a *fact.* So you'd better set me free right after I drink the damned stuff!"

He grunted, ignoring her threat with a nod to the other man. The cup came up to her lips. She resisted a moment, sniffing cautiously. It smelled like dandelion milk, with that greenish, bitterish aroma that spoke of lawns and summer days, and the never-ending battle between parents trying to eradicate the weed and kids nibbling on the stems and blowing on the tufted seeds to make a wish.

A cautious dip of her tongue into the liquid tingled her taste buds. It tasted even worse than the bitter dandelion juice she remembered vaguely from her childhood, because it tasted like someone had dumped in a tablespoon of pepper sauce and a hefty squirt of lemon juice, and maybe even some dishwashing soap. There was no sign of the leaf the other man had used, or any of the other ingredients she had glimpsed being added to the previously muddy brew. She could just see the smooth, milky white, bitter glop inside the white-glazed cup.

The goblet tipped a little more, forcing her to drink or be drowned. Gulping it down quickly, she struggled not to gag at the repellent combination of tastes. When the last of the thick liquid had been delivered, but for the amount coating the interior, the younger man removed the cup from her lips. He waited until she swallowed the last of it, working her tongue with a grimace to get the thick, coating of liquid off of it, then he spoke to her.

"Do you understand me now?"

A dizzying disorientation struck her ears, her head, and her mouth. Tingling on her tongue. Her ears buzzed for a moment, then everything settled and was still. "What?"

"I said, do you understand me now?" the younger of the two repeated.

And Kelly *knew*, watching his lips move, that he wasn't speaking in English. That unnerved her more than being shaken out of her version of reality and dropped into this one, and even more than waking up with the whole house on fire. "Y-yes, I—"

The man holding her dropped her. Not completely without care, since he dropped her legs first, but he barely allowed any time for her to settle her feet and get her balance before letting go of her upper half. "Good," the slightly taller, loose-haired one asserted darkly. "Keep her away from me."

He turned and strode away.

Kelly, torn between the two of them, turned to the nearer one for an explanation. "How the hell am I speaking . . . whatever this language is?"

"Magic," the younger one with the goblet replied, with a casual shrug. Taking it for granted she would understand, or rather, accept the reply.

She had to accept his explanation. Nothing else made sense, not the change in location, the way they could speak her language so suddenly, and then she theirs . . . she just couldn't *take* it. Not on top of everything else that had happened to her.

"Ma—" she got as far as saying. Unfortunately, Kelly Doyle didn't finish the rest. She was too busy dropping in a dead faint, the second one in less than an hour, and the second one of her life.

Jinga's Balls!"

Saber stopped a yard beyond the workroom doorway and called back to his brother. "Watch your language! I may not want her here, but she *is* a woman!"

"Saber, could you please come back in here and pick her up again?"

Saber turned around, stalked back to the door, and leaned inside. "No," he started to assert. And saw the reason why his brother had made the request. The woman was crumpled on the stone floor once again. His brother was leaning back against the worktable a couple of yards away, all but sitting on the worn stone surface and looking a little pale as well as sheened with sweat, which concerned Saber. "What happened?"

"She fainted. And I'm not feeling too good myself, either."

Concern blanketed his irritation. Morganen was his brother after all, however irritating sometimes. "What is it?"

"Oh, nothing much . . . just two *major* spellcastings in one day, if you hadn't noticed. It wasn't easy, rescuing her from that fire so far away," Morganen added, pinching his brow to avert the reaction-headache he was getting. "And then brewing and casting the Ultra Tongue, which just happens to be the hardest linguistics magic of all."

Saber could see that his brother did look wan. But he didn't want to be any more involved than he'd already been. "I am not going to stand around, holding her all day!"

Morganen set the goblet on the worktable next to him. Sometimes his eldest brother could be a real pain in the potion. "Just pick her up, carry her to one of the empty guest rooms, and put her on a bed. Then tell someone to watch over her. I'd do it myself, but I think I'm going to have to sit here a little while longer. And don't forget to remind the others not to do anything with her . . . since you're so good at that."

Saber gave his youngest sibling a dark look, but strode forward and crouched to pick up the woman again. For a moment her lashes fluttered, as he shifted her into his arms, giving him a glimpse of dazed blue green eyes, then she was limp and unresponsive again. He didn't have to hold her as tightly this time, but he did hold her close. She was a limp, uncooperative bundle, after all.

A bundle of skin and bones, he thought as he mounted the steps two levels, muttered a spell to open the door, and close it again behind him, then headed along the protective outer wall that sheltered the grounds of the castle-like structure to the ramp that would let him walk into the nearest wing of the donjon. *One with very little flesh on her. She looks pale and worn. Starved.*

He didn't want to wonder what kind of circumstances could drive her to such straits. Enemies, his brother had said. Her home and her livelihood lost to her enemies, suggesting the fire had been set deliberately . . . with her still asleep in the building, suggesting a murderous attack in the middle of the night. His arms cradled her a little closer unconsciously, as he traveled along the wing that was a part of two wings halfway out from the donjon at the center, and which joined into a single length the closer he got to the center and the great hall.

We may have lost our rightful home, and with it the right to call ourselves sons of the Corvis line, exiled instead to Nightfall Isle . . . but at least we have a roof over our heads. And our livelihood is now played out in fish and game, birds and fruits, and the occasional magical item exchanged for goods brought from the mainland by those who exiled us. Which is not much different from the estate food and livestock and the magical items we had been making and selling beforehand, so I suppose we have not really lost our livelihood . . .

No, I will not feel pity, or anything else for this woman, he asserted to himself. He was the eldest son, after all, and the ancient Prophecy warned against an interest within him for bedding any chaste woman. To feel anything at all for the fairer sex risked the unnamed disaster that was fated to strike all of the continent of Katan.

Carrying her along the eastern hall of the cross-like outer wings of the donjon, Saber passed into the great, octagonal hall at the center of the ancient keep and turned to the right. From the floor a couple levels below, Evanor's silky tenor voice could be heard chanting some rhythmic song, pure and uplifting, more brilliant than the shafts of sunlight pouring through the stained glass windows set in the ordinal corners of the main building.

Skirting the chamber along the upper balcony, he entered the north wing and mounted the nearest set of stairs. There was only one room that was really far enough away from all of the brothers, for they had spread out throughout the sprawling keep and its outer wall towers, in finding each one's ideal bedchamber suite. The room he headed for now was the one they had dubbed the lord's chamber back when they had first been exiled here. That chamber was located directly above the vaulted ceiling of the great hall, well out of the normal path of anyone traveling through the wings of the mostly abandoned palace. The sheer remoteness of it would help keep her out of temptation's way.

She really weighed too little for her size; she needed to put on at least another twenty pounds, maybe thirty before she would look good. Saber tried not to think about it once he realized that, but it was like being told to not think about pink bears. One inevitably thought about rose-tinted ursinoids.

Mounting the steps that followed the curve of the vaulted ceiling when he reached the next floor, he headed up to the door and used a spare fingertip to press on the lever, nudging it open with his shoulder. It didn't budge very far, though it wasn't locked. An awkward swirl of his hand, his arms still burdened with the woman's weight, and an application of magical force opened the stiff, edge-warped panel.

Cobwebs hung here and there in the chamber, for the room had been pretty much untouched since they had explored it upon their arrival three years ago, and the whole keep had been abandoned for twenty or thirty years before that. No one lived on Nightfall Isle anymore, unless they were a royal or noble family in exile. Just like their own exile.

Naturally, no one had bothered to clean anything when the brothers had been all but tied up, carted across the Inner Sea, and dumped on the western shore with a pile of their belongings. And none of them had really bothered to clean up much of the castle since their arrival, including this remote, highest chamber. Even the bedding on the broad bed before him was visibly dusty.

Too dusty to set her on. Even if Koranen had done something to heal her lungs from any smoke inhalation or searing from her ordeal with fire, they would still be tender. Reaching the bench chest at the foot of the large poster bed, Saber balanced the limp woman on his arm and braced knee and concentrated.

A slow sweep of his hand, a mutter under his breath of one of the spells he and his brothers admittedly used less frequently than they probably should, and the dust and cobwebs slowly stripped away from the bedding. The neglected feather mattress, matching pillows, and woolen blankets fluffed as the spell drew dust out of their interiors, too, pulling it out and pushing it aside in a thickening wall of brownish gray.

Saber had plenty of power in his magic, more than many on the mainland of Katan, but his was more oriented toward the spells of war, offensive and defensive magics, not housekeeping ones. Still, their mother had taught a number of household cantrips to all eight of her sons the moment their powers had manifested. It had been her way of assigning punishments to her rambunctious sons.

It took concentration to open the nearest window on that side of the room and "sweep" the cloud of grime out, without dropping the woman, but he managed. Then, because he vaguely remembered women being squeamish about such things—namely, their mother, Annia, who had passed away nine years ago, when her youngest set of twins had been only fourteen and he and his twin were twenty— he added a rodent-insect-spider-repelling spell. Enough of those squeaked and chittered and buzzed out the window to make even his skin crawl a little, though at least none were dangerous. A fact for which Saber was thankful; they'd had plenty of other, not-so-pleasant infestations to contend with over the past three years as it was.

The woman cradled on his knee and arm sighed, mumbled something under her breath that no translation spell could have interpreted, and snuggled into his chest. Trustingly. Saber stilled. How long had it been since a woman had rested so trustingly against him? More than three years, that was certain. Speculation about the eight of them had always been running since Morganen and Koranen had been born, back when Saber was six years old.

Two of the estate's castle servants had been willing to introduce him to the ways of lovemaking in his teens, and a young woman from a family his parents had approved of had been growing interested in him as potential husband material. But at about the same point in time, Koranen had started displaying a magical affinity for fire when puberty had struck the last pair of twins late, at around the age of six-teen or so. That had started the rumors in full, backing every female off from all eight of the brothers, not just Saber. Morganen's confirmation as a potentially very powerful mage just a few years later had only scripted the final page on the fear the others around them had, because of the ancient "Song of the Seer" that now cursed his family.

To have this woman cuddling against him reminded Saber of two uncomfortable things: how very long it had been since any woman had pressed herself so closely and trustingly to him, clothed or otherwise . . . and how very dangerous it was to let her get close.

He didn't just dump her on the bed, though. Instead, he cast one more spell, a freshening cantrip to make sure the bedding wasn't damp or musty, though the room didn't have any signs its roof had leaked in the past three years. There were still cobwebs and dust films around the edges of the room, but the bed was clean and fresh-smelling when he shifted her into both of his arms again.

Slipping her frail body into the bed, Saber covered her up with a single blanket, since it was a warm early summer day. Then he dusted off a chair, conjured one of the books from his study in the northwest outer tower, and cracked it open. *There's no sense in bothering my brothers to look after this woman. They might do something lethally stupid, like fall in love with her.*

With the weight of his part of the Curse over him—the only one actually worded as a curse in the whole of the Prophecy, his Curse to bear, though some of the other verses sounded bad enough on their own—*he* certainly wouldn't think of doing it.

THREE

❧

A horrible dream, Kelly decided, refusing to open her eyes as she snuggled her head deeper into her fluffy feather pillow. Her alarm hadn't gone off yet, after all, and she had set it, surely. She always set it. *A horrid dream, of fire and pain, confusion and fear, and it was all just a dream, thank god . . . though that blond brute was rather gorgeous. When he wasn't scowling . . .*

A feather shaft was poking her in the cheek. She brushed at it with her hand, rumpling it back down into place with the others in the pillow . . . which she didn't have. Her grandmother's place had once had feather pillows, but that had been while Granny Doyle was still alive; they had been too flat and under-filled for her to continue using, so she had replaced them with cheaper ones stuffed with a synthetic material. No, Kelly simply didn't have any feather pillows anymore.

If I'm sleeping in a bed with feather-stuffed pillows . . . Prying her eyes open, Kelly held herself still, assessing her surroundings.

This . . . wasn't her bedroom. It wasn't the guest room at Granny Doyle's, either. Or any other room she had ever been in before, in the whole of her life. That included the bizarre, frightening dream that apparently *wasn't* a dream, no matter how much she wished it had been.

What first caught her eye were the velvet curtains roped back from the six sets of windows in what looked like an octagonal room. The color of the velvet, perhaps dark red, was grayed with dust and traced with equally dirty, fuzzy cobwebs. There was plenty of wall space between the wide, multipaned windows, with bookshelves built into the walls and wardrobe cupboards, dresser drawers, chests, padded, carved chairs, and even a hassock footstool. Everything was ornate, richly carved, decorated, and appointed . . . and apparently neglected for what had to be untold years.

The bed she was in had been cleaned and aired at least somewhat, and there didn't seem to be any bugs or creepy-crawly things to worry about immediately. However, there was one unnerving aspect of the room she was in, beyond the neglect and the lingering grime. She spotted it as soon as she cautiously sat upright. *He* was in the room.

Sitting in one of those padded chairs, in fact, his boots resting on a footstool, his elbows on the armrests, and a medium-large, leather-bound book propped up in his lap, one knee raised slightly higher to support the old-fashioned, hand-bound spine. Dust motes danced over his shoulder, drifting through a shaft of sunshine slanting at a low angle through one of the windows, probably the western one, given that the sun had been higher in this odd world the last time she had seen it, back in that hallway with the door that had closed on its own and the tiny, arrow-loop-style window at the other end.

The sun made the specks of dust look like dancing stars. It also made his dark blond hair look highlighted with fine-spun gold. As she watched in silence, uncertain whether his presence meant ravisher or jailer or whatever her confused mind couldn't think of just yet, he moistened his forefinger and thumb, eased up the corner of the next page, and slowly glided his hand to the center of the edge. A pause as he finished reading whatever was on that side, and he gently flicked the sheet over. Giving her a glimpse of printed characters that weren't English, though her mind struggled to perceive them as it did English.

The slight headache at the back of her eyes was proof enough that there really was magic at work around her, that she really was no longer in Kansas anymore—so to speak—and not just caught in a dream-induced delusion. She rubbed at her forehead and temples, then drew in a breath and spoke when he didn't acknowledge her movement. "What am I doing in here?"

"Staying in here."

"So I'm a prisoner?" Kelly asked warily.

"You're a nuisance. And a danger. As soon as my brother has recovered, he'll find a place to dump you and send you there."

"Oh, like I *asked* to be yanked from my home and off to a universe full of magic," she snapped back, irritated at the decidedly unfriendly reply to her enquiry. "Mind you, I'm damned glad I'm not dead, burned to a crisp by those bigoted, close-minded, asinine fanaticals, but I haven't exactly had a comfortable time since I arrived here, either, you know!"

He frowned over at her, abandoning his book for a moment. "What do you mean by that?"

She gaped at him. He didn't know? "First you attack me, then you yell at me, then you attack me again, make me drink a horrid potion, and now I'm your prisoner in this less-than-Best-Western room, and you ask me why I'm not *comfortable* with all of it?"

He snapped the book shut, dropping his legs to the floor to sit forward and glare at her. "I *meant*, what do you mean by 'yanked from my home and off to a *universe full of magic*'?"

"My universe doesn't *have* magic potions that make communication in bizarre languages instantly possible! Most people don't even believe real magic exists, where I come from," she added pointedly. "I wouldn't believe it myself if I wasn't suffering from it firsthand, today. I'm grateful to be able to communicate, don't get me wrong, but all of this has been happening without my knowledge, or my fully disclosed consent."

He stared at her. And stared at her. And stared at her.

"What?" she demanded defensively as he kept staring at her with those hard gray eyes.

"I am going to kill my brother," the man stated flatly. "He knows damned well that transdimensional crossings are forbidden, when one of the realms has no magic!"

"Excuse me?" Kelly returned, arching her partially singed brows. "If he's the one who did the bibbity-bobbity-boo thing and dragged me here across the multiverse or whatever, then if you're going to kill him, I sincerely hope there's someone else who knows *exactly* what universe to send me back to. Hopefully not to the exact moment I left, though. I'd rather stay here in loopy Wonderland than go back and die in a really bad case of murder by arson, thank you very much!"

That made him scowl. But not at her. "Someone deliberately set a fire to kill you?"

"Well, I don't exactly have proof," she pointed out. "But there were a bunch of prejudiced, ignorant bigots living in the town I'd moved to, idiots who thought I was involved in witchcraft—whether or not that's a respectable career here, it certainly isn't considered to be by most people back in *my* universe.

"They also hated me simply because I was involved in a group that liked resurrecting the old ways and cultures of our history for fun. So they harassed me, harassed my customers, ruined most of my business, and sent me anonymous hate letters."

The bitter tale spilled out of her as he listened. Even with his lingering irritability, he was still far more receptive to her than the local law enforcement had been, back home. Golden and Irritable was *listening* to her and even seemed troubled by what she was telling him.

"Then they started sending even more threatening notes, about historical witchcraft trials, and how the guilty had been stoned, hung, or burned alive at the stake. And just last week, someone put up a hangman's noose on my front porch," she added, as his eyes narrowed at the gruesome punishment "witches" had received in her world's past. "I found it when I went to open up my shop.

"Maybe the masked man who attacked me last month was just a random mugging attempt and not a deliberate targeting of me, but seeing *that* made me angry," Kelly said. "But I didn't think they'd go so far as to actually burn down my house—not with me still *in* it!"

Damn. The wobble in her voice and the tears were coming back. Tightening her jaw, she looked away and did her best to glare out one of the less-than-clean windows, although there wasn't enough clarity to the glass to be able to see anything.

He didn't say anything, and she didn't dare look at him, in case he returned to glaring at her. She'd had enough of hate being aimed her way with the idiotic folk of that one ignorant town. Kelly didn't want to have to deal with any more, today. Not until the urge to cry had passed again.

For his own part, Saber wanted to throttle her neighbors, even if they were in some other universe only Morganen knew how to find. It was the same kind of unreasoning fear that had forced the eight of them into exile, ordered off the ancestral Corvis land and onto Nightfall Island. Except—if he understood her correctly—magic didn't exist in her home dimension, save in stories and superstitions. The fears of her neighbors were imaginary ones, and not the very real, prophecy-directed ones that haunted his own family. Making the reason for her troubles utterly senseless, and thus an even greater tragedy.

Saber now felt like a brute for adding to her misery, listening to the serious troubles she had already gone through. Running a hand through his hair, he tried to think of something to say to change the subject. He found one as he eyed her profile, doing her stubborn best not to cry, though he could see the reddening of her eyes, the way they gleamed with moisture. When her jaw finally relaxed, he spoke.

"What is your name?"

"Kelly. Kelly Doyle." She did her best to clear her nose without a telltale sniff, but of course there was one. Doyles didn't cry, though, not over little things like prejudice and attempted murder, and bullying strangers from other universes. *In* other universes. Composed as much as possible, given her bizarre situation, she finally looked at him. Trying to be polite despite her circumstances and immediate past with the man, she asked, "What's yours?"

"Saber. Of Nightfall." He waited for recognition to dawn, but of course it didn't. "My brothers and I were exiled to this island. Our neighbors were afraid of us, too."

That made her blink and narrow her eyes with a touch of wariness. "Why?"

"We fulfill the Curse of Eight Prophecy, that's why. Eight sons, born in four sets of twins, all on the same day two years apart each time. Each one fitting in demeanor or gift the verses of the 'Song of the Sons of Destiny.'"

She pulled the covers a little closer, though they were meager protection. "What do you mean, 'Curse'? Do you turn into werewolves, or drink other people's blood, or spawn baby demons if someone gets you wet?"

He frowned, opened his mouth, then shut it and shook his head. For a woman from a land that supposedly didn't have any magic, she had some odd notions of what a Curse was. "No. Not that kind of Curse. My own verse in the song states quite clearly if I fall in love, a disaster will immediately befall the whole of Katan . . . and that is a large land, home to more than a million people."

It was her turn to frown at him. "That's it? No details? Just some unspecified disaster happens if you fall in love?"

Saber scowled at her. "It's more complicated than that!"

"Really? You mean there are specific details such as, 'if this man, Saber, falls in love with a blonde, locusts will plague every field from spring to fall, and none shall have anything to eat'?" Kelly challenged him. "Or 'if this man, Saber, falls in love with a brunette, the seas shall rise up in salty flooding, and every mountain spring shall flow red with soured blood for a full month'? That kind of complicated?"

"I mean, in *this* universe, Curses are real. Prophecies are real. It was written by the Seer Draganna over a thousand years ago, and she has never once been wrong."

"*What*, precisely, was written?" Kelly demanded. "You know, where I come from, about three hundred years before, people were accusing other people of witchcraft, of setting Curses to make the cows dry up and not give any more milk, to wither the crops with a drought or wreck them with a heavy rain and flood, and they were *hanging* people, because of these accusations.

"But you know what?" she demanded rhetorically. "The damned cows dried up because they needed to be studded with a bull again so they could drop another calf and produce milk for it, and droughts and floods are simply a natural part of the weather cycle! So maybe these people of yours got all bent out of shape *thinking* they knew what this Prophecy thing was all about, simply by a misinterpretation egged on by ignorant fear." She glared at him, then folded her arms across her breasts, wishing her pajama top wasn't as holey as it was, and in almost indecent places. "Besides, exile doesn't compare with murder by arson!"

"Well, *here*, a Curse *can* dry up a cow or blight a crop with flood or drought," he pointed out. "The Council of Mages do their best to keep such things from happening, but people do have to take Curses seriously!"

"Okay, fine! Maybe that's the way it works in this universe, but what's the damned verse that's got your undershorts in such a wedgie knot?" she shot back.

"My what in a what?" Saber returned. Not because there wasn't a translation for her last few words, but because he had never heard a woman with her level of educated speech use that sort of terminology before.

"Never mind. I presume you *do* know your own Curse by heart?" she added mock-sweetly, arms still folded where she sat in the middle of the oversized bed.

Saber glared at her. And recited it.

> *"The Eldest Son shall bear this weight:*
> *If ever true love he should feel*
> *Disaster shall come at her heel*
> *And Katan will fail to aid*
> *When Sword in sheath is claimed by Maid."*

Kelly blinked. "Oh." She blushed a little at the blatancy of the last line, but it did sound ominous. *And* vague, disaster-wise. She dismissed it with a shake of her head. "It's still a little too nebulous to get all worked up over."

"Disaster *will* come to the whole continent," he argued.

"No, it just says disaster will come, and Katan will not give aid when it arrives," she pointed out reasonably, settling her arms a little more comfortably. Her stomach was feeling rather empty. "Do you have any food, or am I to be both a prisoner *and* starved to death, while I'm an uninvited guest in your *lovely* home, here?"

Saber blinked at her, ignoring the second half of her speech. Testing the weight and shape of her other words, he could find little flaw in her logic, because it fit the words of the verse even more tightly than the other interpretation had for so long, before. He shook his dark gold hair. "Disaster will still come, regardless."

"Yeah. And your neighbors conveniently shoved you off into exile, so that you'll be forced to deal with it without the benefit of their aid. Whether or not it was intentional, *they* deliberately fulfilled that part of the Prophecy by packing you off into isolation in the first place."

He shook his head. Not to deny her logic, but to clear the cobwebs her logic revealed. "This is unbelievable!"

"Well, that's the way *I* see it," Kelly defended. Then eyed him with just a touch of slyness. "If you really want me to shut up, try sticking some food in my mouth. That usually works, for a little while."

He looked up at her again, finally catching the new topic, though the old one still tromped through half a lifetime's beliefs with its blunt-footed logic. "You're hungry?"

She nodded her head exaggeratedly. "*Yes*. And in need of the local facilities. Chamber pot, garderobe water closet, bathroom, outhouse, whatever you call it. Unless I'm so much of a prisoner that you want me to ruin what's left of this bed?"

He scowled at her, jabbing a finger at one of the two doors in the room, the one located directly across from the entrance. "That door leads to the refreshing room. And you are only a prisoner in that I cannot allow you to wander the halls and bring down the Curse on my brothers by making one of them see you long enough to fall in love with you."

"I take it you don't have any females allowed in this exile of yours," she muttered.

"There have only been the eight of us on the whole of this island for the last three years. And now you're here. One female, eight males. I'm confident your universe is not so strange that you cannot figure out the volatility your presence will cause, if you're allowed to roam around unsupervised. So you will stay in here and keep yourself out of the way, out of temptation, and out of trouble," he asserted, rising. "I will come back shortly with some food. It may be a day or two before my youngest brother is ready to send you back near to where he found you. You will stay in here until he is ready to make you leave."

She snapped a sarcastic salute. "Yes, sir! Anything you say, sir! Roger-Wilco, sir! Permission to drop bomb bay doors and moon you enthusiastically, sir!"

His eyes narrowed, and Kelly realized belatedly that, having drunk the translation potion or whatever the awful white stuff had been, he just might be able to accurately translate her sarcasm. She felt herself start to blush. Hopefully the golden hue of the sunlight shining in through the western windows was hiding some of her embarrassed color.

He eyed her for a moment, then sighed and shook his head—thankfully without responding—and turned to go.

As soon as the other door was closed behind him, she scrambled to get out of the bed and go to the bathroom. Her limbs were shaky from exhaustion and hunger, her head a little dizzy in that way that told her she'd run out of calories once again. Potatoes, peanut butter, week-old discount bread, granola, and tuna fish did not an adequate diet make. Cheap and affordable, with what little she had been able to sell in the past few months, but very inadequate.

Thank god I bought multivitamins, expensive though they always are . . . It didn't guarantee her continued good health here in this realm, of course. Her multivitamins were probably a bunch of little charred lumps inside a melted, black plastic puddle anyway. Unattainable even if she could have reached across time and space.

Kelly made it to the door Saber had indicated and pulled it cautiously open. There were more cobwebs and dust inside. There were even some bugs. Wincing, she picked her way into the smallish bathroom, brushing the cobwebs away as she tentatively explored.

The window was small but glazed, so she pushed it open to get some fresh air in the stuffy, musty room and looked around the "refreshing room" as the grimy glass gave way to fading sunlight.

What was really remarkable was that the place had running water. The local version of a toilet wasn't a sinkhole in the side of the castle like an outhouse or garderobe; it was made from a light blue glazed porcelain, had a bowl of water and what looked like an old-fashioned pull-chain tank up on the wall. Instead of an oval, preformed plastic seat like she was used to, it was a gently rounded, broad section of smooth-polished wood with a rounded but almost rectangular hole in the center. It was also hinged to flip up for cleaning, a familiar touch in such a bizarre setting.

Kelly whacked the seat twice with her fist to scare off any bugs that might be lurking underneath, then faced the sink to give them time to scuttle away. There was a basin with a little shelf that splashed water into its drain like an artificial waterfall, bubbling up from where a stone shelf was carved out from the wall. Above it was a glass mirror, slightly spotty with the tarnish of age and almost too dusty for her to even see her silhouette.

The handle to the side of that miniature waterfall, when she tested it, was a lever that turned the water cold or hot, but did nothing to stop the flow. Actually, it just changed the water from warmish to cool. If the faucet-waterfall was broken, the local equivalent of a hot water tank had probably been running too long to continue to heat the water.

Or rather, if it's a spell, the spell's gone weak with age, she added to herself. *God, if this really is a universe full of magic, real, operational magic, then it's probably the latter. I doubt they have very much in the way of actual technology here, when the local wizard could whip something up approximately as good as a machine shop or a factory could, and for probably roughly the same equivalent price in gold coins, or whatever these people use for their money.*

Kelly realized that the light was fading.

She whacked the seat one last time, used the facilities, pulled on the chain, and washed her hands with a hard-dried bar of soap that rested on the shelf next to the basin. There was even a strip of cloth hanging from a bar under the window to wipe her hands on, though it was dusty like everything else. Using it would probably only smear dirt across her skin. She moved to take it off, shake it out, and use it anyway; everything else was filthy.

Something blackish and roughly the size of her spread hand, but with far more limbs than she had fingers, and far too much body-bulk to be a spider, scuttled up over the window ledge and stared at her with four malevolent, pupil-less, dark red eyes.

Saber heard the scream and burst through the door to the dome suite, barely managing to balance the silver platter he had found and turned into a tray. A second after he rushed into the master chamber, the door on the far wall yanked open and a strawberry-haired blur sprinted out. She spotted him as he set the tray on the nearest flat surface, and all but tackled him. Shrieking, she throttled his biceps and babbled something that resolved itself into:

"Kill it kill it kill it kill it *kill it kill it kill it kill it*!!!"

Saber clapped his hand over her mouth, shutting her up long enough to get a word in edgewise, then removed his palm again when she calmed down somewhat after a moment. "Did you see a bug?"

"No, I saw a *spider*! A freaking *big* spider!" she added, releasing his arm long enough to hold up her hands. At the amused smile curving his mouth—he had a really nice smile, when he finally had the gall to show one—she scowled and whacked him in the arm. "I can *handle* the small ones! *This* one was as big as my—"

She broke off and screamed again, trying to climb his left arm, eyes fixed on the floor in front of the door she had left open. Saber saw it, too, big, black, and scuttling their way, confirming the impending dread her interrupted description had sparked in him.

"*Koddah!*" A thrust of his hand and a dagger of solidified energy shot down at the thing. It stabbed, and the creature exploded, as the energy released with a meaty *pop!* . . . but there were more coming their way, running on way too many legs, as they scuttled through the open refreshing room door; from his angle, he could see they were pouring in from the window she must have opened. *Mekhadadaks. Jinga's Tits!*

Swearing under his breath, Saber grabbed the woman around the waist and beat a fast retreat. She wrapped her legs around his hips, clinging to him as he raced down the stairs, banging the door shut behind them for protection. Skidding at the bottom, he spiraled down the steps of the north wing and burst out onto the upper balcony edging the great hall. His brother wasn't physically there, though. "Evanor! *Evanor!*"

"*Yes?*" that smooth tenor sang back from somewhere else in the castle, without actually being shouted or echoed down the halls, answering his own sung-out cry. "*I'm just about to set out our dinner. Did I forget the silverware for the tray?*"

"Sing everyone into the north courtyard—*now!*" Saber shouted, knowing his brother would hear him, reaching the next set of stairs and taking them two and three at a time, as the woman, Kelly, clung to him. One of his arms held her close while the other flung itself out to keep his balance. "And I mean *everyone!*"

It was a long descent, and a long race for the nearest door, but quickly enough, he bolted outside with his burden, into a courtyard whose paving stones were being pushed apart by weeds. Yet more proof that the eight of them had neglected the whole place in far too many ways. He stopped in the center of the broad courtyard, turned this way and that to check for any more signs of an invasion, then finally stood still, breathing hard and holding Kelly of Doyle in place, as she clung to his hips and chest.

"Either you hate big spiders even more than I do, or that was something I don't think I really want to know about," she muttered, still clinging to him, supported by both of his arms as well as her own arms and legs.

"It wasn't a spider." Saber heard the others coming and realized she *was* still clinging to him. An inch or two lower, and she would be clinging very intimately to him. His body stirred with uncomfortable interest at the thought, as did his irritation; any more of this, and he'd risk becoming decidedly interested in her. Something he couldn't allow to happen. "You can get off me now."

Kelly scrambled to get down, yanking her pajama top down, as the charred hole below her right breast threatened to creep up. Her reply was defensive, to cover her embarrassment. "Well, you're the one who grabbed me and ran!"

"Be quiet," he ordered her, waiting impatiently for his brothers to show.

They all came, Morganen and six more she hadn't met. Formally, that was. Kelly had an impression she'd seen at least some of them in the jumbled images that had seemed only a nightmare at the time, but which had probably been a part of her hour of rescue from being burned alive. Patiently, the man next to her waited until they were all in the center of the courtyard, eyeing the pair of them in the slowly dimming twilight. As soon as the others were within hearing range, Saber addressed them.

"We have another mekhadadak infestation, this time starting in the master chamber above the hall," he informed them bluntly. "Gods know if they're anywhere else, too. We'll have to do a full sweep."

FOUR

Some of the others swore, or started to swear. A couple of them eyed the woman in their midst and elbowed their fellow siblings to shut them up. No two looked exactly alike, although according to Saber, they were supposed to all be pairs of twins. A bit of squinting in the fading light allowed Kelly to pick out the shapes of noses and brows and chins. She discovered they all had a very similar cast in their facial features, though hair and eye colors varied from twin to twin.

Well, at least they're trying *to be gentlemanly and polite in their language around me*, Kelly thought, wondering at the same time what a mekha-whatchamacallit infestation was and how bad it could possibly be. *Just my luck to uncover the nest personally.*

"Morg, do you have a piece of chalk?" Saber asked one of his brothers.

"Always," the one she recognized admitted, though his long, light brown hair was now down out of its knot, and the headband was gone. He dug a small white rock from one of the pouches hanging on his belt and tossed it at his brother. Saber squatted and sketched out a near-perfect circle on the surface of the largest uncracked flag-stone around them, marking almost to the edge of the weeds bor-dering the stone. Straightening, he picked Kelly up by the ribs and set her in the middle of the smallish circle before she realized his intent.

"You will stay right here and not move until I give you leave to. *Su-bah makadi deh,*" he added as he pulled his hands away. He lifted a chalk-smeared finger and pointed at her. "Do not move."

"What did you do?" Kelly asked warily, glad it was a warm eve-ning. She tugged her pajama top down a little more, then folded her arms across her breasts to hide them further. Most of the other seared spots were mid-thigh or lower, and there was that rip he'd made ear-lier under her armpit, but that one over her ribs was embarrassingly close to revealing something she didn't want revealed. She might be borderline starvation-thin, but her endowments weren't all *that* starved-looking.

"You are in a repellent shield. So long as you stay within the cir-cle, you will be perfectly safe."

"What's a mekha . . . mekhuda—?"

"A mekhadadak is a carrion-eater, and more," one of the other brothers informed her, the most blond-haired of the eight men. "Nasty things, too."

"They were designed over a thousand years ago to eat the bodies of the fallen in a massive war—ecologically sound cleanup," the one clad in lightweight, dark-dyed velvet added wryly.

"But some twisted bast—uh, impolite person of a mage," a slen-der third corrected, as a fourth elbowed him sharply in the ribs, the largest one of the eight with a massive, muscled figure, "—remade some of them to seek out the living, not just the dead, and eat them. They are very efficient eaters."

"We have enemies who would see us dead, and not just exiled," Saber added grimly. "Though thankfully few of them. One of those enemies must have conjured a nest of them into the castle . . . but since we don't go into every one of the hundreds of rooms here, they apparently haven't been drawn out by our movements until now."

Kelly thought about being attacked while she had been using the facilities and blanched a little. "Ah."

"If she faints, I'm not catching her," one of the brothers muttered, about as surly sounding as Saber had already proven he could get. This one had midnight black hair and a somewhat leaner figure. He didn't even deign to look her way, this darkest-haired brother.

"I'm not going to faint!" Kelly snapped, shoving her hair back from her face, then quickly refolding her arms again as several of them eyed the bare flesh of her abdomen, which had been exposed by the action. "I take it you're going to use some kind of magic to drive them out of the castle, and if I stay exactly where I am, they won't be able to get at me while you're getting them out?"

"No, we're going to drive them to the center of the castle and kill them there," Saber corrected. He started to give the order to spread out to begin the spell-wrought driving, then eyed her. "And every other insect, spider, rodent, snake, and bug inside the actual palace, though we should leave the necessary beasts in the gardens alone."

His gruff addition made her arch a brow. "Thank you, Saber. That's very considerate of you."

It was growing darker and getting harder to tell if that was a slight flush on his cheeks, or if it was just a trick of the fading light. "We're behind in our spring cleaning," he growled, obviously not wanting her to think he was being kind. He turned his attention back to his brothers. "Spread out, each man to his tower. We'll link first to set a repeller spell on the outer wall to keep anything from the outside getting in, then work our way toward the center. Drive everything into the great hall, and do not forget to assert yourself everywhere. Just in case. Open doors and so forth. Koranen, you can flame them when we get there."

"Why can't Morg do it?" the auburn-haired brother asked, puzzled.

"Because I'm tired, and he knows it," Morganen returned. "I have enough strength left to drive a bunch of bugs out of our home, but not enough to dispose of them today."

"And if I burn down the Hall, and with it, the whole castle?" his auburn-haired twin shot back.

"Then I'll take it out of your hide," Saber retorted. "Okay, everyone, spread out. And be wary when you open each door."

"Wait!" Kelly watched as they all returned their attention to her. "Do you guys have a flashlight or something I could hold?"

"A what?" the biggest and most muscular one asked.

"A source of light?" she rephrased. "It's getting darker out here, if you hadn't noticed."

"I'll get her one," the auburn-haired one stated, and jogged toward the nearest wing. The others dispersed, scattering across the court-yard. Traveling, she noted, outside the massive, overgrown mansion of a building they had been inside of just a short while before. Within moments, Kelly was uncomfortably alone. There was a half-lit moon overhead, but it wouldn't be enough to banish her uneasiness at being left alone in a strange place with strange things scuttling about.

The auburn-haired one came back a couple minutes later, as she peered through the dark at the ground around her for more of those spider-not-spider things with the impossible-to-pronounce name.

"Here." He snapped his fingers and thrust an opaque white sphere at her, just a little smaller than the size of a volleyball. It looked like the ones she had seen in that workroom she had first arrived in, but it was dark, not bright, just a plain, opaque white globe that didn't have any buttons or switches, or anything to show how she was supposed to turn it on.

"Hey! How does it work?" she asked quickly as he snapped his fingers a second time and turned to go. "And what was the snapping for?"

"I lowered and reset the wards. And you just tap it. Softly for a little light, harder for more, and twice hard and quick to shut it off—don't worry, it won't break, unless you throw it off the highest tower in the castle . . . though I doubt it would break even then; I'm very good at making them," the redhead added with a hint of pride and a grin as he walked backward, away from her.

"Got it. Thank you," she offered, but he had already turned away again, picking up into a light sprint with lithe grace across the now-deserted courtyard.

Holding the white ball in one hand, she hesitated a moment, then gave it a soft rap with a knuckle. It started glowing dimly, like a translucent glass ceiling cover wrapped around a lightbulb. Except it was a smooth sphere, with no openings for a battery or a lightbulb. The surface was smooth and glassy, but it weighed more like lightweight plastic than glass would, and yet felt solid instead of like a hollow sphere. It was a comfortable weight in the hand, actually. Even comforting, because it felt just solid and heavy enough to make a good throwing weapon.

Not that she was going to throw away her only source of light. That would require her to step outside the chalked circle to retrieve it. Since she was alone, and nothing was happening yet, Kelly experimented with the globe. After several tries, she figured out that it had roughly eight levels of light: from nightlight dim to blindingly white. The lattermost, she discovered when she smashed it as hard as she could with her fist, almost dropping it.

Hitting it twice rapidly after that left her blinking from the sudden darkness, big spots dancing in front of her eyes in an after-glow image.

As she blinked, adjusting her eyes, her ears picked up buzzing, rustling, even hissing sounds. Rapping medium-hard on the sphere, Kelly held it up over her head, turning to look at the outer wall behind her, where the noises were coming from. Things moved through the night, mostly small and fluttery, some larger and scuttly. A snake slithered past no farther than a yard from her feet, making her carefully scoot closer to the center of the chalk-mark. It was striped somewhat like a harmless garter variety, but Kelly had no idea what kinds of snakes in this world were the ones best to be avoided. *Better to be safe than sorry . . .*

She felt sorry for the serpent, since it was probably going to get charred when it got to the center of the castle—but then something fist-sized and black surged out of the shadows, grabbed the snake in way too many limbs, and tussled with it until the curling, writhing serpent went limp. It was all she could do to keep from twitching back out of the chalk circle as the mekha-whatchamacallit slurped up the snake like it was a piece of oversized spaghetti.

It paused for a moment, tensed, and dropped something small and black and multilegged out of its back end, and then scuttled on-ward, vanishing out of the reach of the light within moments. Its offspring immediately pounced on the nearest beetle, devoured it almost too fast to see what it was eating, then raced on as well, following the ragged course of its parent.

At least everything was swerving away from her by a good two feet beyond the chalk circle she stood in, proof that Saber's repulsion spell was working.

Amazing. I'm standing on another planet, in another version of reality, another whole dimension, with a glowing magical ball in my hands, a warding spell around me, and gobbly things are eating snakes and insects on their way to a magic-made immolation on every side ... Just ... amazing.

It was a miracle she was taking it so calmly. Relatively. Her shadow kept shaking from the trembling of her hands, as they held the globe, and her breath hitched unsteadily as three more of those black things scuttled on by. They were remarkably fast and remarkably ugly.

The largest was the size of her head and froze her in place as it eyed her; it headed deliberately her way, then swerved at the two-foot-from-the-circle mark. It remained focused on her, too, side-stepping to keep her in view with several tiny, dark red eyes, before pausing for a long, disturbing moment on the side of the repulsion field closest to the massive castle. Finally, it moved on its way. Driven off by the protective magic the man Saber had cast around her, or more likely by whatever spell the brothers were wielding against all the icky things in their home.

The flow of creepy crawlies slowed to a trickle. Half a minute after they ended, one of the men came back through the courtyard at a slow stroll. It was the one with the hair so black, the lightglobe in her hands gave his locks only bluish highlights, nothing red. He had the same nose as Saber, long but not overly large, and the same stubborn chin, but his eyes were flat and dismissive as he glanced at her and continued walking without pause.

He was the one who had sounded about as grumpy as Saber, claiming he wouldn't catch her if she fainted. Kelly didn't yet know his name; she didn't know most of the brothers' names, for that matter. But as he passed through the brightest reach of the light, she knew she wouldn't forget him quickly. Not when his eyes were eerily as dark as his hair, surrounded by black lashes and fine black brows that were lowered slightly in a look that would have been very intimidating, if Kelly didn't think he was just concentrating on his spellcasting. Well, she hoped that was why he was frowning like that.

Clad in a black, long-sleeved tunic and equally black trousers, making his hands and his face pretty much the only things visible against the shadows of the night, the mage strolled past her. His arms were lifted, his palms facing out, a sense of energy like the looming of a storm about him, as he moved through the courtyard without a word to her. Kelly thought it was probably best not to disturb him by asking how much longer she would have to wait. The night certainly suited him; with his dramatic, contrasting coloring, she could almost picture him with fangs and a black, satin-lined cape.

That thought made her choke back a quick laugh, since he was still within sight and sound of her. Clutching the lightball to her stomach, Kelly shifted her weight in the cooling air of the courtyard. It was a long wait. She eased her feet on the hard flagstone underneath her and did her best to endure the whole thing as stoically as she could, waiting for someone to return and tell her it was safe to move.

Only the moon kept her company now, besides the lightball in her hands.

After a while, a glow above the outer wall off to the side caught her attention. Studying it, she finally figured out what it was. Amazed, Kelly watched as a *second* moon gradually rose, smaller than the first one shining its bluish light down from overhead, but clearly a moon that was three-quarters full. Switching her gaze back and forth between the two moons, Kelly didn't give any further thought to any mekhada-whatsits the brothers might have missed. Those two moons were far more fascinating, and in a way far more alarming, than anything black and scuttly that an invisible wall was clearly protecting her from.

She really *was* in another universe, on another world. She was, as the people of her world liked to say, definitely *not* in Kansas anymore. Glancing at the orb in her hands, glowing like a third, even more tangible moon, Kelly Doyle did her best to come to grips with what had happened to her.

* * *

Thankfully, someone had thought to open the upper windows of the donjon to let out the thick, roiling black smoke. Morganen, Dominor, and Evanor supported Koranen both physically and with metaphysical energy, as he concentrated his fire-based magic on his task. Saber, Trevan, Rydan, and Wolfer contained the beasts within a sphere-shaped shielding that kept the bugs in but allowed air and smoke to pass out, to keep from smothering the searing white core Koranen had created at the center of the hall.

It was unnerving, watching those mekhadadaks snap and snarl and devour the rodents, snakes, and insects being compressed within, growing larger and dumping new versions of themselves. Within an uncomfortably short stretch of time, it was mostly mekhadadaks, and very shortly after that, just the warped carrion-eaters alone.

A pity they will not simply eat each other, Saber thought, holding his quarter slice of the sphere-shield steady. The original version would only breed once a year, unless a more than adequate food supply was on hand. Such as on a battlefield. They also lived only two years. These things bore young anytime they ate ten times their own body-weight, once their central bodies were as thick as a man's fisted hand and their legs longer than that by a hand's length.

A mekhadadak would eat anything that moved and caught its vision, heading straight for it while it moved and relying on its sense of smell when it got within a yard or two to tell it if it were actually edible meat or something indigestible, like a curtain swaying in the breeze. The fact that they were silent even while they burned, unlike the hisses and shrieks their more vocal prey had issued while being devoured or burned, was unnerving. Saber grimaced, watching the immolation as he held his part of the shielding.

Gods, I hate mekhadadaks! I'd love to know which bastard keeps sending them to us. And now we have a woman on the isle, a magicless one with no clue as to what's dangerous or safe in this world, to worry about, too.

Rydan had nodded at him when he arrived, reassuring him silently that the woman hadn't moved from the ward-circle he had cast around her, that she was still safe and unharmed. Not that Saber really cared if she was or not. He couldn't allow himself to care. Whether or not her viewpoint on the meaning of his Curse was more accurate than his own, he couldn't, daren't allow any woman to stay long enough to risk bringing that foretold disaster down upon them all.

It didn't help that he lived in a universe where disasters foretold by true Seers had a bad habit of coming true.

I will not *fall in love with her. She isn't even my type.* Of course, it would help if he could remember *what* his type was. That was what happened to a man after three years of involuntary celibacy. *She's sharp-tongued, screams too much, and doesn't even dress properly—no, don't think of how she's not dressed!*

Firming his attention, he held the sphere until Koranen finally ended the burning hot fire at the center of their sphere. The second youngest of them slumped into the waiting arms of three of his brothers, the white-hot fire dying out at the same time. Saber nodded, and his brothers lowered their linked shield. Only the finest white powder drifted down to the floor from the incineration site, and not much of that. Koranen had been well named, when the Prophecy had labeled him the Son that was Flame.

"I'll get him some food," Evanor offered, heading for the kitchen.

"Trevan, Wolfer, sweep the woods outside tomorrow. Rydan, scry through the night, make certain we missed nothing. And keep the wall shields up all night, until we can sweep the land outside during the daylight."

Dominor smiled slightly, but not out of humor. "I suppose we'll be cleaning the castle, next? Doing all the dusting, sweeping, cobwebbing, and polishing to please our guest?"

About to suggest that himself, Saber stiffened his resolve. "No. If she wants her chamber cleaned, she can do it herself. Get to work on getting her out of here as soon as you can, Morganen. She doesn't belong here."

Leaving the others, he strode out of the great hall. When he reached the courtyard, the woman Kelly of Doyle was still standing there, indecently clad in those charred, loose trousers and that ripped, singed tunic-shirt of hers, instead of a proper skirt and blouse, or a gown. She was idly rolling and shifting the lightglobe someone had fetched for her from hand to hand, lost in whatever thoughts had occupied her in the intervening time. She looked skinny and strange. And yet she wasn't an ugly female. Even Saber couldn't lie about that.

Her head snapped up as he moved into the globe's field of light, spotting his approach.

"Saber? Are they all gone?"

At least she wasn't hysterical anymore. "They're gone. I will take you back to your room."

"Are you *sure* they're gone?" she asked.

"I swept your chambers myself." He turned on his heel and headed back toward the palace.

"Hey!"

Saber stopped and looked back at her. She was still standing in the chalk circle. She hadn't followed him as he'd expected. *Women. They're too damn contrary! Especially this one. Gods, get her out of here quickly!* "What?"

Kelly folded her arms more tightly across her chest. "You didn't say I could come out and play, you know. You said I had to stay right here until you told me otherwise."

She's actually obeying? Saber found himself arching a brow at that. "Are you asking my permission to move?"

She lowered her golden-copper brows and hefted the glowing

ball in her hand, narrowing her eyes in menace. "Do you want me to bean you with this?"

There was the temper of the virago he remembered, though he wasn't sure what beans had to do with her threatening to throw the lightglobe at him. Truth was, he had forgotten she could not dispel the simple warding spell on her own, like any of his brothers could. Three years was a long time to be away from those who didn't also possess the gift of magic in one form or another. He snapped his fingers. "You can move, now. But if you hit me with that—"

"Yeah, yeah, I know; you'll do something gruesome to me, or chain me up in the dungeon or something," she muttered, stepping over the circle and making her way past the weeds growing up through the flagstones. "Warn me if we have to pass any broken glass. I didn't exactly have time to look for myself on the way down here, and you guys certainly aren't the poster boys for Housekeepers of the Year."

"Is that your way of asking to be carried?" Saber demanded, glaring at her for being such a nuisance.

"That's my way of asking if there was any glass, to avoid bloodying my damned feet!" she snapped back. "I don't think you have anything to worry about, regarding that Prophecy, Mister Grumpy. No woman in her right mind would fall for a surly ass like you!" She stomped past him, heading for the bulk of the castle to look for a door—then hissed and hopped on one foot. "Ow, dammit!"

"What is it? Glass?" Saber asked, instantly at her side. He didn't think any glass had been broken and scattered this far out into the courtyard, though some of the palace windows had cracked with neglected age long ago, and none of the brothers had repaired anything beyond what was absolutely necessary since their arrival.

"No, it's a thistle thorn! You're lousy groundskeepers, too!" She let him balance her, as she cradled the lightball in one hand and picked the thorn out of her toe with the other, her heel braced on her thigh with limber dexterity.

"Well, I am not weeding the whole damned courtyard just to satisfy Your Pickiness!" he shot back, concern adding an extra edge to his tone. She dropped her foot and limped forward, pointedly ignoring him. He let out a disgusted sound and picked her up, swinging her over his shoulder again. "The faster I get you back, the faster I can be rid of you!"

"Well, why don't you run, then?" Kelly demanded sarcastically, gritting her teeth from the bruises on that side of her body. There were plenty of others elsewhere, but did he have to slam her face down over his shoulder and hit the ones on her stomach again?

Unfortunately he took her seriously. By the time they got up to the room she had been placed in before, Kelly could barely breathe from all the painful jouncing. He dumped her on the bed, and she curled in on her stomach, eyes squeezed shut.

Saber, turning to leave, looked back at her. She was lying on her side, her bottom lip once again pinched in her teeth, her expression lit at an awkward angle from the lightglobe she had dropped on the bedding next to her. "What, for the love of Jinga, is wrong now?"

"I was being *sarcastic* about you running, you idiot," she managed tightly. "After having a ceiling beam drop on me and God knows what else, and your rough handling before, you think I *wanted* more bruises and pain?"

Torn between irritation at her scolding and anger at his compassion for her, Saber glared at her, whirled, and stalked out. Slamming the door behind him.

When her stomach stopped hurting enough to breathe easily once again, Kelly crawled off of the bed and went around rapping on the crystalline lights—now that she knew how to activate them—until the room was well lit against any missed insects or gobbly bugs. Nothing moved but herself and the occasional breeze-wafted cobweb, though; Saber and his brothers had been very thorough. Not very clean where the grime was concerned, but very crawly things thorough.

It would have to do.

He had also brought her a fair amount of food to eat earlier, Kelly discovered when she investigated the dome-covered platter that had been set on a chest near the door. No silverware, but there was a mug of something that looked and smelled like stout ale, and a plate piled with cooked vegetables, shredded meat, and half a loaf of delicious-smelling, garlic-buttered, toasted bread. Whole wheat, plus rye and oat flours, she decided from the look and the smell.

Ducking into the bathroom, she washed her hands, flapped them to air-dry, and returned to eat. The medieval society had taught her how to eat gracefully with her fingers, thankfully. The lack of silverware was merely an annoyance, not an actual problem.

It had also taught her to be adventurous and open to new experiences, when it came to her taste buds. The herbs and spices used were partially familiar, partially unfamiliar, giving the otherwise plain meal an exotic edge. The meat tasted like duck, which she'd had once for Christmas, years ago when her parents had still been alive, and had been flavored with savory, sweet basil, and something peppery that wasn't quite pepper. And while she wasn't normally very fond of beer or ale, the stout Saber had brought up from the kitchens of this place did have a nutty flavor to it that was kind of appealing when she sipped it.

The hot foods had cooled, but were still flavorful. She couldn't finish it all, though, and had to replace the cover. Her stomach was too small these days to handle such a sudden wealth of calories. Wisely, Kelly didn't eat as much as she wanted to; that way, she didn't make herself sick. The leftovers would still be under the bowl Saber had picked out for a lid whenever she grew hungry again, though she would have to ask him about refrigeration and preservation spells.

When she used the refreshing room again, wanting to wash her hands, Kelly first cautiously checked every corner and nook. Only then did she relax enough to wash up, rub her teeth with a bit of thoroughly rinsed cloth, since she lacked a toothbrush, and retire for the night. Not even a tiny bed mite disturbed her, as she stretched out on the somewhat lumpy, feather-stuffed mattress.

She couldn't sleep, even with one of the globes glowing at half-strength. Of course, she'd had half a night's sleep before the fire, and half an afternoon's sleep after her arrival, though not quite enough to make up for her over-exhausted, underfed, now-sated state. It was the thought of more creepy-crawlies coming back that kept the redhead awake. And awake. And still awake.

Giving up an hour or two later—this universe not only lacked technology, but also clocks—Kelly got up, found the age-hardened bar of soap in the bathroom, and a rag that looked like it might have once been a scrap of non-terry toweling cloth. There was even a bucket and a stiff, hair-bristled scrubbing brush tucked under the basin sink. Soaping up the water, she used another rag to tie her hair out of the way under the makeshift kerchief and started scrubbing the half-bath attached to "her" room.

A good, thorough cleaning would scrub away the memories of being attacked by something that slurped garter snakes like spaghetti, as well as make her less hesitant to touch anything around her. That was the Doyle way, anyway—to confront the bad things, memories included, and get past them any way one could. Not to mention her nature was a lot more fastidious than her surroundings. She wasn't afraid of dirt. She just didn't like it.

So she scrubbed away the bad memories, exchanging them for a thoroughly clean bathroom, hoping to tire herself out so she could sleep without thinking about black things with too many legs, grumpy spell-casting men, nooses, muggers, hate-mail notes, or ceilings collapsing on her in flames.

FIVE

⚜

She wasn't in the bed, when Saber brought up her breakfast on another platter. The room was brightly lit by the globes scattered around the chamber, even though the morning light was already gleaming through the windows to the east, and the bedding was shoved back on one side, proof she had risen at some point after he had left her. Guessing she was in the refreshing room, the mage-smith set the second tray next to the first, then lifted the original tray to remove it. And then set it back down again for a quick peek under the makeshift lid, because it felt almost as heavy as the tray he had just brought up.

His suspicions were confirmed. She had barely eaten half of last night's dinner. Irritated that the fool woman wasn't taking care of herself right, half starving herself to death for the gods alone knew what idiotic reason, Saber stalked over to the bathroom, hesitated, then rapped lightly on the door. No answer. In fact, it swung open slightly the moment he thumped on it.

Pushing it open cautiously, he stuck his head inside. Empty. Clean, and startlingly so, by the standards of the rest of the abandoned palace rooms . . . but empty. If she wasn't in the bedchamber, and she wasn't in the refreshing chamber, and yet last night she hadn't moved until he'd given her leave to move—something had happened to her.

Or she had disobeyed his order to stay up here and had decided to go and explore. The aggravating, petite woman did have that willful virago streak in her that matched the tint of her hair. It seemed that, in her universe, the temperament of their redheads was more or less the same as it was for the ones who lived here in Katan.

Turning to head back out the door and track her down, Saber spotted her. She had been hidden by the near side of the bed, lying on the floor, which was partly scrubbed clean of its accumulated years of grime. Innocently curled up on her side next to a bucket of dirty water, a scrubbing brush, and a half-dried rag, was the woman who just might be the Prophesied downfall of his people. Looking like a cross between an orphaned waif and a limp, strawberry-blond, striped rag.

Saber leaned back through the doorway behind him, reexamining the refreshing room. Clean and grime-free, from floor to ceiling. The age-worn, velvet curtains and linen drying cloths looked like they had been soaked, washed, and hung back up to dry. Neither a cobweb nor a speck of dust occupied the refreshing room, even up by the ceiling. Water splashed serenely from its fall into a clean-scoured draining basin, missing only its stopper-cork; otherwise it was virtually pristine, as if it had been attacked by a troupe of maidservants being paid by the dirt-speck. Even the windowpanes had been scrubbed until the glass gleamed in the morning light.

Walls, door, necessity seat, even the ceiling—all of it had been cleaned. Considering the level of grime he recalled from earlier, that would have taken more than a little effort to get rid of nonmagically. This cleaning spree would have taken a *lot* of nonmagical effort, in fact. On half a meal's worth of food, in an underfed, almost skin-and-bones body.

Angry—righteously angry though he didn't stop to think why—Saber stomped over to the soundly sleeping woman. Scowling, he squatted to shake her hard, to blast her with his opinion of her idiocy the moment she was awake. Two things stopped him.

For one, Saber could now see the bruises she had complained about, visible as dark stains on her freckled skin through the various holes in her clothing. He could even see shadows of them underneath the thin, light, worn material of her odd garments. Dark bruises that clearly lay under the aging fabric. Many of which *he* had probably put there, or at least worsened while constraining her in their fight earlier, and in carrying her about like a sack of refuse thrown carelessly hard over his shoulder last night.

The other thing that stopped him was how she slept so peacefully, so exhaustedly in the gleam of daylight reflected off of the patch of scrubbed hardwood floor around her, limply comfortable in spite of the hardness of her makeshift bed. Or at least oblivious to any discomfort in her exhaustion. And it was exhaustion, confirmed by the shadows visible under her peacefully closed eyes.

Gently, taking care to not wake her, Saber picked up Kelly of Doyle and lifted her onto the bed. He did his best to not look at the curving underside of her breast, indecently revealed where the singed spot in her tunic-shirt rode up a little too high on her deeply sleeping body. Pulling the covers over her, he prodded his memory to try to remember if there were any women's clothing anywhere in the castle.

Perhaps in one of the solars? Or maybe in a bedchamber we haven't examined beyond whatever was necessary for monster-cleansing . . . Leaving the woman to sleep, he made sure both trays of food were covered, double-knocked all the globes off to conserve their magic, and went in search of something much less distracting for her to wear than garments that looked like they would continue tearing if he so much as looked at them wrong.

If he remembered right, if nothing else, there should be a sewing chamber in the north wing that should still have cloth leftover from their last shipment from the mainland. Saber's cloth-sewing spells were about as mediocre as those of the rest of his brothers, save for Evanor, but it shouldn't be too hard to whip up a simple dress. *If* he couldn't find anything already made . . . and if he could find enough intact, sturdy fabric for her to wear.

He just hoped he could find something already made.

Ⓦhat in Jinga's Name are you doing, woman?"

The abrupt shout made her jump, splashing the water she had been using to rinse the scrubbing brush. Heart racing, Kelly watched Saber throw down a bundle of cloth, his face smudged with grime along one cheek. He stalked toward her, and she scrambled to her feet, yanking her pajama top down just to be safe. His unreasoning anger made her nervous, because she had no idea what he was mad about this time around. Kelly backed up a step as he approached, then stood her ground, tugging on her pajama top again. "I'm scrubbing the floor! What does it look like I'm doing?"

"It looks like you're wearing yourself to the bone, dammit!"

His concern, delivered in a half-roar, made her blink. He *cared* about her? *The big lug is concerned about me?* she thought, surprised. He grabbed her arm, making her wince from the bruises that had already blossomed there. Which made him flinch, then he swept her off of her feet, scooping her swiftly into his arms.

She bit her lower lip as he stomped across the floor, away from the bucket and puddle of soapy, dirty water on the floor. But not from his grip. This time, his muscular arms cradled her remarkably gently. Rather, her teeth sank into her bottom lip to keep from smiling. *Why, the big, blond lug is actually concerned about me!*

It was kind of cute, in an annoyingly macho, overly demanding sort of way.

He set her on the chair at the desk the two trays were on and yanked off both tray covers. She had already explored the food and eaten some of the leftovers from the night before. And some of the eggs, potatoes, and onions that someone had fried together for breakfast, plus more of the nut-brown bread, this time slathered with butter. A mug had been filled with fresh-squeezed juice of some sweet-tart, non-orange kind, and she had managed to drink about half of it an hour ago, when she had woken up in the bed. That was when Kelly had realized new food had been brought and she had somehow been tucked back into the bed. She couldn't remember anyone putting either the new food or herself into place.

The only explanation was that Saber had done it for her.

Saber clanged the silver lids on the desktop across from the tray. At least she had eaten some of the damned food since it had been brought up, but some wasn't nearly enough, in his opinion. "Eat!"

She blinked and looked up at him with those blue green eyes. "I already ate. About an hour ago."

"Eat the rest of it!" he elaborated, jabbing a dusty finger at the breakfast plate.

"I'm still full!"

"You haven't eaten enough to *be* full!" her host snapped at her.

"Compared to what little I *have* been eating, I *am* full! I don't want to overstuff myself and throw up," she added, looking up at him again. "You don't force someone who's been starving for a year to eat a fourteen-course meal the first day there's enough to eat."

"Then you're an idiot for starving yourself!"

That was it! Kelly jumped to her feet and lifted her chin belliger-ently, glaring up at him as she gave him back what she had just re-ceived. A full-throated roar.

"I didn't have any *choice*, you big, overgrown ignoramus! Between those prejudiced asinines ruining my local customer trade, and hav-ing to pay off the mortgage on my house and shop, just so I could *have* a house and shop, I was lucky to be able to afford any food at all! And half of *that* I had to grow myself in my tiny little backyard!"

Her pint-sized, completely fearless version of his own roar made him blink. He recovered after a moment, though, and jabbed his fin-ger at the chair. "Sit! Eat anyway!"

"I'm still in the middle of cleaning the floor!" she snapped back, planting her hands on her hips and tossing her shoulder-length hair.

The action, Saber realized, threatened to raise that one hole high enough to make all the other holes and tears positively decent by comparison . . . though it looked like she had wrapped cloth around her flesh underneath for a pass at decency. Saber dug his hands into his hair, then swept one out at the room with his demand. "Why in Jinga's Name were you even cleaning, last night?!"

"Because I couldn't get to sleep!" she shot back, folding her arms over her breasts.

Tired of running around without a bra, she had bound her full curves with a strip of cloth torn off one of the ratty, aging towel-cloths hanging in the half-bath, but that hole still made her uncom-fortable. The moment she found needle and thread, and some cloth that wasn't more moth-eaten than her singed pajamas, she'd make herself something less embarrassing to wear. Even if it had to be out of the velvet curtains hanging in this room, which were in desperate need of washing.

"I couldn't sleep with that bathroom a mess, because I kept think-ing of all those cobwebs, and those mekha-something-or-others crawl-ing around," she added defensively. "So I cleaned out the bathroom, floor to ceiling, then had to clean the floor again from all the drips, and the next thing I knew, I was out into the bedroom, scrubbing the rest of the floor. So I just kept going!"

"You're too damned skinny to be working so hard! Sit down and eat something before you fall dead at my feet!"

"Oh, *trust* me—my *last* intention is to fall at *your* feet!" she shot back, but dropped onto the cushion-seated chair anyway, unfolding her arms. At least this second time a fork had been added to the tray, so she didn't have to use her fingers. He stood at her side, arms folded across his light blue-clad chest, watching every bite she took with those gray eyes of his. "Do you mind not looming over me like that?"

"Obviously you cannot take care of yourself. I will stand here until you finish every last crumb of this food."

"Have fun," she retorted flippantly. Five minutes later, when she was full once more, she stood up to leave the desk-table and return to scrubbing the floor. His hand came down on her shoulder, pushing her back down onto the chair. Kelly rolled her eyes. "Do you mind?"

"*Every* crumb," Saber warned her in a growl.

"I'm full again!" she protested, glaring up at him. "I was full to begin with! I'm not doing this because I'm anorexic, I'm doing this because I haven't had a full meal in months!"

He resettled his arms across his chest, flexing his array of muscles in silent male warning.

"I can't sit here all day! I *won't* sit here all day," she added firmly, getting up again. He unfolded his arm to push her back down. She pinched him on the arm as she landed on the embroidered cushion once more. "Stop that! I don't need my bottom bruised, too."

When she thrust back to her feet the moment his hand was removed, Saber glared at her. "Sit *down*, woman!"

"I don't feel like sitting!" She tossed her shoulder-length hair, planting her hands on her hips once more.

Glaring in aggravation, he picked her up by the ribs and carried her over to the bed.

"Hey!" She thumped him on the shoulders with the edge of her fist, a physical demand to be let down.

"If you will not sit on the chair, then you will lie in bed!" He put her on the bed. She bounced away and rolled to the far side. "Be still!"

Feet slapping on the clean side of the floor, she glared at him from across the bed. "Stop telling me what to do! And stop yelling at me!"

"Either you get in that bed, or I'll *spell* you there!"

Aquamarine eyes narrowed to glittering slits, as her pale, freckled cheeks turned pink with rage. She stomped up onto the mattress to tower over him, taking advantage of the only extra height she could find. "You wouldn't *dare*!"

"Do not try my patience again, woman!" he asserted, starting in a growl and ending in a roar. "Lie down in that bed!"

"You know, this room was built to be proof against most sounds between it and the donjon hall below," a third voice interjected dryly, making both of them whirl toward the doorway to the stairs. The blond haired, brown-eyed brother leaning in the doorway studied the pair of them. "But I could hear you all the way down in the scullery. Not even my lungs are usually employed that loud."

"*He's* being *impossible*!"

"That's because *she* won't *eat*!"

Their audience winced and wiggled a finger in his ear. "Okay. Since the two of you are only making volume headway, I'll play mediator." Brown eyes glanced toward gray. "All right, Saber, what is the problem—softly, if you please?"

"Look at her, Evanor!" Saber demanded, jabbing a finger in her direction. Which she batted away, giving him a dirty look. "She's all skin and bones and eats less than a bee, but works eight times as hard as one! She's been trying to clean this place on less than a third of a meal!"

A golden brow lifted, as the man eyed the partially cleaned room around them. The cobwebs had been batted down, the floor mostly scrubbed, and the dust whacked at least somewhat from the curtains.

"It's indeed a tough job for someone without magic to speed and aid them, but not that overly laborious. And women are often not as fragile as you profess this one to be. Many are often expected to clean and keep house without a speck of magic . . . though I'll admit ours is one of the worst-kept ones around, despite the efforts I've made in the more used rooms. Now," he added, giving his brother a "shut up" look before switching his gaze to the other person in the room, "tell me, lady—well, first, what is your name?"

"Kelly Doyle."

He bowed slightly. "A pleasure to meet you, Lady Kellidoil, despite the circumstances. Now—"

"No, it's just Kelly. *Then* Doyle. Doyle is the name of my family, Kelly is my own name," she corrected, folding her arms across her chest with a brief tug at her top.

"Ah. Well then, Lady Kelly, tell me why you think my brother is being impossible?"

Kelly debated telling him she wasn't a titled lady, but decided she didn't mind finally being treated nicely by someone in this bizarre universe. "He's demanding I either sit in that chair over there and eat more than I physically can, because my stomach's been shrunk from too little money to buy too little food for too many months. Or that I lie here in this bed and do absolutely nothing. I'm not the kind of person who can do absolutely nothing!

"Back home . . ." Her voice wavered a moment at the thought of there being no more "back home," but a pile of charred wood and ash. She firmed it and went on. "Back home, I always had about two dozen projects going at any one time. Lace-making bobbins, embroidery hoops and thread, clothing and dolls and pillows to sew— laundry in need of washing, floors to sweep, a garden to weed, that would hopefully give me more food than I could afford to outright buy, with those idiots pressuring my regular customers away from my shop, so I had to rely on infrequent tourist trade. A Doyle doesn't 'do nothing'! And as I'm the only one left, I cannot 'do nothing' even less!"

Evanor frowned as Saber listened to her confession. "Your family is dead?"

"Yes. They died in an auto accident, a couple of—" Breaking off at their puzzled looks, since the word *auto* didn't seem to make sense to them, something the translation spell didn't seem to be able to handle according to their own tongue, Kelly tried a different tact. "Your people have carriages, right? Drawn by horses?"

"Yes. And some have wheels that turn by magic, though they are expensive to purchase and costly in spells to maintain," Evanor affirmed in his smooth, wonderful voice. "We, of course, make our own for use on the isle, as we have no horses for pulling regular carriages, and we are all mages enough to maintain them. They can go faster than horse-drawn carriages, providing the road is smooth enough to be traveled upon that fast, and can haul almost the same weight in their load as a pair of horses, and they don't have to be fed grain or hay, though they still have to be maintained."

That was close enough for her to make them understand what had happened to her own family. "Yeah, well, in *my* universe, where I come from, we've got machines that do the same thing as your magic carriages, and lots of smooth, straight roads to go really fast on. And three years ago, some idiot had too much to drink, lost control of his horseless carriage, and crashed into their carriage with his own, fast and hard enough to kill all three of them instantly."

"Then you have my condolences for your loss, and Saber's sympathies, too," the younger man added, lifting his chin at Saber, who scowled at his brother for the presumption. "Our own mother, Annia, died in childbirth with our stillborn sister. When our father,

Saveno, grew ill from a fever not a month later, he lacked the strength of will to live on without her and succumbed, despite our efforts to heal him and make him better. So we are more or less orphaned, too. As well as outcast for the simple crime of being born."

"I'm sorry to hear that," Kelly added honestly. That sounded like a lousy way to lose one's parents, too. She refocused on the problem at hand, reviving her earlier irritation. "But that doesn't change the fact that he's being unreasonable in his demands—he even threatened to use a *spell* on me!" she added, jabbing a finger in Saber's direction.

"That is because she is a stubborn fool who doesn't know what is *best* for her!"

"Oh, like *you're* an expert on women, Mister We've Been Exiled Here for Three Whole Years!" she shot back, flipping a hand at him, the other on her hip.

"*Enough*." It wasn't loud, and it wasn't forceful . . . not exactly, but the single, hard-voiced word cut their argument dead. The younger Nightfall brother eyed Kelly, eyed Saber, then straightened, his gaze returning to the first real woman all of them had seen in three years. "He is right in that you should rest, Lady Kelly, and eat, and regain your strength while you are a guest in our home— you do not have to worry about where your food comes from as our guest, or that you must conserve it for another day's meal; we gain more than enough in provisions, both locally and for our trade-goods, than twice our number could eat. So eat your fill whenever you can take another bite, so that you regain whatever in your hard-ships you have lost.

"And *she* is right," he added as Saber folded his arms and took on a smug look, "in that *you* are being unreasonable in expecting a woman with her obvious natural energy to simply lie abed with noth-ing to occupy her hands and mind. You also need more appropriate garments, Lady Kelly," Evanor continued politely but pointedly to their strawberry-haired guest. "My brother and I will go look for

some. And as we do so, we shall look for something in the way of embroidery, or lace-making, or even simple clothes-mending for you to
do . . . *if* you promise to rest in bed, eat your fill whenever you can,
and not scrub any more floors today or tomorrow. Agreed?"

"I already brought her some clothes," Saber pointed out gruffly,
nodding at the pile of cloth discarded on the floor near the door.

"Then we will leave her to try them on—a nontaxing event for
any woman, surely even you will agree—and go in search of needle
and thread so that she can alter them to fit her better, giving her
something nonstrenuous to do with her time here. *Now*, Saber," he
added pointedly.

"You do *not* order me around," Saber asserted, moving toward
the door anyway. "I am the elder brother, and I—"

"—I do when you're acting like an a—uh, fool," the slightly
shorter man asserted with a wary, genteel flick of those mahogany
brown eyes in Kelly's direction. "We will return in an hour, my lady."

"She is *not* your lady," Saber growled, as his brother pulled the door
shut behind them, leaving their unwanted guest inside the lord's chamber. "She is leaving the moment Morganen can safely rid us of her!"

"I am merely being polite, Brother," Evanor returned calmly, as
they descended the steps. "She is not my type, anyway."

"We don't *have* a type, remember?" Saber pointed out. Hating
that he had to say it. "None of us dares have a 'type.'"

His brother carefully said nothing to contradict his words.

W ell. At least she had something to do—try on the clothing he'd
brought and then thrown on the floor. *Clothing that's in serious need
of a heavy scrubbing, though I'll have to settle for a dust-beating, for now*,
she decided, moving to the nearest window. Thrusting the panes
back on their stiff hinges, she returned, picked up the large pile as
best she could and carried it over to the open window.

Several hard shakes of each garment, and they were made somewhat more wearable, as specks of dust billowed out onto the sea-scented breeze. Or at least more presentable than her pajamas had become, between fire, holes, scrub-water, and general grime. Once that was taken care of, Kelly sorted the pile, examining each piece and reluctantly admiring the stitching. Tiny, straight, and entirely machine-free.

But of course they'd do it by hand, here. Assuming not everyone has magic to do mundane tasks by, or even if there is a spell to stitch fabric by.

There were two sets of underdrawers and three corsets. Five skirts, four blouses, three chemises, two gowns, three overgowns. Eight stockings that ranged from a fine-spun woolen pair that would be too warm to wear in this summer-like weather, and silk so thin, aged, and fragile, it tore under just the pressure of her fingertips when she picked it up to give it a good shake. There were already larger holes in the hosiery, which she guessed had come from Saber's handling of them.

Tossing that pair aside, she looked over the shoes. Five sets of those in different sizes, some a little worn, but all more or less fit to wear. The second-best pair looked to be approximately her size, when she held one up to the sole of her bare foot. She set those aside and returned her attention to the clothes.

Some of the clothing was moth-eaten, with little holes here and there, but most of it smelled of some kind of peppery, cedar-like storage material, proof that they had been preserved for at least part of the time, and were probably even older than they looked. There was a hip-length, sleeveless camisole that fit her and seemed sturdy enough that it wouldn't rip just from her breathing. It would do for an undershirt, though it was a bit sheer for a medieval tank top.

Rummaging a bit more, Kelly sighed. There weren't any pants. She didn't mind skirts, but she preferred pants. Everything was of a different size, proof he had grabbed a variety for her to try on, but it was all skirts and such. Slipping into the smaller set of underdrawers as soon as she was naked, she tightened the drawstring. It promptly snapped, making the shorts drop, unable to stay on her hips. A test of the larger pair, and that string broke, too, making Kelly sigh in exasperation.

Kicking them aside, she gingerly tested the corset strings. The smallest and medium sets broke, but the largest stayed taut and firm. Unlacing all three corsets, she held each one up to her ribs, gauged which one would be roughly the right size to support her breasts— even half-starved, she still had a full enough figure in that respect— and laced it with the good strings salvaged from the large corset. Pulling it on over the sleeveless camisole, she tightened the garment, glad it laced in the front. Glad these people did believe in some form breast support in their archaic sense of fashion.

Given how medieval these men dress, I wouldn't have been surprised if there hadn't been anything for holding up a woman's breasts. But I'm glad there is; I hate going braless for too long. The only boning in the garment came from the tightly flat-felted seams from breasts to hips, but it was fitted like a bra in many respects, if just a little loose for her currently undernourished size. And unlike some corsets, at least this style had shoulder straps to take up some of the weight of her flesh, rather than trying to rely on compression alone for support.

She tried on the skirts and blouses next. Unlike the plain, beige muslin of the underdrawers and corsets, the rest of the clothes were dyed in light, pastel colors, some with flowers embroidered at the hems, some with woven ribbon trim stitched in stripes. One of the gowns was too tight for her upper body, not to mention simply too long to be practical without some serious reworking, and the other was too loose to even stay on her shoulders. Namely, because the drawstring broke.

Kelly rolled her eyes. She just wasn't having much luck with strings, today. She knew how to make them, but she didn't have any of the materials she'd need. Sighing, she checked the remaining garments for size.

It was the same with the blouses. The skirts were better; one fit, though it bared her ankles halfway up her calves. Somehow, she guessed that would be "scandalous" to Katani sensibilities. Not that it would stop her, of course. The blouses were too small, save for maybe one that was spotted with mildew, which she refused to even try.

Sighing, Kelly stripped off everything and tried the floor-length chemises next. One fit, but was a little too short in sleeves and hem, the latter of which only came to her knees, shorter even than the skirt she'd tried. The rest were baggy and threatened to trail. As for the oldest-looking garments, the overgowns, those were simply too long, even if that was supposed to be the proper style for whatever era that had been. She had no clue, however. They were all cut *sort of* like the medieval clothes she was used to re-creating in the society, but there were enough differences to make it difficult to say exactly what era and culture these things resembled most closely.

Using just her teeth and her fingernails, which took a lot of time, Kelly managed to work free the thread at the armholes on the short chemise, stripping the sleeves. Paired with the shortish skirt and the corset-bra underneath, the garment would make do as a sleeveless blouse for light summerwear; unlike the camisole, this chemise wasn't sheer. Hopefully it would be decent; it certainly was by her own standards. If it wasn't suitable by Katani ones . . . well, it would just have to do while she reworked the other clothes with the promised thread and needles. Hopefully, her two hosts would remember to fetch scissors for her as well.

She had the now-sleeveless chemise bunched up on her arms and her back to the door, when she heard its hinges squeak. Gasping, she struggled the chemise over her head, yanked it down past her thighs, and whirled to face the intruders. Saber stood in the doorway, a smallish chest gripped in his arms. His gray eyes wide and sort of stunned-looking, were fastened on her figure.

"Haven't you ever heard of *knocking*?" she demanded, blushing as he continued to stare at her.

The dark blond man blinked, then managed to move the rest of the way into the room, his brother entering behind him. The one named Evanor blushed at finding her in a chemise, even if it did cover her from shoulders to knees. Quickly setting down the bolts of fabric he carried, he thumped his brother in the arm to get him to set down the chest, and dragged both of them back out again without a single word.

Kelly blinked when the door slammed shut behind them. Actually, it was kind of flattering, since she had glimpsed the reason why Saber had been lost in that stare . . . as revealed in the slight but distinct bulge that had thrust against the otherwise smooth fall of his thigh-length tunic. Normally the fabric would have concealed that part of his anatomy.

Normally.

Hold on, Kelly Doyle—aren't you forgetting the fact that this is a realm of magic, and that, if he falls for you, some unspecified disaster will befall? Unspecified or not, do you want that on your conscience? You have enough troubles right now without having to worry about something like that!

Yes, but . . . he's a hunk! And he was ogling me! the most feminine corner of her brain retorted. *You're not dead yet, you know!*

It had been undeniably flattering. With her back to the door, without underwear of any kind on, and bent over a little in the act of putting on the chemise, which she had tossed on the bed while changing into the various clothes . . . she must have given him an intriguing view. Very intriguing. Just thinking about him thinking about her in *that* kind of way made her warm and a little breathless, and damp.

She might not have ever been physically touched, but Kelly had grown up around the end of the twentieth century in her own universe, and she knew lots of things about men and women. Things she had unfortunately been too busy making a living to experiment with, other than in her imagination. She bit her lip and sported a little feminine smile as she finished dressing and began exploring the sewing materials the two had brought up to her, thinking about the mindless stare Saber had given her just minutes ago.

Very flattering, indeed . . .

SIX

strawberry carrot. A deeper red gold than her hair, with freckles all the way down to there, by Jinga . . .

Saber bit his lip, trying not to think. Trying not to groan. At least Evanor had left him alone, free to retreat to his bedchamber in the northern spur of the west wing. But he kept seeing it in his mind: shapely legs, despite her unseemly thinness, pale and flecked everywhere with a scattering of tiny spots, if thinly scattered on the back of her knees, buttocks, and thighs. Those thighs had shifted just far enough apart in her struggle to stay balanced and dress, that he had seen that the *cinnin* brown spots were scattered even on that white, soft, inner flesh of her legs. That they dusted the ultra-feminine curves of her hips, a fascinating, speckled contrast below the age-yellowed edge of the corset she had worn from the waist up.

There was such a lush contrast between her underfed but flared hips and her naturally nipped waist, with those almost full breasts jiggling just barely in view beyond her corset-covered ribs and bunching arms, Saber could still feel the urgent demand that had gripped him at that first, lascivious sight. To clasp her waist and bend her over even farther. To grip her hips and pull her close. To thrust home into the heart of those golden carrot curls, again and again, with his impatient manhood.

Groaning, Saber covered his eyes with his arm, fruitlessly trying to block out the image in his mind. Unfortunately, it only made it seem more real, when he closed his eyes. His other hand, resting on his belly, slipped down to the ache that was his groin. He caught himself with his first stroke through the fabric of tunic and breeches, and fisted his hand. He shouldn't do that. He'd done it a few times since their arrival, but mostly only shortly after their arrival, before his body had grown used to the idea of being completely alone, without female companionship.

Without feminine temptation.

It wasn't going away on its own, though. Memories kept turning over in his mind. The feel of her breasts against his body as he had rushed her down the stairs, rescuing her from the mekhadadak attack, and the way her legs had wrapped around his waist, her whole body clinging to him intimately. The feel of her squirming in his grip to get free at their first meeting, the resiliency of her rump when he had smacked it . . . and that backside, bared at last to his view, about forty pounds shy of being properly lush and ripe, but still soft and beckoning with its smooth, freckled skin . . . those seductive, enticingly textured nethercurls.

Swearing, unable to resist any longer, Saber dropped his arm, shoved his tunic hem out of the way, unfastened his breeches, and covered his face with his left forearm once more, shutting out the daylight. He lay there on his bed, torturing himself by imagining her hands, small, pale, freckled, and deft, doing with her fingers what his own hand had to do as a pallid substitute. Imagining without that much effort what it would be like to do as he longed to, to grab her and take her, again and again, until she hollered at him from ecstasy, not from anger—from the pleasure he alone would give her. To spit in the eye of the Curse and its ominous Prophecy, and sheathe his sword in his strawberry-haired maid, over and over and over . . .

It was a hollow pleasure, when he found his completion. He couldn't, daren't do any of the things he longed to, and shouldn't even have done this much. Because, while it had scratched the first itch, it just ignited several more. Not all of them were physical itches, either. Lust might be just lust . . . but sometimes lust led to the dangers of love.

When he came again to her room, it was evening; both moons were up, casting odd, double-silvered shadows through the windows. He smacked the new tray on the desk, checked the old ones to make certain all the food was gone, and took them out with him again, all without a word. Kelly looked up briefly from her hand-stitched re-tailoring—tedious, but necessary—and watched him stomp around the room, glare for barely a quarter of a second in her direction, presumably to make sure she wasn't doing anything strenuous, then stomp out again.

Five seconds later, the door banged open again, and he stalked back inside, glaring at the floor underfoot as if she had committed the highest offense in his land. "You *scrubbed* it!"

"I don't like leaving jobs half done," she returned pointedly, managing to stay calm in face of his fury. "I finished scrubbing the floor, *and* ate a ridiculously large amount of food, compared to what I've been used to. Since then, I have been sitting here, sewing. *Just* working on the sewing I need to do."

He planted his hands on his hips, narrowing his gray eyes. "Where are they?"

She picked up the tiny embroidery scissors that had come with the remarkably well-stocked sewing chest he had brought, and snipped a thread. Sewing and embroidery calmed her, were familiar to her in her new, unfamiliar surroundings, even if she didn't have a sewing machine and plenty of electricity to power it at hand. "Where are what?"

"The bucket and the brush. If I take them away, you cannot use them!"

"They're under the sink. But do not snarl at me because your housekeeping abilities leave so many things to be desired," she added piously, knotting the thread remaining on her needle and shifting to the next seam to be taken in. As soon as she had a little more to wear in the way of decency than a chemise and skirt, she would start on a pair of harem-style pants, full enough to pass for a skirt but much more comfortable in the way that trousers were. Not to mention some underwear. The two Nightfall brothers had certainly brought her enough thread and fabric to make herself a decent number of clothes on their embarrassing visit. No matter that the cloth was aged a bit in both durability and coloring. "I cannot help it if my realm holds higher standards of hygiene and cleanliness than your own."

He snarled something under his breath, yet another curse to that "Jinga" person she had already heard about a couple of times before, and stalked into the bathroom. When he stalked back out, brush rattling in bucket, the curved handle of the latter clenched in his hand, she spoke again.

"I will require a bath sometime soon. That "refreshing room," as you called it, doesn't exactly suit my needs. Do you have baths in this version of existence?"

Gritting his teeth—for he was growing hard just being in the same room as her, proof he should never have unleashed his long-neglected needs by releasing himself mere hours ago—Saber crossed over to one of the windows and pulled away a broad section of jointed, carved wood covering a stone box she had mistaken for a platform, or maybe an odd-looking table of some kind, though it had steps on one side leading up to the carved surface.

Rising from where she had curled up on the bed, pillows piled behind her against the headboard for back support, Kelly padded over in curiosity as he swiped the cobwebs out of a large, stone-lined bathing tub. Yanking on the chained cork jammed into a dry waterfall-spout like the one in the bathroom, he swatted the rest of the cobwebs out of the way as water began spilling forth.

Saber leaned over as she approached and pulled out another cork, one down at the bottom of the basin. "It won't do to fill the tub before it has been rinsed, at the very least," he said. "To stop the water, you simply cork it, like this. To make it cold or hot, you turn this." A wiggle of the lever, a splash of his hand under the flow to gauge the temperature, and Saber frowned. "Great. The spell's worn out."

"So's the one in the bathroom—uh, the refreshing room," she corrected herself, since these people apparently had a different meaning for the first term. Kelly had seen a similar handle next to the sink faucet, but had lost interest in it when it had failed to control the temperature. She peered into the grimy tub and reached into the bucket, wrinkling her nose. Cobwebs, dust, and probably a patina of soap scum, too. "I'll need that brush for just a few more minutes—"

"*Jinga's Balls!*" he exploded, grabbing the brush back from her. Saber gritted his teeth, turning a little reddish in the face in his effort to control his temper. Yanking the bucket out of her reach, he pointed at the bed, carefully mastering his volume, if not the force of his words. "You. Will. Sit. *There. I* will scrub the damned tub!"

"Fine! The soap's by the sink!" Flouncing around him, she stalked back to the bed and crawled back onto it. Flopping down against the pillows, she glared at him as he stared at her. "Well? If *you* don't do it, you know that I'm going to!"

He glared at her, then threw the brush in the bucket and carried it out with him. Biting her lower lip to hide her smile, Kelly returned her attention to her sewing. A tiny part of her attention. The rest of it snuck many glances at him as he came back a few minutes later, muttered something lengthy and complicated-sounding that made the water quickly steam as it splashed along the fall, and corked the waterfall again. "I'll fetch you a new cork for the sink in the refreshing room."

She had to bite her lower lip hard to control her smile as he walked away three steps, then quickly darted back to the edge of the tub, grabbed bucket, soap, and brush, and took them with him to make sure she couldn't do anything with them while he was gone. Choking, she averted her face as he stalked out, slamming the door shut behind him. She really shouldn't laugh at him, but it *was* funny, and Kelly bit her lip and quivered with suppressed laughter until she was sure he was out of earshot, then had to wipe tears away from her eyes as gales of laughter rang through the octagonal room.

When he came back, stripped off his boots and tunic, and crawled halfway into her tub to scrub it, she didn't feel like laughing for long. Drooling, sighing, moaning, and grabbing maybe, but not laughing. Lightly tanned muscles rippled, dusted with dark blond hairs in front, streaked with a faded white scar in back that was jagged like it had come from lightning, down past one shoulder blade. Or maybe it had been caused by the rough-slashed tip of someone's sword or dagger, given the kind of universe he lived in. As she watched, breathless from the view, his muscular arms flexed over and over, his firm backside lifting into the air as he scrubbed the near side of the rim. Those near-full, entirely kissable lips muttered as he worked.

Unfortunately, he must have been muttering a cleansing spell, because it took him less than two minutes to make the damned stone tub gleam like it probably had during its very first polishing. Judging from the amount of accumulated grime, she figured it would have taken her at least an hour to achieve the same results. Swiping at it one last time with a scrap of cloth, he thrust that cloth into the emptied bucket with the soap and the brush and headed for the door.

"I'll need the soap to wash myself," Kelly pointed out quickly. "And a rag to wash with, and clean towels to dry myself with. And if you could use your cleaning-spell thing on . . . these . . . clothes . . ."

The heated, dark look he aimed her way made the words dry up in her throat.

She swallowed. "Never mind. I don't want to be a bother."

He muttered the Katani version of "too late" under his breath and stalked out the door. Forgetting his shirt and his boots, his dark gold hair rippling halfway down the taut, flexing muscles of his back.

As soon as he was gone, she flung herself back against the pillows with a grin and a sigh, running her hand up from her thigh to her breast, needle and garment abandoned on her crossed legs. There was something exhilarating about sparring with him, now that she wasn't frightened, confused, or exhausted. And something even more exciting about being in the same room as a half-naked *him*. She just wished this world didn't have to believe in Curses, or it could have been his hand cupping her breast. Without that silly verse and the local fears against such things, she could well have been the sheath for Saber's sword. Certainly he was the first man in a long time to even tempt her . . . and oh, boy, was he a temptation.

She just didn't have time to do anything about it right now, not when he was due to come back soon.

Ah, well, a girl can always dream . . .

* * *

Kelly was sedately upright and working once more on her stitching, still smiling to herself with secret amusement when he came back a little while later. The wizard Saber—though he looked more like a warrior to her, especially coupled with that name—set half a dozen bottles on the edge of the tub. He added a stack of plain cotton sheets from the crook of his elbow, though they were not the terry cloth towels she was used to. He tromped into her bathroom to shut off the constant flow of water, using a large, oval corkstopper he took from a pouch on his belt. Then he came back and started rapping on all of the lightglobes in the chamber, with the spiral-carved stick that had been hanging on a hook by the door.

The chamber needed the light, Kelly realized; the two moons didn't shine brightly enough, and the single globe she had lit was inadequate for illumination.

She had studied the scenery beyond the windows, earlier, taking in the semitropical forest that cloaked the castle, its grounds, and the line of water beyond the greenery, glistening in the distance. It was more or less the same view, she had already learned, whether one looked east or west out of the walls of the octagonal room. A couple of miles of land sloped down to both the east and the west, away from the peak that the towered outer wall, donjon, and palace wings perched on; horizonless water lay beyond that. They really were exiled on an island far from anyone else.

To the north and south, the island rose into much more mountainous peaks than the modest saddleback hill the brothers' exile-home sat on, stretching the island out across an unseeable distance in those directions. It was a large castle, and, from what she could tell, it was a fairly large island, certainly big enough to have supported a medium-sized town, even by modern standards. That included enough space for farmland, if one cut down some of the jungle out there, but she had yet to see any other signs of civilization beyond Nightfall Castle itself.

One thing was for certain, though: She was in the southern hemisphere of this world. At least, from her perspective, the sun seemed to be traveling from east to west across the northern part of the sky, and that suggested a land that lay south of the local equator. There was also the spell or whatever it was that was allowing her to understand everything translated as being that way: east as east, north as north, and so forth.

I suppose I could be in a miniature, magical version of New Zealand, though these boys don't seem to have the right accent.

As he knocked the last lightglobe into glowing, Saber returned the rapping stick to its hook on the wall, fetched his discarded tunic and boots, then gestured in the direction of the bottles he had placed around the stone tub. "There are your soaps, and some scented oils, too. Do not blame me if they turn out to be dried beyond use."

"Thank you, Saber," she murmured, making him pause at the door. Kelly had done a bit of thinking that afternoon. "I do appreciate this . . . and I apologize for being a trial these past few days. My only reasoning is that maybe the troubles I've been suffering lately have cut my temper a little too short."

He stayed there, one hand on the door handle, absorbing her words. Finally, he spoke. "Trevan swears his rare but hot temper is linked to the red in his hair. And Koranen agrees about his own, calling it as heated as a flame. I . . . apologize for being related to them."

Kelly bit her lip, trying not to chuckle at his roundabout apology. She nodded and kept her gaze carefully on her stitching. "I understand."

"Kelly of Doyle . . ."

She looked up at him and lost the urge to smile at the sobriety in his gray eyes.

"Do not fall in love with me. Do not make me fall in love with you. Do you understand?"

She gave his warning, his order, his request due consideration. "All right. No falling in love," she added in clarification, staring out the western windows beyond the foot of the bed. "I have no problem with that." Then she looked at him, shod but still shirtless, and said the first thing that came into her head. "Want to have hot sex instead?"

He twitched. The eyelid, the throat, and the chest muscles, the whole left half of his body *twitched*. Somehow he left her room. Somehow he shut the door behind him. Quietly. And roared something she did *not* want translated, before he descended the stairs beyond the solid panel between them.

Morganen heard that roar in a way that would have done his sound-oriented brother, Evanor, proud, and smiled. Evanor cocked his light blond head and one of his golden brows, and eyed their beaming youngest sibling. Morganen shook his head and addressed the others assembled in his workroom while their eldest was distracted and safely out of the way.

Everyone was there, except for Saber, of course, and Rydan, who was even less happy about the idea of women on Nightfall than the eldest of them was. Their night-loving brother didn't care for the claim made in his particular verse, that he would fall into ruin at the hands of his own female-sent Destiny. Still, Morganen's remaining five brothers weren't nearly as woman-shy, not even the arrogant Dominor, who fancied himself his Prophesied namesake, the sole Master of his Destiny. Morg smiled again, this time just from looking at the five older men in his workroom.

"My dear brothers, this is working *beautifully*. Especially since our eldest is so unenamoured of the thought of any of the *rest* of us attending her, and maybe falling for the woman, he's forcing himself to spend more and more time with her."

"You may be the most powerful of us, Morg," Wolfer asserted in his low voice that was half a growl, "but is it wise to tempt the Curse that is our Destiny?"

Morganen met those golden eyes levelly, wisely with his younger, aquamarine ones. "It is our Destiny; thus we cannot escape it. We can, however, control it. So when the 'Disaster' comes, as foretold in Saber's verse," he added, "the rest of us must be prepared for anything. We will not be able to rely upon aid from the mainland to help us in dealing with it, here in our exile—even if the threat could possibly destroy the whole of Katan, it will be up to ourselves alone to handle it, so we must be ready.

"If I read the verse right, this woman Kelly will be linked somehow to the Disaster that will appear shortly after Saber's eventual claim of her. If and when he falls for her, it is her heel, after all, which is linked to its appearance—though *not*, as some might assume, the cause of it," he added as even his twin scowled, unhappy at the possibility. "If that were so, the verse would have claimed 'from her heel,' as a result of something she did, not 'at her heel,' something that follows or chases after her of its own volition. A difference of simple, coincidentally timed circumstance, and not through any deliberation on her part.

"I have two excellent reasons, then, to forestall returning the woman to her own universe: to get the coming Disaster over with, and to make certain the woman associated with it is on hand to be able to help us recognize and handle it. Because make no mistake, she *is* linked to it, even if she won't start it," Morganen reiterated. "Delaying her return to her own homeland will buy us time, and wear down Saber's innate, stubborn resistance. But I can only stall for so long. So do what you can to throw the two of them together . . . and to maybe prick his protective jealousy. Carefully, of course."

Some of the brothers smiled wickedly at that last part. Some frowned with worry. One, Dominor, sneered slightly. Morganen dismissed them before their eldest could think to search for any of them and wonder that all were missing from their usual haunts at this hour. They scattered.

Only Koranen lingered. The redhead waited until they were fully alone before speaking. "Morg, are you sure this is a wise thing to do?"

"Of course it is, Kor," Morganen reassured him confidently, moving to crack open one of his spellbooks.

Koranen shook his auburn head. "No, not the defiance of Destiny—I mean, starting the whole thing off." He eyed the door, closed behind the heels of Dominor, last of the others to leave, and shook his head again. "I don't think the others have yet realized what I instantly knew."

"And that would be . . . ?" his slightly younger twin prompted.

"Once Saber falls for a woman, the rest of us will topple, one right after the next."

"What's the problem there? I'm actually looking forward to it," Morganen added, grinning and briefly rubbing his hands together in anticipated glee. "I like women!"

His twin perched on the edge of his stone-topped, experiment-scarred worktable, swinging his legs in their gold-and-red boots and trousers. "Have you considered how rough some of the wooing will be? We can all hear Saber and this woman Kelly going at it, and that's just verbally. Wolfer's too strong, too intense to be trusted with any but the toughest of women physically, but we obviously don't have any female warriors or women smiths on the island.

"Dominor would need someone who could simply match him, let alone best him, and he's the third-best mage in the family, which means one of the best in all of Katan itself, beyond all others, save for yourself and Rydan. But Rydan's power surges that great only with the coming of a storm, and he doesn't bother to play competition games with any of us, least of all Dom, so Dom's the equivalent to second strongest.

"He certainly has the attitude to match his strength. Dom's woman would have to be a virago of power, competitiveness, and manipulation." Koranen arched a skeptical brow at his sibling. "Not exactly a recipe for a gentle wooing, Brother."

"But Evanor's search will likely be a gentle one," Morganen pointed out, abandoning his books for the moment. "The quest for two lonely hearts to join together is not one that calls fierce arguments to mind. And Wolfer has already met the mate Destined for him, though he knows it not, yet. She will come to the island at the appropriate time, in accordance with his own Destiny." That raised his twin's reddish brows, but Morganen merely continued, "Just as Dominor and Evanor will find their own women coming to them—it's not as if we have any that *we* could go to, exiled here on this otherwise deserted isle."

"And back we are again, to Trevan and his catlike ways," Koranen returned. "He of all of us has been the most restless without a woman on the isle. If it were not for his respect for Saber's warning to stay away from her, and our eldest brother's possessiveness toward her, Trevan might have seduced this woman already.

"Rydan's version of courtship—I can picture that in my mind right now, Brother," Koranen stated bluntly, running his fingers through his hair. "He'll toss the woman out the nearest opening, whether it's a window or a door, in the fear that love will sap his powers. He's very proud of being the second-strongest mage of all of us, even though he's not very vocal about it, like Dom is. Or worse, the woman might demand he start acting like a civilized man and walk around during daylight hours."

This time it was Morganen who reacted, though mostly to smother a smile behind his hand as his twin continued.

"He'd call up a storm himself in retaliation, not just wait for one to fuel his powers, just so he could blast the poor woman off the island and return to his solitary, night-loving ways—smile all you like, Morg," Koranen warned him. "You know he'd do it."

"Perhaps, and perhaps not. Prophecy is Prophecy, after all. But then there's *you*," Morganen pointed out quietly, thoughtfully. "You need a woman your passion cannot accidentally but quite literally burn, as we have unfortunately seen in the past. You will grow as restless as Trevan in your own way, longing for something you cannot find . . . but it will find you."

"You speak like a Seer, Brother," his twin returned dryly. "No Katani Mage can ever be a Seer, no Seer ever a Mage. Or have you broken the laws of Magic and Destiny set down by Kata and Jinga at the dawn of our Empire? Perhaps you have found some way to have yourself reborn as the scion of another land, with another set of magical rules that only you can obey?"

Morganen smiled, if more to himself than to his brother. "I have merely meditated a long time on this matter. Never fear; I, too, shall fall beneath the true-struck arrow of love. I think it will be an easy wooing, too, or at least I hope it; my verse speaks more about my playing the part of Kata-the-Love-Maker with all of the rest of you. It does say very clearly that I'll be the last to clasp hands over the eight altars." His smile quirked a little on one side, turning wry with envy. "I have nothing to do until then, but meditate on how I can first help the rest of you. As quickly as can be, else I will be an old bachelor too long neglected upon the shelf for any woman to want to reach for my time-withered hands and step into the altars with me."

"Oh, boo-hoo; I weep a whole river for you," Koranen muttered under his breath. His brother swiped at him, and they mock-tussled as twins and brothers often do, lightening the mood.

SEVEN

❊

"Come in!" Kelly called from her seat at the table-like desk, responding to the knock on her door. Saber was back to looming over her, watching her eat every morsel, since she hadn't managed to finish the previous night's dinner when he had left it with her. Once again, he was overseeing her as she ate her food.

With her hair and skin bathed clean, with the long, light blue overgown rehemmed and the drawstrings of the underdrawers and corset replaced with ones that were sturdier, with the scent of something faint but flowery lingering from one of the age-thickened bath oils Saber had found and the best-fitting pair of slippers he'd brought settled on her feet, Kelly felt almost human. She even felt ready for company. Any company that wasn't the man glowering and carefully keeping his distance from her, while somehow managing at the same time to loom practically over her shoulder from his place in a nearby chair.

She wished her friend Hope was with her. Hope could make any situation cheerful and usually could say just the right thing to make someone smile. But that wasn't very likely, given she was more or less trapped in this alternate reality.

The door opened with a slight creak, and Morganen entered. He was the youngest and, if she remembered right, one of the two shortest of the more or less tall Nightfall Sons. His light brown hair was caught back with the same headband she had seen him wear before, but not confined in a bun. It spilled down over his shoulders to midchest in the longish style all eight brothers wore. Glancing at his eldest sibling, he stepped the rest of the way into the room. "Good. I was hoping I'd catch both of you here. I have some good news, and some bad news."

"About what?" Kelly asked.

"Of what?" Saber questioned at the same time.

Morganen shrugged. "About her being sent back home."

Saber grimaced slightly at that. He told himself it was because his brother didn't sound hopeful of being able to do it soon. Morganen's words as he crossed to the desk and perched his hip on the edge confirmed that hypothesis.

"The good news, Lady Kelly, is that I *can* send you back to your own dimension. Perhaps even to a place and time of your own choosing, instead of into the burning remnants of your former home. Provided it's past the point of your leaving, of course; not even I dare meddle with Time," he added, gentle in his discrete mentioning of her near-death by fire. "The bad news is . . . I cannot do so for another five of our months."

"Five *months*?" Saber all but roared. "But you said—"

"Would you shut up?" Kelly demanded, twisting to glare up at him. His attitude hurt. The idea of her not being able to go back today was not something she wanted shouted in her ear. "I'm sick of you grunting and snarling around me like some damned, idiotic *caveman*!"

Morganen whistled softly, waving his hand between the two of them as he leaned over her partially eaten breakfast. "May I have your attention again, please?"

"You had best explain yourself, and this so-called 'five months' you claim," his oldest brother growled.

"Pay attention, O Lesser-Powered One," Morganen chided, his voice chilly for a moment. Saber might have been the eldest brother, but he was not the most powerful mage in the family by any means, and the youngest of them made no bones about reminding his siblings whenever he had to. "Her realm has very little magic. Think of it as trying to wield your sword in a tiny, imprisoning box made of stout wood. You have to plan each swing and thrust carefully, or risk splintering the walls. Ours is a broad, open battlefield by comparison, where you can not only swing your sword, but move about very freely, able to attack and defend from many different angles."

Saber studied him with a lingering touch of suspicion, but nodded in comprehension at the younger man's analogy. "What has this to do with why you cannot send her back for five whole months?"

"Because the 'wood' has splintered and poses a danger to the sword-wielder. The aether of her world must settle for at least five months by my calculations, before I dare touch it again—Brother, I ripped her from her world with none of the subtleties I am normally famous for," Morganen added, flicking his fingers before folding his arms across his chest. "I had no time and no choice; it was either save her immediately, or watch through my scrying mirror—and please forgive me for mentioning the undoubtedly unpleasant memories of this, my lady—as she would have been scorched to a screaming, dead crisp."

Kelly set her fork down. Apology or not, her appetite wasn't feeling cooperative at the graphically phrased reminder.

Saber growled, flipping his hand at her. "Great! Now you've made her lose her appetite!"

"She'll have plenty of time to recover it," Morganen countered mildly. "Plus plenty of food to eat, plenty of time to eat it in, and plenty of time to get plenty of rest. She should consider it a chance to relax and not have to worry about a single care while she's here." The youngest of the brothers trailed off and peered at his brother. "That is, I'm presuming you're not going to toss her out of the castle and make her live in a hollow tree somewhere for the next five months. Or worse, send her down to the western beach."

"I wouldn't do *that*," Saber returned gruffly, glaring at his brother for even daring to suggest it.

"What do you mean by that?" Kelly asked at the same time. The two men glanced at each other, and Morganen let his eldest brother explain.

"For a woman to be found on this isle—among us, the exiled eight brothers of Corvis—the penalty has been declared as death," Saber stated grimly. "Since we are too strong, individually and collectively, for the Council to face and kill, by any but the most indirect routes—"

"Such as those mekhadadaks and other beasties anonymously inflicted on us every few weeks," Morganen interjected helpfully.

"Yes, well, the Council of Mages has decided that it would be simpler to kill any woman foolish enough to come here instead," Saber continued. "We receive a shipment of trade supplies once every two weeks, at the new and the full of Brother Moon; the traders are men only, and they bring the foods we cannot grow or catch ourselves, and other things we cannot easily make.

"In exchange, they take away in trade some of the excess food we can be bothered to harvest, hunt, or catch, and the magic items that each of us makes. Corvis-made magical items—our former bloodline, before we were exiled from our rightful lands and stripped of its name for the duration of our generation," Saber explained, "—have always been of high magical quality, from long-lasting lightglobes like these ones, to those horseless carriages Evanor mentioned, and other things. Now, it is Nightfall-in-exile that is known to produce the best. *We* are the best."

"And we make certain the traders pay for it," Morganen added. "Myself, Rydan, and Dominor are the three most powerful mages in all of Katan. We're also among the most skilled. We can craft items to order, as described on parchment and brought by the traders, and are able to make things that few others can successfully attempt; we are that strong in our individual and combined ability. So we can, and *do*, charge extra-high prices, partially to make up for the fact that we must ship in the raw materials and manufacture everything ourselves, and partly in a monetary revenge for being exiled here. And . . . some are thrilled by the idea of owning even something so relatively commonplace as a lightglobe from the 'notorious Nightfall Isle,' made by the exiled 'Sons of Destiny.' The novelty is appealing.

"But to get back to the problem, Brother," he added, looking up at Saber. "I essentially broke her free of her realm with a sledgehammer, not just a sword. Hence the 'splinters,' and the five-month wait, so that none of those involved are afflicted by the disturbances in the aethers between our two existences. So. This brings us to an important question. What are you going to do with her while she's here?"

"Me? *You* brought her here. She is *your* responsibility!"

"You are the eldest," Morganen pointed out deferentially.

"You deal with her," Saber ordered, as Kelly frowned, wondering exactly what was going on here, why *she* wasn't being consulted one way or another.

Morganen smiled. Slyly. "Fine. I will take care of her from this point on, Brother." He glanced down at the bewildered woman seated between them and gently picked up her hand. Lifted it to his lips, he saluted it with the gentlest touch before smiling at Kelly of Doyle. "*I* am not afraid of *my* Destiny, or of any woman come to this isle. My lady, if you permit it . . . I would be in raptures if you gave me your permission to court you. With the most honorable intent to walk the eight altars of marriage with you, should it turn out that we are compatible and agree."

"*Get out.*"

"I beg your pardon?" Morganen asked, raising his head and his brows at his brother, still gently holding on to Kelly's fingers.

Saber glowered. "Get out, and don't you ever touch her again! *No one* will be courting, or wooing, or wedding in this house!"

"*Excuse* me!" Kelly tugged her hand free and stood. She glared at both men. Enough was enough, and she was going to let them know it! "I think *I* have a rather big say in the whole of this—and quite frankly, I want *none* of you thickheaded, chauvinistic brutes. Not you, Morganen, nor Evanor, and not any of the others I've seen, but which no one has even bothered to introduce me to—and certainly not *you*!" she added, glaring at Saber. "If anyone is going to get out of this room, it's *both* of you. I refuse to put up with your asinine manners any longer—get out, right now!"

"Kelly—"

"Out!" Stamping her foot for emphasis, she jabbed her arm at the partially open door.

"Keep in mind my offer, my lady," Morganen asserted smoothly as he stood and bowed, backing up to the door in question. "With the most honorable of intentions—"

"Out!"

Saber reluctantly followed, his attention more on making sure his brother left than on her command to leave. "You, Morganen, will leave her alone—"

"I said get *out*!" Picking up the lid that had covered the platter Saber had carried in for her, she flung it at him. It bounced off of the barely visible energy barrier that reflexively hardened between them with a flick of his hand; the lid clanged to the floor, denting slightly as it landed. Kelly glared at him. She was too outraged to be afraid of his magic, though she knew later she'd be trembling. "You'll get what you want, Saber—I fully intend to abide my time well out of the way of *all* of you—or at least the asinine, grumpy ones among you! Of which *you* are the bloody *king*!"

"You—"

"*Out!*"

He left, closing the door, his expression unreadable. She dropped back down into her seat, her anger abruptly deflated. Her limbs trembled, as anticipated. If he'd had the same level of temper as her, Saber of Nightfall could have easily swatted her with a spell, as casually as he would hit an insect.

She didn't have much appetite for food at all. Getting up again, she crossed to the dented dome, picked it up, tried straightening the small flattened spot on the otherwise perfect curve, then gave up and dropped it over the food with a clatter. Something about the man just . . . just set her strawberry blond temper on fire, that was all.

Abandoning the re-covered food, she crossed to the window seat, where she had set up the lace-bobbing form that Evanor had found for her. Kelly punched a couple of pillows into shape for back support, dropped onto the cushions, and propped the velvet-covered bobbing board on her lap. It had a hard-stuffed roller that pivoted along the center of the board, providing a firm place for the pins to go in, yet was broad enough that it provided plenty of surface for wide or narrow lace, whether it was for something short and simple or for more long and complex patterns. A parchment pattern-strip was still carefully pinned in place around the roller, yellowed with age. And there were plenty of cotton-wound bobbins to play out the unfamiliar pattern with.

It was just the sort of absorbing task she needed to help herself relax. Peering at the weave of the fine-spun threads, she refamiliarized herself with which distinctively notched bobbin-spools were associated with which part of the pattern overall, and she started weaving the threads among the pins, occasionally shifting the glass-tipped pins downward into the next set of pre-pricked holes to further the hearts-within-hearts trim along. Lace-making was soothing, exacting, attention-grabbing work, and that was exactly what Kelly needed, dammit.

She did *not* need a pigheaded, asinine, know-it-all occupying her thoughts . . . a lot.

Morganen slammed against the stone wall of the upper level of the north wing, back-first. Saber's hand had gripped his throat the moment they reached the bottom of the steps up to the lord's room. "You will leave her alone. *Is that understood?*"

"Let . . . go—" Morganen choked, grabbing at the fingers threatening to crush his windpipe, "or . . . turn . . . you into . . . *toad* . . ."

Saber let go. Then slammed his brother against the wall again, this time grasping two fistfuls of his tunic, rather than his throat. Gray eyes bored into aquamarine. "I *mean* it, Morg! You will stay away from her!"

Morganen shoved his brother's grip away, though it jerked roughly at his dark blue tunic. "Stop thinking of yourself, Saber! She's free to choose or not choose as she damn well pleases! *I* merely wanted her to know that *I* was interested, if she ever decides to be interested in me—which I am perfectly free to be!" He straightened his tunic and started for the stairs leading down into the rest of the castle, speaking without turning his head. "Frankly, given how you've yelled and bullied and treated her, Saber, I'm not surprised at the way she reacted to you, with your constantly telling her what she can and can't do."

"Morganen—" Saber warned him in a growl.

His youngest brother, twenty-three going on fifty-three, turned and pointed his finger. "*You* listen to me! *There is no escaping Destiny.* Fate arranged itself that I caught sight of her predicament while I was idly scrying through the other universes out there. And by the touch of that distant, Threefold God, I was forced by my conscience to rescue her, and thus bring her here, since I could not make my magic work well enough in her own universe to send her immediately elsewhere there. *If* she must be *here*, then it is plainly Fate's will that she will complete the verse for one of us. And if it is not to be you, then I have a one-in-seven chance of it being *me*.

"I *like* women," Morganen asserted. "I liked being around them back when we were still in Corvis lands. I liked being with them, conversing with them, seeing the pleasure in their faces as I gave them flowers and little trinkets, back in our old home. I liked the way they usually insist on everything being clean and neat—instead of a mekhadadak's nest, like this place—and how sweet they smell when they are freshly bathed, and how pretty they look when they are neatly dressed. I like the way they think, and how they talk, and their sense of humor!

"Kata's Breasts!" he swore, clenching his hands toward the ceiling. "I have every *right* to want to have a woman in my life, Destiny or no! So if *you* discard her by word and by deed, *I* have every right to woo what you leave behind. As do all of your *other* brothers, *Eldest*," Morganen added, slashing his hands between them. "You cannot kill us for exercising our rights as living, breathing men. And if you *ever* attempt to threaten me again, I *will* turn you into a toad!"

"I am the first of the brothers in that damned Prophecy," Saber growled as his sibling turned to head for the stairs again. "The first maiden goes to *me*."

Morganen stopped and turned around. He gave his eldest brother a contemptuous, disgusted look. "What makes you think she *is* a maid, Saber? Have you *asked* her about her level of chastity, or even if her culture and people value such things? Have you asked her *any-thing* that hasn't been punctuated by a demand or a shout? Perhaps that is the way *you* woo, but for myself, it is not! And it has not been so long, nor myself so young at the time, that I cannot remember what women *do* like in their courting!"

Turning once more, the youngest of the brothers entered the north wing stairwell and descended out of sight. Frustrated, Saber took himself along a different path to his own tower. To think on Morganen's blunt words, to not think; it didn't matter. No one could do either successfully, not with their thoughts in the kind of chaotic currents his own were drowning under.

She didn't care when no one brought up her supper by the end of the day. She still had enough food left over from breakfast, eaten partially by lunchtime, to have for her evening meal. And plenty of sewing to occupy her attention, including reworking the neckline of the blue gown to fit a lot better than the shapeless way it was originally designed, stitching it into something much more flattering for her figure. But when no one came up with breakfast shortly after dawn, as Saber had done before, nor for a while afterward, Kelly hitched up the rehemmed skirts of her completely reworked gown, and went in search of sustenance.

Or rather, tried to. The first obstacle was a door that wouldn't budge. She found an age-worn bronze brooch in one of the drawers of the otherwise empty desk, and attempted to jimmy the lock with its pin. That didn't work, but that was no surprise, because she really didn't have more than a vague idea how to go about it, other than it involved somehow shoving tumbler-levers this way and that. Failing at that, she peered out the windows assessing her next option.

Aside from the sloping, forested hills and the distant water, there was the view of the castle itself: the octagonal outer walls that had to be fifty feet tall, each massive tower at the corners rising a good thirty or forty feet more above the top of the encircling guard wall. She could tell that much by counting arrow-loop windows and gauging the size of the doors at their base and the doors she could see that opened onto the ramparts; by comparing the evenly sized crenellated battlements lining each side of the rampart walkways to the overall view of the outer wall.

As a seamstress, she had learned long ago to gauge measurements by eye. Yet the towers and outer wall didn't look all that imposing, because the whole of the compound was so large-scaled overall. But taken as a whole, the place was a veritable palace of sprawling stone. Neglected gardens filled in the space between most of the main wings of the castle and that outer wall; the wings themselves were built interestingly—kind of like a snowflake, she decided, with four and eight branches.

From the octagonal main tower her room was perched on top of, there were four wings of four floors each, if one counted the high-sloped attics with their gable-style, glazed and shuttered windows. Those four main wings spread out due north, east, south, and west. If one didn't count the fact that there would inevitably be at least one basement level, that was already a very large number of rooms to explore. The height of each floor had to be at least twelve to fourteen feet on top of that, with high ceilings designed to keep either candle smoke out of the eyes, or the heat of summer away from the inhabitants; it wasn't as if Kelly knew what season this place was experiencing, though it felt like summer.

After about a hundred yards or so, each one of the four main wings branched into a *Y*-shape for about sixty or seventy yards more. From there, columnar towers supported sculpted sky bridges that stretched out to the rampart walls, with carved wooden drawbridges that could be retracted in times of war—beauty and efficiency, all in one. The bridges looked fairly sturdy, too, despite their gray-weathered age.

Most of the rooftops of the wings were peaked and stoutly tiled in a darkish, gray blue glazed pottery, much like the homes of the southwest desert of her own world, but each roofline that she could see had a broad parapet walkway at the edge of each section, and little towers at the corners that looked like stairwells.

The roof that her room perched on top of was a curved one, as opposed to the straight-angled ones of the outlying wings. A bit of leaning out and looking down confirmed that the dome the room perched upon did terminate in a walkway parapet, the same as the straighter rooflines. Shoving the window open, Kelly hitched up her skirt, made sure her loaned leather slippers were secure on her feet, climbed out onto the almost flat surface up at the top where the room was located, and started inching her way down. Heights had never bothered her, thankfully. She did have to half-slide, half-fall the last few yards to the parapet around the domed roof, cushioning her landing with bent knees, but she didn't hurt herself.

Straightening up and shaking out her skirts, she made her way to the right, exploring as she went. The walkway, like all of the others, was broad enough for three people to have walked along together, with gray blue tiles to one side and light gray granite stone to the other. The battlements staggered up and down like little steps, and where each peak rose head-high to her, there was an arrow-loop carved into the stone; between each stepped peak, the gaps were only waist-low at most. Even though it wasn't likely that many people would go for a stroll all the way up here, the edges of the parapet were beaded and carved with weatherworn, elongated stars.

Stars with eight points, I see, Kelly realized with a touch of wry amusement. *These people really take the number eight seriously!* She found one of the four stairway towers set next to the main tower and tried the lever-style door handle. It opened easily. Skirt in hand so she wouldn't trip—she couldn't wait to make herself a decent pair of pants—Kelly descended the age-worn steps.

Sounds of conversation lured her out at the first landing, into a hall and through an ornately carved, center-pointed archway that led to a broad balcony. One that overlooked the great hall of the castle, apparently. In the sunlight streaming in through the southeastern windows, clearly seen from above the carved railing in front of her, six of the eight brothers were seated at an octagonal table set up in the middle of the floor far below her.

Eating breakfast.

Or rather, the remains of breakfast. Yet no one had brought any up for her! Growing mad, Kelly found the square-spiraled stairs again, hurried all the way to the ground floor, and strode into the great hall, ignoring the attractive patterns of the polished stone tiles underfoot. Ignoring the beauty of the stained glass windows on the four ordinal walls of every level of the hall's balconied tiers. Ignoring the artistry of the carved columns, balustrades, and archways. She was too angry to truly appreciate the architecture at the moment.

Kelly stomped down the final four steps between the column-lined section under the broad balconies and the main floor of the hall and strode straight for the men, who had fallen silent at the approaching, clearly angry *slap slap slap!* of her slippered feet.

Forks hovered in the air. Mouths were caught quirked to one side in the act of chewing. Six pairs of eyes, ranging in shade from brown to blue—lacking only in gray and black—stared at her as she approached them across the great, broad floor of the hall. Six handsome men. None of them the one that she wanted to be the source of her ire, but all of them qualifying as substitutes.

None of them swallowed. None of them spoke. None of them did anything but watch her storm right up to the table. Then again, it might have been the way she had restitched the front-lacing gown to conform to the flare of her hips, past the nip of her waist, up to the full roundness of her corseted breasts. And perhaps especially the sweetheart neckline that replaced the boring, high-necked, rounded collar that had been there before. The carrot-haired brother stared the most, in fact, but that only irritated her further.

Planting her hands on the blue cotton cupping her hips, Kelly glared at them, taking advantage of their stunned silence. "First you rescue me from a fire, then you kidnap me from my home universe, then you yell at me to eat, and now you lock me in my room and *starve* me? What the hell kind of men *are* you?"

Morganen swallowed the mouthful of bread he had been chewing and thumped the nearest of the other five in the ribs, shoving quickly and politely to his feet. The others did the same, belatedly being gentlemen. Morganen spoke as chairs scraped back. "It was not our intention to starve you . . . and I was not aware that anyone had locked you in that chamber, my lady."

"The door might have simply been stuck," Koranen added quickly, looking at his brothers, then at her with a shrug. "Many of them do, in the donjon and its wings. Even sometime out in the towers."

Kelly, not entirely appeased, held up her hands and ticked off her fingers. "Lousy housekeepers, lousy groundskeepers, lousy gentlemen, and lousy *hosts*—you *really* need a woman to straighten you out!"

Dominor took her challenge, folding his arms across his dark purple clad chest. "And you think *you* are that woman?"

"Since I'm the only one here, it has to be me," she pointed out sardonically, and flipped a hand at the table. "No woman in her right mind would allow their home to turn into such a pigsty—just look at this table!"

The six brothers all looked at the tabletop. It was covered in dirty dishes and bits of uneaten food, fruit cores and rinds, bread crusts, and the inevitable stains associated with years of use. From the stains under the placement of the goblets, it looked like their users didn't care about mopping up spills, and from the browning of some of the apple cores, it was clear that they had not been cleaned away since the last meal eaten in this place.

One of them shrugged, the one with hair more coppery than her own strawberry blond locks, lifting his green eyes to hers. "What about it?"

"It's filthy!"

"We have been eating off of it," the tallest, most muscular of the brothers reasoned in a rumbling-low voice, his own brown hair shaggy as it fell in layers to just below his collarbone. "Naturally it is dirty at the moment."

"I mean it should be scrubbed and sanded and refinished, rather than let bits of things clump into dark, sticky spots," Kelly returned. She wiggled her toes in her slipper, letting them hear the almost velcro-like sound of her shoe adhering to a similarly disgusting spot underfoot. One that she had stepped on in her approach. "The same goes for this floor. And I haven't seen so many cobwebs and dust bunnies since *Dracula Needs a Wife*, on the old movie channel!"

"The what?" one of them asked. "And who?"

Kelly shook her head. "Never mind. If I'm going to be stuck here for five months, I insist on a certain standard of hygiene and cleanliness. And you *will* be thanking me for it before I am done with you," she added, pushing up her light blue sleeves in a no-nonsense manner. "Now, the first thing we will do is—"

"The *first* thing we will do," Morganen overrode her, coming around and urging her into the nearest empty chair, "is see that you are properly fed. And then we will place ourselves at your disposal for the rest of the day." The others started making noises of protest. At a pointed look and an equally pointed throat-clearing from their youngest, they muttered under their breaths and sat back down as soon as she was seated. "It may be a little cool, but the food is still quite palatable, which you will soon see.

"Of course, Rydan would be here to accept your praises," Morganen added, serving her on Saber's untouched, empty plate, "but he shuns the day and only stays long enough to prepare at least part of our breakfast, usually the rising of the bread and maybe one or two other things; he takes his own plate back with him to his tower, which not even we are allowed to enter. Well, not beyond the chamber up at the parapet level. He does join us for the evening meal, though, which we always hold after sundown to ensure we actually get to see him once in a while."

"That's the black-haired one, with the black eyes?" Kelly wanted to clarify, thinking of the grumpy one that had passed her during the mekh-something cleanup, the one who had seemed like a part of the night, a storm of barely contained power sweeping past her.

"Yes—don't just sit there like lumps; introduce yourselves!" Morganen added to his brothers, pouring her some more of the sweet-tart, greenish juice she had tasted before. "Everyone, this is the Lady Kelly of Doyle."

"I'm not a lady," Kelly pointed out with quick honesty. That wasn't entirely true; she had a couple of honorariums from the medieval society that had come with a title or two, but now was not the time to explain the difference between real and make-believe. "I'm a citizen of the United States of America, and thus the equal of anyone else. That's all I need to be."

The one with the coppery-blond hair, darker and redder than her own, if sun-streaked with cream, the one with the cat-green eyes who had ogled her despite the fury of her approach, smiled charmingly. "Oh, but any woman who braves the dangers of Nightfall Isle is the most noble and worthy of women."

"Dangers?" she asked, arching a brow. "Little black mekha-whatchamacallits, cobwebs, and sticky spots on the floor, and grumpy men who have let their gentlemanly manners slide into oblivion in, what was it, the past three years?"

"Mainly the lattermost," Morganen agreed dryly, resuming his seat. "You have already met me, more or less; I am Morganen the Mage, youngest of the Eight and the one who brought you here."

To him, she would be polite. She did owe him her life and the ability to converse with her hosts, after all. "And for my timely rescue, I thank you again, Morganen," Kelly returned with a polite nod, glad *someone* was willing to be civilized and talk, not yell, with her. She looked at the man seated on her left, the one with the dark brown hair and the blue eyes, clad in dark blue. "And you are?"

"Dominor, the Master, third of us. And I serve only myself. Prod the others into aiding you," he added with cool disdain. "I will not bow to an outlander woman's will."

EIGHT

❊

Kelly glanced around the table, seeing how the others took his comment. Her determination to stay on top of this bizarre situation hardened the moment she realized most of the others were silently agreeing with him. Morganen was the only one who met her eyes with any real encouragement for her presence among them. He even gave her a slight nod; from the encouraging look in his eyes, she knew it wasn't an agreement with his brother's pronouncement.

Braced by that silent permission, Kelly snapped her hand up and attacked the man next to her in a lightning-fast movement. One taught to her by her grandmother, not by her martial arts instructors. Her fingers pinched the curve of Dominor's ear in an unshakable grip: the infamous Granny Doyle maneuver.

"Ow! Let go, woman!"

Kelly tightened her grip and stood, towering over him, only because he was seated. "Get used to it, buster. Where *I* come from," she added, exaggerating quite a bit, "no man would dare treat a woman in that insulting and condescending manner. If I say you're going to scrub the floor with your favorite toothbrush, you *are* going to scrub the floor with your favorite toothbrush!

"Women are the keepers of civilization, and by all the gods of both this world and mine, you *will* become civilized again!" She jerked on his ear while he tried futilely to pry her hand off of it, and glared at the others. "Do any of the rest of you have a problem with being civilized in my presence?"

"Let go of my ear, woman, or I'll turn you into a toad!" he demanded, glaring up at her.

Kelly yanked him half up out of his chair by his ear, tugging his handsome, grimacing face close to her own. "Have you ever heard of the word *please*? Or *thank you*, or the phrase *if you would be so kind*? I am sick and tired of being yelled at by you overgrown, immature men!" she yelled herself. A thrust of her hand, and he dropped back into his chair, rubbing at the ear she had roughly released. Planting her hands on her hips, Kelly glared at the rest of them. "I solemnly swear, the next man who raises his voice to me, or threatens me, or behaves with anything less than civil courtesy to me, will end up eating dirt!"

"And how are you going to make me behave? *Especially* once I have turned you into the toad you are, woman!" Dominor growled, shoving to his feet to tower over and glare at her in turn.

"That does it!" A hitch of her skirts, and she kicked with her slippered foot. Not at him, but at the chair behind him, then at the one behind her, scraping them both out of the way. Before either piece of furniture had finished rocking from her rough shoves, she grabbed the bigger man by the arm, whirled, twisted, and flipped him onto the floor. A torque of the arm still caught in her grip, a shove of her slippered foot on the back of his head, and she pinned him face-down, almost effortlessly.

"Ow! Dammit, woman!"

She wiggled her foot, making his cheek bounce more or less in the same sticky spot her slipper had found mere moments before. "Do you *feel* that crud on the floor? Do you *like* the feel of that crud?" she added pointedly, almost perversely cheerful in this hearty release of all her anger and frustration at her situation. "Congratulations, Dominor! *You* just volunteered to clean it up!"

In spite of her racing heart, in spite of the acknowledgment that he probably could literally turn her into a toad . . . Kelly found the stunned looks on all of their faces to be quite exhilarating. She took ruthless control of that fact, and the situation. Doyles didn't waste a good tactical advantage, after all.

"You see, I don't need magic to beat the crap out of you . . . but you have to use it to equal me. You know what, Dominor?" she added, addressing the brother under her foot. "I *like* it, that this fact sticks in your throat—*and* to your face. The fact that I can make you eat dirt without having to use magic like some kind of crutch!

"Oh, and I wouldn't ever again threaten to turn me into anything I wasn't meant by God and nature to be in the first place, mister," she added sweetly, torquing his arm a little more, making him gasp. "You see, I would still be a woman inside of that toad shape you threatened to turn me into, and all the darkest powers of Hell have nothing on a woman who's gotten good and mad at some stupid, idiotic man!" Another yank, and he grunted from the pain. "Now, are you going to shut up and obey me? Or shall I tie your body into knots with my otherworldly knowledge and extradimensional ways?"

He muttered something.

"Excuse me; *what* did you say?" Kelly asked, tweaking his arm a little more, though not quite to the point of dislocation. It got the results she wanted, more or less.

"*Truce!*"

"I didn't hear a 'please'; I specifically requested civilized words like *please*, remember?" she asked him mock-sweetly, as his brothers stared, not daring to interfere at the sight of the second most powerful of the brothers present at breakfast being pinned so helplessly to the floor.

"Truce . . . *please.*"

It was said through his teeth, but it was a please nonetheless. Kelly released him, stepped back, smoothed out her skirts, and hooked her chair back into place with a toe and a hand, as he scrambled to his feet. One brother down, the rest to go. She remained on her feet while the third-born of the brothers straightened his clothes, glaring at her.

"Does anyone else care to challenge my status as a woman and therefore the keeper of civilization for the duration of my visit in this household? No? *Excellent.* Do not yell at me, do not threaten me, and do not treat me with anything less than the respect I am due, gentlemen, as your peer and your equal. Or I will redefine this universe's version of the meaning of holy terror. As is my right, as a woman."

Reseating herself, she picked up the fork at her place setting.

"Actually, I am quite easy to get along with, under most civilized circumstances. Treat me nicely, and I will do the same to you. It's that simple."

"I still ought to turn you into a toad," Dominor growled, but he reseated himself, dragging his chair back into place. Morganen watched him, but the third-eldest brother merely eyed the woman in their midst for a long moment. A sigh, and he spoke. Politely. "How did you manage to pin me down like that? You barely weigh half of what I do!"

"Like I said, it's my otherworldly way. Should you be unkind or uncivil to me again, I would be delighted to demonstrate both that and several other painful techniques on your various extremities," Kelly offered smoothly, mock-sweetly. "But only if you act impolitely."

Dominor stared at her a moment more, then looked elsewhere. "Thank Kata she's not *my* Fate . . ."

The green-eyed, coppery-haired brother choked on a laugh, caught in the middle of a sip of his juice. Since he was the next one seated around the table, Kelly focused on him, narrowing her eyes in warning. "Yes? You wished to introduce yourself, politely?"

He coughed, and the male seated next to him, Evanor, whacked him helpfully on the back until the copper-haired man shoved his brother away. "Uh, yes. Please. And, uh, thank you—oh, and if you would be ever so kind . . ."

Green eyes gleamed with humor at that last part, flashing with his quick, charming grin. Kelly rolled her own, not that impressed. "Your name, then, if you please?"

"Trevan the Cat, fifth of the former family Corvis, now the family Nightfall . . . and it will be my *pleasure* to please you in any way you wish, my lady," he added in a tone that was almost a purr. A seductive sound, actually . . . but not *that* seductive. Kelly had been hit on before in her life by suave, handsome men, and was as little impressed by this male's efforts now as she had been back then. He was cute, but his manner was just a little too contrived for her tastes.

"Uh-huh. Thank you for your kind and polite introduction," Kelly allowed him with brief but unimpressed politeness of her own, then looked at Evanor. "I know you are named Evanor—"

"Evanor the Song," he agreed mildly, tucking a strand of his light blond hair behind one well-shaped ear.

All of the brothers had straight noses, high cheekbones, firm jaws and foreheads, well-shaped brows, and small, perfect-for-nibbling sized ears . . . including the eldest brother. *Stop thinking about the big lug*, Kelly ordered herself, suppressing the urge to wince. *Pay attention! These are your hosts for the next ungodly stretch of time.*

Evanor continued with a soft smile. "I am the younger twin of Dominor, and the fourth Son of Destiny. If you have need of my aid, my lady, you need only sing out my name—sing it, not just speak it—and I will hear it and reply, wherever I am on the island."

Kelly eyed him at that admission. "That sounds like a rather neat trick."

He gave her a wry smile, dipping his blond head in a slight, seated bow. "I am something of the household herald in that regard. But then sound and song are my domain, as they have always been. *I* have no objections to helping you clean up the castle, for that matter. If you will lend your experience as a woman in directing us what should be tackled first in this pile of age-grimed stone, that is. I simply could not do it all on my own and freely admit I saw no need for any real effort to do so, save occasionally in the main rooms, when it was just my brothers and I who occupied this place.

"Now that we have a woman in the place . . . I confess I'm a little ashamed at our housekeeping skills," Evanor admitted with more grace than his brothers seemed comfortable at hearing. "We have indeed degenerated from being truly civilized in the last three years, I'm afraid. So feel free to tell *me* what to do, and I'll make *them* do it, too. What would you recommend?"

"Dusting, cobwebs, and floors," Kelly recited immediately. "The kitchen and this table need to be scrubbed spotless, all the 'refreshing rooms,' as you call them, need to be scrubbed bottom to top, then tapestries, windows, and the surfaces of anything that isn't a floor. Bedding needs to be laundered, cushions beaten free of dust, and their covers washed. Every piece of splintering wood will have to be sanded and smoothed, all the curtains washed and mended or replaced, all of the sticking doors and stiff windows need to be planed so that they work smoothly, the hinges and handles oiled, and all the furniture polished.

"Plus the courtyards need to be weeded, paving stones as well as garden beds, the overgrown grass lawns cropped and neatened, the bushes and vines cut back to something less than a jungle state—as you can see, there are obviously *many* things to be done to make this place livable, and hopefully enjoyable."

"And you think we will do these things for you willingly?" Dominor groused from his seat beside her.

"I have already made impressive headway on the rather grimy room your eldest brother stuffed me into," Kelly pointed out. "And, I might remind you, *I* don't have magic to speed my efforts in each task. You have all been living far too long as bachelors, and it more than shows." He didn't look convinced, and the others looked reluctant at best. She drew in a breath and smiled through her teeth. "Let me put it this way . . . if I have to stay for five more months before Morganen here can send me safely home, which do you think would. be better, a couple weeks of cleaning, with your cooperation, or five whole months of me carping incessantly about how much the castle still needs cleaning?

"Hmm? No countering comments? I see you're finally showing some degree of wisdom. All right, who's next?" she added firmly, looking at the young man with the darker auburn hair than Trevan's copper-strawberry locks. The auburn-haired one introduced himself as soon as her gaze fell on him.

"I'm Koranen, Morganen's slightly elder twin. Nicknamed the Flame," he added in the same ritualistic introduction the others had started. "Seventh of the family, and obviously associated with all forms of magic involving fire, whether directly or indirectly—I was the one who healed your burns when you first arrived. You were badly burned in several places, especially on your lower legs, but I could reverse all of it; the few remaining pink spots on your skin should fade within a couple more days, if you were worried about the marks lingering."

Kelly shook her head. "I'm simply glad to be alive and in one piece. Pink spots aren't a major concern. Thank you, by the way. That was very kind and compassionate of you. Now, *you* are Morganen—"

"The Mage," he agreed, smiling at her. "Strongest of all eight of us, magic-wise, though I'm the youngest in age. After seeing you make my brother there, 'eat dirt,' as you put it, I hereby adamantly refuse to turn you into a toad. Or to allow anyone *else* to turn you into one," he added, eyeing his older brothers pointedly before returning his gaze to Kelly's. "That looked rather . . . uncomfortable, what you did just now to Dom. I'd rather not test my arcane powers versus your extradimensional ones, firsthand."

"It was meant to be uncomfortable." She glanced sideways at the glowering Dominor, catching his scowl. "That is precisely what I mean, gentlemen. You have lived way too long without having to deal with women in your lives. Most of us prefer respect and courtesy over threats and bullyings. Keep that in mind for whenever this stupid exile of yours finally ends.

"There's enough similarity between your world and mine to know that the rest of this world isn't going to take kindly to arrogant bullies of men, should you ever leave this isle. Or have more visitors dropping by." She looked to her right, across the empty seat on that side, at the only one left. "I know that Rydan is the one who shuns the light, and I've more than met Saber already. So you must be . . . ?"

"Wolfer," the brother with the biggest body, height, breadth, and muscles, introduced himself on a rumble.

His hair was brown, somewhere between the dark brown of Dominor's and the light brown of Morganen's, with an unruly wave to it that made it even thicker than the others' hair, save for Trevan's thick, sun-streaked strawberry waves. He had amber gold eyes and looked like the wolf his name echoed. He even gave her a wolfish smile, confirming it in his deep voice as he played with the thin, braided bracelet looping his left wrist, gently touching what looked like a plait of hair, of all things.

The last of the brothers to be introduced, he added, "The Wolf. Saber's twin. And I think you just might be a match for him, Lady Kelly." His gold eyes gleamed briefly with humor. "Certainly it is interesting to listen to you try."

She narrowed her aqua eyes. "Are you trying to matchmake us? Because I have had my fill of that arrogant, bullying, pigheaded, confusing, yelling—let's just not talk about him, shall we?" she asserted, breaking off that topic to keep her temper cool and her thoughts from getting lost in a whirl of confusion over the irritating, too damned attractive, and way too grumpy missing man. "Morganen informs me it will be five months or so before he can send me back to my universe. Seeing as how I'm the only woman on the island, that means we're going to have to go over a few ground rules for the duration of my stay."

"Rules?" Dominor asked, arching one dark brown brow. "What have you been spouting until now, if not rules?"

She cleared her mouth with a sip of juice. "First of all, I'm not interested in hopping into bed with any of you—that includes you, Trevan, so you can turn off the charm; I'm not impressed by it. Any attempt from anyone to rape me," she added bluntly, blandly, "and I will cut off the offending organ, stick it in a jar, and keep it on a shelf somewhere in that lovely chamber over this hall that I presume will be my quarters for the duration of my stay. I might even take it with me when I go back home. That's rule number one."

Evanor choked on his juice, as she said that. Wolfer choked on a piece of jam-smeared bread. The others all blinked. Coughing,

Evanor recovered first. "Lady, I assure you that rape is the farthest thing from our minds. The very shades of our mother and father would rise up from their graves and do the exact same thing to us, *for* you!"

"Well, then I needn't have to repeat myself on the matter," she stated primly . . . a little unsure if he meant literally or just figuratively in this magic-soaked realm.

She debated asking for a moment, then shook it off. Glowing lightballs, translation potions, and chalk-drawn invisible walls keeping out hideous mekha-gobblies were enough for her to deal with at the moment. Parental ghosts rising vengefully from the grave would be a bit too much to handle.

"The next rule is no one locks me in my room. Or in a dungeon, or in chains, or in any other way. I don't like that."

"You'll have to argue with Saber on that one," Koranen pointed out. "But none of the rest of us will bother. Right?"

"Speak for yourself," Dominor muttered.

Kelly whapped his arm with the back of her hand, and he glared at her. He did, however, look away when she pointedly arched her brow and glanced at the floor. Instead of repeating himself, he muttered something under his breath about turning her fingers into flimsy feathers.

Ignoring his grumbling, Kelly continued. "The third rule is, I don't take charity. So if any of you have clothing in need of mending, or refitting, or wish for the addition of embroidery or trim, I will sew it for you in exchange for my room and board.

"And if someone is willing to show me how to cook some of these foods, half of which I admit are rather unfamiliar to me, I might be willing to help—*just* help, *not* do it all by myself—with some of the cooking chores, and of course with my share of the cleaning ones. I'd help in the garden, but I've seen too many plants

I'm not familiar with, and I wouldn't be able to tell a weed from a prize-winning whatchamacallit, so it's indoor work for me for right now. Now, rule number four is—"

"*Kelly! Kelleeeey!!*" Footsteps echoed from overhead, pounding into the hall. "Evanor, she's gone missing!" A body high overhead, on the topmost of the three tall balcony tiers, had flung itself half over the railing to shout down at them. Saber froze at the sight of her. "*You!*"

"Rule *four*," Kelly emphasized, rolling her eyes, "is that I don't like people *yelling* at me all the time!" she asserted, raising her voice and her head briefly to holler up at the yeller in question. "If you don't have a damned good reason, you will keep your voices quiet!—I'm certain your mother explained to all of you the vast difference, long ago, between an 'indoor' voice, and an 'outdoor' voice?" she added, dropping her tone once more into a normal, mock-sweet one, as that dark blond head disappeared from above them, bringing the sound of racing feet again. "So unless you're warning me of a danger to myself, or trying to get my attention across a long distance for an important reason, please refrain from shouting at me.

"I can be quite reasonable when treated in a reasonable way," she continued, "but not if I am yelled at constantly. It makes my red-headed temper get all mean and nasty. Rule number five is that I reserve the right to make up more rules as we go along, in case any more might be necessary. Now, I've actually managed to hold my temper in check quite admirably, at least so far today, despite being trapped in my room and denied any food until now. Can you all handle all of that, or do I have to get *really* mean and nasty?"

She got a more or less unanimous collection of nods and murmured agreements. Trevan spoke for the rest as he stood and started clearing the table. "I think so, Lady Kelly . . . so long as you realize none of us speaks for Saber or Rydan. I can say with fair certainty my twin, Rydan, will more or less behave around you for the few moments his hours coincide with yours, providing you leave him alone the rest of the time and do not attempt to enter his domain . . . but none of us speak for Saber. Right, Wolfer?"

The largest man at the table raised his hands defensively. "This is *his* Destiny, not mine! I admit I am generally of the same mind as Dominor," he added, glancing at her as his fingertips touched the braid looped around his left wrist, caressing it with a feathery gentleness that seemed almost strange in this largest and most physically powerful of all of the brothers. Kelly wondered briefly what it meant to him, but he spoke again, recapturing her attention. "I am not much inclined to follow another, woman *or* man. We only tolerate our brother leading us, because he is the eldest, and the head of our family. And I tolerate Morganen's occasional fits of temper, as I respect his power. But I am my own man, most of the time. I am the Wolf, after all."

"Then think of me as the alpha female of this pack, since you're so wolf-oriented," Kelly pointed out firmly as Koranen stood and started helping his brother. "I am the only female, admittedly, but even if I weren't, I can and *will* be the toughest bitch around."

Wolfer grunted and picked up his mug, neither agreeing nor disagreeing with her suggestion.

Dominor frowned at her. "How old are you, anyway?"

"Twenty-seven. I'm also used to being in charge of my life," she added. "It's the only way a Doyle survives."

"Survives what?" Saber demanded, scowling and striding into the main hall in time to catch her last words.

"The disasters in life," Kelly returned without thinking. All of them stilled a heartbeat, including her.

"That's it!" Trevan exclaimed, balancing his stack of plates in one hand so he could point with the other. "*She's* the Disaster! Gods know no one of Katan will help us to survive her, so obviously it's up to us to do it on our own!"

Some of the brothers choked on laughter, while others blinked in bemused shock at the possibility.

"Oh, ha ha, very funny," Kelly retorted, though her mouth twitched up involuntarily on one side. Behind her, Saber stiffened. "If you really want to know how to survive 'Disaster Kelly,' shape up or ship out! As the ranking female of Nightfall, I intend to order you about until this place is up to my standards of living. A woman's standards, gentlemen, not those of a bunch of lawless, lazy bachelors. This place is to no longer be kept under the grime of your own 'ideals,'" she added firmly, looking at the men around the table. "You have half an hour to attend to your affairs and report back here for cleaning detail."

"*You* will be going back to your chamber! You will *not* be ordering my brothers about!"

Kelly piled scrambled eggs between two slices of cheese and two slices of toasted brown bread. "Wolfer, kindly inform your twin that I refuse to listen to anyone who shouts at me. Rule number four, you know."

Those golden eyes studied her a moment speculatively . . . then gleamed, just a little bit. He was apparently enjoying the humor of the situation. "Saber, the Lady Kelly wishes me to inform you that she is not listening to you, because you are shouting at her. That's rule number four, you know."

"*What?*—Get up! You're going back to your room!" He reached down over the back of her chair to grab her under the arm and haul her out of her seat.

"Rule number six!" Kelly asserted, quickly swallowing her mouthful of makeshift egg and cheese sandwich, refusing to cooperate. "No one grabs me without it being absolutely essential, such as to *protect* my life! *Not* to maul me around like a brute. Wolfer, tell this brute to let me go!" she added, clinging hard to the arm of her

chair with her free hand, doing her best to keep her makeshift sandwich together with the hand of the arm he had a hold of.

"Saber, the Lady Kelly requests that I convey her wish that you
let her—"

"I heard her!" Saber dropped her arm, thumping her back down
the few inches he had managed to lift her. For such a lightweight
woman, she was rather strong. Or rather, very determined. Slapping
a hand on the tabletop, the other gripping the back of her seat, he
loomed down over her. "You are going up to the master chamber,
and I am going to lock you in there!"

"Wolfer, inform your brother that he is attempting to violate
rule number two. Oh, and gentlemen, rule number seven: Anyone
who breaks the rules four times in one day eats dirt."

"Brother," the largest of the eight men around her recited as
solemnly as he could, with those wolf-gold eyes gleaming openly in
amusement, "you are attempting to violate rule number two."

"What in Jinga's Name are you two talking about?" Saber demanded, glaring first down at her, then looking up at his twin. The
others were clearing the table quickly and silently, staying out of
the verbal field of fire between the three of them, yet clearly too
drawn by this three-way argument to leave without seeing it to its
conclusion.

Wolfer said nothing to his twin for a moment, then almost as an
afterthought turned to Kelly, who had deliberately not acknowledged Saber's demand. "Lady Kelly, one of my brothers wishes to
know what we are talking about. What would you like me to tell
him?"

"Inform Mister Grumpy that my number one rule is no rape; my
number two rule is no locking me up anywhere; number three is I
intend to work at sewing and other various skills to pay for my room
and meals during my stay; number four is that no one is to yell at

me; number five is that I reserve the right to make up more rules as situations warrant; number six is that no one grabs me gratuitously; and number seven, so far, is that anyone who breaks the rules four times in any combination in one day gets his face pinned to the floor, so that he is forced to 'eat dirt,' as I like to call it."

"Brother, the Lady Kelly wishes to inform you that her first seven rules are—"

"I heard her!" Saber grunted darkly, scowling at her.

"Do inform your eldest brother that he has already violated three of the rules, but as rule seven has just come into effect, he has been granted leniency this one time. Also, inform him that, as he is being graciously given a second chance to start over"—her chair skidded across the floor as Saber hauled it around so that she was facing him—"he should take this opportunity to start off on the right foot," she continued blithely, staring past his shoulder, "and act from this moment on as a perfect gentleman."

"Saber, Lady Kelly wishes to infor—"

"Shut up, Wolfer." Saber stared down at her, his hands braced on the ends of her armrests. She refused to look at him, peering deliberately over his shoulder as she ate her strange meal of cheese, crumbly eggs, and bread slices. "Look at me. Look at me, Kelly!"

"Lady Kelly, I believe my brother has conveyed a request for you to observe him directly."

Kelly cleared her mouth, calmly reaching for her mug of juice and sipping from it, ignoring the cage of his arms. "Did your brother say 'please' in this request?"

Saber tightened his grip on the armrests of her chair, but played along. To have wrestled all night long with his hard-awakened desire for her, with his fear—yes, *fear*—of the Curse hanging over their heads, to have finally given in and gone to fetch her breakfast from the kitchen to take to her, however belatedly . . . only to find her gone, completely gone, with no clue of where she had gone or how, had made him sick with dread.

Any mage familiar enough with Nightfall and strong enough to have sent so many of the mekhadadaks and other creatures to plague them over the past three years could have used memory, or even a painting, to scry and spy with and look in upon their activities. If they were strong enough, that same enemy-mage could have somehow discovered her presence. His brothers and he made damned sure all of the mirrors in each and every room, even the ones they never used, were enspelled against scrying to prevent such attempts on their lives . . . but two hundred years ago, Nightfall had been a thriving duchy, and not just an island used to exile the most unwanted of Katan. Someone clearly had a painting or two of the castle left over from that time, one marked with identifying images still good enough to transport creatures via spells.

Good enough to maybe realize there was a woman in the castle and snatch her away . . . or perhaps even kill her. Finding her gone when Saber had expected her to stay put had nearly stopped his heart. So, faced with her obstinate, incomprehensible female behavior, he played along with it.

"Wolfer, would you kindly pass along my request to the Lady Kelly, here, that she *please* look at me?" he asked graciously as she finished her sandwich and drained the last of her juice.

"Lady Kelly, my brother waxes eloquent in his request, replete with a most courtly 'please,' that you favor him with your full attention."

"If he is gentlemanly in his behavior, then naturally I shall acknowledge him," Kelly allowed, wiping the corners her mouth with her fingers, since there were no napkins—another oversight she would have to correct as a part of her womanly duty to more or less uphold civilized behavior wherever she was. She shifted her gaze from one of the abstract stained glass windows of the hall to the man whose shoulder blocked half of that windowed view. "See how easy it is to get my attention, Saber? Even *I* deserve some display of kindness."

Her words, accompanying that shift of aquamarine blue into his steel gray, pierced him with her simplicity. With her soul. Saber forgot how to breathe as he drowned in that clear blue green gaze, as the world shifted around him abruptly, primed by his unwilling proximity to her and nudged by the sudden fear she had left. He didn't want to breathe; not on his own. Not looking into her eyes.

There was a tie between them that made each of her exhaled breaths an indrawn one of his own, each exhale of his her inhale. The scent of her body, musky and feminine, and the faint aroma of *tisi* flower oils mingled exotically with each breath she gave him, drew him far more than any need for oxygen could. He had been drawn to her from the first, against his will, in spite of his will . . . because of his will. Just a shift of his hands, and he could touch those blue-clad arms, where her elbows rested on the armrests and her forearms draped into her lap. An inch, maybe two, and he could touch her.

Claim her, in the ways his imagination had come up with, despite his resistance to everything she stood for. Sitting there, still too hardworn and thin but ripe with curves, blatantly woman, with a will as strong as his own and a determination to face the disasters of her own life head on, Kelly of Doyle was worth risking the Curse for. Worth loving and caring for . . . and Saber was a world-class idiot for ever thinking otherwise.

She was right, though. He had treated her like a brute. He didn't deserve her, and not just because of the Curse. Because he ran from his fears, while she did her best to face hers. If he loved her, she could be killed by the other Katani in fear of the Curse, by the Disaster foretold and now quite possibly linked to her, or taken from him by his youngest brother and returned to her rightful home. Because there was most likely nothing she wanted here.

Not even him. A base brute.

"You wish to ask me something, Saber?" the outworlder woman prompted him as he continued to stare at her, keeping his expression completely unreadable and everything he was feeling carefully on the inside, where it could freely reel and shift everything into a confused mess he knew he would have to climb out of somehow.

There was no escaping one's Destiny; Saber realized that now.

He shifted away from her and her chair, unable to meet her gaze anymore. "Never mind."

Confused, Kelly watched him turn and walk away. She arched a puzzled brow, but he didn't explain his actions. He just left the hall.

"If you will not be needing me until the assigned time in half an hour, Lady Kelly," his slightly younger, more muscular twin rumbled in that deep voice of his, "I'll need to attend to a couple of things before I report for housecleaning duty."

She craned her head over the back of the chair and looked at him. "Thank you, Wolfer. I *think* I got through to him finally . . . but I'm not sure."

"Perhaps you did. Perhaps *he* is the one who is not sure," the second eldest of the Eight murmured, his golden eyes wolf-wise. Of all of the brothers, he was the one who knew his own twin best, after all.

The others wisely said nothing.

NINE

ꕥ

Even Dominor cooperated. Reluctantly and with the assertion he was doing it because it was *his* opinion that the castle needed cleaning, and thus needed the strength of his magic to help . . . but he cooperated. The first day, the brothers, under her direction, scrubbed the floor of the great hall, eradicated its cobwebs and dust, scrubbed and polished the table, cleaned and polished the chairs, and made the large kitchen a short distance away positively sparkle—a chore greatly enhanced in its ease and success by the application of their version of magical elbow grease.

Cleaning the kitchen was her biggest priority, once the main hall was done. That at least ensured that their meals would be up to Kelly's otherworldly standards of hygienic preparation . . . which was a big relief to her. Once it was all done to her satisfaction, Kelly delivered a lecture to all of them about frequent hand washing and safe cooking practices while handling and preparing different kinds of foods. The last thing she needed was a bout of Montezuma's revenge, or worse.

On the second day, counting from the point she escaped her room and joined the household in full, the six of them—minus Saber and Rydan—marched behind Kelly, accompanying her back up to her given chamber after breakfast. They not only cleaned her rooms more thoroughly than she already had with the aid of their magic, they redecorated, stripping away the not-exactly-inviting scheme the room originally presented. At Evanor's suggestion, and under the most domesticated brother's direction, they cast several spells in her chambers to alter colors and lighten the overall feel.

It was fascinating to watch them work their magic. A flick of a wrist, a mutter of strange syllables that her ears couldn't translate, and they methodically altered everything in the room. From the dark, dirty red velvet curtains, which were replaced with shades of pale blue and green, heavyweight linen rescued from a storeroom by the fourth-born brother and cleaned with their ubiquitous cleaning cantrips, to scrubbing and painting the stone walls a room-brightening shade of chalk white, it was all done with sparkling lights and shimmering waves, and the occasional sizzling sound.

Painting and dyeing literally with magic, the six brothers enthralled their nonmagical guest with this display of their powers. They quickly took some pride in competing with those powers, too, as she stared, wide-eyed and wondering. Her amazement even drove them into cooperating in rearranging the furniture and removing some of it so that it wasn't as cluttered with chests and tables as before, but rather had better flow around the largish room. *Amazing*, she thought as she watched them working on restoring the suite to its former glory, *what one can do with a properly appreciative audience to spur them onward* . . .

They left the bed where it was, though they moved the massive piece of furniture via magic just enough to make sure the wooden floor was scrubbed and wax-polished directly underneath it, at Kelly's insistence. The head of it faced to the east, and the foot to the west, leaving the entry door to the north and the refreshing door to the south. To the right of the bed, they removed a moth-eaten tapestry from the wall and uncovered a modest fireplace set in the corner of two of the eight-sided walls, over by the refreshing room door.

They made that corner into a sort of sitting area, with a carved and cushioned loveseat couch Trevan located from somewhere else in the palace. Kelly admire it; the small couch had just the right kind of leather-padded, curved arm, perfect for leaning on while curled up with a book. Not that she expected to be loaned a lot of books, but what was good for reading was also good for sewing.

Wolfer added a matching chair from somewhere. Both the chair and the loveseat were scrubbed soundly with more cleaning spells to remove the dust, and the dark, cherry-like wood was polished with beeswax to restore its shine. The hearth and its furniture stood on the left of the refreshing room door. To the right of that door, clockwise, was the bathing tub in the southwestern corner, which Saber had already cleaned. Of course, Dominor—ever the perfectionist—gave it a second going-over just to be sure it was up to his standards . . . once his standards had been roused by the challenge of Kelly's own exacting level of cleanliness.

Koranen brought up two folding screens, silk painted with snow capped mountains and flying birds, for an illusion of privacy, once they were positioned between the door and the bed and bathtub. When Kelly described what terry cloth was like, compared to the plain, sheet-like cloth they used for drying themselves, Evanor disappeared for two hours and came back with cotton cloth he had magically rewoven to approximate what she had described. He then promptly found himself promising his brothers, on threat of torture, to make more of the marvelous material for each of them. It was an immediate hit when Kelly demonstrated how much more effective the loop-nubbed, cotton cloth was at mopping up water, compared to what they had been using.

By the time he came back with the first try at the new cloth, the others had shoved the desk out of the middle of the room and into the northwest corner between the tub and the entryway door, clearing out some of the dusty chests that had cluttered that area. The brothers then helped her fix up the northeast corner between the door and the bed as a working nook for her various sewing projects. Well, *helped* was a misnomer. Wolfer picked her up and set her aside, insisting on doing all of the physical labor after a pointed look from Morganen, when she tried dragging around one of the tables herself.

When most of the room was settled, the six brothers brought in piles of clothing for her to mend. They did so while mock-complaining that now they had nothing to wear worthy of the fancy donjon below her chamber, now that the main hall had been cleaned. Joking with each other, the six of them started competing to see which one had the garment with the most holes in need of repair. Kelly had begun to take note of each brother's personality in her observations over the past two days, and she noticed that Dominor was not only arrogant, but competitive as well.

The third-born brother bested the others by finally dipping his hands into his sack of laundry, bringing out his fingers so that they were partially pinched together, and holding his hands up in the air about a foot apart. With nothing dangling between them but his smirking expression, he smugly explained, "Your shirt is mayhaps *second* worst, Wolfer, but I defy this woman to fix *my* undertunic! Why, even the holes clearly have holes of their own!"

As the others gave the arrogant mage dirty looks and laughed, Kelly tossed a cushion at him. "I'll have to stitch your very hide, then, you utter fraud! Come here, so I can set my needle!"

The amount of sewing they had brought was overwhelming, a rounded mound on the floor almost as tall as Kelly herself. She complained that she didn't think she had enough thread and such, and they listened. The six of them trooped down the stairs, cleaning the stairwell as they went, promising good-naturedly to tackle the sewing room next on their list of chores.

True to their word, that was the thing they did the very next day, Kelly in tow. She came up with a list of how she wanted the longish room remade once she saw it, then the rest of that floor in that section of the palace wing. Each brother attended to his best-suited task. Koranen cleaned every hearth in the room and tended to all of the lightglobes, making sure they were still good, and polishing their stands. Trevan polished all of the wooden furniture, and Wolfer took care of bringing down and setting up the curtains and tapestries between laundering them with Dominor's help, being the tallest and most muscular of them; he also worked on restoring the cracked leather coverings of those furnishings that were not cushioned in cloth.

Dominor polished the windows and replaced the cracked and missing panes, removed the grime from the oil paintings, and tackled those cushions that were made from fabric. Evanor scrubbed the floors and walls quite cheerfully, even scrubbing at the ceilings with the aid of a levitating mop, humming as he worked. Morganen did most of the wall-painting. He was faster and neater at it than the rest, and seemed to have an endless supply of whitewash paint to cover the plaster, as well as plaster to repair the occasional crack or flake.

And, in every room they entered and worked, the six of them plopped Kelly down in a comfortable chair as soon as they had cleaned a spot on the floor for her, with a small table at her side full of supplies and tidbits of food, and piles of clothing waiting to be mended at her other side. At least one garment at all times was constantly in her lap

and an enchanted needle in her fingers—one that set four short
stitches for every long one that she actually made, courtesy of Evanor.
Indeed, she was refused the chance to get up for anything but a trip to
the nearest refreshing room, so that she could eat, rest, and pay her
way, according to her own rule number three, while they did all of the
hard labor.

The brothers also did their best to clean up their language
around her, but they were delighted, if a little unnerved, when she
gave as good as she got in both good-natured insults and cleaner
jokes alike. And though she made up a pair of skirts for herself out
of spare fabric found in one of the chambers and a pair of long-
hemmed blouses to belt over them, they grew used to the way she
preferred wearing pants to a skirt whenever possible, once she made
herself a set of trousers. Indeed, the whole mood of the castle
brightened, not just with each room cleaned, but by the efforts of
the cleaners themselves.

Evanor inevitably sang as he worked, for he claimed his magic
was based in resonances. That made the work more bearable, for he
had a smooth, sweet tenor voice. Of course the others got into several makeshift competitions to see who could clean the best and the
fastest. Dominor led the main competition: Who could come up
with a creative idea to make what supplies they had work best for
restoring each room, while repositioning the antique, eclectic tastes
of other eras into some arrangement that all of them liked.

The only rooms her chair, table, and self weren't placed into as
the days of rapid, magic-speeded cleaning turned into one week,
then into two, were the personal chambers of each brother. There,
she was left out in the newly cleaned and painted hall in that section
or wing, and allowed only to supervise by general advice from the
hallway.

"Because it isn't proper for a lady to be in a man's bedchamber, if you aren't going to be wed to him soon," Morganen had explained with a little smile. And then promptly spoiled it with a grin and a tongue-in-cheek, "So, which bedchamber would you like to go into?"

Saber's, her unruly mind had instantly asserted. Except Saber never quite got close enough to join the others. That was the only pall cast on her days, aside from occasional bouts of homesickness. Sometimes he left them alone for hours at a time; sometimes she caught glimpses of him. He acted like a ghost, hovering a little way away, usually just beyond an open door. Watching his brothers laugh and have a good time in her company. But he didn't come near, and she didn't seek him out. She looked for him, but she didn't go to him.

So, Kelly replied simply, if a bit tartly, "My own, of course. *Alone*."

She felt a little confused, actually. She wanted Saber, but he aggravated her. She missed him, but she didn't want to get into yet another argument with him. And she missed sparring with him, but couldn't back down from the stance she had set. Nor could she see a way to bridge the distance between them. It wasn't hard to understand his fears about that Curse-verse looming over him and so clearly associated with her if he took her into his bed, but Kelly still wished this universe didn't have to take such things so seriously.

His brothers were fun to be with, once they were all more or less being nice to her. But as fun as these cleaning sessions were, they were . . . well, just a little bit flat.

Saber hated his brothers.

He knew they assumed the woman among them was destined for him as the eldest, and he actually wanted her to be destined for him . . . but there was a gap between the two of them now, and he didn't know how to close it. So he spent part of his time working on projects for the suppliers, and part of his time taking out his frustration on the practice pells in either the salle or the training courtyard where the brothers exercised their nonmagical defensive skills. And he spent part of his time following their progress through the wings of the donjon palace.

He had to take most of a day off to ferry all of their completed projects from the storage room at the western gate down to the shores of the western cove. That was so that when the new moon meeting-time came and passed, he would be ready to barter with the traders who came by. Unfortunately, without his brothers' help, he found himself repeatedly driving one of the several horseless wagons his youngest brother had created for their own use back and forth to get everything down to the trading warehouse.

All on his own, Saber bartered for the goods they needed and hauled those goods back up to the castle in the magic-powered wagon, while six of his seven brothers catered to Kelly's cleanliness and orderliness whims. Of course, the last one slept through the day, as usual, but that was still six brothers too many who were not paying attention to the usual twice-monthly trading routine.

Then again, Saber's mind hadn't been entirely on supplies when he had been bartering. Five days after the exchange, an extra chest still sat in his room, a room the others had swept into and cleaned up without his permission or will, simply because, "It must be done, same as the rest!" an order delivered by Nightfall's copper-haired, temporary mistress. That chest, tucked neatly to one side of the whitewashed, scrubbed, polished, and generally neatened room that otherwise hadn't been changed, contained things not purchased to be shared among his brothers, nor things for his own use.

It contained a silver-chased grooming set of comb, brush, and a hand mirror enspelled against scrying, respelled by his own hands to be doubly sure it was safe to be used by her. Nestled next to it was a box of yards and yards of silk ribbons rolled into looped bundles . . . for while they did have some old woven trims and scraps of lace, there were no ribbons, and he knew women liked ribbons, especially the ones who could sew. Essence oils pressed from flowers and other fragrant things occupied part of the box, too, bought under the guise of "magic ingredients." He had carefully selected those scents to go with her personal scent, caught permanently, it seemed, in his memory.

There were softsoaps for bathing and lotions to soothe her skin after drying, lotions he kept thinking of having the chance to apply to her smooth, freckled skin himself. And a full bolt, over thirty yards' worth, of aquamarine silk almost the same shade as the blue and green richness of her eyes. It had cost him three expensive vorpal-edged swords and two missile-reflecting shields, items he hadn't intended yet to sell. Certainly not for silk cloth . . . and yet the moment he saw it among the goods offered for sale, Saber had bought it without a second thought, heading back up to the palace to fetch the items requested by the traders in trade for it.

All of these things waited for Kelly Doyle; Saber himself waited for the courage to give them to her.

He was still awake late into the evening, five days after purchasing the carved cedar chest and its contents, when someone knocked on the door of his chamber. Heart thudding hard at the thought it might be her, however unlikely, Saber closed the book he had been trying to read and opened his door.

It wasn't her. Instead, Rydan stepped inside, a foreboding figure dressed in his usual stark black. His eyes swept over the changes in the room, noted the chest on the floor by the window, and finally faced his brother. His night-black gaze silently questioned the eldest of them.

Saber shrugged defensively, though he didn't know why. Rydan was an odd one, even for the eight brothers—one of whom was a wolf in man's clothing, one of them a cat, one a living torch if he wasn't careful to shield his abilities every single day of his young, adult life, one a nonstop singer, one a determined competitor, one a too-wise, too-young, too-powerful mage . . . and one who was an overprotective, stubborn, bullying fool, according to a certain red-head. To say, therefore, that Rydan was odd, even for a son of Corvis, was saying quite a lot.

The sixthborn, night-loving son of the eight of them simply nodded at his brother, then wandered over to one of the windows in Saber's room, peering out at the night beyond the reflections of the lightglobes. Probably seeing things no one else could see in the dark of the night. Saber had only asked once what Rydan saw in his night-borne life, since the younger man had finished passing through puberty. His brother had not replied.

But then, that wasn't too unusual for the sixthborn of them. Rydan rarely spoke at all these days; he had begun shunning the day and roaming the night more and more when his powers had started to grow in puberty, and he had only intensified his strange habits since being branded a Son of Destiny and exiled alongside his brothers. The darkest-haired of the eight of them had endured the daylight hours of their journey to get here under the constant shelter of a full, dark cloak and a deeply cowled hood. There was no medical or magical need for him to do so. Just his own peculiar preference for it.

Saber had insisted he join them for supper each night after the sun was down, simply to make sure his brother was still alive, and still in Rydan's equivalent of "all right." Kelly had managed to get a few words out of him the past few evening meals, but for the most part he had ignored her. It was simply Rydan's way.

Not so the rest of his brothers. Saber, watching from the balcony during the past few weeks of meals, exile within an exile, had watched the rest of them banter with her and recount their days, explain the rules and ways of magic as best as each of them could, though she had trouble, considering her nonmagical background, understanding some of their terms. She'd also had trouble believing some of their tales. His brothers in turn had encouraged her to talk about her own realm, most asking her question after question, trying to understand her very strange, nonmagical, yet magical-seeming world.

Rydan had been almost as much an outsider as Saber, asking very little, responding to very little . . . but then, Rydan had always made himself an outsider, by his own choice. Saber didn't know how to end his own isolation. It wasn't natural for him, but he couldn't seem to escape it these days.

"Perhaps you should shun the daylight, too."

Saber jerked out of his thoughts. "What?"

Rydan turned and looked at him with his dark, dark eyes, then returned his gaze to somewhere beyond the window. "I said, perhaps you should shun the daylight, too. Since you seem to want to have little to do with the others anymore."

"I . . ." Saber didn't know what to say. That was probably the longest personal speech he had heard from Rydan in half a year. He was in for more surprises, though, for Rydan wasn't through.

"Perhaps it is that woman you seek to avoid. You cannot, you know; she is your Destiny. Mine is to rule the night, until I am destroyed by a woman at dawn. Thus I avoid the daylight, and especially the dawn. But I need not avoid *her*." He glanced at his brother again. "She is not my Destiny. For which I thank both moons."

"She therefore must be one of the others' Destinies." He fell silent a moment, then shrugged slightly and spoke again. "She is not Wolfer's Destiny, either; his was begun long ago, before the beginnings of our exile."

Considering Rydan rarely shared any of his insights, unlike the ever-cheerful, talkative Evanor or even the occasionally close-mouthed Morganen, Saber didn't know what to make of that straightforward comment. His own twin had a Destiny already clearly predetermined? Saber couldn't imagine who it could be. "Are you certain?"

"Eyes that can see in the dark see the clearest of all, even into the shadows of mystery." Those eyes stared confidently out into the night beyond the diamond panes of the window in front of him, as Saber studied his sibling.

That was more like the Rydan his eldest brother knew. But Rydan wasn't quite yet done. There was more to be heard from this least-communicative of the eight brothers.

"Morganen will fall the last, and as no other women have appeared to deliver us to our fates so far, she is clearly not the one for him. The woman is not water, so she cannot quench Koranen, and she does not run; she confronts boldly. So she is not Trevan's.

"She has a pleasant singing voice, and probably knows many unknown and unusual melodies from her own realm, but she is not Evanor's Fate; her heart might be lonely for one of us, but even I can see she is not lonely for him. And she is too blunt to correctly master the Master of Manipulation . . . though I wish I had been there to see her make Dominor 'eat dirt,' as the others have teased him about in these past few weeks," he added with a brief smile.

Saber felt unnerved by the sight of that unsober curve. The sixthborn Corvis son almost never smiled anymore. Even as Saber considered the shock of that, Rydan sobered again. Or rather, shuttered his emotions, as if closing stout wooden panels against the threat of a high wind or against whatever dark storm plagued him from within.

"So, if she is not for the rest of us . . . then she is for you. You were the Lord of Corvis, and now you are the Lord of Nightfall. Why have you not claimed your lady, Brother?" Rydan turned and faced him fully, his dark eyes pinning Saber's gray. "Don't give me that *trakk* about suffering your part of the Curse. We all have our Fates to face, however much we may strive to set them from us as far away in time and place as possible," he added with a faint grimace. "Seer Draganna has never been wrong. Only Katani perceptions of her words have faltered and needed to be corrected through the centuries. So . . . why have you not claimed your Maid, Son who is the Sword?"

Saber glanced at the chest, then down at the scrubbed hardwood floor underfoot. There had been *one* addition in recent days beyond the paint and the polish and the general cleanliness, and that was a slightly worn but hole-free and still quite usable carpet laid down to cushion the hard wooden floor under his feet. Just one of many examples of what the woman among them had done . . . and how she had been thinking even of him, in her mass-cleaning forays. Out of kindness, out of pity, he did not know, but she had been thinking of his comfort.

As odd as it was to be discussing this with Rydan, of all of his brothers, Saber knew he was right. "I don't know *how* to, Rydan. I . . . just don't know how."

His brother, hands clasped lightly behind his back, snorted. It was such a strange sound to hear from the normally quiet, reclusive man, Saber looked up at the scoffing sound. Black eyes met and held gray, in a dark storm of brotherly irritation. "*Woo* her, you imbecile!"

"How?" Saber challenged him.

Rydan gestured at the night-dark world beyond the windows, the simple, sparse gesture showing his agitation far more than all the arm-waving and ranting that could be delivered by any other man. "It's summer! I haven't been so long in my realm of darkness to think that flowers no longer bloom in the summertime. If you cannot find anything to say with your lips, speak to her with flowers. Women usually like that sort of thing.

"Pay attention to the things that she likes to do, the tasks that give her a feeling of accomplishment, and compliment her on them,"

Rydan instructed Saber further, surprising his eldest brother with his insight. Annoying him, too, in the next breath. "And then retreat before you stumble and stick your foot in your mouth, for even *I* have heard some of your shouts all the way out in my tower. In the daylight hours I *normally* try to sleep through," the younger man added sardonically. "Women like an air of mystery, so if you keep it short and simple, safely abbreviated, she will be intrigued. Since even I have heard how you locked her in her chamber—"

"I didn't lock her in; the door was stuck!" Saber interjected truthfully, if defensively. It was bad enough that he was the recipient of so much eloquence from the most taciturn of them all. Certainly the others wouldn't believe Rydan could say even a tenth so much, or be so eloquent about it. But he hadn't locked the door on Kelly of Doyle.

He'd been tempted, but he hadn't done so.

Rydan restated his meaning. "You still ordered her presence confined up there. Take her out in one of the wagons and show her the island. Take her to the eastern beach so that she may safely enjoy the sand, the sun, and the surf without being seen by any passing sailors. And show her that you do not resent her.

"*If* you do not resent her," his brother added pointedly, drifting toward the door. "She has asked to have the outer wall and towers cleaned, since the others have made such headway on the donjon and its wings that they are almost done. None of us are willing to allow her near our towers and all the magical dangers therein. Not until all of us have met our Fates and the Prophesied damage is done, at the very least." Rydan paused by the door. "So, she will need something else to keep herself occupied. Until then . . . there is still the risk that she might be my Destiny, and not yours. As seems clear even to me.

"It is up to *you*, Brother, to keep her out of my tower." He regarded Saber a long moment, then turned away. The door—as did all doors for him—opened of its own volition. "*Do* keep her out of my realm."

Moving as silently as ever, with nothing more to say, Rydan let the door close behind him, leaving Saber speechless but with a lot of thinking to do.

Oh! Oh, my," Kelly murmured as she entered the sewing chamber, with its now thoroughly dusted and cleaned pair of looms, several spinning wheels, other assorted cloth-making equipment, and chests and drawers of cloth-bolts, lace and trims, scissors, threads, embroidery floss, and even jars of dye components. But it wasn't the sight of her mostly orderly workspace that had caught her attention.

Someone—male, obviously, since she was the only female on the whole of the island—had brought in two large vases of flowers plucked from the still somewhat wild and overgrown gardens. Roses had been stuck in with bluebells, delphiniums nestled next to eight-petalled, curled flowers that bore a vague resemblance to the normal six-petalled tulips of her own world, interspersed with tiny buds of what looked like pink baby's breath. The colors ranged the whole palette of the rainbow, even to bits of decorative greenery tucked in here and there among the many blooms. The two vases rested on the broad cloth-cutting table set in the center of the half of the longish room she usually worked in, as Evanor was now using the looms in the other half to make more of the highly popular terry-cloth towels she had described.

Kelly reached out and caressed one of the blossoms, feeling the smoothness of its blue and yellow petals and smiling at the effort one of the brothers had gone to. "This is so pretty!"

"Thank you."

The voice replying to her murmured delight wasn't one of the six she had grown used to hearing of late. It was the voice she had perversely longed for, a voice that had usually only shouted and yelled at her, but which now came out soft, even gentle, plucking at her nerves and making her turn toward the source. Sure enough, Saber sat in one of the deep-set window embrasures, one booted foot up on the bench with him, his elbow resting on his knee. His other hand cradled a smallish box against his stomach.

"Saber," she acknowledged. And suddenly wished she had a camera and a means to process the film, or any talent at all at painting, more talent than mere crude pattern-sketching could produce. Because, limned along the edges of his silhouette by the midmorning sun pouring in from the northeast, he was a vision of masculinity.

Black fabric hugged his muscular calves and thighs. White material draped against the breadth of his chest, caressing the occasional ripple of muscle down to the black leather belt girding his hips; the sleeveless tunic he wore showed off the definition of his arms—masculine, tanned, and strong—and a strip of his chest, at the slit-and-laced neckline. His dark blond hair gleamed with honey-golden highlights, rich with the play of many shades in the backlighting of the sunlight, ranging from the much lighter blond of his brother Evanor to hints of the dark shadows of the elusive Rydan's hair. He was a vision of masculine beauty, really, though there was nothing posed or artificially enhanced about him.

As she watched, that upraised thigh flexed, lowering his boot to the floor. That twisted his body upright and off of the padded, cushioned bench. Her mouth dried a little as he approached, then salivated as he stopped about a yard away, bringing his warm, freshly bathed, wonderfully masculine scent with him. Her senses were teased with a scent similar to the musk of male exertion and sweat she had been around over the past few weeks, but different in that this was a wonderful, pleasure-inducing thing to inhale, not just a sometimes strong, nose-wrinkling one. There was no reason why he should smell nicer than his brothers, but he did. A lot.

He held out the star-carved box in his hand. "Here. This is for you."

He said nothing more, just held it out until she took it. Unsure what it was, Kelly opened it gingerly, balancing the box in the crook of her left arm.

It was packed with brightly colored ribbons, made from silk and from cotton, from linen and woven wool, in every shade of the rainbow, and a few were even woven with handspun gold and silver thread—the real kind of gold and silver thread, not the mylar kind she was used to seeing back in the other universe. From her medieval society days and her historical research into clothing, she guessed the box contained a small but serious fortune in expensive trims. "Oh, Saber . . ."

"You don't like any of it?" he asked warily, as her voice wobbled unevenly.

"I *love* it," she breathed, touching the thick bundles of looped trims, examining each one. It was sort of like being dropped in the ribbon-and-trim section of a fabric store and given a four-figure gift certificate—every sewing fanatic's dream! There were trims narrower than her smallest finger and two that were half the width of her palm; the rest were woven of sizes in between, with what looked like many yards of each, enough to trim a dress here and there, perhaps even down at the hems in some cases. "Wherever did you find all of these?"

"I bought them. From the traders a few days ago . . ." As his words trailed off, she looked up at him. He had turned his head to the side, and a muscle worked in his jaw. Without warning, without another word, he turned and strode for the door.

"Saber!" she called out. He slowed his steps, long enough for her to continue. "Thank you. For the ribbons and for the flowers," she added. "They're both beautiful."

His head dipped once, and then he was out the door. One of his brothers called out, beyond her view in the hall somewhere.

"Ooh—look at who's wearing his *best* tu . . . er . . . ah . . . right . . ."

A moment later, as Kelly was still envisioning the teasing brother being fixed with a steely glare, Koranen and Evanor entered the sewing hall, brows still raised at the undoubted vehemence of their encounter with the eldest of them.

"And I thought *my* glares could get hot," Koranen muttered, as he glanced over at the sole woman on the isle, mock-wiping his brow, though he spoiled the drama with a grin. His older brother touched the flowers in their vases, admiring them, and Koranen whistled. "Well! It seems a certain *someone* has finally deigned to notice you."

Kelly felt a little defensive, a little protective. She closed the box in her arms and set it on the table. "You had a reason for coming in here . . . ?"

"The basement storerooms, my lady," Evanor reminded her. "You keep claiming *everything* has to be cleaned, and those are next on our list. So grab your mending for the day, and be prepared to sit and sew!"

"If I don't do *some* manual labor, and soon, I'll have to let out all of my new clothes inch after inch, until I run out of fabric," Kelly retorted. "I'll be the size of a cow!"

Koranen shrugged and eyed her plumping curves. "Oh, I don't know; I think you look even more wonderful with a little more flesh on your bones than what you had when you first arrived."

Evanor elbowed him. "Shush. Be circumspect, remember? No ogling her curves."

"Ogle all you want," Kelly retorted lightly, hand on her hip to accent it, enjoying the brief, lighthearted repartee. "We may not be wed, but neither are we dead. Just don't *touch*."

"My hands are tied at your service," the auburn-haired brother swore, raising them wrist-to-wrist in front of his chest before extending them toward her. "I'll just tie them to your sewing chair for the moment, shall I?"

"And I, my own to your sewing table. Can you get the mending, my lady?" Evanor prompted her.

Sighing dramatically, as if her work was never done, though she had made a distinct dent in all of their piles of clothing—even Rydan's and Saber's—Kelly moved to fetch the latest basketful, shaking her head and smiling. Magic realm or not, it was lacking in many of the amenities she had taken for granted most of her life. Still, Kelly was enjoying her days on Nightfall Isle . . . more than she had enjoyed the last year or so in the other world, that was certain.

Today certainly felt brighter, after Saber's brief, intriguing visit.

TEN

＊❦＊

Two weeks turned into three, and the cleaning of the palace proper finally came to an end, leaving Kelly plenty of time to sew new clothes, not just repair or remake old ones. Saber gave her the silvered grooming set he had bought, presenting them to her with a handful of words at most, then leaving again just as he was on the verge of saying more than a handful of words. A few days later, he gave her the perfume oils, again with little explanation. But he did hover a little closer now, and a little longer, too.

The others went back to their neglected projects, the sources of their livelihoods, but they did linger an hour or two each day in the gardens when the weather was nice, weeding, scouring, and uncorking the fountains and ponds under Kelly's watchful gaze, as she finished the last of the mending and started on sewing new clothes for each of the brothers.

As she watched and cut and stitched, they worked hard at cutting back the overgrown vines and pruning the wild-grown trees, pulling up weeds and raking the flower beds. The exiled world of the nine of them, kept mostly within the outer curtain wall, finally began to look orderly. With that order, the palace keep looked rather nice. Kelly had a hard time even remembering to think about her old life, this new one was so much more real, so much more interesting to her. Especially since she really didn't have to do anything more strenuous than what she loved to do, which was all things textile. It was wonderful, a hobbyist's daydream.

At one point, a storm whipped up from the sea, halting all outdoor activity. It was then that Rydan stalked the halls during the day, when the windows rattled their panes as every brother raced to yank in the shutters and secure the stout wood. The brothers, giving thorough attention to the various home repairs that had gone wanting since the last exiles had lived there, had made sure those storm shutters hung straight and sound during their many repairs around the place. They had even made sure that the latches were tight and that the windows gleamed. Now, at the start of the storm, they hurried to close and latch shutters and windows alike against the increasing wind and rain.

Though he appeared in the heavily overcast daylight, Rydan didn't aid his brothers in securing the palace against the storm; he was too busy with whatever he was doing to participate with such mundanities. It was the most animated Kelly had seen the apparently night-loving man in daylight hours—the only time she *had* seen him in daylight hours—but he didn't speak with her, didn't address his brothers. They certainly didn't get too close to him, for he crackled with an energy that literally made his long black hair move unnervingly on its own, flaring with each flash and crash of energy outside. And all he seemed to do was to walk up and down the corridors, as the storm intensified and progressed.

She watched doors eerily open and shut around him. He didn't touch them; didn't lay a finger on a single doorknob. It was then that

Kelly realized she hadn't ever seen him touch one of the lever-like knobs in the donjon palace. In fact, she thought that the doors might be a little intimidated by him. She certainly was, feeling the way he made even her nonmagical senses tingle with the energy radiating from him.

Rydan the Storm; she truly learned his name then, and wisely stayed out of his way by several wary yards, as his brothers did. Even at that relatively safe distance, though, the hairs on her arms still stood and prickled. He only stayed in the palace wings for the darkest, wildest parts of the storm . . . though *stayed* was a misnomer.

When all of the windows were shuttered, when everything rattled, the rain splattered and the wind howled, he paced through the halls restlessly, his dark eyes alight with something Kelly knew she was not meant to closely examine. Something she was thankfully not meant to know. Somewhere out there, according to the other seven Prophetic verses the brothers languished under, there *was* a woman who was meant to know. Kelly was just glad it wasn't her and stayed well out of his way just to be sure.

After the worst of the storm had passed, after Rydan had retreated and the shutters were swung open once more, it still rained steadily beyond the windowpanes for hours after the hurricane-like storm had passed, and continued to do so through the night and into the next day. It was then that Saber came to her once more, on the day after his brother had stalked through their huge, exiled home. This time, it was with a bundle in his arms of the brightest aquamarine blue she had ever seen, yards and yards of fine, soft-woven silk, folded into a neat, thick bolt.

"For me?" she asked softly, as she rose from her sewing nook, reaching the middle of the room and the cutting table that sat there, just as he approached it himself. He stopped just beyond touching distance, just like before. They stared at each other, gray eyes meeting aquamarine.

He finally looked down at the cloth piled in his arms, and Kelly caught the hint of a blush bronzing his cheeks. "It matches your eyes."

He held it out for her to take. Kelly got the feeling he was going to disappear again. She took a step back, not reaching for this latest gift.

Lifting his dark blond head at her action, he searched her with a questioning look. She turned and trailed her finger over the cutting table, trying to think of something to say. With that dratted Curse hanging between them, this was an awkward moment she had no idea how to get past. Not unless she suddenly turned into a mega-powerful mage with the ability to avert a preordained Fate. Of course, if that hadn't happened by now, she figured it never would. *And the Doyle way is to confront and overcome* . . . "It's very nice of you to bring all these—"

Evanor's voice rang urgently in that non-echoing way in both of their ears, cutting her off, though neither of them were anywhere near the other man. Breaking the fragile mood. *"Wyvern attack! Three wyverns from the west! Koranen, Dominor, Morganen, to the roofs!"*

"Wyverns?" Kelly asked in confusion, then widened her eyes as a shape swooped past the third-floor windows of the sewing hall. It looked like . . . "Are you sure they're not dragons?"

Saber dumped the expensive-looking silk on the table and snapped his fingers with a magical command, instantly summoning his best-made sword to his hand as he explained. "Dragons aren't native to Katan. Wyverns are."

"Aren't you going to go help the others?" Kelly asked him, glancing his way as he placed himself between the windows and her, where she stood next to the cutting table in the middle of that half of the room.

"Evanor would have called for me, if I was needed up above," he admitted over his shoulder; this was an attack his brothers had faced twice before and had plans laid to face such a danger once again, should it ever occur. As it now had. "My sword is better served guarding you."

Seeing his broad shoulders between her and the rain-spattered windows *was* reassuring, but Kelly wasn't one to cower behind another. That wasn't the Doyle way, after all. She cast about her for a weapon.

The shears on her sewing table might work, but they weren't much of a weapon. She crossed to the wall by the hearth, unlit because the weather was still warm despite the rain, and hefted one of the longer lengths of lumber Dominor had found for her, a scrap she had intended to turn into an inkle loom for making woven trim. It was a stout piece of oak she selected, a couple inches thick one way, the width of her hand the other way, and as long as one of her legs in the third direction, yet not too heavy for her hands to grip and hold.

"What are you doing?" Saber demanded, frowning at her.

"Oh, you know me. Stubborn and determined to do my fair share," she quipped. And flinched back as one of the wyverns—grayish and shaped like a dragon-headed, snake-tailed, way oversized bat—flapped over to the bank of windows in front of them and hovered there with a bit of effort.

She held her board up in front of her, prepared to flinch and flail protectively if it burst through the window. Fire flared down from above a moment later, shooing it away, but since its spellcaster, presumably Koranen, had to flare it in the face to get it away, Kelly flinched and turned her back to protect her eyes from the burning ball that exploded beyond the window . . . and saw movement where there shouldn't have been any, inside the room with them.

"Saber, behind you!"

He whirled, saw the rope-like shapes slithering toward them, and swore. "By Jinga! Watersnakes!"

Kelly didn't even wait to ask him what he meant; his agitated tone was enough for her. She flailed her makeshift weapon at the nearest slithering, yellow brown beast. It dodged with cobra speed, and she whacked again, thumping more successfully with the end of the thick board, smashing it mid-back, leaving a bluish smear on the floor and the end of her board. Light flashed to her side, where Saber was shouting and hurling what looked like streaks of fire with one hand and stabbing and slashing with his sword in the other. Ambidextrously, he wielded the blade in his left hand, freeing his right for casting his magic.

A shape darted at her ankle. Kelly leaped quickly and stomped two-footed on the snake, as she came back down, jouncing several times on the squishing flesh to make sure she got it good and dead, then did her best to whack another one with her board. It crawled up onto the narrow wood and twined around it when she missed, working its way up the thin beam toward her hands. She had to ignore it while she smashed at another one, then quickly dropped the board and leaped back when the serpent on the wood lunged at her fingers.

That bumped her into a lightstand; Kelly quickly fumbled for one of the globes. Grabbing and hurling with a well-aimed arm, despite being several years out of practice from her old high school softball team, she smashed one, two, three, making the tough balls glow brightly at the impact, increasing the light in the chamber by several degrees. She raised a fourth ball, but there were no more snakes near her. Certainly there was enough light down on the floor to have seen any of the odd snakes, if there were any more, but she at least was free and clear for the moment.

With the fourth ball cradled in her hands from among the five that had been cupped in curved twists of wrought iron in that particular stand, she turned around quickly, making certain no snakes were anywhere near her. Kelly heard a sharp cry of pain. Whirling back around, she saw Saber shake off one of the arm-length serpents from his hand, his sword clanging to the floor, and hurled her oversized missile with the furious accuracy of a Junior Varsity All-Star softball pitcher. It hit the snake while the thing was still in midair, and both smacked into the edge of the cutting table, creating a smear of something dark blue and a flare of blinding light. "Saber!"

He had conjured a steel dagger and was frantically slashing at his hand and arm around the bite marks, forcing a strange, thick purple ichor out of his flesh along with blood from the wounds. All of his focus was on removing the venom, and none on the remaining, yellowish-scaled serpent slithering straight for him across the floor. Kelly darted forward, stomped down hard, and thoroughly fouled her age-worn, thin-soled slippers, smashing the thing to death under her feet before it could reach him.

"I need water!" Saber gasped as she turned to him. Kelly saw that, though his arm was cut several times, it hadn't even bled. The flesh was in fact beginning to wither and turn a sickly purple. Desiccating.

Whirling, Kelly grabbed one of the flower-filled vases he had taken to filling every couple of days while she wasn't around. Flinging out the flowers, she shoved it at him. He thrust his arm into the pot. Kelly grabbed the second one and poured its contents into the first. Both were almost full of water, but the only water that spilled out of the first pot when she poured in the second was the small amount she splashed in her haste. Instead, something purplish had filled the pot.

"Thir . . . thirsty . . ."

Hanging on to the second vase, she sprinted for the nearest refreshing room; Saber lurched after her, gritting his teeth against the venom infecting him. She got there first, yanked out the upper cork, jammed the vase under the fall, and cursed impatiently while the thing filled. When it was full, she rushed outside again.

He had staggered almost to the door and was now leaning against the wall, looking about as sickly as she probably had when she had first arrived in this crazy realm. Tipping the vase to his mouth, she half drowned him while he did his best to swallow several mouthfuls, then she filled the first vase again. That revived him enough to get into the half-bath refreshing room.

When he pulled his hand out of the first jar, it was thick with purple slime. The venom-ichor of the watersnakes apparently latched on to the water in blood and other bodily fluids, Kelly realized sickly, making the blue venom and the red blood turn into that thick, purple substance. Too thick to allow his blood to flow. Only water diluted it enough, apparently. Scrubbing his arm under the flowing water, she got as much of it off of him as she could, while he used his good hand to scoop up mouthful after mouthful to swallow.

Kelly started feeling a little dry-mouthed and dizzy herself, as she worked. Soaping her hands quickly, afraid the stuff had been absorbed through her skin, she drank her fill, then drank again; both of them drank and drank and drank until they felt waterlogged and yet still dry at the same time. And then to the borderline point of heaving it back up again when the dryness finally eased.

Saber panted, flexing his injured left hand. Blood was beginning to flow sluggishly again, running more red than purple. "I think you saved my life."

"You told me what to do," Kelly panted back, feeling green from all the water she had drunk. Or rather, purple. She looked at her skin. It was dry, far drier than it should have been. Her feet felt sluggish and numb. A glance down showed her slippers soaked with blue. "God—!"

Kicking them off, she hitched herself onto the stone ledge of the sink and stuck her slightly purple-tinged feet under the water. Saber helped her scrub her soles and the sides of her feet, dousing his still purple-oozing arm at the same time. "It gets in through the skin and stays in the blood a long time. We need to get into a bath and soak in as full an immersion as possible, as quickly as possible," Saber added between palmfuls of liquid. "Water is the only thing that flushes the poison out."

"Great." Already her mouth was beginning to feel dry. "Race you to the nearest bathtub?"

He managed half a laugh. "I think that would be your own, from here."

"Well, it is big enough for two," she pointed out, taking her feet out of the sink and scooping more water into her mouth. Rinsing out the second vase, she filled it with water and poured it over her head, soaking her loosely gathered, linen blouse and cotton trousers. Then filled it again and doused him, too, ignoring the cold of the water and the way it splattered over the wooden floor, coughing a little as the liquid dripped down her face. "Think that'll do?"

"It'll get us there. Fill it again," he added between more mouthfuls, "just to be sure."

She did, and both of them half squished, half staggered out into the hall and headed for the stairs. The sewing hall was in the western wing, on the north side to get the most light, right next to the central hall. It really didn't that take long to climb to her chamber, the nearest source for bathing, since all other bathing chambers were farther away, in the bedchambers beyond the *Y*-junction of each longish wing of the castle.

They had almost drained the vase dry by the time they reached her door, however, and hurried to reach her bathtub for more.

"Saber? Kelly? Where are you?"

Saber, hitching himself onto the top step next to the large bathing tub, answered as he pulled out the oversized cork stopper; the other cork was already stuck in the drain, thankfully. *"Evanor!"* he sang, activating his brother's magical listening ability. "We had water-snakes in the sewing room. We both need to soak out the poison."

"Both of you?" the unseen brother asked, shock carried in his Song.

"Yes, from bite and skin contact. We think we got them all in the sewing room, but we were a little distracted at the end." He added as Kelly made it to the refreshing room ahead of him and refilled the vase from the waterfall spout there. "The wyverns were used to spot-scry. They may have done so elsewhere in the compound. Be careful!"

"We're on it. Will you survive?"

Saber half-laughed again, though since he had scooped up a double handful of the warm water splashing into the tub, he half-choked. "Yes, we'll survive. More or less, for the next few days."

"You have my deepest, waterlogged sympathy for both of you."

"What did he mean by that?" Kelly asked, coming back with the refilled jar. Evanor had projected that last part of their conversation to her ears as well. She poured a little of it over her face, then drank from the rim, not even waiting for a reply, she was that dry.

"The only cure is a long and *wet* one. Full submersion, anywhere from several hours to several days, depending on the severity. With short breaks for bouts of purple diarrhea, as the venom works its way out of the body," he confessed with a grimace, trying to untie his boots with his one good hand and not quite making it. "Can you get that? I can't heal my hand for another hour or two, to make sure the poison's soaked out through these cuts as much as possible, first."

While he scooped up water with his good hand and drank, Kelly removed his boots, then peeled off his socks. Her skin was beginning to hurt, it felt so dry. She removed her belt, yet another treasure found in a dusted chest somewhere, and crawled into the tub as soon as it was half-full, since it was a nice, broad, deep one. It even had a sloped back to rest against. Saber climbed in after her, his own belt also removed.

It wasn't a matter of modesty that kept them clothed. Neither wanted to wait long enough to remove the rest of their garments. A touch of his bare toes on the handle upped the temperature a little, then he dropped his foot back underwater with a little splash, their elbows bumping. Kelly ducked under the surface, soaking her whole head, then surfaced with a sigh. Water soaked every needy pore.

"Ohhh, that feels good . . ."

He did the same and came up, blinking against the water dripping down his face. Then curved his mouth and laughed. "And to think I wanted to complain about cleaning this thing!"

She had to laugh at that, too. His arm slipped behind her shoulders as they rested side by side in the deepening water. She didn't protest, in fact felt a little thrill at the companionly moment between them. "Aren't you glad I bullied you into it?"

"Bullied?" Saber shot back, mock-narrowing his eyes, grinning at the same time. "You *tricked* me into it!"

"I was wondering if you'd ever notice."

He looked at her; she looked at him. Both of them licked their drying lips at the same time, with identical little grimaces. And ducked under the water to fully wet their skin. When they came back up, both were laughing. Choking a little, Kelly floated free to the foot of the large, deep, two-person tub and wedged the cork back in the waterfall spout. For all that it delivered a very good volume of endless freshwater, it was surprisingly easy to cork and keep corked. *Yet more magic, probably*, she decided. *I wonder what my friend Hope would say if she could see me now . . .*

Ha. Probably something like, "You lucky woman!" She'd love to be stuck in a tub with a handsome man . . . But thinking about that would only lead to thoughts neither of them were in any condition to have her think about. Even with what seemed like his recent attempts to court her, it probably wasn't a good idea. Kelly pulled her attention back to the water, a safer topic to think about, and wondered about its source. "Saber?"

"Mm-hmm?" Uncomfortable though his near-brush with death still was, he felt great to be alive.

"Where does all of this water come from? The mountains don't seem high enough to be able to collect enough rainwater to sustain a building of this size, if it were fully inhabited."

"From the sea, of course."

"The sea? But it's not salty," Kelly pointed out, turning around to face him with a soft, puzzled frown. "By its very definition, a sea is usually salty."

"The original creators of Nightfall Castle knew there was no way to find enough freshwater on the island to support a duchy-sized population—the island is fifty miles long and twenty miles wide, and the castle sits in the center of the two mountain ranges that form its two lobes," Saber informed her, sketching on the surface of the water between them. "Nightfall has enough rainfall to keep its streams running more or less year-round . . . but only enough for the local plants and wildlife, and maybe about fifty, sixty people more, without having to ration during the driest parts of the year.

"So the duke-to-be called in several large favors with one of the most powerful Mages of the day—someone Morganen's equal, maybe even his superior—and that man created a permanent saltwater conversion facility on one of the low rises nearest the bay that lies directly west of here, plus pipelines across the isle to the homes that used to be here.

"Permanent magic is extremely rare," Saber added, enlightening her as he scooped water over his face to moisten it. "Only the most powerful can cast it, and it usually takes a full year of preparation and many costly materials, the gathering and preparing of which sometimes takes even longer, beforehand . . . so you can see it was a very big favor to the original settlers, creating a system that could process a lot of fresh, drinkable water."

"So, where did all of the original inhabitants go?"

Saber wrinkled his nose. "They were Cursed off the island."

Kelly rolled her eyes.

"Groan all you want, Kelly; it's true. This Curse, however, was deliberately set by the original inhabitants."

"Deliberately?" That caught her attention. "How so? Why?"

"It happened with the fall of Aiar, an ancient and once-powerful empire far to the north of here. I don't know all of the details," he cautioned her, "but they say that Gods and Mortals waged war over the Truth, many years ago. One of the northern Gods died in the confrontation, and the entire empire was cracked asunder. There used to be a Portal here on Nightfall, linking the duchy to Aiar—there used to be a lot of them, across Katan," he added. "There was a Seer living at that time who warned that the Portals and the land for a day's ride around them would be destroyed if they were not shut down beforehand, but it takes a lot of power to shut down a Portal safely.

"Nightfall was the last one the Mage Council was scheduled to visit. They arrived, began the process . . . but the battle had already been engaged in Aiar even as they started, and the last bit of destructive force tried to come through the Portal. They couldn't stop the power, only transmute it, so the duchess who ruled the isle—a powerful Seer herself—transformed the energies into a Curse that basically forbade any permanent settlement larger than one hundred people from living successfully here. If she hadn't done so, of course . . . the center of the island would have been destroyed, killing everyone.

"As it was, the inhabitants had to hurry and migrate to the mainland, for the water turned sour, the animals stopped eating, the crops withered in the fields . . . all manner of disasters. After they left . . . Nightfall became perfect for exiling people. I think the conditions for the Curse being lifted were something about 'when sound becomes silence,' among other things. I haven't looked at it in a while."

"Charming." She frowned at him, ducking briefly under the water to keep her face wet and blinking from the streams of soothing moisture. "How did you learn all of this? I thought you and your brothers only came here a few years ago."

"You cleaned out the castle library, what, eighteen, twenty days ago? There's a set of several thick books of Nightfall Island history in there, bound in white leather; you may have seen them. They cover the past two thousand years. Plus a new one that's had a few pages written in it about the last group to be exiled here, and about ourselves that I've tried to keep updated. Though nothing much ever really happens here, aside from our occasional attacks from our unknown enemy. We'd probably know who it was by now," he added wryly, "if we weren't forced to stay here. But we are."

She wanted to ask if she had been written into the books by now, but the original topic was safer. There was still the bit about her presence foreshadowing some unspecified disaster, after all. "So . . . this fountain-thing draws water from the sea?"

"Yes. It draws water from somewhere deep in the bay, purifies it of salt and plankton and other things, until it is sweet and clear and perfectly safe to drink, and pumps it to the palace," Saber confirmed, pausing politely as she dunked herself again. "Some of it also goes to a freshwater lagoon that used to be a part of the original Nightfall port city, back when this island was a duchy.

"The lagoon is actually a giant stone basin that the water used to be stored in and piped to all of the various buildings and homes," he added, pausing to dip under the water himself. He continued when he came up again. "Even when there isn't anyone in exile here, mainlanders always come out as close to the new and full of Brother Moon as the weather allows. That's to pick up the compressed blocks of salt the fountain produces, extracted from the tons of water purified every day.

"To keep the magic permanently active, the water must always be in the middle of being processed," he explained at her look of curiosity. "The algae blocks make good fertilizer, too, so nothing's wasted in the system. Both types of blocks by law belong to the duchy of Nightfall, but since there hasn't been a duke or duchess of this island in hundreds of years . . ."

He shrugged, so she filled in the rest. "So . . . those who are exiled here are doubly punished, because they can't profit from the salt trade. And if your world is anything like mine was back in its medieval-style period, salt can be worth quite a bit."

"Med-what?"

"Medieval—it means 'middle ages,'" Kelly explained. "Back in my world, between our ancient empires, when everything was still fairly new, ideas, inventions, and such, and our modern era, where everything is being reinvented all over again and new ideas flood the world every day, there was a lengthy period of almost a thousand years where everything pretty much stayed the same. The people wore clothing very much like you wear, for the most part," Kelly confessed. Then frowned slightly. "Though your furniture is more Queen Anne than medieval—a couple hundred years old instead of several hundred, according to the timeline of my world.

"Personally, I *like* sitting down on a cushioned surface, instead of a hard wooden one like my people used a thousand years ago, so don't think I'm complaining," she added quickly. "I'm just . . . observing."

Saber regarded her, sunk nearly to his nose in the water. He doused himself, waited politely for her to dunk as well, then lifted his mouth out of the water and spoke, studying her. "You actually like it here, don't you?"

· "Well . . . now that everyone's stopped yelling at me, yes," she agreed candidly, making him flush. "But then I was rather stressed out, too, at the beginning. Mind you, watersnakes and wyverns and mekha-whatsits aren't exactly restful to experience, but they're a lot better than hate mail, hangman's nooses, and burning to death in your own bed."

She smiled a little, drifting back to stretch out beside him, smiling a little more when he extended his arm to give her head a cushion support against the stone of the tub.

"You have good brothers, Saber. A little weird, but then I *am* in a magic-soaked realm, and that does still take a little getting used to." She flashed him a grin.

"You certainly look healthier than you did when you first arrived a month ago," he pointed out, eyeing her. Then smiled wryly. "Well, you *did* look better . . ."

She splashed him a little. "Thanks a lot!"

He splashed her back.

She started to get into a water fight with him, and someone knocked on the door. Breaking off, she clutched the rim of the solid granite tub. "Come in!"

Trevan and Koranen entered, both carrying trays. They slowed at the sight of both Saber and Kelly up to their necks in steaming water, then blinked and stopped. Thankfully, both men realized the pair were still more or less fully clothed under the water and finished their approach. Trevan with a cat-spotted-the-canary grin, and Koranen with a small smile of his own. And slightly flushed cheeks.

"Well . . . Glad to see the two of you fishies are enjoying the ducal suite's hospitality," Trevan purred, setting his tray down on the broad stone shelf at the foot of the tub. "You managed to kill all of the watersnakes, at least. But our unknown assailant used one of the other two wyverns before we destroyed them all to Gate three demonlings from the Netherhells into one of the empty guest rooms."

"Your efforts at slave-driving us in cleaning and tidying that particular chamber have gone to waste," Koranen explained to Kelly, setting his own tray on the shelf at the head of the stone tub. "Morganen caught the teleportation as it was happening and managed to send the fourth and following demonlings back on their master, but the portal was shut too quickly for him to get a location fix. Even Morg has trouble doing all of that on top of rebounding demonlings back on their original summoners, *and* fighting off the wyverns. But the other three were captured and banished back to their plane of existence the moment he was free to deal with them, so we're safe for a little while."

"And we have some nice kindling and shredded rags in the east wing, and dead wyvern bodies to dispose of before they start stinking up the gardens," Trevan continued, picking up their tale. "But in the meantime, Evanor—culinary genius that he is—has cooked up two bowls of soup guaranteed to take the anemic edge off of your suffering, plus pitchers of blood-bolstering, water-absorbing juices. But he says you don't get the newest, largest set of his otherworldly, fluffy toweling-cloths until you're both healthy and well. We'll check on you in an hour; we've got cleanup duty in the sewing hall, and that'll take literal tons of water to sponge away, even after we scrape off most of it."

"At a nice, safe, magically assisted distance," Koranen added with a little smile as the brothers retreated back to the door. "There's not enough room in here for more than the two of you to be cosy together, I think."

A glance at Saber as the two brothers left showed Kelly that he was blushing. A glance at Kelly showed Saber that she, too, was blushing. She splashed him. He splashed her. It felt good both water-wise and tension-wise, so they splashed each other some more and grinned like fools.

Eventually, they floated over to investigate the food brought to them. When the edge had been taken off of her hunger, when she felt bloated but somewhat hydrated, Kelly realized something felt odd. Setting down the half-emptied mug she had been drinking from, she touched herself through her soaked blouse, then up underneath the hem.

Even though it felt damp on the outside, the inside of her corset was dry. While it was completely submerged in water.

"I'll be damned . . ."

"What is it?" Saber asked, breaking off from drinking his soup.

"My corset's dry! Next to my skin, I mean. You weren't kidding about this absorbed-through-the-skin stuff, were you?" she added, twisting in the water to face him.

Saber shook his head, trying not to think about her corset. "You'll, ah, have to remove it—it's probably not letting in enough water next to your skin to help neutralize the poison, so your skin is drying it out."

She blushed and turned her back on him, batting her blouse up out of the way where it floated in the water. It kept drifting into her line of view, though, while she was tackling the laces of the bra-like garment. "I'm, uh, going to have to take my shirt off for a few seconds."

"I should probabl—" Saber broke off abruptly.

Kelly peered at him over her shoulder. He had a funny look on his face. "What's the matter?"

He blinked and scrambled to get out of the tub, water sloshing everywhere. "Excuse me!"

Bemused, she watched him snatch up the vase on the edge of the tub and splash in a beeline for the refreshing room door, ignoring the water he dripped all over the floor. *Oh. Probably the onset of the diarrhea he warned me about* . . . She waited until the door was shut, then ducked to wet her drying head, and shrugged out of the blouse. With it out of the way, it was easier to get the corset off. Tossing the corset over the rim, she struggled her damp blouse back over her head, then squeezed out the fitted undergarment and draped it on the wooden steps leading up to the stone-lined tub to dry.

At least she hadn't had to take care of laundry. Dominor usually did that chore for the rest; he would go through the castle once a week, gathering up a basket from each brother, then use a tub much like this one in the laundering chamber in the basement of the castle to soak the clothes, add some soap, and poke at it with a stick and a spell for a little while until everything was fresh and clean. Then he dried it with another spell as he drew each article out of the water and applied other spells for freshening, de-wrinkling, pressing, and folding.

She had been highly surprised at first when she learned of him handling that particular chore. After a bit of thought, and given that he was the greatest clothes-horse of the eight of them, always dressed in very expensive fabrics dyed and trimmed in tasteful jewel-tones and thread-of-silver, Kelly didn't blame him for wanting to make sure none of his brothers accidentally shrank anything with the wrong cleansing spell. Since she didn't have a spell to make the work quick and easy for herself, no one had asked her to do it for them.

Frankly, Kelly was *not* about to volunteer. It was more than fine by her; she had always hated doing laundry, though she did love making the clothes that inevitably ended up needing to be washed. That was the perennial sewer's dilemma, of course.

Saber came back a few minutes later, looking gaunt and dry-skinned, though he had apparently soaked himself with the vase at least once while he was gone. A look at the water all over the floor, and he grimaced and snapped his fingers. It whipped up all around him and arrowed back into the tub with a splash. Climbing in beside her, he drew in a deep breath and burrowed under the slowly cooling surface. He emerged with a gasp several seconds later and half-crouched, half-floated shoulder deep for a moment, then ruefully shook his head.

"This isn't working. I need to get my clothes off. I'll, uh, go find another tub."

"And suffer, waiting for it to fill deeply enough?" Kelly shook her head. "Go ahead and strip. I won't be offended. You probably won't have anything I haven't seen before."

·ELEVEN

Saber blinked at her, mouth slack and brows raised, gaping a little. Morganen's words from weeks earlier came back to haunt him, now. "You mean you're *not* a . . . a . . . ?"

"A virgin?" Kelly finished frankly for him, raising her own brows. "Technically, I still am, but since it's not overly valued in my culture, I have seen my share of male nudity. I simply haven't done anything about it, yet. So you won't shock or offend me."

She wasn't even going to try to explain the whole confusing concept of television sets, VCRs, bachelorette parties, and stacks of naughty videotapes, viewed with lots of giggling, popcorn, blushes, lewd comments, and shrieks of laughter.

"You . . . *are* a maiden?" Saber wanted to confirm, digesting her words.

"Technically, yes," she agreed. "I'm just not innocent." As he continued to stare at her, she rolled her eyes and turned around, giving him the privacy of her back. "Oh, just get your pants off and get it over with!"

Saber heartily hoped the water had cooled enough to cool him off as well. A lot more. To the point of loin-numbing cold. He wrestled with the ties holding the front of his breeches together, then inched them off under the water.

A tug on the thigh-length hem of his tunic proved futile to keep from revealing himself, since the fabric simply floated aimlessly upward in the water, but at least she had politely turned her back. When she ducked under the water to soak her scalp and face, he wrung out the pants, then tossed them past her shoulder as she surfaced. She flinched back from the unexpected apparition, and Saber had to grab her waist to keep her from backing up too close to him.

As much as he needed to remove his tunic, since it, too, restricted in some places how much water soaked into his skin and neutralized the poison, he couldn't remove his hands from her flesh. Her own blouse floated loose in the water, caressing his wrists.

They stayed like that a long, breathless moment, only the water moving around them in residual ripples. Both of them were aware of the intimacy of their situation. Then she moved, her arms shifted . . . and her hands pulled on the hem of her blouse, lifting it up over her head. Saber released her, shocked and aroused as she matter-of-factly stripped the garment over her head. Baring her back to him.

"I don't think I got the same amount of venom, but I think I got more than en . . . uhhh . . . Oh, *god*!"

He knew that exact same feeling that was striking her now. A moment later, she exploded out of the water, slipping on the rim in her scramble to get to the refreshing room. She darted back when halfway there, snatched up one of the terry toweling cloths she had introduced them to, and disappeared through the door. Oblivious to the clear view he had of her glistening but rapidly drying breasts as they jiggled in her haste.

Groaning, Saber sank back under the water and concentrated on massaging his bitten and slashed left hand. It was finally starting to bleed normal red blood, not reddish-purplish ooze, so he muttered a healing chant to get the puncture marks and self-inflicted wounds to close. Cursing the unknown mage who insisted on plaguing them so lethally, he wondered yet again who could hate them all so much.

Mekhadadaks and watersnakes, wyverns and demonlings . . . Whoever hates us would be flayed alive by the Mage's Council for keeping so many highly illegal, magewar-bred beasts. If they could only find her or him! And because we're Cursed, they're not even going to try.

Kelly came back out, wrapped from armpit to thigh in the now soaking-wet towel, her wet trousers and equally dripping under-trousers bundled in her hand. She had wrung them over her naked body to dampen it and now dropped the sodden clothes in her laundry basket, woven by Trevan and provided by Dominor for tidiness. An indrawn breath made her look up at Saber, who was staring at her. She folded her arms defensively. "I see no reason why I should sit in my clothes in a tub full of water, when it's just uncomfortable and awkward. We're both adults, after all, so there shouldn't be any problem."

"That . . . *is* the problem," he managed, swallowing to get his heart out of his throat, more than to get any actual liquid down. "We *are* adults."

"Well, this is the only bathing tub that's this close to a refreshing room, in this section of the sprawl you call your home. Unless you think you could make it to a suite out at the edges of the wings somewhere," she pointed out, mounting the steps daintily. She sat down on the rim, then looked at him. "Are you going to turn your back?"

"I don't think I can," he admitted honestly, bluntly, his gray gaze fastened intently on those wet, nubbly clothed curves.

"Oh. Okay."

Her own heart pounding, her body aching for more than just the soothing touch of the water, Kelly managed a blasé shrug and opened the towel. Her nipples, topping her lightly freckled breasts in strawberry-pink tips, hardened under the intensity of his stare, the flush of his skin. She slipped down into the water, revelling in the combined caress of it and his eyes as they followed her progress into the clear liquid of the large bathing tub. He bit off a curse and sloshed around, bracing his arms on the edge of the tub and dropping his head onto them.

"You know," Kelly offered thoughtfully when she came up from dunking her head, "I think we've been avoiding this whole moment fruitlessly, Saber. You want me. I want you. There's one clear solution to that particular dilemma."

He thumped his brow against one forearm, his hair clinging in wet lines to his shoulders, throat, and cheeks. "I cannot take you! Even if we were to just touch with hands and lips . . ."

"You'd risk everything, because of the Curse," she finished quietly. Disappointed. She bit her lower lip, thought a bit, and cut out her feeling of rejection firmly. A Doyle didn't obsess over things a Doyle couldn't change. No matter how much skin she flashed, it wouldn't change the Curse. *Stupid magical fantasy world rules . . .* She sought for a way to make amends for the awkwardness of the moment. "You know, I'm not as bad off as you are. I'll go find another tub; you can stay in here and soak."

He turned as she stood up to get out again, catching her thigh with his good hand. Kelly stopped and shivered from the intimate curve of his fingers and wrist, palm hooked around her flesh. He stared at the coppery tangle of curls just above his fingers, visible through the rippling water, then managed to drag his gaze up past her breasts to her face. "It isn't just the Prophecy . . ."

Frowning, Kelly tried to grasp his meaning. "It isn't?"

He tugged slightly on her thigh. Coaxing her back down into the water, he locked his gray eyes with her aquamarine. The eye contact was bold; the cheeks, however, were distinctly pink. "I simply cannot spare the . . . the *liquid*."

She blushed. Her forehead blushed, her cheeks blushed, her throat blushed . . . even her freckled breasts blushed, Saber noticed, dropping his gaze once again to the waterline.

"*Oh*. Right."

"Neither can you," he murmured, shifting his hand from her thigh to her waist, pulling her deeper under the water. As she nodded, he released her flesh and reached for his tunic.

He twisted the fabric over his head to dry it out a little and dampen his skin at the same time. A second squeeze, and he aimed the trickling fluid haphazardly over her head, generously sharing the moisture. Kelly drifted under the splash, tipping her face up, her eyes closed to enjoy the stream. He trickled some of it over his own head and shoulders again, then lobbed the garment onto the floor somewhere beyond the tub.

Hooking her gently around the ribs, Saber drifted both of them to the sloped back of the tub across from the corked waterspout, and drew her just close enough to be comfortably intimate. The end result was borderline tolerable between his need to hold her close and his need to hold his desire firmly in check. She was also no longer quite so thin and fragile that he had to worry about bruising her with a simple touch, but he still didn't want to risk grabbing her too hard, either.

Kelly nestled her cheek against his bicep, one of her arms behind his back, the other hand resting gently on his chest, and tried to think of something to say. Anything that had nothing to do with sex. "So, tell me, what do you like to do with your days? I know Evanor's about as domesticated as a heterosexual male can get, and Trevan and Wolfer like to do most of the hunting, Rydan acts like an odd sort of bat out in his tower-cave, Koranen makes the lightglobes . . . *you?*"

"I, ah . . . I make magical weapons and armor and associated enspelled items, usually," he confessed, flexing his arm to get her a little more comfortable—*comfortable* being a relative term, with his groin turgid, longing for a touch, any touch, of her own flesh brushing against his rod. "My tower, the northwest one, has a smith's workshop attached to it along the inner wall. Though I have to drop my manly pride in honesty and admit I'm not the absolute best swordsmith out there. Sometimes I get swords shipped to me by the best in Katan, so that I can enspell them, since I *am* one of the best magesmiths . . . but I'm not the best forgesmith."

"Poor baby. I'm sure you do the best you can," she added soothingly with a watery pat to his chest.

"Don't call me a baby. Hold your breath," he warned her, and drew them both down under the surface briefly for a soaking when she complied. They came back up, and he blinked water from his eyes, not bothering to wipe it away, because his skin still needed moisture. "If you were wondering how long this treatment will take, we have to stay in here until our skin finally prunes."

"Ah. So that's how we know when we're done soaking," she murmured.

He held up his hand, showed the skin of each one taut and unwrinkled, despite the fact that they had already been soaking up to their throats and higher for a good half hour. "See? Not yet."

"So you'll only make love to me when I'm more wrinkled than a great-granny, is that it?" she teased lightly, her cheek resting once again on his shoulder.

Love? His heart skipped a beat as he studied her snuggling into his chest. *Yes . . . it is love, isn't it?* It was a terrifying thought. Only a small corner of it was for the Curse, though. The real Disaster, Saber realized, was if something actually happened to her. *I think I finally know what Father felt like, preferring to die rather than live without Mother. And I don't for the life of me know how my feelings for this outworlder happened.*

He loved her strawberry-gold hair, her occasional flares of temper, her freckles, her unceasing demand in everything she did to be treated as an absolute equal. He admired her independence, her fiery streak, her quick grin, and the way she bit her lower lip. He loved the way she was unafraid to discuss just about anything, and how she was a maiden, yet sat naked in a tub with an equally naked him, without shrieking or shrinking away. He just . . . loved her. Damning though it was.

"So. Do you have any idea what Disaster you'll bring when we do eventually make . . . *love*?" He lingered slightly on the last word, meeting her eyes when her water-spiked lashes flicked up quickly in surprise. Saber couldn't resist. Dipping his head, he brushed his mouth against her lips, once, twice, then forced himself to pull back again. They really couldn't do anything for the rest of the day, and in his case, maybe even through the night and into tomorrow.

"Not a clue," she breathed. Then licked her lips, twisted up over his arm—pressing her breasts into his chest and bicep, making him close his eyes and stifle a groan—and poured more juice into one of the mugs his brothers had brought. She dropped back down and drank half of it, then pressed the mug on him so he could drink the rest. She watched him swallow, then put the mug back. "Saber, is it really—?"

"Do you think you could—?" he asked at the same time, and broke off. "Ladies first."

She nodded and looked down at the water. Seeing a rippling image of her breasts, his manhood, and quickly fixed her eyes elsewhere, across the room. "Is it really love? The verse you recited said 'true love' . . . I've never been in love before, so I'm not sure how to tell."

"Can you forgive me for being an ass when you first arrived?" he asked her, instead of answering more directly.

That returned those aquamarine eyes back to him with a frown. "Don't be an idiot!" Kelly paused, blinked, then grinned. "I actually *mean* that; *don't* be an idiot, next time. And I've already forgiven you. I know I wasn't the most likable person when I arrived, either. Can you forgive me?"

He brushed back a wisp of her shoulder-length hair from her cheek, where the water had adhered it and her need for the liquid had begun to dry it. Teasingly, he tugged on the lock. "You had every reason to be a termagant."

She wrinkled her nose and splashed water at him. He grinned and splashed back. They doused each other, grinning and laughing. Until splashing limbs entangled and their bodies floated too close together. Stilling with a groan, Saber gently pushed her back, forcing himself to abandon the pleasure of her touch.

"We cannot *do* this, Kelly . . ."

"You want me to change tubs?" she asked reluctantly.

His answer was very satisfactory. "*No.* But . . . we should be more careful. Even if there wasn't the threat of drowning—"

"But what a pleasant way to go, you'll have to admit," she interjected with a touch of a smile.

His gray eyes smoldered like the smoke from a forge fire. "I do not think it will be merely 'pleasant' between us."

When she blushed, he smiled. A mixture of maidenly shyness and mature boldness, she was enchanting, in a nonmagical way.

"Even if there wasn't the threat of drowning, I would prefer to be feeling more fit and capable of handling whatever comes afterward . . . once I, um . . . once I sheathe myself in you."

Her pink mouth parted, her blue green eyes growing dazed for a moment, her freckled cheeks blooming with color. The warm water felt distinctly cool, compared to the heat of the gaze they shared for one long moment. Saber finally broke the look, backing off and bracing his arms along the stone rim of the tub behind him.

"Right," Kelly murmured, looking elsewhere as well. She was in a bit of inner turmoil, now that the shock of his barely discussed confession was fading off.

If he loves me, physically and emotionally, I'll apparently bring on some Disaster, though no one knows what. If we make love . . . I might finish falling in love with him. I think. And yet, if I'm to go home again in four more months . . .

But there wasn't much for her to go home to, really. She had everything she wanted here, except for maybe some female companionship. His brothers were fun to be with, and she had always gotten along great with males and females alike in her twenty-seven years. Once she had firmly established herself as the "alpha female" of their otherwise all-male household, as she had put it to his twin, Wolfer, everything had smoothed out and gone great. She just longed for a bit of female companionship, too. Like her friend Hope.

It was a little stressful, not being able to talk to a fellow female, to commiserate over the more alien ways of the opposite gender, to be able to share arch feminine in-jokes that no male could readily comprehend. But that was all that was really missing, here. She missed her friends and her family, and some of the technological amenities, but that was all.

Even suffering through her period two weeks ago hadn't been all that bad. Morganen and Evanor had put their heads together at breakfast when she had come down snappish and miserable from cramps. The pair had dared to ask her a few delicate questions, then had gone off for about an hour and concocted a miracle drink that took care of all her symptoms—and would have made them absolute billionaires back in her own world, if their herbal magic could work there.

Even using cotton rags and dried sections of sea-sponge instead of more modern products hadn't been too awkward . . . though of course knowing how medieval women had handled the whole thing without modern conveniences had helped Kelly a lot in dealing with the matter.

By now, she could only think that if all her old friends and few distant relatives had heard about her house being burned down, they probably thought she had died and vanished in the fire. Or that she was hiding from the people responsible. As much as her gut twisted with the urge for some kind of vengeance for ruining her house, her livelihood, and the attempt to kill her so gruesomely . . . she *was* glad it had happened. After all, she was *here*, in this wonderfully strange, new world. *If only there were other women here. Though I suppose if I get together with Tall, Blond, and Not-So-Surly-Anymore . . . and we survive whatever the Disaster is . . . then I've got seven sisters-in-law to look forward to meeting, don't I?*

She scooped a double handful of water over her head and thought some more, trying to see a way out of having to leave this world when the time came.

"What are you thinking?" Saber asked.

"That I'm glad to be here," Kelly admitted quietly. "That . . . I don't want to have to leave, in four months."

"Kata's T—!" He broke off before he could offend her with the indelicate oath. Grabbing her shoulders, he twisted her around, the sides of their thighs brushing together as she turned. "I *love* you and you are going to *marry* me and *stay* here! Is that clear?"

Her hands swished through the water, going straight to her hips as she bobbed on her haunches in the water, doing her best to stay hydrated despite her sharply stirred ire. "Oh, really! And you *think* I'm going to marry you, just because you *tell* me to?"

Idiot! You should know better by now than to rile her temper! Wincing, Saber shook his head to negate his mistake. He drew her close and brushed her mouth gently with his lips, switching tactics completely as he kissed her between words. "Forgive me, Kelly. Please, *please*, stay and be my wife? Marry me and make me miserably happy for the rest of my life?"

"Um . . . well . . . if you absolutely *insist*," she muttered against his mouth, twining her arms around his ribs.

Someone rapped on the door, breaking them apart with a startled splash. Saber cursed; his brothers were back. They knocked again, but he would be damned before he let them see his future bride naked. "Hold your gods-be-damned horses!"

Kelly giggled at his choice of phrase. Some things, it seemed, were the same whatever universe one was in, however it was rephrased.

Giving her a brief, brow-raised look of bemusement at her humor, he dunked himself, then climbed out, grabbed the damp towel she had discarded, and wrapped it around his hips. Padding over to the privacy screen positioned somewhat between the tub and the door, he pulled it more fully into place. Only then did he approach the door, which had been carefully planed and sanded several weeks ago until it didn't stick anymore.

As one of his brothers knocked again, Saber opened it a mere crack. Kelly couldn't quite hear the conversation he was having with whomever was on the other side, and she couldn't quite see any of them since one of her privacy screens was in the way . . . but she could certainly hear the tone of their conversation.

It went something like, "What the hell do you want?", "Why, dear Brother, are you *naked*? Are felicitations in order?", "Mind your damned business, give me whatever you brought, and go away!", followed by rich male laughter from the other side of the opening as he pulled his head back. Kelly could see the top of the door opening wider for a moment. Shutting the heavy panel, Saber eyed it a moment, and passed his mostly healed hand in front of it, muttering under his breath. Probably locking it with a spell.

He padded back to the tub with a large pitcher in his hands. With a sigh, he poured the liquid—a fruit juice cocktail, probably rich in a gazillion ingredients since it was an indefinite sort of brown green color—into their mugs and rested the flagon on the steps. Shedding the towel, he climbed in, dunked under, then came up and slicked his rewetted hair back from his face. Kelly had only a few seconds at most to admire his groin; he wasn't fully erect, but he wasn't flaccid, either.

Proportionate was the word that came to mind, in fact.

He sighed, wiping his face. "Jinga, I think I'm finally beginning to feel human ag—"

A familiar, funny look rumpled his handsome features, giving her a glimpse of what he must have looked like as a boy when making faces at his younger brothers.

Kelly grinned into her replenished mug, as he splashed right back out of the tub again. No doubt she would have that *urk!* expression on her face all too soon, herself . . . but it was funny for the moment. It was also guaranteeing through their mutual misery that there would be no way the two of them would feel physically awkward around each other. Not by the time the watersnake poison was finally out of their system. Not with the torture it was putting them both through.

Sort of like a case of the stomach-flu, but in our case, it's trouble from the other end, and caused by a venom, not a virus. Drowning the urge to laugh with more liquid for her insides to absorb, she drank the surprisingly palatable juice and floated in the water, waiting for his return, and for her turn at making a dripping dash for the bathroom. *Or rather, the refreshing room. Keep using the local vocabulary, Kelly . . .*

They touched, little brushes that carefully stayed free of important zones. They made funny faces every once in a while, sometimes from the excess of water that had to come out one way, sometimes from drinking too much of it in the other way. They checked fingers and toes occasionally, to see if anything was beginning to prune.

And they talked. Of her childhood, growing up in the Pacific Northwest, of what bicycles, television sets, movies, and roller coasters all were. Of his childhood, of his first lessons in riding; learning how to hold a wooden sword; growing up knowing that, as the oldest, the County of Corvis would eventually be his, before it had been taken away with their exile.

They compared her solitary childhood with his having not only a fraternal twin, but four sets of twins, always having plenty of brothers to play with or pester. He spoke of that special bond of being one of a twin set, the bond of understanding between him and his twin, Wolfer. Kelly spoke of her ending up between the generation gaps in her neighborhood, stuck between the older neighbor kids, who didn't want to play with her because she was too little, and the younger ones she found herself "herding," because she was older and therefore responsible for them.

He talked about his first battle, against bandits at the age of fifteen; she talked about fighting off that mugger and school yard bullies when she was younger. He revealed that the scar on his back came from scraping a tree limb during a fall when he was young and wasn't supposed to be climbing the tree. He'd hidden the injury, and the local mage-healer hadn't seen it until a few days later, when he developed an infection fever, after the flesh had begun to scar. She confessed that she'd had a mole lasered off of the underside of her breast, the site of which he just had to see, though very carefully did not touch.

There was nothing to do *but* talk, after all, and soak, dash to the refreshing room and back, and soak and talk some more.

They drank, they ate, they drained and refilled the tub with more water at twilight, as the rain continued to drizzle outside in the lingering edge of the storm; they rapped the lightglobes for illumination as night fell, and talked some more. They had many things in common despite their literal universe of differences, including the way both of them felt they were responsible for themselves and those around them. And Kelly and Saber admitted that, after a bit of teasing and hesitant confession, they both liked sparring verbally with each other. Not all the time, but some of the time they had both enjoyed their battle of wits.

There was no real way to tell the hours, since the eight brothers had never needed to keep appointments and didn't need a way of keeping time beyond the general position of the sun. But sometime after midnight, Kelly lifted her hand to cover one of many yawns she had begun smothering some time before. She rubbed her fingertips idly as she lowered her hand again, disliking the texture of them. Wishing they didn't have to stay in the water all night long, where the risk of falling asleep and drowning was a serious one.

Saber finished his own yawn, triggered by hers, blinked and stretched—and blinked again, grabbing her wrist with a little splash of lukewarm water. "Prune! Prune!"

"What?" Kelly woke up a little more and twisted her hand toward her face. Sure enough, the tips of her fingers had finally achieved that wrinkly, pale, waterlogged complexion that she didn't particularly like. This time, though, it was a wonderful sight. "I'm pruny! I'm all wrinkly and *pruny*! I can get out now!"

Releasing her wrist, Saber checked his own fingertips and sighed. Firm and solid-surfaced. "But not me. Not yet. Watersnake venom injected directly into the blood takes longer to flush out than when it is absorbed through the skin."

"Would you like me to stay in here and keep you company?" Kelly offered politely.

Saber shook his head. "No. Go ahead and get out. Dry yourself off—and keep drinking liquids." He glanced at her, lowering his hand back into the water. "But, if you could still keep me company . . ."

"And make sure you don't drown?" she agreed, floating over to the edge with the steps. "You know, you're actually pretty fun to be with, Saber, when you're not constantly yelling at me."

He arched a brow at her, soaked but still handsome. "I could say the same for you!"

She grinned and splashed him. He splashed her back, then dunked under the surface as she started climbing out. He came up in time to squint against the streaming water moisturizing his face, and caught a glimpse of her many feminine parts before she started rubbing them dry with the odd but clever terry-cloth towels Evanor had made. The sight of her made his mouth dry, and he wasn't entirely sure the watersnake venom had anything to do with it.

Reminded of their continuing need for liquid, he ordered, "Drink, woman!"

She peered over her shoulder at his command, then dropped the towel just low enough and jiggled impertinently in his direction, her backside prominently displayed. Even though it was meant as a wordless, rude disagreement, it was an incredible sight. Dropping his forehead to his arm, he groaned. Kelly laughed and continued drying off.

"Are you *certain* you're an untouched maiden?" he demanded, his nose and mouth barely an inch from being submerged in the water, his head still resting on his arm.

She came back and stroked the top of his damp head. "Poor baby. Not sure if you can handle an Earth-girl, are you?"

He lifted his head and caught her arm with a snap that proved, toxin or not, he still had warrior reflexes. Tugging her wrist close, he pressed a kiss to her palm. "Not tonight, my dear; I am still feeling the poison. And don't call me 'baby.' I am a fully grown man. Which, since I know you stared at me blatantly several times as I came back from the refreshing room, I *know* you have noticed by now."

She laughed at that and crossed to the wardrobe bureau where her clothes were stored. Drawing out the sleeveless chemise she had made, she donned it. Then she wrapped her hair in a dry towel, dragged a chair close to the tub, sat and poured herself a dollop of the remaining juice from the third flagon brought to them by his brothers. She poured him some, too, and watched as he downed it with a waterlogged sigh. Kelly admired him as he dunked under the water yet again, then sighed herself as he came back up.

Saber wiped at his eyes and studied her. "What was that for?"

"Not tonight, dear. You're poisoned," she repeated wistfully.

"Kelly . . . if you are twenty-seven, and yet you said your culture doesn't value virginity," Saber asked, knowing by now after all their talking—and thankful for it—that she preferred more direct conversation than most other people did, "why are you still a virgin?"

"Overprotective parents, lack of real enthusiasm, busy making a life for myself . . ." She rested her chin on her hand, her elbow on the rim of the tub, and thought about it. "I did promise my parents I'd try to wait until my wedding day. Maybe . . . I kind of also felt like I was born in the wrong time. I mean, I went to college, got a degree in business administration and office work, and had a couple good jobs from early on, but there weren't that many girls my age who were interested in the same things I was, such as when I first got hooked on needlepoint and embroidery at twelve, then interested in the medieval society at thirteen, when a friend's family took me with them to a local event.

"Things just deteriorated from there," she added with a mock-shake of her head. "Sewing my own medieval-style Halloween costumes, making my own prom dress, rather than buying one premade—I'd rather embroider than watch TV, though I didn't mind listening to the radio. Of course, your brother makes a pretty decent radio," she added with a little smile, meaning Evanor. "Especially since I like folk and classical, and that's the kind of music that he sings.

"At least, from my perspective." She fell silent a moment, then eyed him. "Mind you, I've kissed and been kissed, and done a little, um, fully clothed fondling, and I've had five boyfriends—swains, you'd probably call them, where we indulged in flirtations and light courtings, but nothing overly serious. Plus I had a very thorough theoretical education in the pleasurable arts, thanks to my many friends' attempts to enlighten me. But I never really felt the *urge* to pick out a lover and rumple the sheets with him," she added honestly. "At least, not as strongly as I've been feeling around you. You're rather handsome, intelligent, and even funny—when you're not yelling at me. I not only find you attractive, I'm also attracted to you. So . . . how about you? May I presume, being male, you aren't a virgin?"

He blushed at that, charming her. Especially since she knew now he was two years older than her. They had talked about a lot of things, after all.

"No, I'm not. But I've only lain with a few. They were castle servants, and it was mostly their idea," he added. Then shrugged with a twinge of honesty. "Okay, I coaxed some of them into it sometimes, too, but what can I say? It's quite enjoyable. It has been a few years, though. On top of the exile, I mean," he added. "I was often too busy or too exhausted, learning how to run the estate from our father, then running it on my own. And I'd even gotten used to it—being celibate—until shortly after you showed up."

"Poor baby. Did you have to stop at the self-service gas station of love?" Kelly asked with a sympathetic, feminine purr.

He quirked a brow in uncertainty at her odd phrase. Some things were translated by that potion she had drunk, but others simply weren't. "Did I have to *what*?"

She grinned, but blushed at the same time. "Did I make you, um . . . want to touch yourself?"

He blushed a sort of bronzed red as his lightly tanned face colored deeply. "How did—?"

"So you *did*?" she inquired as she leaned closer, wide-eyed and avidly curious.

"Kelly!"

"Oh, don't be scandalized, Saber! I do it myself," she pointed out, flicking drops of water at him with her fingertips. "It's perfectly natural . . . and it totally beats abstinence hands down."

He colored again. Two seconds later, Kelly realized how her common-phrased cliché *could* have been taken.

And laughed out loud, throwing her head back so hard, the towel wrapped around it slipped free, tugging on her still-damp hair as it fell to the floor. Saber grinned back, flashing his nearly even teeth at her. Then grimaced and splashed quickly out of the tub, heading for the refreshing room door once more.

TWELVE

H is fingertips finally pruned three hours later. Despite her promise to stay awake, Kelly had drooped about an hour and a half ago onto her forearms, and was dozing lightly while slouched in her chair. Tired but elated over the proof of his cure, Saber pulled the plug, drank the last of the juice as the bathtub drained, patted himself dry enough to climb into bed, and mustered just enough strength to swing her up into his arms and take both of them to her bed.

Her mattress was less lumpy than his own, he discovered. Not that it was exactly comfortable, trying to fall asleep while holding her lightly clothed body against his naked one. But he wouldn't have let go of her if the whole donjon was on fire . . . and when she snuggled closer in her sleep, murmuring something indistinct, he knew his annoying youngest sibling was right.

One couldn't escape one's Destiny.

He wasn't even going to try anymore, and he was content with that. Pleased with it. She would make him one hell of a wife. A hell-raiser, though thankfully not a literal one. *Actually, she's like a cat, fiercely independent, unafraid to unsheath her claws if needed, yet capable of purring and nuzzling whenever she is pleased.*

It's a good thing I admire and like cats, he mused as he drifted off.

When Saber woke again, her chemise hem had risen to the top of her thighs, which were tangled with his own; his hips, in a morning-roused life of their own, were flexing, rubbing himself intimately against her dampness.

He jerked back, cursing himself under his breath as he crawled free of her body. She woke and blinked sleepily, while Saber quickly stripped the bedcovers back and checked for virginal stains. Nothing. He hadn't sheathed himself in her yet, though he wanted to. Oh, how he wanted to, especially looking at her, pushed half up on her elbows, her knees splayed, her sleeveless chemise nightgown pooled at her waist, giving him a torturous glimpse of copper-curled heaven between her thighs.

One minute she was blinking sleepily at him, making him hard and randy just from the sight of her. The next moment, her eyes snapped wide, her knees slapped together, and her hands yanked down the muslin of the undergown in belated decorum. Her lightly freckled cheeks turned a little more than pink; they turned decidedly red, in fact. Then she rubbed her fingers through her already rumpled hair and gave him a wry smile, still blushing but recovering her composure.

"Good morning. Nice to see you're alive." Her gaze drifted down to his naked hips, and the corner of her mouth quirked up. "*Very* alive . . ."

"Quite." Even though he knew his own cheeks were heating at her blatant innuendo, Saber *did* feel incredibly alive. And thirsty. He backed up, found his trousers—mostly dried where he had tossed them to the floor yesterday—and did his best to pull the damp fabric on. He had to turn around, stare determinedly out the window, and wait a few moments to be able to get the lacings fastened, but it didn't take too long, all things considered. He heard her slide out of the bed and pad into the refreshing room; once she was gone from immediate view, he managed to relax a little more, enough to be able to bend over and finish dressing.

A mug appeared around his arm as he finished tugging his tunic down into place, wrinkled but more or less dry, like his pants.

"Water?" Kelly offered, holding up the mug.

Groaning ruefully, Saber took it anyway. He lifted it in a brief, mock-toast before drinking from it. "I think I have seen *enough* water for the next week. May Jinga keep me from seeing more."

"For at least the next month," Kelly asserted, drinking from her own mug.

"The next year!" he saluted, turning and clinking mugs with her.

"Halleluia, Brother, you're preachin' to the choir!" she drawled. At the arch of his brow, she shook her head. "Never mind. Just one of my otherworldly oddities; it's a cultural reference."

"Ah." He finished draining his mug, wiped his mouth with the back of his wrist, then frowned thoughtfully. "I believe I have forgotten something."

"Underwear? You weren't wearing any to begin with," Kelly mused, tipping her own mug up for the last drop. She grimaced a moment later. "I do hope the diarrhea is over with?"

He nodded. "More or less. Though neither of us will feel normal, inside or out, for another day or two. And it's best to keep drinking, to ensure the dehydration doesn't return. Which it has been known to do."

"Oh, that's reassuring." Shaking it off, she eyed him. "So, what did you forget?"

"This." Hooking his left arm around her waist, he pulled her up against him, bent his head, and took her mouth in the kind of kiss they hadn't allowed themselves to indulge in before. His lips nipped hers, his tongue flicked in a taste, and her own opened to tangle with him in a hot, wet, oh-my-good-*morning*! kind of kiss. Her breath hitched, her fingers curled around his shoulders, knocking him in the back with her pottery mug, and she arched against him, burrowing her breasts into his chest, her belly into his groin and let out a little whimper.

Saber liked that sound. He flicked her lower lip, caught it in his own teeth as she every so often did with hers, then sucked on it. Making her emit that tiny mewl of pleasure again. With one arm around her back, he transferred the mug in his other hand to it, then slid his now freed right hand down to the curves of her bottom, lifting and squeezing them to press her in against him. After a month of regular, frequent meals putting on some much-needed pounds, her backside was becoming nicely cushioned, perfect in his palm. He slid his other hand down there, too, feeling her around the handle of the mug.

She liked that so much, she rewarded him by teasing his tongue into her mouth with strokes of her own, then sucking on it. Making him groan.

Bam-bam-bam.

Reluctantly, they pulled apart a little. Saber sighed and dropped his forehead against her own. "Remind me to kill my brothers for their sense of timing."

She shook her head, rolling her forehead against his with a wicked smile. "Nah. It's much more fun when you can plot to do the exact same thing to them, one day."

That reminded Saber of the Curse; not of the coming Disaster, exactly, but of the fact that there were seven more women destined to come into their exiled lives. He tried picturing seven more versions of Kelly and failed. One was exactly enough for him—and only one, no more. He wasn't sure yet what he would do if they ended up having a daughter as boisterous as her . . . or worse, a son with some of her more redheaded traits. Saber tried to picture that, too, and failed again.

One of his brothers knocked on the door again. "Hey! Anyone still alive in there? This door is spelled shut, you know!"

It was Evanor. Releasing his strawberry-haired Destiny reluctantly, Saber crossed to the door, passed his hand over it with a murmur of the release word, then opened it.

The light-haired, brown-eyed brother beamed at Saber the moment Evanor realized he was dressed. "An excellent morning to you! Is it safe to come in?" he added politely, a jug of something fresh-squeezed in his hand.

Saber glanced back at Kelly. She was still clad in the chemise. "Would you put something on?"

"I *am* wearing something," she retorted

"Something more decent?" he asserted.

She planted her hands on her hips. "By my world's standards, this *is* 'more decent'!"

Evanor made a *psst* sound at his brother and whispered to him, "Should we be on the alert for a Disaster, or just another fight between the two of you?"

"*Very* funny," Saber growled. "No Disaster, no fight." He looked back at his bride-to-be. "Find your best gown. We will go to the chapel, clasp hands over the eight altars, and be wed before breakfast."

She gaped at him. Then rolled her eyes and glared at him, hands going to her hips again. "Ha! If I'm marrying you, buster, we're doing this right! Which means you have to wait until I've *made* my best gown." As his brows lowered in a frown and his lips parted to argue, she cocked her hip, hands resting in their usual place, and smiled at him slyly. "Out of that gorgeous aquamarine silk you brought me yesterday. I believe there is even enough of it to make you a matching tunic. That way we'll look like we belong to each other."

"And it would give the rest of us time to finish—uh, *start* making your wedding gifts," Evanor added.

Saber mock-glared at him. He felt too good to give his blond-haired brother the real thing, though. "*Fine*. How long will it take you to make your best gown?" he asked Kelly, twisting to face her. "Two days? Three?"

She gauged the time, adding up the difference between normally having a sewing machine and now having to do everything by hand. Even with an enchanted needle that created four stitches for every one she made. "One month. If I work on nothing else but your clothes and mine."

"A month!" He wasn't going to last that long! He turned back to his brother. "Evanor, you're the best with clothing among us; use your magic to help her. You have two weeks at most."

"Two *weeks*?"

At that too-familiar, dangerous tone in her voice, at the matching arch of her brow and the hands once again firmly planted on her hips, Saber abandoned the door and crossed to stand in front of his bride-to-be. He slipped his hands around her waist, tucking them into the space formed by her braced arms, and rested his forehead against hers, stooping a little to do so. Evanor looked elsewhere, humming quietly to himself, as Saber murmured in Kelly's ear.

"That is as long as I think I can wait for you, my love. As it is, I shall have the torment of remembering how we spent the night in your bed, and how we woke up together, so natural and right together, to torture me for all of the intervening time." He brushed her mouth with his own. "Please don't make me wait any longer—please?"

"All right," she murmured, kissing him back. "Since you asked so nicely."

Ending their exchange before he could do anything that he wouldn't want his brother to see, Saber kissed her brow. Then caressed that ripe feminine bottom because he simply couldn't resist. "Get dressed and join us for breakfast, then. We'll plan for the celebration, among other things."

Hanging in the air at the end of his words was the fact that they would also have to plan for whatever vaguely Prophesied Disaster would come from the fallout of their wedding. But he said nothing more, just nuzzled the tip of her slightly pert, freckled nose with his own straight, lightly tanned one, and left her to get dressed.

Evanor left the pitcher of juice just inside the door for Kelly's use and accompanied his older brother back down the stairs. "So, you finally embraced your Fate, Brother?"

Saber gave Evanor a dirty look. "*Your* turn is coming soon, Brother."

Evanor smiled serenely, and slyly. "Yes, well, we all have our Destiny—in preordained order—to bear."

I have it!" Morganen burst into the great hall four days later, fist raised high. Rydan, in the act of setting out the plates, eyed his youngest sibling.

"Have what?"

"I have the solution to our plague of deadly infestations!"

Kelly raised her brow, setting out the silverware behind the one brother whom she only ever saw at this post-sunset evening meal. "How often have you had these invasions, anyway?"

"About once every week or two," Wolfer rumbled, hefting a keg onto the table and pulling out the knife at his belt to pry the cork out of the bunghole; he wanted to thrust in a new tap so they could pour the stout everyone seemed to prefer for their evening drink.

Not that she could fault their choice of beverage; one, they were men and would naturally want to drink something to put a little more hair on their otherwise lightly dusted chests, and two, proper, thick, dark stouts like this one were usually full of vitamins and nutrients, simply from the way they were made. She even kind of liked the nutty taste, especially with the spicy-sweet honey-nut pastries Evanor had showed her how to make for dessert. But the second eldest's comment caught her attention as his meaning sank in.

"Once a *week*? That often?" Kelly asked as her eyes widened, alarmed by the frequency.

"Not for the first two or so months, but after that, they came, increased, and stayed at a pacing of roughly one a week, though not always evenly spaced. It's only since you came that they have lessened in their frequency. Which makes no sense, if you are meant to be our Disaster-bringer," Wolfer added, though he winked one golden eye at her to show he didn't mean any insult. "Are you certain you're the one meant to wed my twin?"

"No, my dear brother," Morganen all but caroled, thumping his sibling on one thickly muscled shoulder as he strode around the table. "*You* are wrong!" He continued around, and caught up Kelly as she finished laying the last fork and spoon down. Sweeping her around, arm at her waist, his hand catching hers, he hummed a little tune, dancing with her in a rocking little two-step.

"*Morganen!*"

The roar made Kelly jump, blinking at the rage in Saber's voice, as he came into the hall.

"Just celebrating with my sister-in-law-to-be, dear brother!"

"*He's* in a good mood," Trevan quipped to no one in particular, helping Saber fetch the steaming platters of food from the kitchens at the base of the north wing, next to the great hall.

Saber narrowed his gaze, but his youngest brother wasn't touching her improperly; one hand was at her back, above her waist, the other held her hand, and there was a full hand-span of distance between their bodies. He grunted and allowed it. "Why are you dancing with my bride?"

"Because she made us clean the hall!"

Dominor snorted from up on the second balcony level, where he was knocking the lightglobes into life. His voice echoed down to them. "And you *thank* her for it with your little dance?"

Morganen twirled Kelly out, la-la-la-ing to the tune he had swept her into. "But of course, lalalaaaah!" He caught her as she came back again, and dropped a brotherly kiss on her forehead before stepping back and bowing over Kelly's hand in a courtly way, while his eldest sibling glared. Morganen ignored his brother. "My dear lady, we all owe you a *deep* debt of gratitude!

"*Think* about it, my brothers," he added, releasing her fingertips and turning to look at the others. "At first there were no teleported invasions. Then they slowly began increasing, and within a span of five months, were coming frequently. If our unknown assailant had any paintings of this hall, then it would have taken him or her time to adjust to all of the dirt and grime in his mind's eye for accurate, successful teleportation. It would be a painting, since all of our mirrors are enspelled against scrying, and the distance to the mainland's coast is too far to do it easily by such directly scryed means. That would also explain the five or so months it took our tormentor to focus firmly on us.

"*But*," he added, holding up a finger, "once we started *cleaning* the hall, scrubbing and painting the walls and moving the furnishings, it changed the look of all the rooms!"

"And as every mage knows," Rydan added, speaking the most words Kelly had yet heard from him, especially since he was glancing at her with his night-dark eyes as he explained it for her, "only through deep familiarity can a mage teleport something elsewhere, or through an indirect but *accurate* scry, such as a painting."

After a quick double-blink, his twin, Trevan, got over the shock of

Rydan speaking so much to them all at once and continued Morganen's line of reasoning and Rydan's proffered explanation. "But only after deep meditation and with great strength, perhaps even with some forgotten article we left behind in Corvis; it cannot be easily done over any great distance, and not one *noticeable* thing must be different between what is known and what is actually here, which means that the task is exceedingly difficult. There can be some minor differences of the sort that would take a second or third look to register, but nothing stronger than that."

"You cannot teleport anything without knowing exactly where it will fit into the part of the universe it goes to," Wolfer added in his rumble, his mouth quirking up slightly on one side. "Or it will not go there at all. So *I* will thank you, too, Lady Kelly, for working our knuckles raw with so much soap, spell, and water."

"Wait, wait; there's more!" Morganen asserted gleefully, eager to recapture everyone's attention. "It will take a little preparation and a very careful layering of spells and paint, but I have come up with a way to *ensure* that no one not intimately familiar with the new look of Nightfall Castle can ever teleport anything into it from afar! And again, I have *you* to thank, Lady Kelly—or rather, my peeks into your universe to ascertain the settling flow of its aether, to thank.

"They have these boxes," he continued, relating the tale to his brothers now, "that glow and flicker with different images, as if the most detailed of paintings had sprung to life. They call it the *teevee*, and while it does make most who sit before it slack-jawed and witless—no offense, Kelly—it *does* constantly change.

"So I was thinking, perhaps *I* could come up with a type of paint that changes from hour to hour, day to day, in its colors and images—murals of panoramic, pastoral scenes, perhaps, or drifting clouds, or maybe even both. Something subtle and tasteful, but still there, and still *changing*," he stressed as his deeply interested brothers slowly nodded, agreeing with him. "Not enough to distract from everyday life, but certainly enough to change each wall from hour to hour, and thus change the vital appearance of each room, altering them too much for our unknown mage to easily reach us again! Even if he sends more creatures to peek in through our windows, the trick won't work more than just the once, in that very moment!"

"It also explains," Trevan agreed, lingering to hear his brother's words, "why those wyvern were peering into the rooms instead of attacking us more directly, to do a secondhand scry for the mage— one can also scry through the eyes of a largish animal, if one has the right spell for it, and enough power to not only master the will and resistance of the creature for long enough, but also the strength to do so over such a long distance," he added in explanation to Kelly. "The larger and smarter the animal, the more likely it'll still follow orders over a long distance.

"But it's a risky matter, because the size of Gates needed to send such large creatures over such a long distance makes it more likely that the Council of Mages will notice what is going on and put an end to it. These beasts being sent our way are forbidden for anyone, outside of the government, to create or possess in times of peace, for wartime breeding purposes."

"Wasting the energy to hunt us with larger beasts certainly proves we angered our foe by cleaning the castle and thwarting his or her scrying," Saber mused, pulling out Kelly's chair for her.

The chair had been added next to his on his side of the large, eight-sided table they had built for their own use when they had been exiled to the isle. It struck him for a moment that there was enough room at each of the eight sides for two people to sit, not just one brother each . . . enough room on each of the eight sides for a husband and a wife to sit, come to think of it. Morganen had directed the size of the table during its making. Not Trevan, who was the one most talented at furniture making. Saber was going to have to talk to his youngest brother, before Morg's matchmaking tendencies got out of hand . . . or rather, now that the situation had definitely gotten out of hand.

Strawberry blond hair swung into his vision, as his bride-to-be sat down, drawing his eyes to her. Kelly of Doyle, seated beside him, was but the first of the Prophesied brides awaiting him and his brothers. *Or maybe I won't have a talk with him . . .*

"You think he's been angered that much?" Kelly asked, reasoning it out for herself. "As opposed to his normal level of insane rage, I suppose? Was that triple attack the most powerful, so far? Wyvern, watersnake, and demon-thing?"

"Yes," Wolfer rumbled, taking his own seat. "Normally he or she sends only one type of creature at a time. Once in a while, there will be two types of beast to worry about, but not often. They are expensive to create, breed, and maintain, especially when done with the need to keep their existence absolutely secret. So we have clearly angered our foe, that he would waste so much of his or her power and resources in attacking us."

"I'm not surprised he or she would be so chary with the beasts," Morganen asserted, as his twin and Evanor came out of the hall that led to the kitchens with the last platters of food, and Dominor descended into the hall to join them. "The Council of Mages has a policy of severely discouraging the breeding of such monsters; if the war-monsters have killed anyone, either through accidental escape or deliberately being set, the sentence is automatically death.

"This mage would have to maintain a secret compound somewhere, housing and breeding the beasts, but not a very large one, else it would have long since been discovered. And he or she would send the fast-breeding things, such as the mekhadadaks, to plague us the most—as often as one out of every two or three attacks, in other words," he added to Kelly. Making her shiver. "In some ways

I think it a miracle we've survived this long, but somehow we have, and with only a few close calls. Such as your own bout with the watersnakes."

Kelly shook her head as she picked up her fork. "I don't see what the eight of you are harping about where I'm concerned—frankly, you're *already* plagued with a major Disaster!"

"We will track down this would-be murderer. Eventually, following the traces of his or her own power," Wolfer rumbled with the surety of a basalt mountain. Implacable and impossible to deter from its position. "When we do, we will kill our attacker. It is that simple."

"Our foe must be extremely powerful, though," Dominor admitted—and that was something, that the most arrogant of the brothers would admit such a thing about someone else. "Even Morganen cannot find the source of these sendings."

Morganen shrugged at the damned-with-faint praise. "I do work on it, whenever I have the chance to trace the energies through the aether right after an attack. But it would be better, I think, to concentrate on making that special paint first and redo every wall inside the castle with it immediately. It does make more sense that our foe uses a painting for scrying rather than memory or a mirror. It is far more likely for them to have a painting of this castle than to have come to this rarely visited isle prior to our exile.

"But now our enemy has a clear, wyvern-gained view of the exterior of the donjon and similarly clear glimpses into the interior. Painting the inner walls won't work alone. We should probably change our exterior walls as well."

"I am loath to change the exterior blatantly. Especially using the same changing paint as we would use on the interior; it would be easier for them to study and learn the pattern if it were on the outside walls," Saber stated, shaking his head. "I would rather have something more subtle . . . something different. Not as blatant. I

certainly don't want the traders coming and noticing the changes in
the distance and talking about them. But I don't know what."

"*Camouflage,*" Kelly said suddenly, making Wolfer eye her as he
passed a basket of rolls.

"Camo-what?" the second eldest asked.

Kelly smiled. It was about time someone *else* did a terminology
double take! "*Camouflage* is a word in my native language that basically means 'to obscure or conceal through a blending with one's
surroundings.' If we paint the outer walls of the castle in patterns
like the jungle, it will blend into its surroundings and make it difficult for creatures like the wyverns to fly out here, spot the castle
quickly, and attack before anyone knows they are here. They'll be
busy hunting around looking for it, giving us more time to see them
and ready ourselves for a counterattack."

The third-eldest sighed. "I must agree. Painting over the gardens,
courtyards, and all the glass of the windows would be too difficult,
and the shapes of the buildings would still stand out too easily,"
Dominor pointed out, making his own offering to the others. "But an
illusion, cast over the whole of the castle grounds, added to and aug-
menting the warning-and-warding spells we have already cast over
everything, *that* might work."

"A combination of the two would work best," Saber stated.
"Dominor, work on the illusion; you're the best enchanter we have.
If you set it in an object, we can fix it to the storm-vane on the peak
of this hall, and it will be able to spread out like a dome, allowing us
to see everything on the island from within as it actually appears,
but still be able to hide the castle from those beyond its walls. Set it
to work effectively both from a distance and from close up, and
from either the ground or the air . . . and make it so that those who
are given verbal permission from one of us to enter the compound
can actually see the entrance gates and such when they do draw near.

"I would like to be able to find our home from an approach on the ground, but some camouflage at ground-level would still be helpful. Morganen, work on your paint. Try to see if you can make it last a good few decades with only minor touch-up spells. I have reason to hope it will not take much longer to find our foe, now that he or she grows more agitated at being thwarted, and thus potentially more careless. But others may think to do the same later on, if word ever gets out that there is now a woman in our hall."

"I will not have Lady Kelly harmed."

"She is our sister, Saber," Morganen returned, answering the unspoken order in his eldest brother's words. The calm, clear intent behind his words was echoed in the faces of the others around them, even Rydan's. "We will protect her with our very lives."

With the focus of the protective looks around her, Kelly felt a warmth spread through her, from the middle of her chest out. These eight men—real "witches," not just the imagined kind—had welcomed her into their hearts as well as their home. Something many of the folk of a certain Midwest town back on Earth had *not*. This odd world was now more of a home to her than her old one, in that regard.

She cared for Saber and liked his brothers, even if there weren't any other females for company right now. She liked her life here, with nothing but time to stitch and knit and sew, to talk and laugh with men who put up with her occasionally strawberry-haired, tart-worded temper and assertive will. There was even time to look for a history book or two, or maybe a primer on the basics of how magic worked in this wonderful, strange, increasingly less-bizarre world.

Kelly made up her mind. She felt like she was in love, though she didn't know for certain just yet—never having been in love before— but she would marry Saber. Marry him, and rescue him from whatever overblown Disaster all of these otherwise big and strong men feared so much, and do her best to live happily ever after. Doyles weren't stupid, after all.

THIRTEEN

❧

"We cannot get married today."

Saber's words woke her up quickly, cutting Kelly off in mid-yawn. She stepped back from the door she had opened to him, giving him room to step inside, unmindful of how beautiful she looked to him, sleep-rumpled in that sleeveless chemise she used for a nightgown. "What do you mean, we can't get married today?"

"The supply boats are here. They're a day early. They usually camp in the temple, one of the few buildings still standing from the old city that used to be down there, so we cannot use it to wed in," he murmured, tugging her close to drop an apologetic kiss on her brow. "They must not see you, or else they would seek to remove you from the isle. One way or another."

"I can't wait until the damned Disaster gets here, and it's done and gone," she muttered into his chest. "Then we can send them all a letter, telling them they don't have anything left to fear and to just let us be."

He kissed the top of her head, pressing his lips to the light reddish-gold locks that were shorter than his own. Most of the women he remembered from three years before liked to grow theirs as long as was possible, but not his Kelly. He ached with wanting for her, but then he was usually hard when thinking about or standing around her, these days.

Her safety came first, though. This feeling was a long cry from the first ungentlemanly impulses he had gone through when he had met her—wanting to get rid of her in a variety of vaguely plotted, nefarious ways. *But then, I was a fool, when she first arrived. A stubborn, insensitive fool.* "Better that we wait until they are gone and wed the day after tomorrow. They will depart with the last ebb of the dawn tide, tomorrow, but we should wait just a little longer all the same, to be certain they are well away."

She didn't like it and felt a touch of irrational irritability, but sighed and nodded and snuggled deeper into his arms . . . and then felt it. That first warning wave of pain, first dull, then sharp, then dull and hard. Which she hadn't felt for roughly a month. "Um, Saber?"

"Mm-hmm?" he managed, breathing in her feminine scent with a pleasure that was going to have to be delayed two more nights, unfortunately.

"Make that five days from now."

He stiffened. "What?"

"I, um, can't . . . you know," she hedged. "Not for another five or six days. And go ask Evanor to brew me up a strong cup of that cramp-easing tea he and Morganen came up with. I'm going to need it today. And tomorrow. And probably the day after that . . ."

"Oh."

She chuckled at the disappointment in his tone, the slump of his shoulders as he comprehended and flushed, and gave him a little squeeze. "Poor baby."

"I am *not* a baby!"

Kelly prepared herself for her wedding. Bathed and perfumed in a light rubbing of Saber's favorite scents for her, she drew on her new underclothes. She had found a use for the hearts-within-hearts patterned lace she had found and experimented with. Carefully stitched together, the two-inch-wide, soft silk lace formed a bra any bride would be proud to wear on her wedding day . . . and matching bikini underwear. She smiled as she fastened the hook-and-eye closures on the front of her carefully fitted bra; Saber had bent the tiny fasteners for her out of thin steel wire, uncertain why she wanted such odd-shaped, miniscule things.

He's going to have fun playing with them, I think, when he finally gets to see why they were made!

She missed not having a bachelorette party, or even just her friend Hope to attend her as she got ready, but Kelly was glad she hadn't heard a bachelor party going on for her groom last night, either. Not that she would've had to worry about strippers or anything, but still . . .

The newly repainted room slowly shifted in shades of blue and white around her, swirls of "clouds" gradually patterning their way across the formerly white walls. That was the result of Morganen's experiment into anti-scrying wall art. Kelly adjusted the underwear and reached for the first piece of her best-dress, aquamarine silk clothes, as the sun finished setting outside, leaving the painted walls to look like a parody of daylight, though the paint did not actually glow.

For Rydan's sake, they were holding an early evening wedding instead of a daylight one. Somewhere out there, the others were readying the chapel, and the horseless cart that would carry her down the long, winding road that led to the chapel, where she would be wed Katani-style.

As fun as it was to dress medievally, she liked wearing pants for the freedom of movement. Though her assistant, Evanor, had been uncertain about the decidedly un-Katani design, she had first sketched on a piece of yellowed paper, then measured, cut, and directed him where to sew on the aquamarine silk, transforming it into a multipiece garment of her own design.

First, she pulled on the pants, cut on the bias to fit smoothly over her hips and tapered just a little to show off her legs. She had put on some weight, in the past few months. Her legs looked a lot better, with just a little more curve to them. She laced the front in a flap-backed version, which was very like the brothers' style of trousers, since Evanor was familiar with how to stitch the eyelets and plackets. Next she donned her blouse, pulling on the loosely gathered garment until the neckline draped down over her shoulders.

Over that, she fastened a girdle-like skirt, gathered into a yoke at her waist. The hem was uneven, falling back in a diagonal cut from the middle of her thighs, almost but not quite sweeping the floor at her heels. Next came a bodice-vest that laced up the front and covered her bra straps.

Her back-draped skirt and the gathered blouse were both edged with more of the heart-patterned lace, stitched along the hemlines, cuffs, and gathered, lightly ruffled neckline, the delicate white contrasting nicely with the blue-green of the silk. The trousers, vest, and waist-yoke of the skirt were trimmed with a flat-woven ribbon, pattered with white, touches of emerald green, sapphire blue, and thread-of-gold, outlining the cut of the waist-length, fitted bodice vest at the low-scooping neckline, sleeve holes, lacings and waist, and down the sides and cuffs of her pants. And Wolfer, who had the best touch with leather of the eight brothers, had made her a pair of new ankle-high boots that he had somehow managed to dye the same aquamarine shade, plus promises of more pairs of slippers to replace the aged ones she was making do with for now.

Slipping on a pair of ankle-high socks knitted from fine thread in her spare time, her only new pair at the moment, she stepped into the boots, stamping her feet a little to make certain they fit comfortably. They fit perfectly, proof that Wolfer was good at making shoes, much better than the mass-produced shoe manufacturers of her old life. *Then again*, she admitted silently, smiling, *he has magic of his own to make a perfect shoe. He doesn't even need shoe-making elves from a fairy tale!* The thought amused her.

When she was dressed, Kelly hurried into the refreshing room to peer into the mirror and try to do something with her hair. Unlike a lot of redheads, her hair was perfectly straight. It insisted on staying perfectly straight, in fact, and only picked up the slightest curve at the very ends. Perms had fallen out in less than a month during her experimental teenage years. Hot curling irons didn't work. Her hair laughed in the face of mousse, gel, and hairspray, even when combined in countertop-cluttering hordes marshaled against her light reddish-golden locks. Thankfully, Saber didn't seem to notice the lack. Or didn't care.

Picking up the silver-backed brush he had given her, she stroked its stiff animal bristles through her hair. If she couldn't do anything with it, she could at the very least smooth it. Dampening the silver comb with a quick splash of water from the fall-faucet, she ran it through her hair, then used the brush to smooth the dampness into a sleek, shoulder-length, brushed-back style that exposed the lightly freckled planes of her face.

Kelly frowned at her face. She supposed she had a nice forehead, and a slightly pert nose, one with a little bump toward the tip that made her look tart and assertive sometimes. Her cheekbones were nice, her chin okay, her lips just borderline full, and naturally rose pink. Her lashes weren't as thick as Saber's, but then a lot of guys had better lashes than most women did.

Her brows had never needed plucking, which was nice, and she didn't miss makeup, but she wished that just once Saber had told her she was beautiful to him. Of course, he had stared at her several times as if she were, but he had never actually *said* anything.

I guess I'll have to beat it out of him, she thought on a sigh. Then chuckled at her reflection, smiling at the thought of mixing wits with the equally strong-willed man over the next few . . . next several . . . *Oh, god. I think I'm having a bridal-nerves attack . . .*

Forcing herself to breathe through the panic that suddenly clutched at her, she gripped the stone shelf of the sink and stared into her own aquamarine eyes. The light around her slowly faded, as she thought of staying in this realm for the rest of her life. Never again watching a television show, or hearing the radio. Never flying in an airplane, never tasting ice cream . . .

Oh, don't be silly! You have only to tell Evanor about ice cream, and you can bet he'll try to Sing it out of sugar, cream, eggs, and thin air. And as for flying, if these guys can create horseless, magic-drawn carriages, they can learn how to create floating, flying versions. Or you can always play the missing Wright sister and experiment with crafting hang-gliders on your own . . . assuming Saber doesn't go all protective and shouting on you, and lock you in the bedroom for even thinking of attempting something so foolishly dangerous. Though at least you should use his magic to protect you, she acknowledged wryly to herself.

It was nice knowing that she wasn't on her own, that she didn't have to completely take care of herself.

But, to live here—*not for a few years, or even several, but for actual* decades, *until I die* here, *to know that this place will be my home from this moment on, forever more . . .*

It wasn't entirely a panic point. Kelly could picture herself staying at Nightfall with the eight brothers, with Saber as her husband

and the others as her marriage-bound kin . . . but not in permanent exile.

She needed female companionship. She needed other people to talk to, even as interesting as the eight brothers were. She wanted to go *shopping*, even if only in a medieval marketplace. To find her own embroidery thread, to select and purchase her own cloth, to pick and choose what foods to eat, rather than whatever the brothers bartered or grew. And she wanted to sell the things she could make, as the brothers sold their own items, to add her contribution to the household.

That, of course, would have to wait until after the so-called Curse had come and gone. Once it had passed through—and they had survived whatever it was—there shouldn't be nearly as much of a stigma against women living on this isle as there was right now. She hoped.

And then there were children. Kelly really wanted a trained midwife when that point came, as it surely would. Otherwise, she wanted to put it off as long as possible. True, there was a part of her that wanted Saber's children, and in their long talk during the watersnake poisoning, she had learned that Saber wanted children, too. She just didn't want to be the only female around when she had them.

Well . . . I'll just have to do my damnedest, Doyle-style, to end the exile of the brothers, so that I can travel occasionally to other areas of this odd, fascinating world.

She had gone all the way out to the eastern beaches several miles away with Saber for a picnic on the sand last week. Semitropical, lush, and pretty though it had been, it wasn't the same as actually *going* somewhere else. As in, off this island.

There was a knock on the outer door. Kelly abruptly realized she was standing in darkness. Squinting through the refreshing room, she reached up, thunked a knuckle on the lightglobe in its bracket on the bathroom wall for some light, and made certain she still looked good in its abrupt, soft white glow. A woman—if she was lucky and found the right man the first time around—only got one wedding day in her lifetime, after all. Even if she had to literally go to another universe to find the right one.

I hope he's the right one . . .

Her visitor knocked again. Kelly gave herself one last check, making sure her hair looked like it was going to stay in place. Hurrying out, she opened the door on the far side of the bedchamber.

Trevan and Evanor stepped inside, grinning and eyeing her clothing appreciatively; their own was apparently their best wear, given the neatness of their clothes and the fine quality of the fabric. Some of which she had put trim on in the past month and a half, Kelly recognized with a touch of amusement. Behind them came Koranen and Morganen. The auburn-haired mage stopped, stared at her, and whistled appreciatively at the figure displayed by the careful, tailored cut of her clothes. Behind them stood Dominor.

"Work-party, O Beauteous One!" Trevan joked. "We're here to tidy the bridal chamber; Evanor bullied us into it as a last-minute gift."

"Lady Kelly, it is my honor to escort you to the carriage, while these louts figure out the difference between the handles and the feathers on their dusters," Dominor drawled, gesturing toward the stairs beyond. His brothers raspberried him and set to work, stepping around their imminent sister-in-law, as they started casting their magics.

Nodding graciously to the third-eldest, Kelly vacated the room in the company of the dark-clad man, her hand on his forearm. It was a long way down, but the stairwell was well lit. The handrail was decorated with flower-and-leaf garland ropes down both sides. The garlands ended at the bottom, at the doorway into the north wing where the stairs let out, but it was a wonderfully decorative touch that one of the brothers must have added on their way up to her door.

She and Dominor descended the spiraling steps to the great hall, then out through the eastern wing, through the door in the center of its *Y*-split, and into the easternmost courtyard. Most of the rest of the castle lay in darkness, but there were lightglobes illuminating their path and the courtyard where they emerged. There were two magic-steered wagons as well, one no doubt for the others to take down, and one to carry her to the chapel.

The normally utilitarian wagon had been provided with an extra bench covered in cushions and decorated with more flowery garlands. Poles rose up from the four corners, supporting bright-gleaming lightglobes, and more garlands stretched between them, scenting the darkening twilight air. Helping her up into the bed of the wagon, where she was apparently to travel in relative comfort on the cushioned bench, Dominor climbed onto the front bench and picked up the reins. As Saber had done before on their trip to the beach, Dominor pressed the sprung-levered pedal on the floor that made the cart go forward and steered with reins that stretched out to a pole that turned the pivoting axle of the front wheels.

Kelly decided to try to explain rack-and-pinion steering to these men one day, to hopefully get them to switch over to something less hazardous-seeming than the awkward arrangement they currently used. *And shock absorbers*, she added mentally as the cart rattled over the now completely weeded courtyard flagstones, rumbling out the well-lit gate. *Though it would be easier if I had a manual, since I don't quite understand it myself in any real depth* . . . She could explain how to card-weave far better than she could how to build a car.

They trundled down the weathered cobblestone path that led to the western shore. Out here were the lightglobes missing from the rest of the donjon palace, mounted on poles sunk into the sides of the road. Like lamps in a fairy-tale drawing, they lit the curves of the aged, stone-paved road, outlining their descent from the sway-backed plateau on which the castle was perched. Kelly could even see where the road twisted and turned ahead of them, by checking for the hints of lights through the trees.

Dominor kept the cart to a steady, almost agonizingly sedate pace as they descended. When they were not even halfway to their destination, the other cart came rattling along. The men piled in it cheered and hollered, waving as they sped past, hurrying on their way to fill the chapel ahead of them. Kelly had to smile; they were doing their best to give her an impression of a large, boistrous wedding party—whether or not it was intentional—and it touched her.

Dominor, silent for a little while more, finally spoke up. "I really wish you would teach me that 'dirt-eating' trick you pulled on me. It *is* a style of fighting in your realm, is it not?"

"It is," she agreed. "But I'd rather keep my advantage over you. You're bigger than me, and you can cast magic, which I can't." She smoothed the thigh-length hem of her blouse over her lap. "But if you stay nice to me, I'll consider *not* teaching it to your wife."

"My wife will know better than to try to make me 'eat dirt.' She will know her proper place and stay there."

Kelly snorted. "And you think she'll obey your every whim? That's not a wife! That's a *rug*. And *you*, Dominor of Nightfall, would be bored to tears by her if she were! I *have* been paying attention, you know. You're a lot more like Saber than you'd care to admit, in that way. He loves a good fight, and you love a good challenge. So I sincerely hope, Dominor, as your new sister-in-law, that you're whacked over the head, chained to a dungeon wall, and challenged like never before, by the *mere woman* it's your fate to suffer," she drawled. Then added primly, "And I really *do* mean that in the nicest way possible."

He regarded her a long moment, as the cart trundled down a straight stretch of the path. "I believe you actually do."

She snorted again. "You'd be bored with anything less than a struggle. If you're honest, you'll admit at least that much to yourself."

"You may be right. But *my* verse suggests that it is I who will do the whacking and the chaining, and so trap my mate. *If* I ever run across a woman worthy enough," he added, increasing their speed a little as they came down onto flat terrain, leaving behind the slope they had been rattling gently down. "You may be a challenge for my brother, but you aren't one for me."

"Did you just insult me?" Kelly asked mock-suspiciously, lifting her fingers in an ear-pinching pose, mock-warning him with the gesture.

"I mean you aren't the woman for me. The point is useless, anyway," he added with a sigh, for once losing some of the posturing in his voice, exchanging it for a somewhat more thoughtful tone. "Unless Morganen makes a habit of plucking women from other realms—which is forbidden with good reason by the Council, as it can upset the balance of the multiverse—the odds of another woman reaching this isle are extremely slim.

"The odds of one of us successfully returning unnoticed and unhindered to the mainland long enough to find a wife there . . . are also very, very small. Trevan can change his shape into a bird form, but even I doubt he could fly far enough and fast enough to escape pursuit—going there wouldn't be the problem. The problem would be surviving long enough to return. We are bound by laws forbidding us from teleporting anyone to the island, you see, even if the distance weren't too far," he explained. "Nor can we open a Gate, a sort of small-scale, mirror-based Portal. Nor operate any flying carts.

"All we can do is change our shapes . . . and only Trevan and Wolfer can do that." He smirked for a moment. "Wolfer is afraid of heights . . . so his going bears small odds, indeed."

"They couldn't be so impossibly small as Morganen seeing me burning in my bed and rescuing me from certain death. In a realm that doesn't believe in real magic, mind you," Kelly added as they rattled over a bridge and came into a globe-lit clearing, in front of a vine-draped marble building not quite swallowed by the jungle around them.

Rydan was just finishing the lighting of the last lightglobe. He lowered the knocking pole in his hands and leaned it against the side of the building, where it disappeared into the leaves of the vines. As Dominor stopped the cart, the black-haired, black-clad brother mounted the steps at the entrance to the octagonal building, vanishing into the interior without looking their way. Somehow, though, Kelly got the impression that he was very aware of every detail of her arrival.

Dominor helped her down as Wolfer descended the steps, handsome in stripes of velvety gold and brown. The largest of the eight by an inch in height and maybe two in breadth, he gave her a graceful bow and held out his hand, rumbling in that deep voice of his. "We decided that the twin of the brother kneeling to his Destiny should have the honor of presenting the bride, as you have no kin of your own to stand at your side. If you will allow it."

Nodding, suddenly nervous again, Kelly placed her palm in his, letting him tuck it into his, preparing them to mount the steps. She cast about for something, anything to take her mind off of her nerves and the panic she felt at what she was doing, so unbelievably far from home, far from even the memory of her long-gone parents, who would have done anything to be there on her wedding day. The bracelet on his wrist caught her attention.

"Wolfer? A question . . ."

He looked down at her. The only attempt made to tame his wild brown hair had been a leather band that crossed his brow and held most of it back from his face. In the light of the globes around them, surrounded mostly by nature, he looked about as untamable as his name suggested. His deep voice, however, was as gentle as he looked fierce. "Yes?"

"What is that bracelet on your wrist?"

He quirked an eyebrow at her. "Are you having second thoughts?"

"Well, I *am* nervous, but I'm trying to distract myself."

He grunted, nodding his head slightly in comprehension. A gesture of his wrist, and the thin binding of braided, dark blond hair gleamed with golden highlights under the light of the globes set around the chapel doors. Noticing her attention, Wolfer explained simply, "It was a gift."

"From Saber? Is it his hair?" she asked, since it was about the same color.

"No . . . from a friend. And a sort of cousin, removed once or twice by marriage—not a blood kin, but a close friend and former neighbor. Her name is Alys." A muscle worked in his jawline for a moment, then he managed a smile. "I was very angry when we were ordered to leave Corvis. She gave it to me and asked that I wear it and remember her, to remind me whenever I got the urge to smash things again, that there was at least *one* person on the mainland who still cared about all of us.

"She could not do anything to prevent our exile, but she still cared." His memories seemed to warm his smile. "She was a crazy little thing, four or five years younger than Saber and me, half timid, half bold, as if she had to goad herself into tagging along with us against her fears of our young and manly outrageousness—well, when she was young, she was bold," he corrected, urging Kelly to head for the steps once more. His smile slipped. "Something changed within her.

"She started to be more and more timid and withdrawn as she grew older . . . and her boldness stopped being the kind that would have her climb trees with us and became the kind that would bring her to see us at all. But . . . she cared about me. So I keep my pledge; I wear her hair in this braid on my wrist, and I think of her with fondness once in a while. I also think of her in those moments when I would otherwise unthinkingly unleash my rage. She didn't like it much when people were angry."

Kelly couldn't think of a thing to say to that. She wanted to ask him if he wished he could see the young woman again, but he guided her up the steps and into the chapel.

The simplicity of the building pleased her, when she glanced at it. It had just one doorway, but it had many thin, high-stretching, glazed windows that during the day would let in shafts of colored light to turn the white marble walls all sorts of luminescent shades. The interior too, was garlanded, and she guessed the ropes of flowers and leaves had to have been woven by magic, because they obviously would have otherwise taken a lot of time.

There were eight altars spaced around the center, one centered in front of the entrance, and one centered in front of each bank of windows in the other seven walls. Proof once again that these people were culturally crazy for the number eight. The other six brothers were spaced around the outside of the altars, either consciously or unconsciously echoing that pattern. Saber, however, waited within the eight blocks of white stone.

There had been more than enough cloth and trim to make him trousers, gathered shirt, and tunic in the same aquamarine he had given her. With his dark gold hair bound across the brow in the same way as most of his brothers wore theirs, albeit with a thin band of silver instead of leather or ribbon, he was breathtakingly handsome to her. Just looking at him, tall and proud, his gray eyes fastened only on her, Kelly felt her nervousness sliding away. Whatever she felt for him, it was like nothing she'd felt before.

Breathless . . . I feel breathless, she acknowledged, staring at him.

Like I'm at zero-g, in that moment right before the roller coaster takes that first, great, big fall . . . and I've always loved that feeling . . .

She stopped with Wolfer just on the far side of the first altar from Saber.

"Gods and gathered witnesses," Wolfer rumbled, taking Kelly's hand and raising it slightly. "I present to you Kelly of the family Doyle, and Lord Saber of the family Nightfall, the Count of Corvis-in-exile. They come before you now to clasp hands over the eight altars of the gods in solemn marriage vow. Witness their pledge this night."

Stepping forward, Kelly held out her hand, meeting the palm that reached for her own. Evanor had coached her on the proper ceremony during the long hours they had spent sewing together. "I, Kelly of Doyle, take Saber of Nightfall as my husband."

"I, Saber of Nightfall, take Kelly of Doyle as my wife," Saber returned, fighting the urge to tremble at her touch.

They had hesitated so long outside, he had grown nervous that she had changed her mind. His own nerves at what was coming, both the need to be gentle her first time, and the unknown of whatever might happen the moment they did come together, had eased at the sight of her, at the advance of her into the chapel. At the touch of her hand and the firm vow of her words. Their eyes met over the altar, he nodded slightly, and they recited their vows together, turning and pacing around the circle of altars, flanking both sizes of the carved marble blocks.

> *"In Sorrow and Joy . . .*
> *In Trouble and Peace*
> *In Illness and Health*
> *Trading Anger for Love*
> *In Poverty and Wealth*

> *Through each Day and Year*
> *Turning Weakness to Strength*
> *Making Wrong into Right!"*

They passed over the altars as they spoke, circling back around to the one they had started over, completing the circle. Saber gripped her hand a little tighter and gave his half of their oath.

"I pledge myself to you, my lady, my true love, my partner. I give my life to you, my power to you, my heart to you, and my trust to you. You are my wife, and my Countess-in-exile, for I know you will care for my family and watch over them, and lead them as surely and well as they now follow me. All that I have, I give into your hands. All that I am, I lay at your feet, for I am yours, Kelly, and only yours from this day forth."

It was her turn. Kelly steadied herself with a breath, unnerved at this public confession of his love for her; she wasn't sure if she loved him that deeply yet. Loved him, yes, but . . . that much? *It's just bridal nerves . . . I'm sure if I'd had the chance to talk with Hope, she'd be calming and encouraging me . . .* With another deep breath, she pledged her own part in the ceremony.

"I pledge myself to you, Saber, my lord, my friend, and my companion. My . . . heart I give to you, as surely as I have given my hand, for I want it to go to no other. I have nothing else but my skills and my knowledge to give to you, but I wrap them in my trust and tie them with the faith I place in you to be a good husband." Her lips quirked up on one side. The words sounded right, so she let her sense of humor show. "And I will bully your family in the same spirit you would bully me: in their best interests, and only for their own good." His own mouth twitched a little. "Saber, I am yours and only yours from this day forth."

Yes, this feels right . . .

A gentle tug of his hand, and she rounded the end of the altar between them, joining him within the eight-sided circle. Their mouths
met, as Wolfer finished the ceremony for them. "Witness and rejoice!"
his twin called out, from outside the circle of rectangular, carved stones.
"The family that is now Nightfall is made stronger and greater this
night!"

"Rejoice!" the others shouted, lifting their fists. "Rejoice! Rejoice!"

"You can stop kissing her now," Morganen prodded a few moments later, when the newlyweds remained locked together as the
cheering died. "Uh, Saber? Kelly?"

Koranen, more blunt than his twin, strode forward, planting his
hands on the nearest altar stone and giving the newlyweds a firm
look. "*Excuse* us, dear Brother, but we did *not* go to all the trouble of
fixing up your bedchamber just to have the two of you go at it like
rabbits right here in the chapel!"

Kelly broke off with a laugh, while Saber gave his brother a dirty
look over the top of her head. Neither of them let go their embrace
of the other. The second youngest of the twins slapped the stone
slab in front of him.

"Get out here so we can congratulate you two!"

Grinning, both of them came out of the sanctified circle so that
hugs and wishes of good luck could be exchanged. Dominor brought
forward a pair of thin, golden curves. Saber put one around Kelly's
neck, then urged her to put the other around his, wedding torcs with
identically unique patterns stamped in the metal to show they were
wed to each other, their names twined together in the elegant lines of
Katani script. Then they were hustled back out to the flower-decked
carriage, and Dominor once more took the driving bench.

The others, save for Rydan, hurried on ahead of them in the second wagon to finish assembling the small wedding feast meant to follow the ceremony. As they started forward at an again stately pace,

compared with the rush of the other horseless vehicle, Kelly glanced back. Lights were already winking out one by one, inside the chapel. She could also see the garlands exploding silently in a rain of greenery and petals, a rain of flora that vanished even as it reached the floor.

"So *that's* how they did all those flowers. Magic."

Saber raised his brow and peered behind them, glancing through the chapel door getting farther and farther away from them. "Oh. That. You honestly didn't think my brothers would actually weave several days' worth of real flowers together? Most of that's just an illusion."

"But, I did smell *some* flowers . . ." Kelly half pointed out, half asked.

"There probably were a few," Saber agreed, tucking her a little closer into the curve of his arm. "Rydan will dispose of them so that the traders, when they come again to display their wares, will never know we were married in there; they usually display their wares in the salt warehouse in the compound where the water is purified, but sometimes they visit the chapel for prayers and a place to sleep— they are rightfully wary about being on Nightfall Isle, given the many attacks that have plagued us.

"Rydan will clean the hall of our presence during the night so that their sleeping place holds nothing to rouse their suspicions. Then he will darken all of the globes on his way back up the hill and teleport them back to all of the brackets and stands they came from. He'll be fast enough to join us in time for the feast, don't worry."

"That particular brother of yours is certainly an odd one," Kelly observed.

"Tell me about it," Dominor muttered from his seat on the bench, steering them up the gently sloping, zig-zagging road. One more glance behind, and Kelly saw that already the lights on the poles leading back to the chapel were winking out.

It was just as well. *There's no telling when the unknown mage plaguing us with mekhadadaks and other beasts would seek to attack this place again, even if we've repainted in the interim. No sense in lighting up the island like a beacon for any curious sailors to spy upon, either.*

"Why are you grinning like that?" Saber asked her a moment later, studying her in the light of the globes that hung from the wagon and those they passed that were still lighting their path.

"What? Oh—I just finally figured out how to say 'mekhadadak,' that's all." Smug, pleased she was finally beginning to fit into her odd new homeworld, Kelly scooted a little closer to him, rested her head on his shoulder, and enjoyed the leisurely nighttime wagon ride back up to their home.

FOURTEEN

✦❊✦

After the food had been eaten, and after his brothers told several stories and jokes about her groom, and the cloth-and-garland-draped table had been cleared, they opened gifts. Some of the customs of the Katani were the same as those back home, it seemed; the first gifts to be exchanged were between the bride and groom. Kelly was glad she had made what she did. When Saber opened the box she had put everything into, he widened his eyes and carefully lifted out the two most important components.

It contained a largish rectangle of the finest white silk she had been able to find and a roll of paper. The silk was partially embroidered already, though more in outline stitches than anything else. She had already begun his eyes, from nose to brows in intricate detail, with tiny stitches of silk that had managed to capture the mottling of gray for each of his irises. Saber stood and unrolled the paper, quickly spreading it out on the table for the others to see.

The other men exclaimed softly in admiration. It was a delicately shaded charcoal sketch of his upper body, his hair flowing from the crown of his head down to his shoulders. There was no sense of color, since she had been working literally with a sliver of burned wood from the kitchen hearth, but she had smudged it carefully with her fingertips to give it some illusion of depth and shading.

"This is *incredible* . . . You will embroider this image of me?" he asked, glancing at the skeins of embroidery thread in the box, then at her.

"When I have all of the colors and the amounts that I need," she admitted. "My best talent has always been embroidery. I'm sorry I've only barely begun . . ."

"No—do not be sorry," he ordered her, blinking a little, clearly touched by her gift. Rolling up the paper, he tucked it and the cloth back into the chest, which was the one he had first brought to her with sewing materials inside, back when they hadn't gotten along. He sat back down, then blinked again and looked at her, deeply touched. "Only the finest artists have ever crafted the portraits of the Corvis family line, and always before, it was only done in paint.

"You will embroider my whole family, when you are done with this portrait of me. You and I together, when this is finished, then my brothers in turn. And your work will hang prominently in this very hall," Saber asserted, blinking twice.

For once, Kelly didn't mind his autocratic tone; those tears he was blinking back were proof that he was deeply moved. Saber stood again to fetch his own present from a table set off to the side, brought in to keep the gifts out of the way of the feast the brothers had assembled for the newlyweds. Dominor leaned in from her left and murmured into her ear, while his eldest brother was gone.

"Saber was to have been painted as the thirtieth Count of Corvis by the great artist Fenlor of Daubney himself, who painted the current

Council of Mages. The artist had even begun the preliminary sketches, when the Council decreed us the Sons of Destiny and exiled us from our home. Unless a miracle occurs," he continued quietly in her ear, "we will never see our father's portrait again, nor his mother's, her mother's, her father's . . . none of the counts and countesses who governed our ancestral lands. And we would have no hope of seeing our own portraits hanging here on this exiled island, forbidden to have lengthy visits from others as we are. So your gift touches him more than you know."

"Stop whispering in *my* wife's ear," Saber mock-growled, as he came back. Dominor smiled and leaned back.

"*Someone* has to tell her about the time you mooned the Duchess of Elvenor when she was passing by in her carriage," Dominor covered with a deliberately lazy drawl.

"I was eleven years old!" Saber protested, as Kelly giggled, imagining the scene. He sat back down and held out a cloth-wrapped package balanced on top of a bread-loaf sized wooden box. "Ignore the idiot. These are for you."

Taking them, Kelly opened the cloth sack. It held a silver coronet, much like his own, beaded lightly around the upper and lower edges and therefore quite plain, but perfect in its own way. Gingerly, she tried it on her head. For a moment, the circlet felt too loose, then it resized to fit her head perfectly.

"You are the Countess-in-Exile of Corvis," Saber reminded her at her uncertain look, fingers still touching the circlet. "And the Lady of Nightfall Isle. You are allowed to wear one, now."

"Of course, we have no actual use for coronets, when everyone here already knows who and what you are," Koranen added with a shrug.

"And you've already proven you'll take nothing less than absolute respect from the rest of us," Dominor added dryly.

"You're never going to stop jabbing at me for making you eat dirt, are you?" Kelly asked, taking the coronet off and setting it aside.

"Not until you teach me how to do it, too. Which you *will*," Dominor asserted, eyeing her firmly.

"Not on your magic-wielding life! Kung fu is the only way I'll ever have an advantage over the rest of you," Kelly retorted, turning to her next present.

The tiny brass catch on the lid of the box was a little stiff, but she got it open and eased the lid up. Inside, resting in a nest of wadded black velvet, was the most beautiful knife she had ever seen. It had a straight, longish, slightly tapered blade with two blood grooves to strengthen and lighten the steel, and an intricately interwoven mesh of tiny steel wires on the grip of the hilt. An eight-point star was etched into the crosspiece, and the pommel and crosspiece points were set with clear, polished crystal spheres.

"Ohhh . . . this is *beautiful*, Saber! You made this?"

"For you," he added. And caught her hand as she started to reach for it. "The blade is enspelled for eight times the sharpness against all flesh but your own. So be careful when wielding it around me," he added with a little smile. "It is also enspelled against breaking from eight times the pressure it would have as a normal blade, and it is enspelled—"

"Let me guess, eight times for something else utterly magical?" she interjected dryly.

Saber shook his head. "No. It is enspelled to come to your hand when you call it. So you must name it, the first time you touch it. Yours will be the first hand to ever touch it . . . and, I can tell you, crafting an enchanted weapon without touching it is *not* an easy thing to do. Name-called weapons are very rare, and very precious. So long as you can speak its name, it will always come to you. No matter what situation you may be caught in."

"So I have to 'name' it?" Kelly asked in clarification, shaking her head slightly in incomprehension. Just when she thought she was getting used to the oddities of this world. She knew of businesses that would kill for the ability to invest this kind of automatic-return feature into their products. Remote controls, key chains, purses, and wallets . . .

Wolfer nodded in confirmation from Saber's other side, glancing at the blade in the box. "Each of us has our own name-called weapon, birthing-day presents from Saber. Take it in your hand and say exactly what you would call it—something you would not normally say, lest you find yourself accidentally carrying it every time you say 'please' or 'thank you' or 'if you would be so kind' . . ."

She mock-shoved him with her elbow, just a little nudge; he grinned at her, golden eyes gleaming. Returning her attention to the box and its contents, Kelly thought about it. "Well, I've always been a bit of a Tolkien fan—not fanatic about it, mind you, but I've liked his stories, especially the book *The Hobbit*. So, I dub thee"—she paused, grasped the hilt, tightening her hand as it tingled against her skin, lifting it free of the box—" 'Son of Sting!' "

The weapon flared in her fingers from hilt to blade, tingling almost painfully sharp for an instant, before fading in the next moment to a normal, regular-feeling knife.

" 'Son of Sting'?" Koranen asked, glancing around the table with a scoffing look. "What in Jinga's Name does *that* mean? It sounds like an insect with an overinflated ego!"

Shrugging, Kelly lifted the longish dagger in her hand. "There was a story where a hob—uh, one of the characters in the book came across a magic dagger, much like this one, that had certain powers he discovered after fighting off a group of enemies. He 'stung' them with the small blade, since it was not a full sword, but fought them off successfully anyway with it, and thus named his weapon 'Sting.'

And since I liked the story, and I'm not very likely to say 'Son' and 'of' and 'Sting' all in the same sentence, all in a row, not unless I *mean* to say it . . . that's what I've named it."

Saber eased the blade from her fingers and set it on the table, out of arm's reach. "Give it a try, then."

"Do I do anything special with my hand?" she asked, eyeing the dagger on the table. "Is it going to fly at me and stab me accidentally if I don't catch it on the first try?"

He cupped her wrist and held it out for her. "Just relax your hand."

"Relax my hand," she repeated dubiously.

"And say the magic words."

Kelly laughed at that. She quickly covered her mouth with her other hand, mastered her giggles, and relaxed the wrist dangling beyond his gentle fingers. " 'Son of Sting!' "

Instantly, and indeed it was instantly, the blade was firmly clasped in her grip. No flash of light, no flying blade, though there was a soft *pop*, as if the air had slapped in its displacement. And her fingers were automatically wrapped securely around the hilt, through no effort of her own. Saber lifted her wrist and kissed the back of her hand. "There, see? Now you can finally do magic of your own. You can summon your blade to your hand on command."

"Gee, I thought I already could," she retorted slyly. All eight of the men seated around her looked at each other blankly, at that comment, missing the innuendo completely. Kelly grinned wickedly. "I'll show you what I mean later, Saber the 'Sword'."

As Saber flushed in comprehension, his brothers roared with laughter, finally getting it, too. Grinning, his twin rose to get his own gift to the two of them. Coming back, Wolfer dropped the large paper-wrapped package in front of them on the table, amber eyes still gleaming with humor. "This is for both of you."

Kelly quickly tucked her dagger back into its box, pushed it, her embroidery chest, and the coronet to the center of the table and glanced up at Saber. He nodded, and she opened the paper carefully so that it could be conserved and reused later, since there was only so much of it that she had seen in all of the castle. It was a large bundle, requiring a large piece of paper . . . for a luxurious fur quilt.

She knew many furs just by sight and touch already, because they were often used in medieval garb. Of course, she preferred her own furs to be like rabbit fur, the kind that came from something that could be eaten or otherwise hunted for more than mere sport. This pelt had the golden-reddish glow of fox fur, yet clearly wasn't, for it was shorter than fox fur usually was. It was also as thick and plush as mink, even though it wasn't.

Running her hand over the surface proved it was as soft as rabbit fur, but much thicker. It was also, she discovered by running her fingers along the wool-backed quilt, made of four large pieces, trimmed square, not the many small pieces that would be made from mink, fox, or rabbit. "What is it?"

"It's a *blanket*," Wolfer growled, a touch of insult coloring his deep voice. "As any fool can see."

"I could *see* that, Wolfer—what *kind* of fur is it?" Kelly clarified.

"*Jonja* fur." At the questioning looks from his brothers, he shrugged. "I hunted many of them before we left the mainland, and these four pelts are a blend of both of your hair colors."

"Thank you, Brother," Saber murmured. Then smiled. "Though I do not care to have you thinking of us lying underneath it, after this point."

Wolfer's grin was wolfish. "It is meant to be lain on *top* of, so that all the soft fur is against one's skin—but *that* is not an image I care to cultivate in my mind, thank you. I had to share a crib with your ugly hide when you were a baby, remember?" He shuddered exaggeratedly. "I'll already take *that* image to my grave—you as an *adult*? Gods avert!"

Kelly laughed as he pretended to shudder again. "It's a wonderful gift, Wolfer. Thank you."

Dominor brought over his gifts, as the next eldest. "One for you, Sister-Who-Makes-Me-Eat-Dirt. I shall never wed, because I shall never find any woman in this universe who can do that to me again . . . for which I thank all the gods in existence. And one for you, Brother-Who-Yells-Too-Much. May she make you eat dirt once in a while . . . and may he deafen you for making him eat dirt once in a while."

That earned him a dry, sardonic look. "I'm still not going to teach you, Dominor."

The dark-haired mage sat down, smiling. "I can wait."

Saber opened his cloth-wrapped package first. Inside was a pair of bellows. "You did it! You bas—uh, you impertinent son of a mage!"

"What did he do?" Kelly asked, eyeing the squeezable contraption of accordioned leather and hinged pressure plates. The blockish, somewhat geometric figures of Katani writing were embossed into the steel plating covering the wooden pressure plates and wrapped around the handles, but they didn't form words of any language she was familiar with. Saber was too busy playing with the pump-action, puffing air that ruffled the fur quilt in front of him to answer her question, so she glanced at the others for enlightenment.

"They're magic-enhanced forge bellows," Dominor explained, as Saber murmured over them, tracing the words, the design. "Enchanted—with a little help from Koranen, whose specialty it partly is—against fire and heat. So they should not only last a very long time, they'll last at the highest temperatures our dear brother can forge. He has only to speak the first of the words inscribed on them, plus the number he wants, and they'll pump air at the level of the numbers inscribed along the length of the handles. The higher the number, the faster and harder they will blow. Until he speaks the second word on the plate, and then they'll stop."

"This will free up my hands at the most intricate spell-smithing moments, so I won't have to call on the others," Saber added, leaning past his wife to thump his brother in the shoulder with his fist. "You told me it'd be another three months!"

Dominor leaned back out of range and brushed his upper sleeve smooth. "Morganen is not the only mage in the family who can pull off a miracle or two in a short period of time."

Unsure what Dominor could have gotten her—except maybe a box full of dirt—Kelly unwrapped her own cloth-covered package. It was a book, with beautifully tooled white leather and golden cornering plates studded with jewels. She was growing used to reading Katani, which was a little more disorienting than just speaking or hearing it, since ears didn't get dizzy like eyes did for the first few moments under the effects of the translation spell. But it didn't take her very long to puzzle out the title, just the few seconds it took her eyes to adjust to the Katani script.

"*Prime Millenium: The First Thousand Years of the Empire of Katan.* It's one of the history books I've been looking for, these past few weeks! How did you know I was looking for this particular book?"

"As you once said, 'I have been paying attention,'" Dominor returned smoothly. "And it did not tax my genius to believe an intelligent woman such as you would want to know at least some things of our history, so that you understand us better. You are an intelligent woman, after all. If an ignorant one. It's not the original, though; this is your own personal copy. You'll have to teach me how to 'eat dirt' if you want personal copies of the other volumes."

"This is a wonderful gift, Dominor, and very thoughtful. Thank you very much," Kelly added, choosing magnanimously to ignore his afterthought of a gibe, especially prefaced by a compliment as it had been.

"My turn, I think," Evanor stated. He fetched his gift and passed it over, as the others helped gather all of the gifts together in the middle of the table. He set it between them, and Kelly gestured for Saber to open it.

It was a small box, carved like many of them in the castle were, but this one was barely a handspan across, half that in width, and maybe a fingerlength deep. Saber opened the lid, curious to see what was inside. Music spilled forth. It was the sound of several instruments and Evanor's voice; they wafted with delicate clarity from within. Both eyed the box, then its giver. Evanor shrugged modestly.

"You told me, Kelly, what a *raydeeoh* was—a box that, when one activated it, allowed one to hear all different kinds of music without needing musicians constantly around. So I enspelled this box to be a music-playing box, to replace the *raydeeoh* you can no longer hear when you sew." The lightest blond of the eight brothers poked his finger at the metal squares inserted in the grooves lining the box. "Each of these brass tokens contains the music for two songs, one on each side, and their titles and the general meaning of their content is also inscribed on the plates on each particular side, so you'll know what they are and which one you may want to listen to.

"If you flick this little lever here, in the lid, the magic plays the songs from left to right, and to here, from right to left, and here, this third position, left to right and back again, over and over, for as long as the lid is open. The fourth position randomizes the songs entirely. And they can come out, too, the tokens. It holds sixty pieces of music, in thirty token-squares. I'll make more of the tokens for later—you know, I think I could even sell these," he added, touching Kelly's shoulder. "Your *raydeeoh* idea could really revolutionize minstrelling and storytelling."

"Uh, you might want to hold off on that idea," Kelly warned him, as he started to wax enthusiastic. "In my universe, people got so enamored of hearing their favorite musicians, it turned those musicians into celebrities, and that's usually not a good thing. What a celebrity gets put through makes a mekhadadak loose in the house seem mild."

"You sound as if you're talking about some type of evil magic," Saber stated with a slight frown.

"Just because we don't have magic or accurate Prophecies doesn't mean we don't have our own versions of Curses. But this will be perfect to accompany me in the sewing hall, Evanor. And your voice is wonderful to listen to, either in person or from a box," Kelly added, closing the lid and ending the lyrical song. "Thank you."

"A question, Evanor," Saber mused, rubbing his chin and eyeing the music box. "Why is it a wedding gift for the both of us, when *she* is the one who will be listening to it the most?"

Evanor grinned. "Because all of the songs on the tokens in that box are *romantic*, Brother. You *will* benefit, trust me."

All of them had a laugh at that, even Saber and Kelly . . . though it was Kelly's turn to blush.

Trevan's gift came next. Kelly half expected it to be something risqué, since he was a bit of a rogue, maybe their version of lingerie, or maybe bath oils, but it wasn't. Dragging the largest, bulkiest present forward with a scrape of wood over stone as Kelly and Saber twisted in their chairs, he grabbed the cloth draping the object and whisked it away with a flourish. "Enjoy!"

It was a chair. A broad, two-person couch, almost too small to be a loveseat, but too big to fit just one person. Like all of the other furniture she had seen, it had cushioning on its seat and back, the aquamarine silk tacked in place with tiny, round-studded, polished brass nails in the same fashion as most of the other furniture in the overgrown castle. Ornate, fluid carving had been added around its edges.

Kelly narrowed her eyes at the strawberry blond male. "I *thought* a couple yards of my silk had gone missing!"

"All the better to help the two of you blend into the furniture,"

Trevan quipped back fearlessly. "This is for the two of you to sit upon together when taking your meals—you may not know this, Sister," he added to Kelly, "but it was a custom of our mother's province for married couples, especially from the nobility, to sit on the same seat together when they ate. It helped to show that the pair was united in all things. It was not the custom in Corvis lands, but occasionally Father and Mother would sit on a seat like this one during feasts, especially when hosting her kin."

At a gesture from the fifth-born son, Saber and Kelly stood. Wolfer and Dominor as the closest brothers snatched their seats away, and Trevan scooted the double chair close for them to try it. Kelly sat, bounced a couple of times on the springy cushioning of the seat, and smiled. "This is actually comfortable, Trevan! Thank you."

"Yes, it is; thank you, Brother," Saber added. He glanced down where her overskirt brushed his thigh, and smirked. "Now we can do things under the table without having t—"

Kelly elbowed him and he grunted. "Yes, Trev, this is *wonderful*, not having any armrests to get in my way."

The copper-haired man laughed and sat back down. Everyone glanced expectantly at Rydan, next in line of the brothers of Nightfall. He sighed, set down his goblet, and rose, heading for the gift-table. A moment later, he came back with two small packages, handed them over, and sat back down again without a word.

When the newlyweds unwrapped them, they uncovered nearly identical steel-and-iron plaques, no bigger than Saber's palm. The metal was shaped in swirling figures around the edges and the Katani characters for each of their names cast into the center. Saber caressed the metal with a slight frown of concentration, then smiled. "Thank you, Rydan! Now I know what you have been doing in my forge late at night."

"What are they, exactly?" Kelly asked, turning hers over in

her hand, mystified. They sort of looked magical, like oversized amulets . . . or maybe they were trivets for resting hot dishes on. Unfortunately, she couldn't tell.

"They're ward-sigils, to hang over our bed," Saber informed his bride. "No harmful magic aimed at either of us will be able to reach us when we sleep—it's Rydan's way of assuring our protection throughout the night."

Kelly beamed at the man who had created them. "Thank you, Rydan! It makes me wish I had some magic of my own, so I could make the same for you, for during the day."

The light-shunning, dramatically colored, black-clad, unsmiling man . . . smiled. Actually, honestly, openly *smiled*. The shift in his expression from shuttered to smiling transformed him from broodingly handsome to stunningly gorgeous. Unnervingly so; the simple transformation startled his brothers into giving him wary, dubious looks.

"I thank you for the sentiment, Sister." He said nothing more, his expression smoothing out blandly once again within moments— though Kelly noticed a slight softening that continued to linger in his dark eyes, afterward.

Koranen shrugged and got up, the next in line. His pair of packages looked exactly the same as Rydan's. And were almost identically the same once unwrapped, except these metal sculptures were cast in an attractive mingling of copper and bronze and had a somewhat different pattern to the outer design.

Koranen explained their purpose immediately to his magic-ignorant sister-in-law. "These have been crafted to ward against fire in your bedchamber. I made them so you will never need fear waking up in an inferno again, Sister."

"That is a *very* thoughtful gift," Kelly murmured, deeply appreciative of it, as she fingered the polished design. She still had a few murky nightmares of that moment, between waking and being rescued, brief dreams to accompany her brief memories, but all of it felt like it almost belonged to another lifetime, as well as another universe. She traced the entwining, flame-like lines of metal around her name characters. "I think we can hang these from the four posts of the bed . . . assuming Morganen didn't make us a third set."

"No, I didn't," Morganen chuckled.

"Indeed, we'll hang them right away. Thank you, Kor," Saber added. Then looked at Morganen. "Well?"

Morganen fetched the last box, a very small one, from the table off to the side. It wasn't even half the size of a fist. He set it on the table between them and returned to his seat.

Saber opened it cautiously and eyed the contents of the box. "Finger rings?"

"In watching the aether of Kelly's world in these past few weeks to check how it was settling, I noticed that their wedding ceremonies include the exchange of finger rings. Apparently, they don't use necktorcs," he explained.

"They're to symbolize the unbroken, eternal circle of love that enfolds each spouse," Kelly explained at the puzzled looks of the brothers. She touched the thin torc at her throat as Saber fished out the smaller one and examined it, stroking her neckpiece the same way he had the steel set of ward-sigils from Rydan. "Like these torcs you wear, it helps identify who's married and who's not to the others."

"They're not magic," Saber stated dubiously, examining the one in his hand.

"They're not meant to be," Morganen returned. "And I tell you, it is *not* easy getting someone's ring size without them knowing it, since I didn't use a resizing spell like the one you put on her coronet—it goes on the third finger of her left hand, Brother. The one next to the littlest finger."

Saber lifted Kelly's hand, started to push the ring on, then looked up at her. "Is there anything I should say, any ceremony your people use?"

"Most of it is similar enough in spirit to your own ways, though not in the actual words, but, at this part, you just say, 'With this ring, I thee wed,'" Kelly explained to him, touched by Morganen's thoughtful gift.

"With this ring, I thee wed," he repeated, pushing it past her knuckle. Lifting the whole of her hand, he kissed the ring, her flesh, then held up the box with the remaining, larger ring still inside. "I presume I wear one, too?"

"Yes, you do." She wasn't going to give him the option of refusing. She had always believed both husband and wife should wear rings. Picking it up, she slid it carefully onto his finger. "With this ring . . . I thee wed."

Her fingers trembled as she finished it, making their marriage even more real, with this token of her world's ways. Saber folded her hands in his, lifting them to his mouth. His gaze grew dark and heated, and she knew he was feeling that much more bound to his otherworldly bride, too.

"Okay, break it up!" Koranen mock-ordered. "Any hotter, and those amulets I made will have to start working!"

Wolfer kicked their double chair in the nearest leg with his boot heel for emphasis. "Take it upstairs, you two."

"As you wish." Standing up immediately, Saber tugged Kelly up, then scooped her over his shoulder. She shrieked and thumped his back with a fist . . . but not nearly with as much vigor as she had at their very first meeting.

Her lips brushed his back in a kiss, not in a bite, before she pretended to demand, "Put me down, Saber!"

"You heard my twin. Not until we're upstairs." He strode for the north archway, then did a U-turn back to the table. Grabbing the four ward-sigils, he tucked them into his overtunic, adjusted his bride on his shoulder, and took his burdens out of the hall.

FIFTEEN

❦

Saber crossed to the bed as soon as the door shut behind them. The covers, just a sheet and a blanket to ward against the cool summer nights, had been turned down slightly on both sides, while bedposts and headboard had been wrapped with real garlands of sweet-smelling flowers. Tossing the bedding down over the flowerless footboard, he lowered Kelly from his shoulder to the floor, then fished the sigils out of his tunic. Sorting them out, he handed her the ones with her name.

"I think on opposite posts would be best," he murmured, gesturing at the diagonally opposed ones. "I'm not certain which side either of us will end up sleeping on, night after night; I have no preference, myself, and this way the wards will enclose both of us completely."

She nodded and crawled onto the bed instead of going around, pausing only long enough to toe off her ankle boots at the edge.

He eyed her backside, draped in soft aquamarine silk, then shook his head and quickly hung up the fire-ward sigil on one of the nearer posts. Saber then bent and removed his own boots and crawled onto the bed to reach the far post to hang up the night-peace amulet. When he sat back on his heels, the task done, aquamarine-clad arms slipped around him from behind.

"This silk may be lightweight . . . but I'm feeling rather warm and overdressed," Kelly murmured in his ear. "How about you?"

Just feeling her warm breath against the curve of his ear made him hot. Feeling her palms flatted against the muscles of his chest, stroking upward, then down again, brought him to an instant boil. Because her fingers went all the way down to his belt and started working on the buckle. "Kelly . . ."

"I may be physically a virgin, but I paid attention in my sex-education classes," she murmured with a smile, tossing his belt away. "Did I tell you it was my favorite subject?"

Turning in her arms, Saber cupped her face and kissed her. Sweetly. Gently. Doing his damnedest to go slow instead of now, now, *now* like his body demanded. "We have all night, Kelly . . . and we may only have one time of it before the verse is fulfilled."

"If your universe knows what's good for it," she asserted in a low, feminine growl, "that damned Disaster will stay away until *after* dawn." She shifted her fingers to his overtunic, which laced down the front.

Out of self-defense, Saber pulled her fingers away. "You are the one wearing the most clothing; we will remove your garments first. Though I am not sure what to *call* your odd mix of clothes."

"I thought I'd start a comfortable fashion trend," she sighed against his lips, leaning forward to kiss him again.

"Women wear skirts, in Katan," he pointed out between kisses.

"We're not in Katan. We're on Nightfall Island," she reminded him, pulling back so he could attend to the laces of her tunic-vest.

"And I like pants more than skirts; my thighs sometimes get chafed, in skirts."

He stopped with the ties halfway loosened to glance down at her aqua-clad thighs. Her legs were shapely, feminine and wonderful, the kind meant to wrap around his hips . . .

"Chafing my thighs is *your* job," Kelly added with a grin.

Saber closed his eyes on a groan. When she chuckled, he snapped his eyes open again. She was drawing out the laces the rest of the way, teasingly sliding one out of a hole, then the other, then back to the first for the next hole down the row. It aroused him; not because it was an innocent, ordinary undressing action, if done torturously slow, but because her smile while she was doing it was pure feminine temptation, knowing exactly what he was longing for beneath the slowly removed garment.

When she pulled out the last bit of cord, she slipped off of the bed and stood next to it, leaving on the unlaced vest. But instead of removing it, Kelly slipped her hands under the front of her skirt and long-hemmed blouse, and did something there that, moments later, dropped her trousers. Peeling them off delicately one leg at a time, she took off her socks in the same graceful motion, then reached under the edge of the blouse and removed the half-skirt.

He couldn't get enough of her legs. Pale, softly muscled, and dusted with freckles below the hem of her blouse. The sight reminded Saber of that first, torturous glimpse he'd had of her femininity, the first day he had brought her clothes to wear. There had been plenty of skin on view during their incarceration in the bathtub, but this hinted at the illicit and forbidden, rather than the blatant. Saber held his breath as Kelly loosened the ties of her blouse at the lace-trimmed wrists, but she didn't remove anything else, yet.

"Your turn. You're wearing more clothes than I, now," Kelly reminded him with a smile.

Slipping off the bed, he stripped tunic and shirt in one motion from his chest. Then cursed with a rueful laugh as the sleeves stayed tied to his wrists. Laughing openly, she helped him, since his hands were trapped inside the sleeves, forcing her to tease out the laces and unknot them.

Saber grinned and tickled her hands with his fingertips, making her narrow her eyes at him. As soon as both hands were free, Saber stooped and slid his fingertips up the backs of her thighs, then cupped her buttocks in his palms. And frowned and wiggled his fingers, feeling the odd texture there. "What are you wearing, under there?"

Kelly giggled at the ticklish sensation. Squirming free, she backed up a step, then finished loosening the ties holding the gathered sleeves and neckline in place. A shrug out of her vest, a tug on the fabric underneath, and the blouse loosened completely. It dropped, pooling at her feet, revealing the see-through lacework of her homemade lingerie.

At the highly provocative sight, Saber stiffened instantly. In every way. "By the gods!" He stared at hearts-within-hearts, woven in the same white intricate openwork that had trimmed her clothes. The lace-made fabric did nothing to conceal the underlying dusky pink of her nipples, or the coppery-blond curls of her mound. "What is *that*?"

"Undergarments. In the wedding-night style of *my* world," she added, resting her hands on her hips, with just a slight, coquettish cock of one hip to the side, emphasizing the curves that had filled out over the past month and a half. "I take it you like it?"

Like it? His manhood was straining so hard at the exotic, erotic sight, he was surprised the lacings of his trousers hadn't broken! Under the intensity of his gaze, her nipples tightened, thrusting against the stitched-together lace that she had somehow made into fabric.

His knees gave out along with his control, and Saber dropped to the hardwood floor. His hands caught her hips, his head tipped up as she swayed, and his mouth caught one of those tight buds through the textured lace. Suckling greedily, he heard her gasp and tried to gentle his pace, but the texture, the warmth and taste were driving him too hard to be ignored. Cupping her other breast, he latched onto its peak, too. He suckled her through the lace, inflamed by the knowledge she had deliberately worn such scandalously arousing garments just to walk the eight altars with him.

Her strained cry cracked the fever in him, and he tore his mouth away to look up at her. Caught in her teeth was her lower lip, which Kelly did any time she was worried or overwhelmed. It reminded him that, enthusiastic or not, she was still physically innocent. Breathing hard, Saber scooped her up and laid her on the blanket-stripped bed. He pressed a kiss to her soft, lightly freckled belly, heard her in-drawn breath, and licked the skin of her stomach. She gasped, breath hitching in her lungs. This close to the core of her, the scent of her heat made him dizzy with need, as all of his blood pooled in his loins.

"Beloved—these garments have to go. *Now*," he added, drawing the very brief undertrouser-like thing down over her hips, trying to be careful with the flimsy garment. "Before I rip them from you."

If he had been anyone else, Kelly knew she would have been nervous to have even that nonexistent barrier stripped away from such an intimate location on her body. Saber, however, had seen her waterlogged and rushing to the bathroom, thanks to the water-snake venom. Hardly the most decorous of moments in which to be naked . . . and they had been naked in their misery literally for hours, together.

The only thing she longed for now was for his hands, his mouth, his body touching her where the lace had been only moments be-fore, the underpants tossed to the floor. His comment about ripping her hard work made her fumble at the hook-and-eye fastenings be-tween her breasts. This wasn't her old universe after all; garments like these were clearly one of a kind, from his dumbfounded, impassioned expression. She couldn't just skip down to the nearest department store's lingerie section to buy more, if anything happened to this set.

He helped her sit up and peel the upper garment away, tossing it aside like he had the panties. Then he dropped her onto the feather-stuffed bed by cupping and suckling both of her breasts hungrily one after the other, making her groan and fall on her back. He divided his attention greedily among first one breast, then her mouth, then the other breast, licking with his tongue, scraping with his teeth, nipping with his lips. Panting, Kelly arched her back into the arousing actions, holding his arms where they were braced on the bed to either side of her, then cupping his head when he shifted up and kissed her mouth.

Just when the sensations within her started to be frustrating, Saber kissed his way down her ribs, along the soft dip and curve of her belly. He reached the ticklish zone around her belly button, and she giggled, then laughed, then gasped as he discovered how much it stimulated her by nuzzling and licking the dimple in her flesh with his nose and tongue. As she squirmed under him, alternately calling out his name and ticklish protests in half-moaned, half-giggled pleas, the blond mage worked his body down between her knees, parting her writhing thighs with his wrists.

When she was gasping with each breath from the ticklish nips of his teeth and lips against her thighs, he pulled back with a smile, sitting up on his heels between her calves. His fingertips stroked from her ankles to her thighs, slowly, over and over as he sat there between her legs, the front of his silk trousers blatantly tight with his arousal.

First over the outside of her legs from ankle almost to waist, then up the tops of them, shin to knee to the tender skin where leg met hip. Then farther and farther to the inside of her twitching legs . . . until his fingers stopped mere inches from their goal. Deliberately as she watched, he stared right there. Let her feel the cool air of the room on her private core as his fingers pressed against her flesh, slightly parting her nether lips. Letting her feel the heat of his stare as he looked nowhere else, sweat beginning to bead on his slowly tightening muscles. Letting her know just how ready he was for her . . . and how hot and slick and ready she was for him, just from being looked at so intensely.

Finally, slowly, in agony of waiting and wanting, she watched him dip down. Felt the cool, silken caress of his chest-length hair brush her thighs. Felt his fingers inch closer, then part her even more. Felt the hot, wet glide of his tongue against her most intimate flesh. Her moan slid up into a tight cry, as his tongue flicked once, twice, then suckled intensely at that one special spot, and her back arched as her eyes squeezed shut, as she wailed with the first, full-blown orgasm a man had ever given her.

Saber couldn't get enough of her. He nipped with his lips, he licked every inch with his tongue; he even thought about using his teeth, but her hips were twitching too much with involuntary need to safely try. Then she bucked without warning; in fact, she nearly broke his nose, but it was worth the brief pain as his otherworld-woman cried out, clutching at the covers in the need to anchor herself in her climax. Delving back in, Saber dragged out her pleasure as long as he could.

Only when her cries, her gasps, her groans had slipped back down into moaning pants, her body quivering and drained for the moment, did he reluctantly kiss his way back up to her belly. Saber drifted his mouth over her breasts for a few moments and then finally up past her Katani-style marriage torc to her parted lips. He groaned himself, when her tongue flicked out and tasted herself on his mouth in little licks.

Her energy came back. More languorous than before, but it came back, and it was strong enough to push him over, onto his back in the middle of the bed. He groaned again when her naked weight settled against his half-clothed body.

His hands occupied themselves with her backside as she mated their mouths together in devouring kisses. Somehow, Kelly got her own hands on his biceps, pinning his arms and upper body down so that when she slid her mouth down to his throat, then to his collarbone to nuzzle around his own thin, stiff marriage torc, he couldn't successfully drag her back. She brushed her lips against his chest, enjoying the tickling of the sparse dusting of dark golden hairs across his skin. Saber loved the sensuality of the act.

When she reached his nipples, Saber groaned and gripped her arms, unsure he could take such incredibly delicious torture. Each lick, each nip, shot straight to his throbbing groin. And when she did the equivalent of what he had done to her breasts, sealed those kiss-swollen lips around him and sucked on the flat, rosy-brown disc of one of his nipples, he arched up with a shout. But she wasn't done with him. He rasped her name out in desperate warning, when she trailed all the way down to his belly button, bared just above the waistline of his new trousers, and he shuddered, every muscle tightening against the urge for release when she dipped her tongue into his taut navel.

He breathed a quick sigh of relief when she swayed up his body again, then caught his breath when she tormented his other nipple. Abandoning his grip on her arms, he focused as hard as he could and unlaced the front of his trousers, removing them while he could without ripping off the silk garment. His manhood poked free of the opening, brushed against her waist and hip, and he tensed yet again as desire threatened to surge uncontrollably through him. She abandoned his other nipple, scrambling back down the bed, and quickly peeled off his trousers.

Just as he started to sit up, to retake control now that he was fully naked like her, she tossed his pants to the floor and gripped him. Boldly. In her hand. Saber jerked and flopped onto his back, his hips involuntarily thrusting up.

"*Kelly!*"

With her fingers firmly wrapped around the velvety-warm base of his shaft, she dipped her head and tasted his reddened, moistening tip. His own lower lip caught between his teeth, as he grimaced in a struggle for self-control. Proving herself no innocent indeed, Kelly deepened her contact with him, as she took in more of him. As her tongue swirled around him. And when she closed her mouth around as much of him as was possible, and then sucked—

"Jinga's Balls and Kata's Tits!" The oath ripped from him as he bolted upright and reversed their positions lightning swift, slamming her onto her back and coming down hard between her thighs. He pinned her to the bed with the whole of his body, his hands pinning her wrists, his manhood right *there*, at the hot, moist-weeping opening at the apex of her thighs.

Kelly would have giggled at the oath, if she wasn't caught on the verge of a major moan. Because she could *feel* him. Throbbing. Against her. *There*. Right where she wanted him to be, even more than he already was. Involuntarily, her muscles twitched, instinctively hungry for more. He shuddered as her flexing hips rubbed her core against his very tip.

"Do. Not. Move," he growled in her ear, panting, desperate to regain some control of his raging need. This was nothing like touching himself and finding release. After this, such sparse pleasure would never be enough. If he could only survive long enough to gently—*gently*—breach her and get fully inside . . . he could have this for the rest of his life.

With his face buried in her hair, in the curve of her throat and shoulder, he breathed hard, mentally reciting the names of every one of his ennobled ancestors that he could remember. It helped, a tiny, tiny bit. So he pulled out the big sword, so to speak, and tried to picture his mother and father making love. The most instinctively repulsive thing any offspring could think of.

That helped. A lot. He even started to breathe easier, to relax against her . . . until he thought about how his parents had made nine children. That was a lot of children his parents had made, even if birthed in twins . . . and their no doubt untold numbers of tries in creating them. Which made his mind think of how he and his bride could make even half that many of their own, and the untold times *they* could try. Groaning, he lifted his head, sought her mouth, and kissed it in apology. He found her bottom lip caught in her teeth again, and he teased it free with his own, then groaned as she moaned and wriggled.

"I can't wait anymore—"

"Good!" Kelly panted, and hitched her hips up closer, impatiently. Pushing him against her willing, feminine flesh. "Now!"

Groaning at his bossy wife's demand, Saber kissed her hard and deep, then braced himself on one elbow, making certain he was in the best position against her with his free hand. Then, slowly— excruciatingly slowly—he pushed inside. Kelly forced herself to breathe, as he stretched her flesh painfully, then slipped back out a little. He came in a little bit more, then eased out.

Breathing hard but steadily, in rhythm with each indrawn and exhaled breath, he breached her slowly and gently, over and over, until he was finally all the way inside, as far as he could go. He rested inside her for a little while, the sweat from his effort turning his skin slick against the arms she had wrapped around his ribs, then he eased out and back in a little. And again. And a little sooner, a little faster each time. Each stroke a little longer and deeper than before.

His head dipped down to hers; his lips plucked and nibbled at hers. Her tongue swept up to taste him, and he moaned as she boldly imitated with her tongue what he was doing with his manhood. Determined to give her pleasure before he finally took his—which would hopefully not be long, with the feel of her sultry heat smothering his need—he freed a hand and slipped it down between them, tickling that budding pearl that had made her go wild when he had licked and suckled it before. She shuddered, her throat tightening on a keen. Her legs hitched up instinctively, hooking around his waist and allowing him greater access.

That allowed him to slide even deeper, gloriously deeper . . . and he gave up his control.

Bracing both arms, Saber surged into her, pleasuring her with perfect friction, invading her over and over as man was meant to know woman, as woman was meant to know man. Her hands slipped down to grip the flexing muscles guiding his hips. It built between them, their shuddering, striving pleasure. Head arching back, Kelly cried out, straining up into him, tightening around him; he gasped and bucked into her, flooding her as she milked him for his seed.

It took a long time for the convulsions to relax, for the trembling to ease. For him to stop pushing into her and just accept his home in her body. His sword in her sheath.

They rested together, until he finally found enough strength to twist to the side, taking her with him so that he didn't crush her any further. He had slipped out of her with the maneuver, but at her mumbled protest, Saber shifted a little and slid his still somewhat hardened flesh back into her depths. Grinning at her contented sigh, he cradled her close.

The quiet night air was filled with the scent of their musk, the heavy, rich scent of sex and sweat. Kelly buried her nose in his soft hair, breathing in the aroma of his soap, his sweat, their satisfaction. Every once in a while, her body would involuntarily contract around him, proof she had just had a really big orgasm. That thought made her smile. Feeling him jerk, hearing him suck in a sharp breath at each contraction, that made her laugh, though she tried to stifle it.

"What . . . what's so funny?" Saber managed somehow, since with each chuckle, her body convulsed like a little slice of the afterlife around him, making him tremble. With shock as well as pleasure, because he could have sworn he was dead; blissfully, satedly, wonderfully dead . . . but no, she had to prove he was still very much gloriously alive.

"It's a female thing." She tightened deliberately around him, he moaned and shuddered, and Kelly giggled again.

"Oh, sweet Kata! Do that again," Saber begged, feeling his body tighten and harden again. "Please!"

"Okay." Kelly did it again, tightening her Kegel muscles, as they were called in her universe. He gasped, swore, and rolled her under him again.

Just that fast, he was gliding into her, a deep friction that made her catch her breath with each delving, exploring thrust. Concentrating, she tightened when he first entered, over and over. Then when he pulled out part of the way, again and again, then alternating the two somewhat randomly. His breath hissed against her temple, his chest reverberated against her breasts, and he groaned when she returned to the first rhythm again. He hitched into her, stayed deep and tight, while he arched his back a little and braced himself more solidly over her, then he thrust again, ducking his head and taking a hand-plumped breast into his mouth for a bit of suckling.

The double stimulation shattered Kelly. Arching her head back into the feather mattress, she cried out and clenched tight around him. He let loose an oath, releasing her breast, and thrust hard, once, twice, thrice into her depths. That was all it took for either of them, and it took all that both of them had.

As they both sagged in repletion, Saber slipped gently out of her and onto his side, cuddling her against him protectively. The last thing he heard after dousing the light was his name on her breath, the last thing he felt was her heartbeat thudding in time with his own.

The first thing he felt an untold while later was her mouth, warm and wet and completely unabashed, once again doing exactly what she had done earlier to him. Only this time, ambushed and on his back, Saber tensed even as he came fully awake, arched his back in sheer pleasure, and spasmed with a shout, thrusting up into the glorious suction of her mouth. Thankfully, she gentled her ministrations; otherwise, he might have grown too tender.

As it was, his wife kept licking him through all of it, keeping him hard. Saber reached for her in the darkness of the room, twisting to get himself properly over her. His attempt didn't work; she simply pushed him back down. She clambered up his body, hidden in the darkness of the lightglobes she must have extinguished at some point, and positioned herself over him. That allowed her to straddle his hips most indecently as she pushed his shoulders back into the bedding. Taking the initiative *very* boldly.

"Gods! You may have been a maiden," Saber managed to gasp as she sank—sweet gods in heaven!—onto him, "but you are *no* innocent!"

Her laughter, rich, full, and feminine, tightened her flesh around him. His hands found her thighs, gripped her hips and buttocks as she moved on him, and he discovered the joys of guiding her in that position, of deliciously, deliriously enduring her leisurely, experimental rhythms. Of feeling her collapse on his chest when her pleasure swept over her in a swift-building wave, igniting his own ecstasy as she tightened around him, crying out.

Their heavy breathing meshed in the darkness. Stretching up, he felt for one of the garland-wrapped bedposts, found one of the protective pendants, then managed to reach the cool, glassy curve of the lightglobe in its bed-reading bracket. Saber flicked the smooth surface with his fingertip. The faint glow that sprang up illuminated just the two of them, and dimly at that, but it was enough for him to see her. He didn't want to stop looking at her, this amazing woman his youngest brother had brought into his life.

"I love you, Kelly," he murmured, gazing at his sated wife.

Kelly roused from the temptation of another doze. She didn't know what to say. She cared for him, she lusted over him, she was more than content to marry him, but she honestly didn't know if she outright loved him yet. Not the true love he was Destined to feel for her. Guilt made her bury her face against his chest as he stroked her hair. She couldn't say the words without knowing for sure. She *felt* that she loved him, but . . . was she *in* love with him?

Her silence wasn't exactly reassuring, yet he knew she wasn't asleep. "Kelly?"

"My heart is yours," she finally murmured. It certainly wasn't going to anyone else, so it was about as accurate as she could get, given her inner uncertainty. And she couldn't just let him say that he loved her, without giving him something truthful in return. She did care a great deal for him and couldn't imagine being with anyone else like this.

Perhaps that is the way her people say it, Saber decided as she said nothing more. It wasn't as if he knew everything about her universe, her people's culture; certainly she had done several things that were as alien to his Katani-raised ways as a woman could get. Wearing trousers, for one. But he didn't really mind them, even the more incomprehensible things.

His thumb rubbed the plain gold band on his third finger, working it around a little. He could feel the beat of her heart against his, where her breasts were crushed by her own weight to his chest, see the pulse in her temple flicker a fraction after each beat against his chest. Still buried inside her intimately, his manhood was reluctant to finish diminishing with his release, reluctant to leave the sheath of her flesh.

Without his consent, he had fallen for her. In the face of the Curse and its Disaster, he had fallen hard for Kelly Doyle of Earth . . . wherever that was. Among all of his brothers, most of whom were less surly and less temperamental than he had been at the beginning, most of which surely would have been less awkward in their wooing . . . she had fallen for *him*.

"My heart is yours, too," he murmured. She burrowed a little closer to him. The night felt warm, especially with the drapes and windows closed and the season now thoroughly into summer. At least, he felt perfectly warm with her draped over him, but she might not feel that way. "Are you cold?"

She shook her head against his chest and burrowed her fingers under his back, holding him closer.

Sighing, Saber wrapped his arms around her a little more comfortably and closed his eyes against the dim glow of the globe. He didn't care if the Disaster was the imminent collapse of the donjon roof supporting this aerie of a bedchamber; he was not about to dislodge her.

SIXTEEN

He was already inside her when he awoke—or, given that she was still draped over his chest with his arms still locked around her, he had likely never slipped out—so Saber didn't have to do very much to ease the deep, hard hunger that had awakened him every morning since first finding his release by himself. Before that moment, if he were honest with himself. It had started the time he had pinned her against the wall in Morganen's tower, since he had first reluctantly admitted he lusted for the woman still sleeping peacefully on his chest. Unlocking the hands clasped over her back, he slipped them down to her hips and pulled her gently down onto him just a little bit more, filling her fully instead of just partway.

She made an indistinct sound against his chest, wriggling a little against him, and he eased her up and tugged her back down, gliding into her slick core with moisture left over from the pleasures of their gloriously late night. Kelly mumbled again, digging her chin into his chest in the effort to bury her face there, as if he were a pillow. He hitched up in three demanding, upward thrusts . . . and had the satisfaction of seeing her eyes jerk open in three ever-widening stages. When he relaxed his grip on her backside, her lids slid down again, as he slid part of the way out of her body, sliding back into the limpness of sleep.

That was interesting.

He did it again. She reacted the same, wide, wider, widening . . . and then drooping. Smiling, Saber arched his back, sliding himself out to the very tip, to the point just before he might fall out of her. She mumbled and sighed, a sound that was almost a whimper, and wriggled her hips, threatening to free him. Gripping her pelvis, he pulled her down firmly as he thrust up strong, burrowing into her hard and deep and full.

Instant orgasm. Kelly gasped and convulsed, coming awake in more ways than one. He jerked into her again, finding and spilling his pleasure in the tightening of her own as she writhed and gasped. Both of them slumped and breathed hard.

Looking up at the canopy over the bed, Saber felt his racing heart slow down as his eyes focused on a drifting, dancing dust mote. His brothers, in preparing the chamber for their wedding night, had tactfully drawn all of the curtains, though no other point in the castle was as high as their room above the donjon roof. Or rather, they had almost drawn all the curtains. A shaft of sunlight was streaming in from the northeast, from behind and to one side of their heads, proving that dawn had already come and gone. From the angle of the light, in fact, it was probably even several hours into midmorning.

The roof hadn't collapsed. No mekhadadaks had chewed on the furniture in their frustration at being unable to get past his brothers' amulets. No demonlings were buzzing around the rooms, looking for things to destroy. The donjon hadn't burned down around them.

Feeling good, Saber lifted his head a little, lazily following the trail of sunlit dust particles with mild curiosity, while his wife—blessed gods, his *wife*—mumbled and snuggled closer. No Disaster had occurred, now that Sword was sheathed in Maid. And most satisfactorily sheathed, at that. Beyond satisfactorily. He smirked to himself. In fact, he felt about as liquid gold as that shaft of light. Idly, Saber followed it with his gaze.

The sunlight, just a narrow little shaft worming its way through a gap in the curtains, terminated on her heel, making it glow pink and gold, with little pale brown freckles around the anklebones and tendon.

Her heel.

"*Jinga,*" he swore, and rolled her off of him, pulling out of her with acute physical regret. She groused something under her breath as she dropped onto the bed, and woke up enough to brace herself on her arm, while he examined that patch of sunlight, careful to avoid getting caught in it. The ray of light was now on the bed, not on her foot, but that didn't necessarily mean anything. He caught her ankle, but the briefly sun-touched limb was no different than the other one, now that the sun was off of it.

"What are you doing?" Kelly grumped.

"Your *heel,*" he explained, but only that far.

That made her frown in confusion. "My what?"

The sunlight—it has to be the sunlight, or something about it. Gingerly, he waved his fingers through the light. Nothing happened. It felt warm and glowed on his skin, like regular sunshine should. Climbing out of the bed, feeling muscles twinge that hadn't been exercised in more than three years before their glorious wedding night, Saber stepped around the end of the bed and swept aside the blue and green linen curtains that had replaced the old, grimy, red velvet ones.

Sunlight flooded the room in a broad shaft. Kelly grunted and buried her head under the nearest feather-stuffed pillow. Her body ached. She knew the only thing that would make it feel better was exercise; she even wanted to exercise it in the same way that made it ache, and exercise it some more. She just craved a little more sleep first to make up for her late-night adventures, and to give her enough strength to have some more marital fun. She didn't know what had gotten into Saber, but if he didn't come back to the bed and make love to her again, that was his loss. It was either sex or sleep, and if she didn't get one, she was going to claim the other.

Squinting into the sunlight at the window, Saber shaded his eyes with his hand. The sun still didn't seem to be the source of the Prophesied Disaster, so he blinked and lowered his gaze to the rest of the palace castle. The courtyards and gardens, the eastern wing and outer wall, all looked normal. The jungle beyond seemed ordinary, with the usual handful of birds flying among the treetops, the rippling canopy of green echoing the terraced hills hidden beneath, sloping out and down to the eastern bay in the distance.

Nothing looked out of the ordinary; not even the dark-and-white blot of a large sailing ship in the distance disturbed the tranquility of the morning-blue ocean—

"Ship!"

Kelly grunted.

"Ship!" Saber whirled, looked about for his clothes, then reached over the low headboard of the bed and grabbed the pillow from her head. "*Ship!*"

So she was to be denied both sex *and* sleep. Propping herself up, Kelly glared at him. "What about the damned ship?"

"Kelly, it's the *quarter moon*! And it's coming from the east—the east! Get up! *Evanor!*" he sang out, crossing to the chest of drawers his brothers had brought up from the bedchamber he was abandoning in favor of this larger, better one his wife had already claimed.

"Good morning!" his unseen, distant brother caroled back cheerfully, projecting to both of them, judging by the way Kelly grunted again and reburied her head under the pillows, clamping the nearest one over her ears. *"Shall I finally bring up a tray of breakfast for you two? It won't take a trice to reheat it, after all . . ."*

"Shut up, Ev!" Saber ordered, yanking on trousers and a sleeveless tunic in shades of green, colors that would blend well with the forest. His brothers had already brought his wardrobe and chests up, arranging them to share space with Kelly's belongings. "There's a large ship on the horizon, heading for the *eastern* harbor . . . and it's the wrong time and direction for traders. And I noticed it only *after* I saw the sun on my wife's heel!"

Kelly blinked herself more fully awake at that, sliding out from under the pillow and off of the bed. "You mean that's my Disaster? My Disaster is a *ship* on the horizon?—What kind of a Disaster is *that*?" she demanded, tossing her head. " 'Hi, we've got scurvy, and if you don't give us all your lemons, we'll run you through'?"

Saber smacked her lightly on the nearest buttock as he passed her. "Get dressed—wear green, so you'll blend into the jungle. We may have to confront them, and I certainly don't want them making it all the way into the castle."

Kelly wondered if he even realized he had assumed she would be coming with him and his brothers; it was a far cry from the overprotective demand that she remain behind she would have otherwise expected from him. *I'm going to have to reward him for that*, she decided, though she wasn't sure yet if she would tell him why. It was more fun keeping men on their toes, guessing what went on in a woman's mind.

"Everyone's assembling in the great hall, save Rydan, of course," Evanor announced on the heels of his order. *"I'll bring you your breakfast there; Morg's bringing his best scrying mirror, to try to see who and what our visitors are."*

"Good." Saber finished tugging on his calf-length boots and cast about for his belt. A scrap of exotically sewn lace lay draped over the tooled leather; it reminded him with a rush of blood to his groin how she had looked while barely clad in it, last night. Straightening, his belt in one hand and the highly abbreviated undertrousers in the other, he looked around for its owner.

She was lacing herself into a half-length corset with efficient, quick yanks to tighten the undergarment. Given that it was all she was wearing at the moment, he felt his blood quicken at the sight of her mostly bared curves for one moment, proud that he had such a desirable, beautiful wife. Even if her heel had led him to discover their now looming, unknown, Prophesied Disaster.

Tossing the undergarment onto the bed, he buckled the belt around his hips then watched her pull on more normal, Katani-style undershorts after the corset had been knotted in place. Within another minute, she was clad in loose green trousers, a slightly darker, sleeveless tunic like his own, and one of the pairs of leather slippers his twin had made for her earlier, in a utilitarian light brown. Finding her belt, Saber tossed it at her. He remembered to rap twice on the lightglobe by the bed to conserve its energy, and hurried her out of their chamber.

Kelly wiped her mouth with her napkin and peered past Saber's arm. He had barely touched his food, so she pinched him, making him glance back and scowl at her. His eyes followed her imperiously pointing finger, and he shifted his dark look to the scrambled eggs on his plate. They had come from the fowl yard in one of the gardens, one of the only two sources of domesticated food on the island, the other being the chickens that had lain the eggs themselves. If he could demand that she eat more when needed, she could bully him about the same thing, too.

Sighing, Saber sat forward and picked up his fork, digging into the rest of his half-forgotten breakfast. Kelly arched back behind his shoulders and managed to catch a glimpse of the oval mirror braced at an angle in Morganen's hands, seated in Wolfer's usual chair so that the two newlyweds could eat on their shared seat and still view the goings-on. Which were finally beginning to get interesting. The ship had finally sailed all the way into the broad bay and had furled its sails, drifting forward under mere momentum.

"They're dropping anchor," Morganen muttered a moment later.

"It's a very strange-looking ship . . ." Trevan murmured. He squinted and peered past Wolfer's shoulder, who was standing with him on that side of their youngest sibling. "By Kata! There's a naked woman bound in chains to the front of that ship! But . . . it can't be! I can see the people on the rigging, and they're very tiny in comparison, and that woman is *huge*."

"Let me see," Kelly asserted. She tried to lean past Saber's broad back, then elbowed him into picking up his plate and leaning back so she could lean over his lap while he ate. The ship looked something like a Spanish brigantine in the outline of its hull, to her . . . except the sails were more like the kind found on a Chinese junk, braced by thin lines that stuck out on either side every few yards, suggesting sail-stiffening poles. She lowered her gaze to the front, where the naked lady was chained to the ramming spar. And smiled. "Ah. That's a *figurehead*, nothing more."

"A what?" Morganen asked, tapping the surface of the mirror that at the moment wasn't a mirror, somehow focusing the image in tighter on that part of the foreign ship.

"It's a special kind of carving; they're put on ships under the ramming spar partially to strengthen it, partially to decorate the ship, and partially—at least in my universe's past—to provide the idea of spiritual 'eyes.' It's meant to represent whatever friendly spirits might have a vested interest in the ship and its crew, to protect it against less-friendly forces.

"We may not have actual magic like you do, but we do have superstition, and the faith of believing in it." She studied the ship a little longer, then spoke again. "This ship looks like a mishmash of styles of ship building that are a couple centuries old, by my era's standards . . . but it's not exactly like any specific style from my world's history."

"We mark our ship hulls with magic sigils to guard them against foundering on reefs and sandbars," Saber stated, pushing her down slightly over his lap so he could put his emptied plate back on the table. He leaned over her, sipping on his mug of juice, and studied the image over the top of her still sleep-tousled head. "You say you're familiar with the different parts, or at least their styles?"

"Yes, more or less . . ." she agreed, distracted slightly by the way her side, pressed to his lap as she peered over his youngest brother's elbow, could feel the warm bulge there.

"Do you know what those little wooden squares are for?" he asked, pointing at the single row of shutters below the main deck rails, but above the round, glazed portholes. "Their portholes farther down are round and glazed much as ours are, but I see no use for having a shuttered window that would surely leak."

"Those aren't windows. I think . . . I think they're *gun* ports."

"What ports?" Dominor asked from where he stood behind Morganen's back.

"Cannons, to be more precise, but still a type of gun—a technological device in my world that, using a naturally explosive combination of ignitable powders, hurls an object along a tightly fitted, metal aiming tube at a target. Cannons are big, heavy, dangerous, early types of guns. They hurl lead balls as big as your fist, sometimes even as big as your head, usually too fast for you to see before it hits you . . . and too fast to readily dodge, even if you do.

"*Pistol* is the term for the small, hand-sized version that shoots lumps of lead about the size of the tip of your finger, and rifles are longer, arm-length versions that can shoot their bullets quite a distance with a good amount of accuracy. But I could be wrong," she added frankly. "This is a world of magic, not technology. So they're probably some sort of magical weaponry port—maybe instead of housing cannons behind those shutters, they have magic wands that shoot lightning at their targets; I don't know."

"With our luck, they have these *cannons* you describe, but ones that shoot mekhadadaks, instead of lumps of lead," Koranen muttered. Then grinned. "But if they do have an *explosive* powder—"

Saber stretched between Morganen and Dominor and whacked his second-youngest brother across the back of his head. "Behave. We don't know exactly what kind of Disaster this arrival is."

"They're lowering the longboats," Morganen observed.

"Then we're going down to the beach to greet them before they can finish rowing to shore," Saber announced. "Kelly, you'll stay here. Koranen, you'll stay w—"

Kelly elbowed him in the gut, straightening up. *There* was the protectiveness she had been expecting, earlier. She gave him a pointed aquamarine look. "It's *my* Disaster. I'm going."

"This isn't a picnic!" he argued, reminding her of their last visit to the eastern shore.

"And I'll still have *you* to protect me when we get there," she returned smoothly, with irrefutable female-soothing-male logic. Averting their next argument with sweetness, as he himself sometimes did these days, since he had started courting her instead of cursing her.

"Saber, she did drink the Ultra Tongue potion," Morganen pointed out. "You and she are the only ones who can instantly hear and speak with these people, and two sets of ears are always better than one. I'm going to stay behind and whip up another batch for the rest of us to drink. But may I suggest you get there quickly and hide the cart and yourselves, so that you might observe them for a little while first? See what they're doing, and what they want."

Kelly stood and snaked herself quickly out of the double chair. "First one to the cart gets to drive it!"

Saber abandoned his urge to argue and scrambled after her. No way was he letting her do something that potentially dangerous! "You don't even know how to drive it, woman!"

"I'll help you with the potion," Dominor offered his youngest brother as the others took off, Koranen included. "I've cast it before. And I know it worked successfully when I did; I speak Ultra Tongue, too."

Morganen raised his brows at that piece of information . . . but he shouldn't have been surprised. The third-born of the eight exiled sons could get rather competitive sometimes. Even if no one was actually competing with him at the time.

After a joltingly fast drive in one of the rein-guided, magic-propelled, horseless carts, the five of them hid the cart off the track a short distance from the beach and eased themselves through the forest. Even Kelly managed a modicum of stealth, but it wasn't all that necessary. When they got close enough to peer through the undergrowth and have a fair view of the beach, the longboats were still being rowed toward the shore.

The tide was going out, slowing their progress, and the ship spawning the three packed longboats had been forced to drop anchor quite a ways out, given how the cove was shallow. The ship's occupants had clearly not wanted to risk being grounded and stuck in place, should the tide run a little too low and their need to leave become urgent . . . but they were still clearly intent on reaching landfall as soon as possible.

Kelly edged a little closer, finding a patch of brush to crawl under that would hopefully get her closer without being seen. Gritting his teeth, Saber caught her calf and crawled after her. "What are you doing?"

"Getting close enough to maybe hear whatever they'll be saying over the sound of the surf," she murmured back. At some point while he had been distracted with her underpants, she had remembered to bring along a scrap of dull green cloth, and had wrapped it during the bumpy cart ride—Saber driving—over her colorful strawberry blond hair.

"I was going to use a spell to make their words seem louder."

"Wouldn't another mage be able to detect that spell?" she asked.

"Not easily; it is a mostly passive spell, affecting only those it is cast on. This is close enough," he added firmly. "Until we know their intentions are both good and trustworthy, none of us are going any closer."

"Fine. Cast the spell now, while they're still occupied with rowing, just in case anyone out there knows a detecting spell that you don't."

Rolling his eyes, wondering when his foreign bride had grown so comfortable with the idea of magic, he muttered under his breath and flicked his fingers. At her, at himself, and at his brothers, who had spread out a little, also wearing shades of green and brown to blend in with the foliage. Kelly realized with a start that, wherever she focused her eyes now, she could hear the sounds from that spot clearly. The rush of the surf, the hook-claw scraping of an insect climbing up the bark of a nearby tree . . . the loud beating of Saber's heart when she glanced at him. *Sort of like my own universe's parabolic listening gear, isn't it?*

She grinned. "Thanks."

He looked at her, glanced at the longboats that were almost to the beach, and leaned in for a quick kiss. Then he returned his gaze to the shore.

Kelly looked that way, too.

Some of the men—for there appeared to be no women among them—splashed into the water as the longboats reached the part in the surf where their boats stuck instead of floated. Dragging the wooden hulls forward with each recession of the water and sprinting a little with each surge, they hauled the boats well up onto the beach.

One of the men in the central boat was clad in clothing different from the practical garments of the others. They wore loose, belted trousers, some shirtless, the others with tunics or shirts with the sleeves rolled up. The other fellow was far less casually dressed.

He sort of looked Elizabethan to Kelly's costuming-trained eye, but instead of the usual doublet or jerkin, he had a short jacket, a waistcoat vest under that, a neck-cravat that was sort of Victorian in style . . . and puffy pantaloons with hose that made her think again about Elizabethan costuming. The costume was completed with boots with what looked like spats from ankles to toes, huge cuffs on the jacket, frothy lace cuffs on the shirt, gloves, and a curling-brimmed, feathered chevalier's hat, like the kind worn in just about any Three Musketeers movie she had ever seen.

He had a thin mustache, a goatee, and definite sideburns. The sight of facial hair on him and some of the other sailors seemed rather strange, after seeing nothing but eight men who used highly convenient cantrips to keep their faces clean shaven. About the only concession to the weather the froufrou dressed man had made in his multilayered, lace-edged, embroidered clothes, was that they were in shades of pastel and white, even to the hat covering his light brown, short-cropped hair. The only dark object on him, besides his head and facial hair, was a longish, bulky, curve-ended object stuck into his belt, next to the sheathed length of a sword hanging by his thigh.

Though medieval history was more her forte than the age of exploration had been, Kelly recognized the object the moment she studied it. It was clearly a flintlock pistol. The shape of the weapon was too unique to mistake. Which meant those square-shuttered sections on the ship *were* gunports.

Kelly winced. There was no telling just how well magic could defend against technology. *This definitely has the potential to be a Disaster.*

Froufrou Man stood and stepped out of the second boat, only when it had reached dry sand. Turning back to the longboat, he held out his hand and demanded something short and succinct. Kelly felt her ears twitch the way they had the first time Saber had spoken to her. Apparently the "Ultra Tongue" spell was still working perfectly. When he faced forward again, her eyes fixed on him as the most likely leader, he strode forward three broad steps, unfurled the long, narrow bundle in his arm, and made his proclamation, as he thrust the butt end of a flag-fluttering pole in the sand of Nightfall Isle.

"I claim this land in the name of the Independence of Mandare, and name it Gustavoland—in the name of the King!"

"In the name of the King!" the other men, the sailors, shouted at his words, some raising their fists.

"Oh, crap!"

Saber looked at her. His brothers were waiting for their report. The men in the landing party were looking around, eager to be dismissed so they could start exploring in depth. "What's wrong?"

"*That's* the Disaster," she breathed, shaking her head. "It's Christopher Columbus, all over again!"

"Cristo-what?"

She squirmed back, gesturing for the others to gather near. When they had retreated and put a heavier clump of undergrowth between them and the men, she explained as quickly as she could, for those sailors were already beginning to spread out to explore "Gustavoland." It was only a matter of time before they found the stone-laid path that led up to the castle's east postern gate.

"Pay attention; we've got very little time before they find the path, realize the island is inhabited, and start looking for us. On my world, there was a continent called North America, where there lived a bunch of relatively peaceful people; much like the people of Katan, they didn't bother exploring elsewhere. Across the sea lived a bunch of contentious people on another, smaller continent who needed to explore and claim land elsewhere, to have enough space and prosperity to expand their populations, and so gain dominance by numbers and supplies over the rest.

"So they explored across the ocean, found this other continent, North America, and used their superior technology—stronger magic, if you will—to decimate the native population, take over their land, and impose their own ways and rules on the natives. This, in spite of the indigenous population's claim on the land. *These* guys are acting a lot like the explorers did, according to my history lessons," Kelly informed the brothers. "They might be here to do something else, something innocuous, but from what that guy said when he planted that flag, I don't think so. So I suggest we beat a very fast retreat, get back to the castle, and lay our plans behind some seriously stout walls, before they can realize just how few of us there are on the island, compared to them."

"I must believe her, if she says this is a serious possibility," Saber agreed, looking at his brothers. "This is her Prophesied Disaster, after all."

"And yours, Brother," Trevan pointed out with a sardonic grin. "Father always said, never let your wife take all the blame, if you want to sleep comfortably at night."

"Your father was a very wise man, then," Kelly praised wryly.

The strawberry-haired man grinned at her. Saber grunted. "Let's get back up to the donjon, then."

With the others nodding agreement, they squirmed back through the underbrush, climbed into the cart, and drove it back up the hill as fast as the magic and the bumpy ride could be pushed. They dropped Trevan off at the stone-faced eastern gate to close and lock it behind them and to coat the exterior wall with an illusion of an impassable cliff instead of an impassable castle wall, extending the illusion Dominor had created to cloak the castle from a distance. Leaving their brother to the task, the rest hurried back to the great hall of the donjon to plan their counterattack.

SEVENTEEN

◦─✖─◦

By the time Trevan rejoined them and Morganen and Dominor came back from their own task, Saber had used Morganen's mirror to trace all of the movement along the path up from the eastern beach. The semi-overgrown road had been discovered, and a group of five sailors, all armed with swords and a few with more flintlock pistols, were now exploring it. By the time the eight of them were together again, the sailors had already walked a third of the way up the granite-lined road.

"Rydan has had his own taste of the Ultra Tongue and has been apprised of the situation," Morganen announced, striding into the hall with a familiar gold goblet in his hand. Dominor came after him, carrying another one of his own. Morganen continued, approaching his brothers. "Of course, he's gone back to sleep, but then he'll be alert and ready to guard us by nightfall, which is a good advantage to have. Here, drink this, Brothers."

The other brothers drank from the contents of Morganen's and Dominor's cups, made wordless faces at the bitter-spicy taste, and returned their attention to the oval mirror now in Saber's hands.

"It looks like they're exploring for supplies, looking for fruit and water here, and over here," Saber informed all of the brothers who didn't have any objections to daylight hours, touching the mirror in the same way Morganen had earlier to refocus it along the beach line. "The men on the road look like they're trying to figure out where it goes. I haven't seen anything that looks like they're using magic to help them get their bearings, yet."

"Some of them are carrying flintlocks," Kelly pointed out. "It's a type of gun, like a small, personal cannon. It's a primitive version, compared to the kinds I know, but still a gun, and still dangerous. I don't know if your magic shields are strong enough to keep out a bullet that is propelled faster than the speed of sound itself."

Evanor blinked at that. "*Faster* than the speed of sound? It would take a *very* strong shield to block something moving that hard and fast! And those are the shields that usually cannot be snapped up in an instant's notice, nor maintained for an indefinite length of time."

"They may or may not have magic, but they're carrying around weapons that are deadly and hard to counter, if Kelly and Evanor are right," Saber murmured. "I'd rather not antagonize them, until we know just what it would take to keep ourselves from being injured in a fight."

"If they intend to take this island for their own, it may come to a fight regardless," Dominor pointed out grimly.

"Diplomacy is the art of saying, 'Nice doggy,' while reaching for a big stick," Kelly quipped, earning strange looks from the brothers, before some of them chuckled at her words. "If there's a way we could present ourselves as a strong enough power to make them back off, I suggest we find it."

"Should we even bother to try contacting King and Council?"

Trevan asked wryly as Saber refocused the view on the men cautiously following the granite road. At their pace, it would be another hour before they reached the illusion of a cliff the copper-blond haired man had cast to shroud their walls.

Morganen laughed, a half-humored sound at best. "Why not? It'll fulfill Prophecy when they refuse to help us. Though I can always hope that they don't 'fail to aid.' Hand me the mirror, Saber."

"It's *my* Destiny," the eldest of them stated, keeping a grip on the carved wooden frame. "*I'll* speak to them." Balancing the mirror against the edge of the table, he concentrated and chanted. "*Domi esto nua sorr; estis adri evalor. Quanno Consi Regi saun; yemi esta yava laun!*"

The mirror flared even brighter than it had when Morganen had activated it the first time, and Saber the second just a short while ago. Then again, the distance was considerably greater, the magic needed to make the connection considerably stronger . . . and this version included sound, since it was a direct link to another, similarly enchanted mirror, not just a peek show into a general place. A pattern in shades from blue to green to yellow pulsed across the mirror, however, not a concrete image of anything just yet.

"What is that, a holding pattern?" Kelly asked. "A magical screen saver?"

"No one is probably in the Council Hall at the moment," Saber muttered back, ignoring her last, odd otherworldly comment. Though he would probably ask her about it later. "But they will know someone is attempting to reach them through the Wall of Mirrors—" The pattern disappeared, and a man in purple and yellow robes appeared. His light brown hair was liberally streaked with gray and pulled back severely from his head, though it looked like it was in a ponytail at least as long as Saber's; apparently it was fashionable among the Katani for men of all ages to have long hair.

"You! You have gall, contacting . . ." The man, the Mage, Kelly realized, trailed off and stared out of the mirror at her, seated at Saber's side. "A *woman*!"

Kelly bit back the urge to exclaim, "No, really? And here I thought I was a kumquat!" while Saber cut to the chase. It wasn't easy, but she did it. Her friend Hope—who loved lecturing Kelly about tact and diplomacy—would certainly have been proud of her. Either that, or Hope would have thought the same thing, had someone so stupidly stated the obvious to her. Hope could occasionally be as sassy as Kelly liked to be. Kelly really missed her friend.

"We do not have time to debate the matter, Mage Consus," Saber stated while the other, older man was still spluttering. "There is a ship from an unknown land, a place called Mandare, that has arrived from the east, on the eastern side of Nightfall Isle. We have reason to believe they are here seeking to claim this land without our permission, and we believe they have a form of weaponry that may be difficult to counter by normal magical means. They may seek to take this island by force. If they take it, they may continue onward to Katan, to claim that which is also not theirs."

"If this is your woman-brought Disaster, then *you* deal with it. Stop them from taking Nightfall yourself!"

"They may go on to Katan even if Nightfall successfully repels them," Kelly pointed out quickly, drawing the older man's attention to herself before he could sever the connection between them. "They're looking for land and resources, and it looks like they're very determined."

"Then stop them outright, or die trying. And pray no one less *lenient* finds out you have a woman on that island!"

"Will you help us to discourage them from any attempts at conquest?" Saber asked.

"It is *your* problem! I have told you this! Katan wants nothing to do with you!"

Kelly's mind leaped into a serendipitous tangent, at that.

"Then do you give us the rightful authority to deal with this matter in our own fashion?" Kelly asked, earning a brief, questioning look from her husband and his brothers. "Do you relinquish all claim to Nightfall, its troubles, and its triumphs?"

"Do whatever you want; Nightfall is not a part of Katan, so do not contact the High Council again!" The mage on the other end of the mirror-link cut the connection with an angry swipe of his arm, popping the image in the glazed surface and restoring it to a reflection of Saber's face.

"What a bastard," she muttered.

"Fear does that to some people," Morganen reminded her. "It is up to us alone to handle this potential disaster, gentlemen, lady, as the Seer Draganna's Prophecy foretold—speaking of which, was there any way those invaders from your own history were successfully stopped in their conquest, Kelly?"

"Greater strength . . . or an *appearance* of greater strength," she added, thinking quickly as an idea unfolded in her mind. "You're going to be very grateful I insisted on having the grounds tidied."

"You have an idea?" Saber asked her.

"You bet I do. We need to present ourselves as that greater power, *too* great for them to want to try to blast their way through. Call up the image of that guy in too many clothes," she ordered him. When he obliged, she pointed to the man's garments. "See all of that? Do you know what his clothing tells me?"

"That he has horrid taste in fashion?" Dominor asked.

"Well, yes, from your viewpoint, maybe; Katani fashions seem to be fairly straightforward, comfortable, and utilitarian. *His* fashion tells me his culture is obsessed with appearances, at least in its upper echelons. The common sailors are clad simply, efficiently garbed for the labor they constantly do. This man is the expedition leader—a nobleman probably, or perhaps someone of great wealth.

"He is someone of far greater standing than the rest, great enough to be highly conscious of that difference in their status, or he would have dispensed with at least a few layers for comfort. He also apparently has the backing of this King Gustavo that he claimed the beach in the name of, with the planting of that flag. And the fact that he dresses in so many layers in the appearance-conscious fashion of his social ranking, despite the summer heat and the supposed emptiness of the beach, suggests that he is *very* status conscious."

"Which means that he'll only defer to someone he thinks is his social superior," Saber filled in, catching her meaning. "The question is, will a count and countess be considered a strong enough social status?"

Kelly shook her head. "Higher, just in case he's as high as a duke, though I don't think he's a prince. We should proclaim ourselves something like King and Queen—"

"I can't do that!" Saber choked, eyeing her askance. "No one of Katan may claim such a position, without actually being the rightful ruler!"

"Technically, the Council of Mages did dismiss us from any association with the realm of Katan," Morganen pointed out helpfully.

Saber shook his head. "I cannot do it. I cannot proclaim myself a king. Even if it would be the strongest status-point to battle this . . . person's arrogance with, I will not do it!"

"Fine, then; you don't have to. I call all of you as witness," Kelly stated, crossing her legs neatly and folding her hands in her lap, straightening her back primly. "I hereby declare *myself* to be your sovereign Queen. As *I* am not of Katan, I have no loyalty to Katan, and therefore no compunction against doing so. Neither do I fall under the jurisdiction of Katani law, social strata, tradition, or custom to prevent me from doing so. Furthermore, all of you as well as I myself have witnessed a duly appointed representative of the Katani government relinquish all claim to Nightfall Island, its resources and its occupants, in the name of the Katani government.

"Therefore, I hereby claim Nightfall Isle and all of its encompassing land, local waters, and many resources as *my* domain, and its lawful, native inhabitants as my subjects, of which currently number myself, my husband, who shall be my consort, and his seven brothers. Plus the chickens in the henhouse," she added primly, to be fair. The chickens were horrible creatures with nasty tempers and sharp beaks, but they *were* members of the brothers' household. So to speak. "Though they're more chattel than true citizens. The rest of our 'population' . . . we can pretend we're all living under a protective don't-see-'em illusion, or something, to explain why these invaders haven't seen anything, as yet."

Saber closed his eyes. He knew she was strange, this woman from another realm, but this was too much. "Kelly . . . you can't *do* that."

"She just did, Brother, and none here will gainsay her," Morganen commiserated with a pat on the eldest's shoulder. "None on the mainland, either, will protest at our secession, now that the Disaster has come and they have learned of it. Personally, I think it's a great idea," he added with a shrug. "I mean, we've got a woman who knows something of these outlanders' weaponry and ways, and a castle that is also a palace—an impressive palace, especially now that it's been cleaned up—and we've got enough of an advanced warning to whip up enough illusions to populate the place with servants and such before they find and breech our walls of illusions, shields, and stones.

"Congratulations on your incipient kingdom, Your Majesty," the youngest of them added with a flourished bow to his sister-in-law. "I place my skills and knowledge at your royal disposal."

"And I," Trevan agreed, smirking at the idea.

"Count me in," Koranen added, grinning.

"I'd rather bow to you, who can make me eat dirt in the blink of an eye, than allow anyone dressed like *that* to try and claim this island," Dominor asserted. "I respect *your* fashion sense far more than his."

That made Kelly smile. "Why thank you, Dom; that's the nicest thing you've ever said to me."

He smiled back slyly. "Don't worry; I'm certain it was accidental."

"I relish the idea of kicking these men off the island," Wolfer stated. "But if their weaponry is as difficult to stop as Kelly thinks, this will not be an easy task. As you said—though I resent the animal you used—one must sometimes say 'nice jonja' while reaching for your stoutest spear."

"What if the Council finds all of this out?" Saber pointed out to his crazy, strawberry-haired wife.

"They gave up all claim to us, and thus to Nightfall," she pointed out. Then caught his hand where it had fisted on this thigh. "Saber, I can as easily *un*declare myself queen as I can declare it. The only reason *why* a person is made a king or a queen in the first place is because it is declared and acknowledged as so by the populace that king or queen rules over. People rule only by consent of the people around them, whether actively by choice, or apathetically through a disinterest in changing tradition."

"Saber, if she declares herself our queen and *we* agree to it as her 'subjects,' she *is* a queen," Morganen agreed. "She's right in that the declaration and the consent are all you need to be one. This isn't shattered Aiar, after all. And personally, I don't mind. *If* it's temporary."

"Only on the occasional weekends, holidays, and whenever we have visitors," Kelly quipped, dismissing their concerns with a flip of her free hand. She rubbed Saber's hand with the other one. "It's a status thing, nothing more."

"I cannot declare myself King," he reminded her, beginning to give in at least a little on the idea.

Kelly smiled. Slow, sly, and feminine. "Honey, any man who can do what *you* can do in the bedroom, is *automatically* a king. At least, in my humble opinion."

The others laughed and slapped Saber on the back, as the eldest of the eight brothers blushed.

"Remind me to give you a royal *spanking* when we get back up there," Saber growled out of the corner of his tight-grinning mouth, glancing up at the ceiling to indicate their chamber.

She patted his knee. "That's nice, dear—but don't tease and make promises you don't intend to keep."

He hooked her around the waist, hauled her up against him, and silenced her with his mouth.

Koranen rapped his knuckles twice on the top of Saber's head, interrupting their kiss. "Shut off that blinding lightglobe of passion, Brother! We have business to attend to, remember?"

Saber did remember. He released Kelly—slowly, because his body refused to accept an abrupt withdrawal of her heady, responsive mouth—and organized his thoughts, dragging them from her tease about wanting him to spank her when they were alone back to the problem at hand. "That flag on the beach . . . if this were a real kingdom, concealed or no, someone would have noticed it by now. We should remove it immediately. To wait would only imply we are slack, unobservant and lazy . . . and that is not the kind of behavior that impresses."

"I think we should replace it with a flag of our own," Kelly offered. "Morganen, do you have any of that paint left from when we redid the walls? Or even better, can you replicate the same thing in cloth quickly?"

"Now that I know what I'm doing, yes—very quickly," Morganen agreed. "The slow part for me is figuring out how to achieve the effect; once the enspelling methods are known, it goes very quickly with each repetition." He grinned. "Especially when power isn't a problem, for me."

"Excellent," she praised. "Since this is Nightfall, the name of our castle, island, and kingdom, I suggest a lovely, color-shifting flag depicting a black silhouette of the land. Trees, mountains, that sort of thing. With stars and a crescent moon in white—two crescent moons, sorry—in a 'sky' that changes from sunset shades to midnight blue and back. Compared to their normal cloth flag down there, a plain red fist on a white background, it should be quite stunning and impressive, I think."

"It can be done easily enough, I think, with the special paint applied on black cloth. Ev, care to help me construct a counterclaiming banner?"

"*I* want to know if I'm going to get a fancy title bestowed on me by our queen, there," the singer-mage drawled before budging. "Seeing as how I do all of the *real* work around here . . ."

"I hereby declare you Lord Chamberlain, with duties including the smooth running of this castle palace," Kelly promptly agreed. "Which you already do so well."

"I want a title, too!" Koranen asserted quickly.

"Lord Secretary, since you seem to insist on wanting us to keep on topic and on schedule," Kelly teased him.

"And me?" Wolfer rumbled, folding his arms across his chest.

"Lord Protector, head of palace defense," Kelly decided, since he was the biggest.

"That's *my* job," Saber growled.

"Sorry. Okay, Wolfer, you're . . . Master of the Hunt, and Captain of the Armies, Saber's first officer. Saber, you're General of the Armies and Lord Protector of my person, as well as Consort. Um, Dominor, you're my Lord Chancellor and Master of Ceremonies; Morganen, as the best of all the brothers, you're obviously my Court Mage; Trevan . . ."

"Stable boy? Scullery maid?" he teased. "Your abject slave?"

"I'd name you Lord Rogue, if I could get away with it," Kelly muttered dryly as Saber glared at his brother, slipping his arm around his wife possessively. She elbowed the eldest of them. "Help me out, here, Saber. What *does* he do, anyway?"

Trevan winced and clapped his hand dramatically to his chest, mock-wounded.

"When he isn't gainfully employed crafting something with magic, and usually working in wood, he changes his shape, sometimes into a bird, sometimes into a cat and goes roaming through the forest, as Wolfer often does in canine form. They are the hunters of the family . . . though my twin is often more reliable," Saber added, digging at his younger brother in retaliation for teasing Kelly in front of him.

"You could be my chief of intelligence, then—for I've never known a cat to not be curious and not want to find out everything, and in a stealthy way at that." At the brothers' blank looks, she picked out a more medieval-sounding title, something they were more likely to be familiar with. "Um . . . you will be my official Lord Vizier, Trevan, for your title, and so advise me on all the things going on outside these walls. And Rydan can be Lord of the Night, since, well, he is.

"Now," Kelly continued briskly. "Morganen, Evanor, go work on the flag; make several of them, since we'll need a few to fly from the towers and such, and to hang here in the hall. I doubt we'll be able to make them go away without a display of wealth and power. The rest of you, we'll need to make sure the palace is looking perfect, since we'll probably have to bring them inside the walls at least once to impress them. And we'll have to change this hall into a grand audience hall."

"I'll take care of tidying the castle from the east courtyard to here, to begin with," Dominor offered as the two left to work on the flag. "That's the most direct path they'll be led along. We can also use your marriage-bench for the throne, since it's fancy enough. Once that's done, I'll set to work on making illusions of courtiers for our 'guests' to interact with, once they get into the castle and into this hall, since it would look odd to have an otherwise empty palace—you can't have a throne room without courtiers attending the throne, after all," he added dryly.

"I'll strengthen the donjon defenses," Saber asserted. "And I can manage adequate illusions of guards on the outer walls and castle parapets, even to the point of them actually defending our home, if necessary."

"I'll help handle the majority of the illusions, since I'm really good at them. Illusions are rarely more than light, and light is a part of fire," Koranen explained to his sister-in-law. "I can also tie some of the illusions into the lightglobes, since I made most of them, so that those images that can stay in one room won't need as much constant, direct supervision from a mage. Though I'll need Evanor's help when he's done with the flags, to make convincing sounds—the spells from that music box he made might be able to help."

"I'll make illusions of animals—of more animals than just the official citizen-chickens," Wolfer amended with a touch of deep-rumbled amusement. "And servants to work in the gardens, and outdoors."

"And I'll go keep an eye on our Disaster-visitors," Trevan agreed.

"Don't be seen. And don't get caught," Saber ordered him.

"I can't believe I have to say this," Kelly muttered, rising from their double seat, as the others started to scatter around her, "but, I have to find something to wear!"

EIGHTEEN

❦

Crouched high in a nearby tree, Trevan waited in one of his favorite feline forms, listening with ears that occasionally twitched from the Ultra-Tongue spell. The group of five sailors had finally reached the end of the road, which now stopped at the base of a virtually sheer cliff face, instead of the stone-covered postern gate of the castle. The sight of the large rock wall, curving gradually to either side, puzzled the newcomers.

There was a break in the tree line between the "cliff" and the forest, one too wide to try and jump from tree to parapet, or in this case, cliff top. That much, the eight brothers had diligently kept clear, in order to find and eradicate any monsters sent their way from beyond the castle walls during their former, weekly plagues. Now, only the illusion of moss and the occasional tendril of vine that he had placed there marred the age-weathered, slightly rugged surface he had created, rugged enough to be real, but too devoid of handholds to try to climb.

The sailors were arguing.

"It can't just *end*," one with a full beard argued with the others, as Trevan listened with Ultra-Tongue ears. "I say it's an illusion of some kind. Why else would anyone put a paved roadway between the beach and a cliff wall, without a reason for having a road? We haven't found that reason, and that's because this wall is surely an illusion!"

"We have only one illusion-dispeller with us, and that's back on board the ship. Lord Aragol isn't about to let it out of his sight," one of the thinner, tallish men returned.

A broader-shouldered, bare-chested one ran his hand over the cliff face. "It *feels* real—if it's an illusion, it's a very powerful one."

"Rights of Man forbid we've come on another land of *women mages*," the fourth one spat.

Interesting way to put it, Trevan thought.

"Trevan, the first flag is complete; would you like the honor of reasserting Her Majesty's claim to this island?" Evanor sang into his ears alone, in that almost-annoying way his next-eldest brother had. *"I'll meet you on the eastern parapet."*

Trevan flicked his ears, *mrraowled* under his breath, and transformed. Coppery-striped housecat shifted to a golden-red hawk. Launching himself from the branch, he flapped through the trees, soared over the cliff that was a wall, and angled just slightly to land on the roof of the tower that looked like a pinnacle of rock from outside. Transforming as soon as he had waddled bird-style into the stairwell, he tripped lightly down the steps, just in time to meet Evanor coming up from below with a cloth-wrapped staff.

"We made it banner-style," Evanor stated. "You have only to plant the pole and hang the crosspiece. And be careful."

"Or what, get myself killed on my very first day as a lord vizier?" he quipped, taking the bundle from his brother. Shaking his head, Trevan turned serious. "I overheard them speak of something they call an illusion-dispeller. They have only one, which is in the position of their leader, a Lord Aragol. The fop, I think. They also have something against female mages, and possibly against women in general, from the tone of the man who spoke . . . though I do not yet know why."

"I'll tell the others. Be careful, Brother."

Trevan grinned. "As careful as any cat."

Evanor rolled his eyes as he turned away.

Returning to the roof, Trevan murmured under his breath, rubbed his hands together, and transformed a third time, into his largest eagle form. Waddling over to the bundle set briefly on the stones underfoot, or rather, under claw, he gripped it in his talons gently, spread his wings, and flapped hard. Taking off over the inner parapet battlements, he soared around the palace with his awkward load a few times, until he had gained sufficient height, then soared to the south, to avoid the eyes of the sailors down below as he cleared the illusion-cloaked wall.

Turning east once more, he soared low over the treetops, until he came close to the edge of the forest that was the beach line. Dropping down under the canopy, he found a broad, thick limb and landed, then carefully transformed again, back to his normal self. The bundle of banner and pole almost fell. Biting back a curse, he grabbed at it, then straddled the limb and listened, peering into the forest floor a ways below.

Even as he and the limb he was sitting on stopped swaying, a sailor came into view. Without a concern in the world, without doing more than looking around at the underbrush cursorily, the man lifted up his shirt, unfastened his trousers, and relieved himself, balancing against the tree he was watering. Trevan waited until the other man was done, turning his head away from the less than civilized display. He might have a variety of animal shapes he liked to turn himself into, but he was as fastidious as a cat.

He was also probably the cleanest of the brothers, next to Dominor, whose only actual claim to superiority in that department was that he preferred to dress in richer fabrics more often than Trevan ever bothered with on this isle—to Trevan's way of thinking, without any women to impress, why should he bother?

Slipping quietly down the tree, Trevan crept through the underbrush until he was at the tree line, where the bushes were at their thickest to take advantage of the sunlight. That obnoxious red-on-white flag was still there, in front of the three boats drawn onto the sand. The tide was now well out. Some of the sailors were clamming, digging mollusks from the bared tidal sands. The rest seemed to still be off exploring the immediate land. Their poorly dressed leader was sitting in the center boat, his back to the shoreline, drinking from a glass goblet that glinted in the sunlight and eating from a pristine white napkin spread out over his lap, without a care for the world.

Trevan slipped out noiselessly from between the bushes and strode across the sand. No one noticed him . . . but then his plain, tan tunic and slightly darker trousers were little different from the clothes most of the others wore. He was far enough away that any of the sailors glancing his way probably thought him just another one of their group.

Stopping at the flag, he pulled it up and leaned the unwelcome ensemble against his chest, shook out the Nightfall banner, pushed its pole into the hole left by the other one, and fitted the hole in the crosspiece bar over the top of the tapered pole so that it sat levelly on the pole. Trevan then twisted the foreign flag and its short banner pole in his hands, bundling it up quickly. As the silhouette-flag of Nightfall shifted from blue to pale green, shades of yellow, peach golds, pinks, and down into deepening, darkening purples with slow, stately grace, around mountain-forest outline and the eight-point star and crescent moons design, he stepped around the marker and strode up to the middle of the trio of boats.

Lord Aragol—it couldn't be any other man, not in that ridiculously fussy outfit—continued to eat his cheese and bread, and sip at his wine. He seemed oblivious to Trevan's presence, even when the strawberry-blond mage came over to the side of the boat, within the man's field of view. Sighing, Trevan shook out the flag, with its red fist, red border, and white background, letting it drape plainly in the man's view. The other man choked on his bread.

"By the Rights of Man! What is *that* doing out of the sands, you oaf?" he demanded in whatever language his men and he spoke, making Trevan's ears twitch as the Ultra-Tongue potion once again translated it for him. The foppish man raised hazel eyes in a glare to Trevan's face, then frowned slightly, apparently trying to recall if he had ever seen Trevan before.

Trevan dropped the flag into the boat. "You left your flag on our beach."

"Of course I left it there!" the somewhat older man exclaimed roughly, twisting to look at where it had been planted only moments before. "I claimed the whole beach in the king's name with . . . it. Where did *that* come from?"

"I put it there. In our *queen's* name," Trevan added, folding his arms across his chest, amused by the man's gaping stare.

The other man whipped his broad-hatted head back around, the soft, fluffy feather tucked in it almost snapping in half with the speed of his turn.

"Her Majesty does not care to have foreigners prancing around on our soil, picking our fruit without her permission. She especially doesn't like foreigners claiming our land. I give you a friendly suggestion, stranger. Do not try her patience with such impolite gestures again."

The other man stood in the beached boat, making it rock slightly in the sand as he sneered at Trevan through his goatee. "You do your whole gender a disgraceful disservice, obeying Queen Maegan so subserviently—like a whipped dog with your tail chained between your legs!"

"Queen who?" Trevan asked, feeling his fur figuratively fluff at the crude language of this fop-man. "I serve Her Majesty, Queen Kelly, she who rules all of Nightfall. Which is the whole of this land you stand uninvited upon." He gave the man in his foppish, sweat-inducing attire a contemptuous look. "We will be observing you for a while. If you can prove yourselves civilized enough, you *might* be granted an audience in Her Majesty's court."

"Insolence! I am Lord Kemblin Aragol, Earl of the Western Marches of the Independence of Mandare, and representative of the king!" He put his hand on his sword-hilt.

"You could claim yourself the king of the whole universe, and I would not care. Leave your arrogance behind you, stranger, when you step foot on Her Majesty's shore." Turning, Trevan strode past the Nightfall banner, which had begun to lighten from midnight to sky blue again, resuming its sunset shift of colors, and headed back up the beach. Behind him, the lord yelled at his companions to go after him, capture and bring the stranger among them back. Unfortunately for the now red-faced stranger, they were all too far away to hear him clearly; by the time they had started in earnest up the beach after the copper-haired man, Trevan had already slipped into the trees.

A glance around, a quick shift into a small, winged form, and he flew up among the other birds perching and flitting in the canopy.

It amused him to watch the men, when they finally reached the spot he had vanished from, beat through the bushes, fruitlessly trying to find him.

I have no idea what words were exchanged with Trevan, but obviously this foppish man has a bit of a temper," Kelly murmured, staring into the mirrored surface Dominor had activated and demonstrated for her. She touched the cool glass of the mirror, pushing and sliding with her fingertip, and the image focused in even tighter on the yelling leader of the landing party.

The man grimaced, and she caught a glimpse of puffy gums, a sign of scurvy; it was caused by a lack of fresh fruit and thus vitamin C in the diet. It wasn't uncommon in the old sailing ship days of her old world, long before her own time and the advent of modern nutrition and medicine. A stroke of the frame and the image backed off, panning around to view the sailors giving futile chase of Trevan. She tapped and backed along one side of the oval, focusing in on some of them next. It was kind of fun, using magic like it was some kind of high-tech surveillance system. She just wished she could have overheard Trevan's conversation with the man.

"Your Majesty, the eastern wing of the donjon has been polished and peopled and awaits only the addition of sound and the activation of the illusions," Dominor announced dryly, Koranen approaching with him. "If you would be so kind as to stand for a few moments, we'll move the table out of view and arrange the donjon hall to look like a proper throne room."

"I think the solar above the kitchen would make a nice dining room—if you can get the table in there," she added as she stood. It was a broad table, too large to fit through most of the normal-sized doors in the castle.

"It comes apart in four pieces," Koranen reassured her, moving to disassemble it, tools already in his hands.

"Let's put the 'throne' over there, first, against the northwest windows," Dominor ordered his brother, and they picked up Kelly and Saber's marriage-seat and carried it there. Kelly took herself and the mirror over in that direction, sitting down on the double-wide seat as soon as it was in place.

She hadn't changed yet, but the moment it was decided to meet with their uninvited visitors, she would don her aquamarine silk wedding clothes as her most impressive garb. Tucking up her green-covered legs on the broad seat, she played with the mirror a little bit more, observing the visitors by sight if not also by sound, since that was something she could do with the mirror while the others used their magic to speed the various other tasks. If she spotted something that needed someone's attention, Kelly knew all she had to do was sing out Evanor's name.

Evanor came in and hung from the upper levels the long Nightfall banners he and Morganen had made, then disappeared again to start adding his specialty of sound to the illusions Dominor, Koranen, and now Morganen and Evanor were making and fine-tuning somewhere else in the castle-like palace.

Lunch was served in the salon just off the north balcony. It was made by Saber, of all people. That was the moment Kelly discovered her husband liked his food spicy. Of course, she discovered the fact *after* taking a healthy bite of the chili-like stew he had made. Two seconds later, she grabbed swiftly for a hunk of bread to neutralize the peppers and a glass of water to drown the rest of the fire turning her freckled face red. Saber only grinned at her as she wiped at her watering eyes, and leaned in close.

"And I thought you could handle anything . . . *hot* in your mouth," he murmured into her ear, sliding his fingers between her trousered thighs. Right up against the warmth of her core. *Much better than a skirt*, he decided then and there, since the folds of a skirt would not have given him such ready access.

She flushed again, and not from the spices in the stew. Setting her cup down, she dropped her hand straight to his lap and cupped him intimately in retaliation for that. "You mean, if you can't stand the heat, get out of the kitchen?"

"Do you two *mind*? I *don't* need to see that! Not while we're eating lunch," Wolfer demanded, his spoon halfway to his mouth, his brow arching as he eyed the two of them. Wolfer, on Saber's right, could see past the edge of the cloth-draped table with his peripheral vision, seeing clearly what the two of them were doing. So could Dominor, for that matter, seated on Kelly's left.

Both of them removed their hands. Both of them blushed. Both of them returned to their meal, and both of them managed to focus on the conversation of how to go about handling the visitors on their eastern shore.

A bit of debate, and it was decided to wait until morning, after finishing their preparations and briefing Rydan when he awoke, before making the next move. Which would be to send a "delegation" from the castle, if the visitors didn't finish taking on scavenged provisions and leave when the tide went out toward midnight again. No one thought that outcome likely, though it would have been nice. Not with the Prophesied Disaster looming.

As soon as the meal was over and the others had begun clearing the table, Saber grabbed Kelly by the hand and dragged her out of the new dining chamber. Hustling her to the nearest stairs and up them, he got them up to their chamber, slammed the door behind them, and yanked her up against him, bracing his back against the stout wood. There they stood for just a handful of seconds, panting from the fast climb up all of those stairs, then Saber hauled her even closer and kissed her.

She met the demands of his mouth willingly, heatedly, hungrily writhing against his body. His fingers dug into her backside, lifting her up against him. Breaking off their kiss, Kelly wriggled down his body, avoiding the hands that tried to pull her back up, and dragged down his trousers with an impatient tug at the laces to loosen them. With the garment tangled at his knees, she took him in her mouth and showed him what *a hot mouthful* really meant to her.

Saber banged his head back against the door behind him. The pain helped; he was determined to not climax, not this way, not when his whole body begged to be buried inside her own for that. Not just when deliciously tortured by her mouth. Shuddering as she cupped his sack, gently fondled the spheres inside his flesh, he gripped her hair, then her head, and pushed her away. Sinking to the floor, dragging her with him, he yanked impatiently at her own pants and undershorts, loosening them with her help.

Shifting onto her bared backside, she shoved the clothing down over her knees, lifting her feet—and Saber pressed her back, her cloth-imprisoned limbs hooked over his chest, as he stretched out over her, probed with his need, and entered her slick center in one sure thrust. There was a moment of stretching pain for her, from the angle and the sudden, filling depth of his demanding member in her only recently breached body, but it was nothing compared to the sweet friction that was the glide of his flesh into hers. He sucked in a breath as she cried out tightly and convulsed around him in an instant release, arms bracing his body above the curled angle of hers. Thrusting over and over into her quaking depths, seeking and yet delaying his own completion, he bit his lower lip as she did hers, and determinedly drove her back up and over the edge of insanity once more. When he fell with her, it was with a shout of her name, as her hips squirmed up into his.

Untangling themselves somewhat, breathing heavily, they curled up together on the floor, limp and sated. A few minutes later, when his body felt capable of assembling liquified bones and muscles back into working order again, Saber scooped her up and waddled over to the bed, since his breeches were now tangled around his calves.

Kelly kicked her own clothing-restrained legs and laughed.

"Does something amuse you?" he panted, getting to the edge of the bed and dropping her on it.

She bounced on her backside and kicked her feet again in explanation, giggling. He grabbed her feet, slipped off her slippers, tickled and nibbled on her toes while she squirmed and giggled, then threw her pants away and spread her legs. Tugging off his own footwear and garments, he dropped to his knees beside the bed, dragged her hips to the edge, and buried his tongue in her slick center with a wriggle. She shrieked and giggled, throwing her feet up, then parting her knees willingly, moaning. He raced his lips across her tender, slick flesh, nipping and suckling mercilessly, until she was forced to grip his hair and drag him away from there.

"Please—please—" Kelly panted, tugging him up over her. "Take me!"

He wanted to. But not like that. Disentangling her fingers from his locks, he climbed onto the bed and sprawled on his back, tugging her into squirming after him. With his hands on her waist, her hips, he got her over him. "Ride me . . ."

He broke off with a moan when she scrambled over his hips, grabbed his shaft without preamble, and sank onto him rather impatiently. Gripping her hips hard, Saber helped rock her down onto him in that exotic way she had taken him in the night. Until her insistence on a slow pace wasn't enough for him. Pulling his wife close, he rolled them over and showed Kelly exactly who was the ruler in their bedroom, with each of his masterful thrusts. At least, until she tightened deliberately around him, squeezing rhythmically.

Pleasure was the true ruler, at least in this particular corner of the donjon.

* * *

Happy and a little disheveled, they returned to the great hall a while later. Transformed completely, it was now filled with people, making both of them slow and stare as they walked out of the stairwell at the ground floor. Men clad in tunics and shirts, some sleeveless, some sleeved; women clad in Katani-style gowns and in variations of the trouser-and-shell-skirt garment Kelly had created; all turned and bowed politely to the two of them as they walked onto a length of red velvet laid down for carpeting. Kelly recognized it belatedly as the curtains that used to hang in the chamber over their heads, washed free of the grime of ages and spell-stitched together into a long runner for their feet to tread upon.

Long banners that slowly changed in sunset colors hung down each of the eight ceiling-supporting pillars, from the highest balcony railing overhead to just brushing the floor, lengths of black muslin treated with Morganen's color-changing paint. And to the right, angled in front of the stained glass windows under the balcony area, was an actual dais. A platform that stood just high enough to place a seated head level with a standing one, and just big enough for the massive, carved chair to safely perch. Trevan—or someone—had been busy; the loveseat had been gilded over and pillowed with yet more of the pilfered aquamarine silk.

Dominor stood next to that dais, talking with a woman clad in a violet and cream version of Kelly's aquamarine clothes, which were currently still upstairs. When the two of them followed the runner to the middle of the room, they discovered it was laid out in four runners, not just one. In addition to the lengths stretching from archway to archway, there was one more runner leading to the dais. The five aisles ran between the wedge-shaped sections of people occupying the hall, who were murmuring around them quietly.

As Saber and Kelly approached, Dominor broke off the conversation and smiled at them.

"Your Majesty, Brother, this is the Lady Felisa of Novella, a barony not too far north of Corvis lands. Lady Felisa, these are Her Majesty, Kelly of Nightfall, and her Consort, Lord Saber of Nightfall."

The woman dipped a little curtsy, knees together and bowing her dark-haired head, streaked faintly with gray at one temple. "Your Majesty, Your Highness. It is a pleasure to see you again, Lord Saber."

Kelly and Saber both raised their brows. Kelly spoke first, addressing both brothers, though it was Dominor's skill in illusion-casting that earned him a look of respect from her. "You both know this woman? The real one your spell is based upon?"

Her husband answered her. "I knew her, when I was younger; she would visit our family occasionally while on trips that passed by our home—I sincerely hope she's an illusion," Saber added to his brother. "She was one of the women advocating that the royal executioner should take our heads, rather than merely exile us to this isle."

Dominor smirked. "Isn't it wonderful that she'll be here to help *save* our lives?"

"You have a wicked sense of humor, Dominor," Kelly praised him. She held out her hand hesitantly. "Is she real to the touch?"

"Quite real," the older woman asserted on her own volition, and held out her arm. Kelly almost jumped at being addressed by the illusion. A very interactive illusion.

"They have physical presence," Dominor informed her as Kelly gingerly touched and explored the flesh of the woman's bare arm. "They have sight, they have sound, they have smell, and they have touch. Some even have a personality, and many have enough conversational skills to answer a variety of questions. The only sense these illusions do not have is taste, and the smell section of the spell is weak at best, but I figured if we burned incense and aromatic oils, that would take care of the first part, and if we made sure none of the visiting men tried to steal a kiss from anyone, that would take care of the second part.

"Now, would you like to be introduced to your courtiers? You'll notice that each one has a piece of embroidery in the trim of their garments that contains the Katani characters for their name, so that even for the ones we've cobbled together out of thin air, you'll know exactly who they are, or who they're supposed to be."

Kelly immediately looked for the name on the woman's clothes. She found it a few moments later near the armhole of the lavender vest-bodice. "It's . . . very subtle."

"We cannot know if these Mandarites have an Ultra-Tongue spell of their own, which allows them to read and write as well as hear and speak a given foreign tongue," Dominor agreed. "Also, each one of these people has a different level of communicativeness. Lady Felisa, because I knew her well, is stronger in the conversational department than most; others mutter pleasantries when spoken to, and seek to go elsewhere if pressed for anything more than their enspelled existence can handle."

"How did you anchor these spells?" Saber asked, curious.

"*Anchor?*" Kelly echoed, confused by the term. It was kind of like listening to a conversation between computer geeks, listening to the brothers talk about the technical aspects magic. She couldn't tell a microprocessor from a soundcard, either. She could guess what they meant, but it would be better to know more directly what each said. This was her kingdom now, after all.

"Unless an illusion is cast by the mage directly, with full concentration, they must be anchored in something," Dominor explained. He snapped his fingers, muttering yet another of the nonsensical, mystical words her Ultra-Tongue spell didn't translate, and the woman vanished. Stooping, the mage picked up a clear glass bead, no bigger than a largish marble, and displayed it on his palm. "Koranen usually uses these to create his lightglobes with, but they're perfect for anchoring the illusions. As are the lightglobes themselves, which cast light to begin with, and are thus easily altered. They're even enspelled with modest mobility powers, so that some illusory courtiers will move from room to room, while those anchored in a particular lightglobe will remain within that room."

"What if someone tries to drag them out of range of a lightglobe?" Kelly asked, worried about that aspect as Dominor returned the bead to the floor and restored "Lady Felisa" back into existence.

"Then they're enspelled to shout the word '*bekh*!,' and they vanish," Dominor stated. "Koranen thought about that one, already. He reasoned that, if our castle could be concealed by illusion-camouflage, then it was likely that our whole "culture" could indeed be based on that sort of thing, as you suggested. For all *they* know, we could have a whole city on the eastern shore near where the sailors have landed, and the outlanders wouldn't even know, because it's hidden. And if we hide our palace and cities, then it would make sense to have the ability to hide our individuals as well.

"If uncertain or threatened, we simply hide ourselves. If our enemies cannot find us, they cannot strike at us. You will be certain to explain this to our 'guests' if they ever ask why our castle wall looks like a rocky cliff at the moment, of course," Dominor added.

"Naturally," Saber agreed. He looked around at the chamber and the seventy or so "people" within it. "You've done rather well, in such a short time."

"You've been gone for almost two hours," his brother pointed out dryly. "*We* have been working ourselves to the bone all this time, putting this 'kingdom' together."

Kelly blushed. "We were in an important royal conference."

Dominor arched one of his dark brown brows. "Right."

NINETEEN

※◦❊◦※

The twinge of his own spells sent Saber quickly from Kelly's side. Hurrying out onto the eastern ramparts of the outer wall, he angled toward the section of wards that had been alerted. The illusion-spelled guards, anchored to certain stones at certain distances along the wall, were busy following the parameters of their spell.

The repel-invaders parameter of the spell had triggered the warning, he noted, watching his soldier-illusions as they unhooked a scaling claw from the battlements and tossed it over the side with their hands. Clad in studded midnight blue leather for both armor and clothing, patterned like the guardsmen at Corvis Saber had once known, they looked real enough that he almost started to ask them what had been happening. But they weren't enspelled to be able to actually reply; there hadn't been enough time for enspelling something as complex as verbal reasoning.

Saber peered over the edge between two of the defensive crenel-lations. A group of about seven sailors stood down there. Two had ropes with hooked claws tied to the ends. One was gathering up his rope into a neat coil, the other was whirling his own in preparation for another attempted throw. The man cast as hard as he could, and the hook sailed up, almost to the top. It fell short by about half a foot. Clearly this was at the edge of the man's throwing ability, with such a long and heavy rope that had to be attached to reach this high. The hook clanged against the stones of the wall, dropping back down in a ripple of rope to the ground.

One of the others, watching the cast, shouted and pointed up at Saber. All of the others looked up and focused where the man was indicating.

Saber leaned his elbows on the broad parapet edge and studied them in return.

"You, up there! How did you get up there?" one of the sailors de-manded in his native tongue.

"I was invited up here. You were not," he stated in Ultra-Tongue reply, as the other man with rope and claw finished coiling and started swinging. "Perhaps it is different in your land, but in this one, we believe in being invited first, before attempting to enter an-other's home."

The one who had spoken gestured for the other one to stop swinging his rope and grappling claw. "Then this road does lead somewhere?"

"All roads lead somewhere."

"So this wall is an illusion?"

"Of course. It is our way. Rather than be rude and needlessly violent when an unwelcomed, uninvited intruder arrives and tries to barge into our home, we simply . . . vanish."

With a flick of his hand, he vanished in a simple illusion. The men down below shouted, calling for him. Saber counted to twenty, then reappeared as the leader ordered his men to scale the "cliff" wall again.

"Are you hard of hearing, man? Or simply lacking in wit? If you ask, and ask politely, then perhaps someone will pay attention to you. I suggest you go back to your ship and think about how you could approach us in polite civility, instead of in rude intrusion. None of us are angry with your foolish attempts. Yet. But I suggest that you do not press your luck."

Flicking his fingers, he vanished yet again from their view. As he watched, unmoving, the men down below argued, then gave up and turned away. They coiled up their ropes and hooks and started marching back down the hill.

Why are you pacing, Sister?" Morganen asked his eldest brother's wife.

Kelly shook her head, wearing footprints along the red velvet path dissecting the floor of the great hall in five stitched-together stripes. "I can't see a way around those guns."

"How do you mean?" he asked, falling into step beside her. "If perhaps you told me how they are activated, I could counter their activation by bringing out some of my own collection of enchanted weapons, some of which are very powerful indeed."

She shook her head. "You're doing the exact same thing. It's a male flaw in thinking."

"I beg your pardon?" the youngest brother of them all asked, for the first time sounding offended instead of levelheaded.

Kelly lifted her head with a blush. "Sorry. I spoke without thinking. It's . . . a matter of thinking that bigger is better. You think a bigger and better spell will cure everything. But it doesn't, not always. Men are more predisposed than women to think that machines—or spells, in this universe—will solve anything if they're just made bigger. Or smaller, or stronger, or faster. They don't think like this always, but admit it: You'd be impressed with me if I could pull off a bigger and more complex spell than you could, wouldn't you?"

"I would be impressed if you could pull off *any* spell, but yes," Morganen agreed. "But isn't that the way of the world?"

"Not always from a female point of view . . . but they're not female, are they?" she added with a frustrated sigh.

"You've lost me again," he pointed out. She stopped in the center of the hall and did her best to explain.

"Sorry. Here's an analogy: If *I* came to you with a better spell, a magical item more efficient, more powerful, far easier to cast and to use than the version you had, you would be impressed, right?"

"I thought we agreed on that, already."

"True. Now, if you had a weapon-spell that was pretty effective, if someone else came along with an even better version of that spell, would you be impressed?"

"Of course."

"And more inclined to avoid angering the person wielding it?" she added, lifting her brows. "To behave and do what they say, including and up to going away if they requested you to?"

He began to get her point. "A weapon that, if you are correct, travels faster than sound itself, too fast to be easily stopped by most magical means. In order to impress these men, you would need a bigger and better gun than what they have?"

"Exactly. Because they're men, and they'd be more impressed by such things than a woman would—that's not to say women aren't impressed by bigger and better things," she added quickly, as Morganen grinned. She caught his meaning a moment later, a marital joke at her and Saber's expense. Kelly resisted the urge to hit him for it. "We're just focused on other things that are important, too. If they were women, I might have a better chance of finding some other way to impress or otherwise reason with them, but they're men, which means I have to find an appropriately 'male' way of dealing with them.

"Now, the next problem is," Kelly continued briskly, "my old universe is unfortunately teeming with 'bigger and better' guns, but that's there and this is here, and I don't personally know enough about how guns work to come up with a better version in this world than the basic flintlocks those men are carrying around. Not in the little amount of time we have to come up with them from the materials that are to be found here. Ergo, I need a bigger and better gun from my own world. Even though I don't like that idea."

Morganen shrugged. "I can fetch one of these 'better' guns from your realm, any time you wish me to."

"I thought the aether was disturbed too much to risk it in her realm," Saber pointed out, making both of them turn around. He had returned from the parapet in time to catch this very interesting end of their conversation.

"A gun is a nonliving object," Morganen returned blithely. His expression was calm and natural, responding evenly to his brother's half-growled remark. "There is little danger in bringing it across the slowly healing fractures in the aether. At least, I presume they're nonliving," he added, turning politely back to Kelly.

She had a thoughtful frown on her face. "How much can you pull across?"

"A few items. Why do you ask?"

"How much information do you need to be able to locate and fetch specific items?"

The light-brown-haired man shrugged. "You could be there in my workroom with me, and point them out in the mirror . . ."

"You may do that in a moment, Kelly," Saber said, closing the distance between him and his youngest brother. He clamped a hand down on Morganen's shoulder. "I must speak with my brother about something, first. Please excuse us."

Steering Morganen aside, he stopped when they were far enough away for an argument. Which meant into the east wing a short ways. Tightening his grip, he narrowed his eyes, pinning the youngest of the twins in place physically and visually.

"You *lied* about not being able to send her back, didn't you, Morg?"

Aquamarine eyes, close in shade to Kelly's own, stared guilelessly back at his brother's gray. "Why would I lie about that?"

"Jinga's Knees! To keep her here long enough for me to fall in love with her!" Saber exclaimed, tightening his grip.

Morganen winced and pried his brother's hand from his shoulder. "You're welcome."

Saber shook his hand free and pointed a finger at his brother. "You *manipulated* me!"

"It could have just as easily been any one of us," his youngest sibling pointed out, folding his arms across his chest.

"No, it wouldn't have been! I'm first in the Song, the first to fall—was she even burning to death in her bed, Morganen?" Saber demanded. "Was that just another ruse, created by you?"

The paling of the other man's skin was accompanied by the darkening of his eyes . . . and by a perceptible crackling of power, eerily reminiscent of their brother Rydan whenever a storm came. Saber, realizing suddenly that he had gone a little too far with his youngest brother, fell back a step. Morganen closed his eyes and visibly mastered his rage at the accusation, quelling the disturbances in the aether. Opening his eyes again, he gave his brother a cold look.

"I will forget you ever suggested that, Brother. Unlike you, I *like* women. I like the idea of having them around, of talking with them, seeing them, and otherwise enjoying their company. I do not deliberately harm them. Not the innocent ones. *Ever*."

"I apologize," Saber offered gruffly. "I spoke without thinking.

But, you still manipulated me—*and* Kelly, even if you did save her life. *No more*, Morg. Do you understand that?"

"I understand," he returned calmly. Without any sign that he would obey his eldest brother.

Saber thought about pressing the matter, but decided against it. Morg was Morg, and no power on this planet short of the Gods themselves could probably stop him. The eldest of them could only be deeply grateful that the youngest was too good a man to take advantage of that fact. Most of the time.

"Now, if you'll excuse me, Saber, I promised your wife I'd help her come up with a way or two to impress our 'guests.'"

Saber had to ask it. Even if it angered the most powerful mage on Nightfall or even the whole of Katan. "Morg—did you have anything to do with these outlander men arriving here?"

Morganen faced him again. A glance told him that only his sister-in-law was close enough to hear them. It was time these two, at least, knew what he could do, and what he had done. "No. But I did see them preparing to leave their homeland, while scrying long and far in my more idle moments. I knew they were determined to head west across the ocean in search of more land," he admitted coolly. "And I did then look more closely at the five women I had seen already in my scryings who might make you a true-love wife. Finding Kelly being burned alive simply solved the choice of which one to bring here to you. Then I sent a few storms across the sea to delay these men from arriving until it was time for them to appear, the only source of the Prophesied Disaster possible that I could foresee."

"You were watching me *before* you saved me?" Kelly demanded. Curious to hear their conversation, she had followed the two men at a discreet, quiet distance. "Just how much did you see of me, Morganen?"

"Enough to know your character would suit his, and that you would be able to fall in love with each other."

"I already figured that much. I meant, how much did you see of *me*?" she demanded, folding her arms defensively across her currently decently clad chest, remembering any number of times when she had been less than decently clad in her old life.

"I would like to know that as well, Brother," Saber added, shifting to join her in glaring at his kin.

"My scrying mirror is enspelled to blank out the impolite bits, and that is the truth. Regardless of your belief or disbelief in it, it is the truth," Morganen added with a hint of primness. "I suggest we return to the topic of fetching what you think you might need from your realm, Sister—and then you can see for yourself what I can and cannot scry with my mirror."

Kelly didn't know what to think. She retired early after dinner came and went, leaving the others to explain everything to Rydan when he joined them. The night-loving one of the brothers had absorbed their information, arching one of his blue black brows at all of the changes in the great hall and the shift of the table to a room in the north wing. But that was earlier. Far overhead, above the curve of the vaulted hall that the others were still working on to transform into a place of impressive power and splendor, Kelly sat bent over a embroidery frame dug out from some storage room, "painting" with thin thread and careful stitches the details of Saber's face, in the promised embroidered portrait.

The work was intricate and consuming . . . for hand and for eye. Her mind and her heart ached, however, free to wander, free to think.

Morganen said I was one in five. If he hadn't seen me burning alive at that moment in time, I would have died. And another woman would be

*here, right now. Someone else would have caught Saber's eye . . . and prob-
ably a lot smoother than I did*, she thought, flushing a little at the memory of how she had hit him, had bitten him, had yelled at and treated
him. *I don't even see why he fell in love with me.*

She stitched a little more, changing threads to a slightly darker
shade of tan-peach to sculpt the shadow of his cheekbone, carefully
blending it into the lines of the other ones for a few passes before
solidifying the color, to blend the two shades without an unruly,
abrupt line between them.

A thought stilled her hand.

*We both drank from the same potion-cup; Morganen could have cast a
second spell . . . a spell to make him only* think *he's in love with me. And to
make me . . . care for him.* She carefully skirted around the topic of
love where it concerned herself. She wasn't ready to examine if she
loved him utterly and unconditionally; she was afraid she might find
out she didn't. Which made that thought even worse. Biting her
lower lip, Kelly forced herself to focus on the tapestry, taking extra
care in placing her stitches while the turmoil went on inside her.
Everything here was just a little too different for her to trust her
own feelings.

Embroidery soothed her, particularly something as painstaking as
portraiture. She switched threads when the current color grew too
short to work any further and began the carefully curved, sculpted
lines of his hair, arcing up and out from the smooth stitches of his
forehead. That meant she had to dig into the embroidery chest to
see if she had enough of the right colors to properly describe his
honey-blond locks. Just after she set the fourth stitch of the new
thread, the door of the master chamber opened and Saber stepped
through.

Saber could tell instantly that something was wrong. She was biting her lower lip, yet he wasn't making love to her, which was the
only other time she ever did that. Closing the door, Saber crossed to

the window seat she was sitting on. His portrait was set in the free-standing workframe angled in front of her, illuminated by a pair of carefully positioned lightglobe stands. When she didn't even look at him as he sat down beside her, he guessed that whatever was worrying her had something to do with him.

"Will you tell me what is wrong?"

Her lower lip trembled; she released it. He was being so nice, it made her heart ache and her eyes sting. "I . . . I'm afraid."

"Of the men in the ship, or of something else?" Saber asked, hoping it wasn't him after all.

"Something else," she murmured, keeping her gaze down. She couldn't even look into the eyes stitched on her embroidery.

He had to ask. "Is it me?"

"No . . . yes . . . I don't know." Her lip went back between her teeth.

That hurt. Saber drew in a breath around the pain in his heart. "I don't want you to be afraid of me—"

She shook her head. "Not *you*—I'm afraid . . . that you don't really love me."

Saber blinked. He cupped her cheek, turning her face toward him, though she didn't raise her gaze. "*Not* love you? How could that be? You are my true love, my Destiny—"

Shaking her head, she looked up at him. "Morganen said it himself: I was one of five! How can I be your 'true love,' if it could have been any one of us?" She stared at him in anguish, her lip catching briefly between her teeth before she went on. "How do we know he didn't slip another potion into that Ultra-Tongue drink? One that . . . that *made* you think you're in love with me?"

Something about the way she put that gnawed inside of him. Met up with other things she had said, and how she had said it. Saber stared at her. "You don't love me."

Bite, pause . . . "I don't *know*. I don't know *anything* right now. The rules of this world are so strange, so *different* from my own."

He got up and paced, leaving her on the bench. *She doesn't love me. I love her, but she doesn't love me . . . How can that be?* He thought it over as she stayed where she was, lip between her teeth, hands unmoving in her lap. Saber turned. "It cannot be, Kelly. Some forms of love can be faked, coerced, or forced by a spell . . . but true love cannot be.

"I saw your heel lit by sunlight, followed the sun, and spotted the ship that now lies out there, anchored in the night," he reminded her, striding back to her side. Nudging the embroidery stand aside, he knelt in front of her and took her talented, idle hands in his; they felt cool, and he rubbed them slightly to warm them. "The Seer Draganna Prophesied that Disaster would come at the heel of my true love . . . and it would not be true love if only I loved you. True love can only exist when it exists on *both* sides. You *do* love me, Kelly."

She tried to tug her hands free. "But I treated you so badly, when we met!"

He smiled, one side curving higher than the other as he held on to her hands. "Then that proves it wasn't a potion, for if it were, we would have liked each other from the very start. Right?"

She raised her eyes to his. Uncertainty and doubt still lingered—though his last comment did make undeniable sense. Heck, she'd even used the same argument herself, convincing herself the potion was safe to drink when it hadn't changed his initial irritation with her one bit. Rising, Saber slid one arm behind her back, the other beneath her knees.

"I will prove that it is true love," he murmured, carrying her to their bed. Flower garlands still wrapped its posts, a reminder that they were still very newly wed. Laying her on the bed, he knelt beside it and picked up her feet, while she propped herself up with her arms.

Slipping her shoe off, he kissed the heel that had been illuminated by Destiny only that very morning, half a day and half a lifetime ago. He told her as he showed her what he meant. "In these past few weeks, I've discovered many things. I've discovered I didn't live before I met you. I didn't breathe before I kissed you. I couldn't think before I knew your name, Kelly of Doyle . . . Kelly of Nightfall, my true love."

He slipped off her other shoe, kissed that heel, too, as he continued with the truth. "I cannot walk without knowing my feet can take me to you, as well as from you. I cannot see without hoping to look at you as I look around. I cannot find peace or relax unless I am touching you, so it *must* be true love."

Murmuring softly, shifting up onto the bed, gently peeling back her clothes, he bared his thoughts and feelings as he bared her body. Somewhere in there, he divested himself of his own clothes, until their flesh brushed and touched, a satin glide of skin against skin, illuminated by the lightglobes still lit, standing off to the side.

Slowly, sweetly, he made love to every inch of her, until she drifted free of her fears and entwined her limbs with his. It was not the hot-burning passion of their previous lovemaking, but rather like the tide of the sea, rising slowly, lapping at the shores of their flesh, until their limbs were entwined like the froth of a wave clinging to a beach.

When he surged inside her, it was not with fervor, not with impatience, but with simple determination. It went on and on, slowly, gently, until her lip caught in her teeth from a better kind of pain than mere indecision, caught up in a delicately, torturously, piercingly sweet agony. When they found their pleasure at that leisurely pace, he held her through its quiet but still overwhelming intensity. And then held her some more, close to the beating of his heart, which he had proved beat only for her.

Kelly clung to him gently, feeling that heartbeat. Feeling his words deep inside. She *felt* loved, so maybe she was loved, truly. And she did feel many of the same things for him that he had whispered to her.

"Do I love you?" Saber asked his strawberry-haired wife in the aftermath stretching quietly between them.

Tears stung her eyes. She snuggled closer, her doubts quelled. "You love me."

"Do you love me?" he asked, needed to ask.

She didn't answer for a long moment, until she felt his heart skip a beat against her cheek. Waiting for her reply. Hoping for a reply. This meant so much to him, one little word.

"Yes."

I think so . . .

She just didn't feel like she *could* know. Not in a realm where even he admitted potions could imitate several forms of love . . . and if they could imitate some, surely they could imitate all. If this was her world, her reality—her stable, immutable, nonmagical, undoubtable version of reality—she might not feel doubt. She might be able to know, if she was there instead of here. But it wasn't, and she wasn't, and she still suffered from a tiny prickling of doubt.

Closing her eyes, Kelly held on to him. Prayed to whatever might listen that she did love him. Because she knew for certain that, after this night, she desperately wanted it to be true love.

TWENTY

※❋❋❋❋❋

Trevan arrived on the eastern wall before the delegation from the ship did, but then he'd headed for the outer wall after he and the others had watched the party making its way up the long, sloping road, in the scrying mirror over their breakfast. This time, he was clad in an illusion of the same midnight blue, steel-studded leather armor the "guards" his eldest brother had created were wearing, pacing tirelessly along their sections of the outer wall rampart. They were spaced evenly all the way around the vast, eight-sided circle of the palatial castle, and had been enchanted to defend against invaders, just in case their visitors attempted to climb another section of the wall.

He waited for them to arrive and announce themselves, leaning against the parapet wall on the inner side, out of sight. It was apparent in their view through the scrying mirror, from the overly fancy garb of their leader and at least two other men, to the clean and neat clothes on the six sailors accompanying them, that they were indeed coming for a polite, formal visit. As it had been suggested they should.

Trevan grinned at that thought. He had done some of that suggesting himself, as had Saber.

A horn sounded, piping a short-long note like the call to a hunt, then a set of trills that sounded a little militaristic, before ending on an uplifted note. Pushing away from the inner wall, he stepped up to the outer one, leaned on the broad stone ledge, and peered over it. The eight towers were each set in the four cardinal and four ordinal directions. The section of wall he was leaning over technically was the east-by-northeast wall, just north of Morganen's private tower, and the walls themselves were slightly curved, softening the eight lines encircling the castle, ensuring that all of the gardens and courtyards held ample space. But instead of smooth, tightly jointed gray white granite, the slightly rugged cliff facade he had created fell below him, still artfully draped in vines and moss.

Peering over the edge, he studied the party of nine waiting at the end of the road for a response to their horn-call. "Did you want something?"

One of the other two foppishly dressed men stepped forward and spoke up. "His Lordship, Kemblin Aragol, Earl of the Western Marches, and representative of King Gustavo the Third, ruler of the Independence of Mandare, requests an audience with your . . . leader."

"What, with my captain?" Trevan asked, playing on the man's distasteful avoidance of the word *queen*.

"With your ruler. This Queen Kelly of Nightfall," the man added with a touch of impatience.

"I'll pass your request along," Trevan called down, then retreated to lean against the inner battlement crenellations once again, hidden from their view, and waited.

He counted slowly, silently to one hundred, then reversed the count back down to zero, then mouthed the names of all forty-four of the phonetic letter-characters of the Katani alphabet, front to back, and back to front. He examined his nails. He drew the knife sheathed at his waist and pared the longer of those nails with its sharp edge. He wiped the blade of all fingerprints, taking care to polish it very thoroughly with the hem of his illusion-dyed tunic before resheathing it. Then, and only then, Trevan stepped back up to the edge and leaned on his elbows once more, peering over the edge.

"Her Majesty states that, as you have asked politely, you may come within our walls. However, as you are foreigners, you must be apprised of the most pertinent laws of the Kingdom of Nightfall, before you can be allowed to see any of its denizens.

"Privacy is respected, here. You will not be allowed to wander off and try a little exploration on your own; if you do so, you will be gently but firmly returned to only the areas that are open to you. Fighting is not allowed here. You may retain your weapons, but if you attack any of the citizens of Nightfall, or damage any of our property, you will either be removed from the premises if you have not yet actually harmed anyone, or thrown into the dungeon to await trial if you do . . . and our punishments are very harsh for those who are found guilty of a violent crime.

"Rape is not tolerated on Nightfall. Any man who attempts to do so will be lashed hard fifty times across the back, or until the blood runs to his knees . . . whichever takes *longer*. Any man who actually succeeds in rape shall have his manhood and bollocks cut off, and all of his possessions and wealth confiscated to support his victim, with a conscripted labor of five years to continue that support if the forced union is fruitless, and a labor of twenty years should a child have resulted, to support both mother and child.

"Murder is not tolerated either, in Nightfall. Commit murder, and you will be executed, and your possessions and wealth confiscated to support the family of the victim. Theft is not permitted here. Twenty lashes and eight times the value of whatever was stolen will be confiscated from the thief, plus the item in question retaken, with half given to the government and half given to the victim of the theft, in compensation for the trauma of the crime; for those who cannot afford the recompense of a theft, they shall be enslaved to labor until the eight-times cost of the stolen items have been compensated, *plus* twice more, for the inconvenience put to the Crown for the cost of maintaining a prisoner-slave. Do you understand these points as I have explained them to you?" Trevan finished.

The men below the base of the disguised wall peered up at him silently.

"Do you understand that you are subject to these laws of Nightfall, and do you understand that there are other laws in this land that, explained or not, you are also subject to, so long as you stay within sight of our land?"

Even from high up on the stout wall, he could see a muscle work in their leader's jaw, from the way it flexed his sideburns. "Yes. We understand these laws. Do you understand that I come as the representative of my own government, and not as some common visitor?"

"If that is what you say. The Lord Chancellor will be here shortly to escort you inside." Withdrawing from the wall, he grinned and headed for one of the sky bridges. Strolling and taking his time, that was; Trevan could shift into many shapes, but cats were his favorite. Cats loved to play with their prey, after all, and part of the playing was making that prey wait for each velvet-clawed pat of the paw.

Dominor finished shifting the second heavy, enspelled bracing-bar aside via magic. Making certain his hands and clothes were still clean, he smoothed the trimmed, dark sapphire silk of his best tunic—which had been in need of repair since shortly after arriving on Nightfall Isle three years ago, been sentenced to enspelled storage all this time, and finally repaired by his sister-in-law just a few weeks ago—and raised his hand. With a murmur and a pass, the huge and heavy but well-hung doors swung open silently, easily.

Behind him, the eastern courtyard and Y-wings of the castle were already showing signs of life, as the activated illusions could be seen in windows and occasionally crossing the large, garden-edged courtyard behind him on nebulous errands. More of the blue-clad illusory guards that were standing up on the wall also stood at the edges of the courtyard, and a pair of guards stood to either side of the opening gate doors. Between himself and the illusions, Dominor was fairly certain they presented an impressive sight. An imposing one would be better, though.

Through the opening came the nine strangers. They stopped just inside the gates, facing Dominor, and looked all around them. There was a lot to take in: the age-worn but still ornate carvings of the castle donjon, the dozen soldiers in immediate view, the men and women moving around in the distance. The sailors were carrying three chests between the six of them, and rucksacks on their backs. The three impossibly dressed, supposedly important people studied Dominor as the most interesting part of their view; apparently the rest of it was quickly dismissible.

"You are the Lord Chancellor?" Lord Aragol asked, staying where he was as he arched a brow under that ridiculously broad-brimmed hat. He eyed Dominor's far simpler outfit of fitted dark blue breeches, deep sapphire tunic, and pale blue shirt, emphasizing the blue of his eyes, and did not seem impressed.

Neither was Dominor. The foreigner's garb was similar to what he had worn the day before, pastel shades, but still far too many layers. There were ridiculously puffy short-trousers above opaque-stockinged legs on all three of them, their version of formal-garb, apparently—trousers with bulges at the front that were too uniform to be real, but too large to escape being anything other than borderline obscene, in Dominor's opinion. Still, he had a role to play, so he ignored their glaring excuses for fashion and nodded his head briefly.

"I am Lord Dominor, Lord Chancellor of Nightfall in Her Majesty's exalted service. I have been informed that you have been given a recital of the major laws of this land, in both expectations and consequences. Is this so?" he asked. The intent was to give the impression of law and order, enough law and order that it would impress these people—who outnumbered them by far too many for comfort, given the number of bodies scried on board their ship— and thus keep them in line by civilized threat alone.

"We have been so informed," the oldest overdressed member of the trio stated. "I am Lord Kemblin Aragol. This is my eldest son, Sir Kennal Aragol, and my second-born son, Sir Eduor Aragol. You will escort us to your queen."

Dominor didn't bother to stop the arch of one dark brown brow. *What an arrogant ass, to command me in my own home.*

"At your gracious convenience, of course," the earl added with an ingratiating smile.

"This way, then, Lord Aragol. But mind what you do and say while upon Nightfall Isle." As he turned, Dominor swept his hand discreetly. The eastern gates swung silently shut behind them, and the bars slid back into place, obeying the silent signal without any sign of help from Saber's illusory guards. It was just as well these people didn't seem to have much in the way of magic; even the three overdressed men looked impressed at that simple bit of magery.

"Is it necessary to lock us in, Lord Chancellor?" the younger of the two fop-clad men asked, glancing back.

"You are not locked in; you have only to ask, and you are free to leave. We prefer our privacy, that is all. The gate is closed so that no one can enter our walls uninvited."

His father had tipped his head back to gaze up at the curved roof of the great hall, visible above the wings of the building before them. "We did not see any of this from the harbor."

"You were not meant to."

"How large is this land, Lord Chancellor?"

"Large enough . . . though we do feel a little overcrowded of late," Dominor added. Playing on the same reasoning the other man had no doubt come, the reasons his new sister-in-law had related. The need for more resources and room.

"Overcrowded?" the elder son scoffed lightly. "Where are your cities? Your harbors?"

"You landed at one. Well, at the fishing port of Whitetide," he added, keeping his smile to himself. "I understand you almost tore one of their *sampa* dragnets with your rudder, sailing between two of our fishing ships, though I heard the owners successfully lowered it in time."

"We saw no ships," one of the sailors asserted firmly as a "guard" opened the door into the east wing.

"You were not meant to. We prefer our privacy."

"Lord Chancellor! A word with you about the silk shipment," a woman in green asserted from a doorway. An enchantment of Dominor's, of course, and one enspelled to give the illusion that they were a prosperous people. She eyed the newcomers briefly, then addressed Dominor, who had stopped politely for the illusion, forcing the others to stop as well. "I told Her Majesty a few months ago that there would only be ten tons of raw silk harvested this year for tithe, but the summer has been exceptionally pleasant, perfect weather for the silkworms, and the Weaver's Guild will be presenting twelve tons at tax time. However, because of the good weather, the *antithi* mushroom harvest has been conversely poor, and scarlet will be in higher demand; I do apologize for that, on behalf of the Guild."

"I will pass the news to Her Majesty's ear, Lady Risia. Oh—Lady Risia of Caston, this is the Lord Kemblin of Aragol, his sons, and some of the sailors from the ship in Whitetide Bay. They come from a land called Mandare, somewhere to the east of here."

The woman eyed the group of nine and belatedly held out her hand. Her smile was polite but just a little distant, the kind reserved for being civil to strangers. "A pleasure to meet you, Lord Kemblin."

"It is Lord Aragol," he returned, taking her hand and bowing formally, coolly over it. "I am amazed that you speak our language, so eloquently and so far from our home."

"The moment you arrived and spoke on our shore, we learned your tongue; all of us speak it now so that you may feel more comfortable. It matters not what tongue *we* speak in, but it does matter to you. We may prefer our privacy, but we try to be polite," Dominor added. Nodding to the illusory lady as the earl released her hand, he continued along the passageway. "Keep together, please. Her Majesty's court is not accustomed to being kept waiting long."

The remade Audience Hall and its illusory audience quietened as Dominor made his way into the center of the quartered chamber, striding confidently along the carpeted, former-curtain runner. He stopped in the center, turned slightly to face the dais, which was placed at an angle from their approach, and addressed the makeshift court.

"Your Majesty, Your Highness, Courtiers of Nightfall: I present His Lordship, Lord Kemblin Aragol, Earl of the Western Marches, representative of King Gustavo the Third of the Independence of Mandare, from far across the Eastern Ocean; his sons, Sir Kennal Aragol, and Sir Eduor Aragol; and some of the men from their ship. Gentlemen, I present to you Her Sovereign Majesty, Queen Kelly of Nightfall, Scion of the Most Honorable House of Doyle, Protector of the People, Fairest Flower of the Eastern Ocean; and His Highness, Lord Saber of Nightfall, Consort of Her Majesty, Count of Corvis, General of the Armies, Champion of the Isle, and Lord Protector of Nightfall."

Kelly nodded regally from where she sat on her makeshift throne. The coronet Saber had given her as a wedding gift, she had set aside, since it was a Katani noble's crown. Even she didn't feel comfortable wearing that particular symbol after declaring herself a queen and claiming Nightfall as her own kingdom, independent of the Katan Empire.

Instead, she was wearing a crown of cubic zirconias, fake diamonds filched from a costume shop—and paid for with a real diamond tucked into an envelope and set in its place, with a brief, block-printed note explaining it was a real, flawless, uncut diamond of roughly ten carats' size, and worth far more than the costume jewelry crown itself. It wasn't as if Morganen had any American cash lying around to pay for the things they had bought, but he did have gemstones to spare. Magically made, no less.

She had been working with Morganen yesterday, setting aside the doubts he had instilled in her to work on acquiring everything that could be needed, and paying for it with the diamonds Morganen had on hand—diamonds that were apparently very easy to make, when one was a massively good mage. In their "panning" through her world, looking for various different props, he had spotted the fake crown in a window display and pointed out that the eight-pointed stars in its design was a sign from destiny that she should wear it today. And when he popped it through and placed it on her head, showing her how she looked with it in a normal mirror, Kelly had been forced to agree it looked perfect on her.

The combs holding it on her head itched, though. A lot.

Beside her, Saber sat wearing his silver coronet, clad in the same aquamarine of their wedding outfits, holding her hand in his. He nodded coolly as well, and lifted his free hand slightly. "You may approach, Lord Earl, you and your sons."

Dominor stood aside and gestured for them to head up the runner, while he waited with the sailors. The six much more plainly dressed men in the center of the hall eyed the color-changing curtains, the colorfully, aesthetically dressed men and women around them, and stayed respectfully where they were, the three chests and rucksacks resting at their feet. Lord Aragol and his sons came forward, stopped six feet from the first step of the wood dais, and swept off their hats in elegant bows.

"Your Highness, Your Majesty . . ." the trio murmured in near-perfect unison.

"Lord Earl, young Sirs," Kelly returned, dipping her head slightly.

"Gentlemen," Saber added, nodding his own politely.

Lord Aragol straightened and passed his hat to the youngest son, who took his brother's as well and held them with his own. The earl glanced at the people around them, then eyed the two on the dais. "We are impressed with your court, Your Highness . . . Your Majesty. And with the extent of your magic, if you can so readily conceal this palace here in the hills and a village at the shore so completely from our eyes . . . though I do not understand why you would squander your magic in such a manner."

"To us, it is not squandering," Kelly countered smoothly. "I am certain you will allow us our reasons for cloaking ourselves from strangers. We are an ancient culture," she added, lying smoothly around the fact that "ancient" in this case meant as of the day before. "This *donjon* alone has stood for more than two thousand years. We respect such a longstanding history and its many traditions. We have moved beyond needlessly making war on other lands, but at the same time we realize some have not matured as far as we have in their own ways and cultures. It is often easier for us to simply 'not be there' while strangers are near our isle, rather than become engaged in confrontations that would lead to pointless annihilations. Stains take forever to scrub out of the carpets, as you may or may not realize."

Saber kept a straight face at her last comment, delivered in a bored tone . . . but only just. He spoke up as soon as she finished with her little speech. "Tell us about your own land, Lord Earl—you call it the 'Independence' of Mandare. Is there a particular reason why?"

The other man straightened with a touch of pride. "We have liberated many of our fellow men from the shackles of oppression in the empire of Natallia. No man is slave to a woman in Mandare," he added, flicking his gaze just for an instant to Kelly and back. "No woman is allowed to practice her magic freely in Mandare. However it may be elsewhere, in our kingdom, men rightfully rule."

Saber looked at him, looked at Kelly, looked back at the earl, and arched a brow, not bothering to hide his smirk. "You think my wife has magic?"

"Your kingdom is rich with it. Obviously it comes from your women, who are the practitioners of witchery," the pompously dressed earl pointed out.

This sounds disgustingly familiar, Kelly thought. *And here I'd thought I'd escaped this kind of prejudice* . . . "You think I am a witch?"

"You are a woman who is queen," Lord Aragol pointed out in return. "Obviously you use your magic to maintain your power."

"I'll have you know I was *elected* to this throne," Kelly returned tartly. "By vote of the citizens of Nightfall, who have confidence in my intelligence and ability to lead them more successfully than anyone else on this island. I rule by the free will of the people; that is the greatest power a ruler can wield . . . and the only power I need to wield.

"As for magic, I cannot even whistle up a wind, save for whatever my own breath might blow. My lord husband possesses magic, but not I. If you think I rule simply because I am a woman, the previous ruler of this island was a man, and the next one might be a woman or a man, whoever is the best person to sit on the throne that day. We of Nightfall see no difference between the genders, save what each person individually has been graced in mind and talent by the gods . . . and we value the talents of our minds far more than the extent of our magics."

"We respect each other, Lord Earl," Saber added, lifting his wife's hand for a brief kiss. She gripped it back, entwining their fingers again as he continued. "That is how one prevents battle. By respecting differences, respecting similarities . . . respecting boundaries . . ."

Lord Aragol smiled diplomatically. "I think, once we have come to know each other's ways, we will come to . . . to respect each other greatly. Perhaps we should be shown to our chambers now, so we can refresh ourselves from the long walk up the hill?"

Saber smiled. It wasn't as diplomatic as the earl's. "We regret that we do not make a habit of providing accommodations for unexpected visitors. But we will provide a ride back down to Whitetide Bay for your belongings and your sailors, and for yourselves later in the day. Lord Secretary."

"Yes, Your Highness?" Koranen asked, stepping forward.

"Arrange to send these good sailors back down to the harbor," Saber instructed his younger brother. "Include a keg of stout to cheer them on their way back down, since they have had such a long walk uphill."

"Yes, Your Highness." He moved off to fulfill the keg part of the task himself, since no one could expect an illusion, however tactile, to be strong enough to lift a keg or smart enough to know where to find it, or to safely drive the horseless wagon afterward.

"You do not provide chambers for us?" the elder son, Kennal, asked skeptically. "When my father is a representative of our king?"

"We would not provide accommodations for the King and Queen of Katan, our best and closest neighbors, should they come here without our direct invitation," Kelly pointed out. "You are still very unfamiliar with our ways; only those who truly understand Nightfall are invited to stay."

"The Lord of Night would not take kindly to strangers wandering the halls in the middle of the night, searching for a refreshing room," Saber added as the young man opened his mouth to argue the point. "There is a reason why this land is called Nightfall. Rest assured, we will be certain you are safely on your ship when night does fall."

"The 'Lord of Night'?" Lord Aragol inquired, arching one brow.

Kelly suppressed a smile, more than ready to relate the tale which Rydan—with his rare sense of humor—had concocted for them in sparse but precise words over dinner, so they could have a plausible reason for keeping the strangers from having access to the castle at night, when their own defenses would be lowered. Night was a time when ambush and treachery were more likely to succeed, because most of the brothers would be exhausted from working throughout the day. Kelly had offered her own extradimensional twist to his suggested tale, which had tickled the most unusual inhabitant of their isle no end, making him actually smile for the second time in as many days. In fact, she had gone back to Morganen afterward and requested he fetch just a few more items from her world, namely, books describing in stories and legends several variations on what she had related, for Rydan to read and enjoy.

The borrowed legend would certainly ensure that their unwelcome visitors remained off the island and away from its "people." None of their illusions could hold up to that length of exposure, and all of the real inhabitants of Nightfall knew it. With a straight face, Kelly filled in the three foreigners on the "legend" in question.

"The Lord of Night rules the hours between dusk and dawn; not even my place as queen is above his ultimate rule, though as a native, I am of course safe from his powers. He has been here since before the Kingdom of Nightfall was founded. In fact, he was here long before then, though none can say exactly how long. He tolerates our presence because we respect him, and we respect his privacy. As per our agreement with him, Nightfall holds all uninvited strangers at bay from our isle, so that none disrupt his rest by day . . . and none dare disturb his path at night, lest they find him drinking their blood."

Saber continued as the trio of men gave her uncertain looks. "The Lord of Night roams the whole of the island at night; he tolerates nothing to get in his way. Those who belong here are as safe as babes in their parents' arms, but those who do not belong here . . ." Saber shrugged lightly. "Stains are indeed hard to clean from the carpets if any dares to resist his hunger, and bloodless corpses are hard to explain if the unwelcome intruder has relatives who might ask too many questions. So we discourage visitors from wanting to stay after nightfall. It is simply easier that way."

"You have our royal reassurances, Lord Aragol, you and your men are perfectly safe while sunlight illuminates this land—provided you are polite and obey the laws and ways of Nightfall, of course," Kelly added as Koranen came back, murmured to the sailors, and led the way out to the eastern courtyard, where Trevan was no doubt waiting to drive them back down to the shore. "We will see that you are escorted safely back to your ship by sunset; it is not our intention to see you harmed in any way, after all. That would be impolite.

"Now, if you wish to refresh yourselves, the Lord Chancellor is our chosen representative to deal with your needs while we finish with the matters of our court; he has our faith and trust to handle these matters well."

"We should be free from the obligations of our court to join you in about half an hour," Saber added. "Since the weather is good, perhaps you would enjoy the delights of the southwestern gardens while you await our leisure? Lord Chancellor, do show them the gardens when they have refreshed themselves. Our gardeners have put a lot of effort into making them bloom, and it would be a shame to let their efforts pass unappreciated."

Both of them nodded regally, dismissing the trio.

Lord Aragol bowed, his sons bowed, and they backed up three steps and turned, rejoining the Lord Chancellor. Some of the illusionary courtiers in the hall nodded politely, some murmured pleasant greetings, and then Dominor led them into the south wing, first to a sitting room with an attached refreshing room so they could refresh themselves, then through a door into the set of gardens that had been already designated as the "holding area" for their visitors.

When they were all out of the donjon hall, the noblemen with Dominor and the sailors with Koranen when he reappeared to escort them away, when only illusions surrounded the pair on the aquamarine-padded "throne," Kelly slumped back into the silk-padded seat. "Whew! That was one heck of a performance—now I see why finishing school is so expensive."

" 'Finishing' school?" Saber asked.

"Where young ladies of wealthy or important background are sent to learn manners, etiquette, and how to sit with perfect, regal posture. To 'finish' their training in manners and deportment. Naturally, I never went," she added wryly, stretching her arms and back. A quick lean forward and peek through the milling, murmuring courtiers that were really small glass marbles, and she dug her fingers into her scalp, freeing the crown and scratching with great relief at her head, mussing her hair. "Boy, am I glad I only decided to do this when visitors drop by!"

"And on weekends, and 'holidays,' whatever those are," Saber added, teasing her.

"When this is over, we'll *need* a holiday. I hope Dominor can handle this part," she sighed. "That Lord Aragol doesn't look like he cares for biting his tongue in the presence of a woman with more rank than him." Kelly frowned thoughtfully. "I wonder what caused this cultural attitude of his, to have such arrogant antipathy toward women."

"*I* wonder when this Disaster will be over with, so I can carry you back up to our room," Saber muttered. "Curse or no Curse, no man should have to be so constantly interrupted on his honeymoon."

His wife flashed him a smile as she stood and stretched. "Poor baby."

Only the more sophisticated illusions appeared to notice the consort hauling the queen onto his lap and giving her a heated kiss. The rest continued chatting superficially with each other, as they were enspelled to do.

TWENTY-ONE

※ ❧ ❧ ❧ ※

Is it true that the woman who claims to lead you has no magic?"
Sir Eduor asked Dominor.

Dominor slanted his blue eyes toward the younger man, nineteen at most and too young to sport any serious facial hair; his brother looked to be about twenty-two, five years younger than Dominor, with a mustache and the beginnings of sideburns and beard, and the father was clearly in his mid-forties, currently the last to use the refreshing room. Dominor wasn't very impressed with them. "She leads us in truth; she does not *claim* to lead us. Be careful how you phrase things, young one. Her Majesty might take offense, and you would not like the consequences of her displeasure."

His brother, Sir Kennal, snorted. "If she has no magic, then there is nothing to fear from her."

Smiling to himself, Dominor wished he could convince his sister-

in-law to teach him that "dirt-eating" move of hers; here was an arrogant young cuss in need of a little soil-tasting. "Then you are a fool.
Magic and gender have nothing to do with power. But tell me," he
continued smoothly, "in the interest of getting to know each other
more, why did you assume our queen has magical power?"

"Because magic flows through the veins of women," the elder
son pointed out, as if it were an obvious fact.

Dominor arched a brow. "Only through the veins of women?"

"Of course!" Eduor asserted. "Except for the rare, blessed man
born with a drop of it in his blood, but that is less than one in a hundred thousand men."

Kennal eyed Dominor, as the door to the refreshing room opened
and his father came out. "You seem surprised by this fact, Lord Chancellor."

"Of course I do. All of the inhabitants of Nightfall use magic,
regardless of gender; even those who do not possess the gift use the
magics of others in their everyday lives," Dominor stated truthfully. Since Kelly could use a scrying mirror that was activated for
her, and had been given a dagger that was enspelled to come when
she called it, it was the absolute truth. "It is the same in the empire
of Katan.

"I myself am the third most powerful mage on the whole of
Nightfall Island, and rank well among the highest on the mainland of
Katan, which has tens of thousands of mages among its five million
inhabitants. But then both my mother *and* my father had magery in
their veins."

"You are a mage?" Lord Aragol asked, hazel eyes sharpening
with interest as he studied the Lord Chancellor standing before him.
"A very powerful one, compared to the rest of your people? How
strong is your magic, exactly?"

"Why do you ask?" Dominor inquired, arching his brow again.

The earl lifted his goatee-covered chin. "The Independence of Mandare could always use strongly gifted men in its fight against the tyranny of Natallian women and their immoral witchery. If you or any of the other magically gifted men of Nightfall come back with us, we can not only finish securing our borders through our war machines, but expand them greatly with the aid of your magical powers, and claim what is rightfully ours: dominion over Natallia. Any magically gifted man who came with us and aided us would automatically become a great lord and gain equally great land and wealth for his service."

"I serve Nightfall Isle," Dominor reminded the man, carefully hiding his offense at the suggestion; he was arrogant, not misogynistic. Still, leaving an opening for gaining more knowledge about these people later on, he amended diplomatically, "But I will keep your words in mind. Come, let me show you the southwestern gardens; they contain a number of rare plants that are quite interesting to behold."

Strolling with Saber and nodding cordially to their "subjects"—a handful of illusory courtiers and a pair of gardeners—Kelly spotted the quartet of real bodies standing near one of the more elaborate fountains in the southwest gardens, close to the outer wall. When she had first arrived here, the water had been stagnant with scum and weeds, moss and vines clinging to the carved figures. Faucet corks had bottled up most of the pipe openings, reducing the water flow to an algae-slimed trickle here and there.

Now everything was pristine, sparkling, polished, and gleaming. She could see the marble and granite tiles laid in pastel patterns lining the pools, where pipes splashed and poured free. From granite carvings of sea horses spouting water in intricate, overlapping, liquid arches, to oversized marble flower petals arranged in bouquet-tiers, from urn-carrying statues of women and men, to friezes artfully depicting scenes of courtly love among the splashing, gleaming pools, the view of these particular gardens formed a sensual delight. Now that they were clean, that was.

Lord Aragol spied them as they came near and pasted on a gracious smile. "Your Highness . . . Your Majesty. These gardens are indeed quite intricate, and worth the time to see them. Were these fountains carved by magic, or carved by hand?"

Kelly raised her brows. "I think I would have to look in the castle records, Lord Aragol," she apologized lightly. "But I would think by both; magic often speeds the labor in our lives, and the skills of hand and eye ensures the artistry that inspired the work is still retained."

He smiled a smug smile between his mustache and goatee. "But labor that can be done by the hand alone is more impressive . . . especially when it is done with the aid of machinery designed by the mind, and not by mere magic alone. How would you raise that stone bench over there, Your Majesty? To lift it completely off the ground?"

She eyed the bench in question, a long, curved, solid granite one that could probably seat six or seven people; it probably weighed four hundred pounds, easily. "I could ask the Lord Chancellor, or my husband, to move it by magic," she pointed out, playing along with his game. "Or many others who are so gifted here on Nightfall; that would be the swiftest way to ensure its movement."

"But what if you could not use magic?" the earl asked slyly. "What if you had to do it without any magic at all?"

"There are plenty of strong backs and hands who would be willing to help me lift it in concert," she returned mildly, "and they would help me to do so even if I were not queen. We of Nightfall tend to help one another; it is the civilized thing to do."

"But what if you were alone? *I* could lift this stone bench using the intelligence of my mind, Your Majesty," he claimed. "Using machinery that I could design and create with just a few simple tools, I could lift it clear off the ground, *without* any magic."

"We are not unfamiliar with the applications of nonmagical machinery, Lord Earl. If *I* were alone," Kelly added dryly, "and for some reason needed to lift that bench, I would simply construct a tripod-mounted block-and-pulley system, probably with a ratio of ten-to-one, so that I only have to lift, what, forty pounds instead of four hundred at each pull? Albeit at ten times the length of rope pulled for the distance required to be lifted, but then that is the mechanics of simple machinery."

The technical terms rattling out of Kelly's mouth made the nobleman's smug look fade a little.

"Or I could lift it with a wedge-style, gear-assisted jack-lift, simply by turning the gears with a handle to achieve sufficient torque through the sprocket shaft to lift that much granite with a minimum of physical effort," Kelly continued, quelling the urge to give him a superior smirk. *You're not going to win this one, Lord Arrogant*, she thought, giving him an eloquent shrug. *My homeworld is vastly superior in its technology to yours.* "And by using two jacks, one at each end, I could lift the entire bench off the ground, as your hypothetical task requires."

The earl and his two sons blinked. Saber and Dominor got that slightly glazed look in their eyes that told her she was talking like a computer-geek to them.

Suppressing the urge to smile, she continued. "Or I could use an air-compression-based wedge of some kind to use the pounds-per-square-inch natural law of air pressure, by simply pumping the handle of the appropriate device to force the bench up into the air on an inflatable bladder of some kind, much as placing an airtight sack under a book and inflating the bag with a strongly blown breath will subsequently lift the book. There are *many* ways to complete the task proposed without using magic, Lord Earl," she added with a shrug. "We are not unfamiliar with them. Technology has many merits. And many drawbacks, just as magic has. Magic in many ways is just simpler to use, here on Nightfall."

"But magic requires a magician able to wield it," Lord Aragol pointed out. "We have very few male magicians in Mandare. We have therefore explored many nonmagical means to do all that we need to do." He looked at his sons, then smiled and stroked his goatee. "Your Majesty . . . could I trouble one of your servants to bring out a melon, or some other large-sized fruit, and have them set it on that pedestal over there, by the outer wall?"

"For what purpose?" Saber asked him.

"I would prove that Mandarite machinery is superior to magic."

And here it comes; I'll bet this is a demonstration of their flintlock guns to frighten us into acknowledging their superiority . . . She and Morganen had already prepared for this moment, however. "Lord Chancellor, would you see to it?" Kelly asked Dominor. "Bring back several melons, please. They would be pleasant to eat on such a warm summer's day, if nothing else."

"Certainly, Your Majesty." With a bow to her, he headed for the nearest wing of the castle. The Nightfallers and the Mandarites eyed each other and spoke of how pleasant the weather was, the delights of the garden, the hope that the weather would continue good for a few more days, until the well of small talk dried up between the two groups.

Saber switched from Mandarite to Katani and murmured in Kelly's ear, tucking her against his side as they waited. "Do you know what the man is up to? I do not like this Earl's smugness . . . though I loved your quick replies. What little I could understand of them."

"I think he's going to demonstrate the power of the flintlock guns each one of them is wearing," she murmured back with a little smile. Switching between the languages sounded to her ear simply like switching between accents. From the puzzled look of their guests, it was a successful, obfuscating switch. "I figured he might, at some point. Guns are very impressive—and *very* loud, just to warn you—when wielded in front of those unfamiliar with their effects."

"Is that your native tongue?" Edour spoke up with a touch of curiosity. "I thought you said you would speak solely in ours while we were here."

"We speak in endearments meant to be exchanged by husband and wife alone," Saber returned smoothly. "We value our privacy, if you have not figured it out by now."

Kelly smiled up at him through the half foot difference in their height as he said it, then returned her gaze to the trio of men before them. "With respect comes admiration, gentlemen; it is a natural progression. My husband knows well that I respond well to sweet words, and poorly to sour. As he prefers me to be a gentlewoman more often than a termagant whenever I am around him, he speaks sweetly to me. And I prefer him to be a gentleman, rather than a bully, so I speak sweetly to him in return.

"We of Nightfall understand this give-and-take," she continued smoothly. "It takes great strength of character to respond to an uncivility with politeness. But then, if one person is polite, it is easier for the other person to be polite as well. Just as, when one person acts in violence, the other is often more inclined out of hurt or spite to act the same. It is simply a matter of overcoming one's base immaturity and responding with wisdom.

"Ah, Lord Chancellor, you have returned."

Dominor, carrying a basket of melons, nodded and moved to place the first one on the stone shelf indicated, one in a set of eight decorative pillars that normally had urns of flowers growing on top; two had lost their urns to weather damage, so the brothers had just cleared away the remains and shifted the other pots so that the bare ones flanked the other six. Now they looked intentionally left bare.

He set the basket of fruit at the base, adjusted the melon on top so that it would not roll, then returned to the others.

"Why do you do this work yourself?" Sir Kennal asked him, frowning at the Lord Chancellor in confusion. "You are a lord of your realm; that is a servant's task, something fit for a woman to do."

"I find myself intrigued to know what your father intends to do, young lord," Dominor stated smoothly, as Kelly's brows drew down at the blatant insult to her gender. "And too impatient to have a servant summoned away from some other, more important task when I could do this all the more quickly myself. We are not lazy, here on Nightfall, Sir Kennal. Each citizen of the isle is more than capable of doing many things for themselves—our queen, for example, is a warrior in her own right."

I just knew he'd work that in, somehow, Kelly thought, doing her best to not smile as she shook her head ruefully. "You flatter me, Lord Chancellor, but I have my husband to champion and protect me these days; I need nothing more."

At her sincere praise, Saber felt his chest swell, expanding a little with masculine pride. Considering that she had made *him* "eat dirt" more times than she had tossed Dominor to the floor—twice to just once—he felt pleasure at her confidence in his own abilities. Saber marshaled his attention back to their surroundings; he wasn't really the Lord Protector of the isle, nor was she the Queen, nor his brother the Lord Chancellor . . . and yet they still had to flawlessly maintain the illusion that they were. "Lord Aragol, I believe you were going to make some sort of point, by having us fetch these fruit?"

"Quite," the earl stated. He shifted over, placed the pillar and its fiber-hulled melon between him and the slightly curved outer wall, then stepped back several paces, putting half a dozen yards between him and the pillars by the outer wall, flanking this side of the many-streamed fountain they had been standing in front of for their conversation. "You may wish to stand behind me, so that you are safe."

His sons quickly moved back behind him, so the other three did as well. Kelly flipped her hand discreetly at the courtiers in the garden, and Dominor and Saber muttered under the splashing cover of the fountains, redirecting the "strolling" illusions to make certain none strolled near them.

"Observe the power of a man's intellect, Majesty, and the might that is our machinery." Drawing the flintlock pistol from the embossed leather holster slung on his hip across from his sword, he aimed the barrel across his forearm and flicked the flintlock lever hard.

BANG!

While Saber and Dominor jumped from the too-loud explosion, Kelly merely winced. The melon jumped and half-exploded in the same instant as the noise, scattering small chunks of itself from the back end. All of them coughed a second or two later as grayish, acrid gunpowder residue wafted around them, dispersing and dissipating slowly in the soft breeze meandering through the garden.

Eyes gleaming at both the sting of the acrid smoke and the triumph of his demonstration, Lord Aragol faced them, the still-smoking barrel pointed toward the sky. "This is a piece of machinery that hurls a ball of iron at speeds far greater than any magical shield can protect against. Lord Chancellor, you are a mage, you said? Please, replace the melon with a fresh one and cast a protective shield around it. Your strongest one if you please . . . then come back here and stand behind me again, for your safety."

Dominor paced to the pedestal, examined the roughly pierced fruit, then shifted and dropped it onto the ground and put a fresh one in its place. He murmured, flexing his fingers, until the air around the melon and pedestal began to glow. Then stepped back from the fuzzy-white ball, reminiscent of a blurry moon, and joined the others as it solidified. Resembling a lightglobe, only on a larger scale, it completely enveloped the melon and the top of the pedestal.

"Kennal, if you would be so kind?" the father asked his eldest son, gesturing toward the spot he had used as he stepped back out of the way. The young man stepped into place, drew his own weapon, aimed on his forearm, and struck the flint with the trigger.

BANG!

Nothing appeared to have happened this time, aside from the very loud, abrupt sound and a second, equally acrid cloud.

"I believe, Lord Chancellor," Kennal asserted as he lowered his weapon, "that when you remove your magic, you will find that the pellet has successfully penetrated your shield. Our flintlock guns fling the pellets so fast and hard, not even magic can stand in their way. *These* are the weapons that give Mandare its independence, so named as our men dared to resume our rightful place in the universe."

Striding to the pedestal, Dominor snapped his fingers, canceling the shield-globe. He stared at the melon, his blue-clad back blocking the view for everyone else. Finally, he picked it up after a moment and carried it back, displaying the hole that came in one side, but did not go out the other. Digging his fingers into the opening, he cracked the melon in half with a display of the physical strength all of the brothers shared, and showed Kelly and Saber how the bullet had lodged almost to the far side of the orange pink flesh.

Kelly plucked the ball from the fruit and examined it. The iron sphere, no bigger than a fingernail, was still quite hot, though not quite enough to scorch her fingertips.

Saber took it from her, examining the pellet. "Interesting."

"Isn't it? And we have more of these. Machines that can hurl iron balls the size of a man's fist," Lord Aragol added.

"Yes. I must admit this has been an interesting demonstration," Kelly added mildly. "Lord Dominor, would you be a dear and put one more melon on the pedestal, for me this time?"

"As you wish, Your Majesty." With a little bow, he strode back, dropped the melon halves with the other decimated one, and put one of the remaining fruit on the stone surface.

"You care for another demonstration, Your Majesty?" Lord Aragol asked as Dominor completed his task and came back. "My other son can demonstrate with his pistol as well, if you wish . . ."

"Your flintlock pistols are very intriguing, Lord Earl," Kelly stated, reaching behind her, under the back hem of her vest-tunic. "I confess it has been some time since I last saw such a weapon. But I must apologize at not being perhaps as impressed as you clearly hoped I would be," she added gently, apologetically. Smiling, Kelly pulled out the 9-mm handgun Morganen had fetched across the dimensions for her in preparation for this event.

Flicking the safety, Kelly checked the chamber. Along with kung fu lessons, her parents had insisted on a course in gun safety when she had gone to college. Now she lifted the weapon, aimed, and squeezed off four rapid rounds.

BAM! BAM! BAM! BAM!

As the echoes and the thinner cloud of smoke died away, Kelly was grateful to see she had hit the melon enough at this distance to tear it to chunks, rather than ignobly missing after being so long out of practice. As more of the acrid smoke cleared—though there was less with the use of her weapon than had been involved with the Mandarites'—she restored the safety and returned the gun to the back of her outfit, tucking it into the holster hidden there. "As you can see, we have long since progressed beyond that level of mechanical technology."

"May I see that weapon, Majesty?" Lord Aragol asked, holding out his hand. For the first time since his arrival, his tone conveyed nothing but full respect for her . . . and it was clearly astonished admiration for the superior gun she had used, not for herself, a mere female.

"No, you may not, milord," Kelly returned firmly, flatly. "Such

things are not meant for the hands of those not yet mature enough
to wield them responsibility. We hold enough knowledge of nonmagical technology to gouge this island right out of the sea, to reduce it to black slag, glass, and ash; we simply do not care to be so
idiotic as to *use* such weapons."

"You have weapons that can reduce this entire, large island to
rubble?" Kennal repeated. "Why do you not use those weapons to
take over the whole of the world?"

"If you pride yourselves on your intelligence, Lord Aragol, Sir
Kennal, Sir Eduor, as you seem to want to impress us that you do,
then you tell *me*—what do you gain from using weaponry on that
scale of power?" Kelly countered, suppressing an impatient roll of
her eyes. "Land? Food? Minerals? Subjects to rule over? The land
itself is blackened beyond use, the soil burned of all nutrients, the
minerals slagged into useless dross, the buildings reduced to rubble,
the plants and animals and people seared to vapor—what, exactly,
would you gain?"

"You could simply threaten your enemies with the use of the
weapon," Lord Aragol pointed out. "If such machinery exists, it could
terrorize a whole continent into your power."

"Or it could more likely frighten them into making a similar
weapon of their own . . . and then *they* would use it against *you*. And
then you would be very, very dead," Kelly stated flatly. "The only
way to gain anything in a war is to *stop* the war, before it starts. Before it goes any farther. The only way to survive violence is to end
the violence. The best way to find prosperity is to encourage peace."

"The only way you can defeat these Natallians you fight," Dominor added, joining her argument, "is to make peace with them. You
say you developed nonmagical ways to fight these magic-wielding
women of Natallia. Even now they could be working on a way to
counter your machinery with more powerful magic, or even nonmagical machinery of their own . . . and then *your* land would eventually

become a blackened crater. It is only a victory when both sides are still alive to realize it, after all."

"We know why you are really here," Kelly stated, seizing on that much information with her quick mind and embellishing. "You came here seeking land to expand into, easy resources to conquer. As yet, your current level of technology prevents you from completely countering the level of these Natallians' magic. You attempted to claim this island so that you could have a land far from their influence in which to raise men to believe that women are inferior to you in all ways. Women are created different, not inferior, nor superior. Just different.

"We feel sorry for you," she continued, "that you are so afraid of such insignificant things as the differences between men and women, you feel you must try and prove yourself superior in such infantile ways."

"Infantile ways!" Lord Aragol protested.

"Yes. Your displays of immature arrogance, and your unjustifiable, barely veiled threats of violence and hostility," Kelly reminded him. "You offered them, thinking we'd be stupid enough to not notice . . . but we have. I can only hope and pray that your intelligence saves you from the course of folly that you currently sail before it is too late, before you destroy yourselves. As you are now, you are blinded to the lethal shoals that currently await you, ahead and below the surface of the tossing waves that are all you let yourselves see," she concluded.

"Nightfall, and the land that lies beyond it to the west, Katan, do not care for your petty quarrels," Saber added, resting his palms on her shoulders as he faced the trio of strangers. "You may come here to trade in peace, or you may go to Katan and trade in peace. But you would do well to not bring your troubles here to our lands.

"It would be best if you left your antiquated weapons behind, when you do come to trade; we will barter peacefully with you, if you come peacefully before us, but if you choose to fight . . . you will not win. As it is, you would do well to tread carefully while you are here," he warned the trio of men. "Nightfall is protected by its superior technology, its superior magic, and the Lord of Night, whose wrath is the most powerful of all when roused to the defense of this land. Katan, which lies to the east, has the combined might of the Council of Mages and its own vast array of resources, magical and otherwise, to defend itself with. Neither land will tolerate violence or aggression aimed its way."

"Do not mistake our words for a threat," Dominor murmured as the trio of men glared at them in affront. "This is the most well-meant of advice only, garnered through ages of wisdom and experience, and offered to you freely in the hopes that you are citizens of a wise culture. One we wouldn't mind trading with in the future, when you are invited to come back to Nightfall again."

"If you *truly* want to get the best of your foe, you must prove you *are* superior. Not by machines and technology," Kelly warned them, "but by being smarter than they are and bringing an end to your conflict through honest, respectful peace. You must prove yourself superior by being willing to compromise at least a little, if others are too stubborn to bend. Otherwise you and your enemy *both* will break, wither, and die, like a tree that snaps under pressure when it refuses to sway in the wind.

"And one more kind word. Do not make the mistake of thinking that the rulers of this other land, Natallia, think the same way that you do. If their rulers are women, then I tell you as a woman that they will not think as you do. Your weapons will not prove your superiority to females, as they might to a fellow male. The use of violence and brute force in the quest for superiority *never* impresses women."

Lord Aragol said nothing; he eyed her with a shuttered expression, eyed her husband where Saber stood behind her. His sons looked as doubting, wary, and skeptical as he did. Finally he spoke, looking at Saber, not at Kelly. "You would not be so lenient and forgiving if you had a foe as arrogant as the Natallians are. You would be at the whims and mercy of your wife, and you would not be accounted her equal. Men are not meant for such humiliation; we would have things restored to how they were in the ancient days, when *we* ruled the land—"

"You mean the days when women were not allowed to learn how to read or to write," Kelly interrupted, "or to own property, or to decide who they would marry? An age when they were sold to the highest suitor in exchange for land and goods in a dowry, in a humiliation that is nothing more than a pretty name for *slavery*, regardless of their feelings? When they were degraded by men and counted less important than sheep, because while women could produce children, sheep at least could produce lambs *and* wool?" Kelly bit back tightly. "When a woman's choices were to spend her life on her back under her husband as a wife, an object, a *thing* used to clean the house and breed sons, or to spend her life on her back under strangers with the coin for it, being *fu*—"

Saber clamped his hand over her mouth. "Please forgive my wife; she has a bit of a temper. Thankfully, it is only triggered by blatant displays of stupidity, so she does not unleash it often on our own populace."

Kelly peeled his hand away. She wasn't done yet, though she did revert her language back to the polite-vocabulary kind. "It is a *fact*, Lord Aragol, of biology, built into the ways of their flesh as created by the very gods themselves, that while men are stronger than women, women are *smarter* than men, on the average. And brains will *always* defeat mere muscles, magic, or machinery in the end. So if you wish to stand on equal footing with a woman, open your fist and use it to pick up a book, not a weapon.

"Your touted ancestors probably beat their wives with their greater strength, until the gods of your lands gave the minds of your women something even stronger to fight back with, that greater magic than your men possess—but therein lies your very problem," she pointed out, striving hard to keep her tone and expression reasonably polite. "Your mind-set probably *made* them strike back at you. Violence begets violence, my lord. Arrogance breeds arrogance. Pain and humiliation begs only for a future revenge. *You* started the cycle; therefore *you* must be the ones to end it. And until you can end this vicious cycle in your own minds, you cannot end it in your lifetime, and you *will not win*. That is the lesson of history, if you are smart enough to learn it.

"Until then, I suggest you pack up your ship and take your immature, arrogant selves back to your excuse of an 'Independence.' Because until you do, you are chained to your own blind hatred, as surely as if the manacles were right *there* on your wrists," Kelly finished, jabbing her finger at his hands. "*That* is not true independence!"

He flinched back from her finger, scowling at her harsh lecture.

Saber tightened his grip slightly on her shoulders, and Kelly straightened and clasped her hands lightly in front of her. He addressed their visitors, taking over and playing the "good cop" to her "bad." "I think you should return to your homeland, Lord Earl. And think—actually *think*, not just react—about the logic of what has been said here this day. If you come to a point where your people can visit here and leave your attitudes and your quarrels behind, you may come again one day and be welcomed in many ways.

"Until then, Nightfall will have nothing to do with the Disaster that is you. And do not look to Katan, until you can stop being a cultural Disaster and be an intelligent people instead; until the day you can approach them, honestly and most civilized, they will want less than nothing to do with you. I'm afraid that *they* will not be as polite about dealing with you as we have been."

"You will not see us again, until we no longer see what we currently do, when we look at you. It is too ugly and immature a view," Kelly added with a touch of disdain in her recomposed, neutral tone. "Lord Chancellor, arrange transportation for these three to be returned to the beach at Whitetide. Be certain they are on their way before nightfall; if *we* have low tolerance for the words these nobles speak, the Lord of Night will have considerably less so. The blood of fools is his favorite drink, after all. It would not be polite to detain them overnight."

"As you command, Your Majesty."

"*Bekh!*" Kelly asserted, flipping her hand in an imperious snap. A beat behind her, Saber blanked them from view with a hidden twist of his own wrist. A moment behind that, and all of the illusory courtiers and servants in the distance vanished from view, triggered by his and Dominor's magics.

Dominor stood alone with the three Mandarites in the garden, silent but for the splashing of the fountains around them.

The third-born, blue-clad son of the island's population sighed, glancing toward the palace as if that were where everyone had vanished to. "I keep forgetting to inform the guards to warn uninvited strangers of the foremost law of Nightfall—don't get Her Majesty mad. She may have a bit of a temper, but that is mostly because she is fiercely protective of her subjects. Blunt though she may sometimes be, her insight into problems is as keen as a healer's knife, cutting away all that is bad.

"I do apologize for her vehemence," Dominor continued diplomatically, "but as you can clearly see, her logic and wisdom are impeccable; *that* is why we choose to follow her and why we tolerate her occasional outbursts of . . . well, to be diplomatic, I'll call it redheadedness," he hedged politely. "Still, she is right in her summation of what our people will and will not tolerate from our uninvited visitors. As Queen, she simply has the right to express herself more directly than the rest of us would deem polite—the privilege of being a monarch, you know," he added to the men still standing with him. "Now, as I choose to obey my queen, this is the way to the eastern courtyard, gentlemen, if you will kindly follow me . . ."

"We're actually being kicked off this island?" Sir Kennal exclaimed, outraged. "Right now?"

His father held up his gloved hand, silencing him. "Inform Her Majesty that we will sail with the evening tide. But we *will* return, and when we do, our *next* meeting—"

The foppishly clad man whirled, stumbled, and flipped, with no apparent reason for his odd behavior. Dominor blinked. His sons stared down at him. The man's hat was askew, his cheek pressed to the paved pathway they stood on. It was a familiar position for Dominor; thankfully, he wasn't the one being pinned that way. This time.

"By the Rights of Man!" the earl exclaimed, startled out of his threat. If a bit mushily, since his upper cheek was pressing his lower cheek into the ground and his arm was twisted up in the air awkwardly behind him. "What is this that *has* me?"

Dominor bit the inside of his cheek to keep from laughing. His sister-in-law had done it again, and he couldn't even *see* it this time to study the moves his brother's mate had made! He managed to recover his composure and speak in a calm tone, rather than an amused one.

"I believe your speech implied a threat toward the inhabitants of this isle, Lord Earl; that threat was most likely perceived by the Lord of Night in his sleep. He is dangerous even in his dreams . . . and you have clearly lost Her Majesty's protection from his wrath, in being requested to depart the isle. Be glad he but only dreams about this moment and has not actually awakened. His terror then would be horrible to behold. His thirst for the blood of the unwelcome and the impolite is legendary in this land."

"Don't just stand there—help me! How do I make it let go?" the frantic man demanded, struggling and gasping when his own movements only increased the pain pressuring him in place. His boots and hose-clad knees scrabbled against the paving stones, the edge of a nearby flower bed, but he couldn't get enough purchase to free himself from the invisible hold pinning him to the ground. His sons hurried forward to help him up, but were thrust back by another invisible force, shoved back repeatedly from trying to even get within a couple feet of their father. Lord Aragol struggled harder, eyes wide as he squirmed around just enough to gaze up at Dominor, but not enough to get himself free. "*Help* me!"

"I suggest, with nothing but absolute honesty and humble sincerity in your speech, that you apologize thoroughly for even thinking of threatening Nightfall . . . and state with the truth of it lodged firmly in your heart that you will do everything in your power to make certain that you and your fellow Mandarites, should you ever visit this portion of the world again, will behave with the utmost of politeness, respect, and civility," Dominor offered smoothly as the earl's arm bobbled a little with his struggles, still caught in the invisible grip twisting it up into the air. The third-born of the brothers added blandly, "Sometimes the Lord of Night is known to extend his protection across the sea to the west, to the shores of Katan, our nearest and best-loved neighbor, if the source of his irritation is great enough to engender his personal attention. It is speculated that he may have come from there, originally, and still harbors some small, lingering affection for the mainland, though Nightfall is now clearly his domain. As you can unfortunately see."

"Apologize?" Lord Aragol managed to gasp through the pressure squeezing his head, and the jerk of his air-pinned arm. His sons gave up and stood a few yards away, unable to get close enough to help their father.

"Apologize. With great sincerity," Dominor confirmed soberly. "For all of your offenses."

"I . . . I apologize for ever thinking less than civilized thoughts about such a powerful island kingdom." The pressure eased slightly, visible by the way his arm stopped being torqued as much. "I apologize . . . for being arrogant around this island's . . . queen." His head was released, though he was still locked on the ground by absolute nothing pressing on his shoulder. The earl worked his mouth, his mustached and bearded lips, then tried one more time. "I apologize most sincerely for implying Mandare would return in force to this isle . . . and I will accept the advice given to me by its people. I will even advise my people to conduct themselves most politely and peacefully, should they ever come here again."

Kelly, invisible even to herself, which was why she'd had an awkward moment in first trying to grab him, released him completely. She backed up, bumped into Saber, who had been holding off the annoying, foppish man's sons, and they both backed up a few more steps to get out of the way. Lord Aragol flexed his arm and worked his neck, then pushed warily to his feet. His youngest son scooped up his broad-brimmed hat, holding it out to him while the earl brushed off his elaborate clothes.

Dominor tipped his head, listening to Evanor's voice projected solely to him. The others not in sight were either watching the ship or watching the three men left among them through scrying mirrors, back inside the donjon. He nodded to the trio of Mandarites.

"I believe there is a cart waiting in the eastern courtyard to take you back down to your ship even as we speak. Please, do not take offense at what has happened, Lord Aragol, young sirs. I *did* say that you should watch what you do and say while you are here," he added as they reluctantly started moving around the outer wings of the palace to reach the eastern courtyard without reentering the palace itself. "It is another reason why we do not encourage visitors. Most end up accidentally putting their foot in their mouth, by speaking without thinking . . . and thus most end up eating the dirt that is clinging to said foot."

Saber held on to Kelly until the quartet of men were well out of sight and out of hearing range. He had felt her start to quiver at his brother's parting words. A murmured word, and they were visible once more.

She was shaking with laughter, not rage. Turning, gasping with the need for silence, she quivered and quaked in his arms, whispering up at him. "Did you see his *face*? When I pinned it under my heel?" she demanded harshly, her freckled features positively red with mirth. "My god—his *face!*"

Tipping his head thoughtfully, Saber had to admit it had been a hilarious sight. But the situation was still a sobering one "Let us just pray that this has dealt with our Disaster. I won't relax until they're gone, either."

TWENTY-TWO

ou will not believe the bargain I struck!" Dominor called out as the cart came back into the castle and the real inhabitants of Nightfall met him at the gate. It was being driven by a disguised Evanor, not Trevan, who was apparently down at the shore, spying on their guests. The third-born of them preened with a pleased, smug smile as he got down from the driving bench. "With the extra water being processed for the fountains and such, we've got a surplus of salt blocks down at the western shore. Salt is something their people cannot process easily, lacking the magic to do it quickly and efficiently—and *they* have a surplus of oil of *comsworg*, which I noticed they use to keep their gun-things oiled and their ship-lanterns lit, and which *we* use in the creation of our lightglobes!

"I am a *consummate* diplomat," the twenty-seven-year-old mage added somewhat arrogantly, striking a pose with his hand splayed on his chest before gesturing at the barrels and keg in question in the bed of the cart behind him. "I have not only smoothed over any ruffled feelings on the ride back to the eastern cove, but I have *also* arranged to trade thirty blocks of salt for two hogsheads and a keg!"

"By Jinga, Brother! Considering the price the traders get for our salt, which they've been taking for free until now, and the price they charge to ship us the comsworg, that's *incredible*, Dom!" Koranen asserted, hazel eyes wide. "That much oil will create . . . a thousand globes per hogshead, plus the keg—*far* more than two thousand lightglobes, maybe even as many as twenty-four hundred!" he calculated gleefully out loud, rubbing his hands together. "And since it's the rarest and most costly ingredient in the artificing process, that means we'll be making a real profit for a full year! And we don't even have to *do* anything to make the salt, other than uncork a fountain or two!"

"Help me get the barrels off the cart—we're going to go fetch the blocks immediately," Dominor added, ordering his brothers with a clap on his twin, Evanor's, shoulder. "*Before* they change their minds and ask for all of this back!"

Kelly frowned; she didn't know why, but something about the bargain sounded a little odd. She didn't stop them when they departed, though. If Dominor had managed to smooth things over enough to arrange a trade of goods, that meant the outlanders weren't going to cause any real trouble, and that was a good thing. Since she didn't know what comsworg-oil was, let alone how or where it was acquired, it was conceivable these Mandarites considered it as common and therefore cheap as the Greeks of her old world had considered olive oil.

For all I know, they might consider salt such a rare commodity, they'd be willing to give up their "lamp oil" for the incredibly pure stuff this island's water system produces daily. Even if their kingdom sits on the edge of the local ocean, salt could still be hard for them to process efficiently. I know it takes a broad, shallow stone beach to successfully sun-dry seawater into salt, without having to burn down all the local forests to boil it off the hard way. Digging into a salt mine might be easier, but first you have to find one.

They don't have magic to speed up the process either way, so they probably are getting a bargain, I guess . . . but I still don't trust them, either way.

Dominor and Evanor came back up from the western side of the isle in half an hour, driving two carts. When Kelly glanced down into the courtyard and saw the size of the salt blocks, each one the size of a perfectly rectangular, grainy white coffin, the seemingly uneven bargain made a little more sense. Even for mere salt versus whatever that type of oil was, that was a *lot* of salt. Perhaps the bargain was worth it.

Turning away from the windows of the great hall, she continued her own assigned chore of picking up all of the illusion-marbles on the ground floor and balcony levels and packing them away in a carefully labeled chest Trevan had found somewhere. The others were going through the castle wings, disabling the illusion-spells set in stones and globes and self-roaming glass marbles, since they no longer needed their castle full of servants and courtiers, nor the great hall to be an audience chamber. Putting away the marbles only required a helping hand, not the magic to dispel the illusions, so that was her job.

It was kind of fun—weird, but fun—to hold up the marbles to the sunlight coming in from the north and see the tiny image of the "person" each one contained reflected in the curved little spheres. A stray thought struck her as she poured yet another handful of illusory people-marbles into the chest, packing them like peas into a box that would be set on a shelf somewhere until they were needed again. The thought made her choke on a laugh the moment it struck, too.

Talk about a canned audience!

Father . . . I'm worried about the salt," Sir Kennal stated, as Dominor and Evanor watched several longboats rowing out to pick up the heavy blocks.

"How so, my son?" Lord Aragol asked, glancing at him.

"We have no magic to keep it from getting wet and being ruined—this is the purest salt I have ever seen, and I would be loath to take it home green from seawater seeping into our hold . . . or stained with the tar of our hull," the elder of the two sons added earnestly.

The earl arched a brow under the brim of his hat and turned to eye Dominor. "You are a mage—is it within your powers to secure the salt in such a way from contamination, in our hold?"

"I could do that, yes," Dominor agreed, pleased at being asked.

"Then we would be very grateful, Lord Chancellor, if you would come out to our ship and make sure our trade stays as worthwhile as it so far seems."

Nodding, Dominor waited with them on the sand for the men to finish getting there. It was a delicate balance that all of them were striving to create, between the need to warn off these men from attacking with their hard-to-stop weapons—that image of the melons exploding, of being pierced even through his tightest shield, would stay with the mage a good, long time—and yet soothing them enough to *not* attack anyway out of overwhelming fear. Watching the waves of the midmorning, outgoing tide, and the broad expanse of wet tidal sand in the way, he nodded toward the oncoming boats. "I will even secure the salt for the longboats, so that it does not get wet between here and your ship. As you can see, when we behave politely and civilly toward each other, cooperation brings far more rewards than others might think."

"Perhaps there is indeed much we could learn from your people," the earl murmured.

"Perhaps there is something we can learn from yours as well."

It didn't take long to load all of the longboats, though they were awkward loads; Dominor's protective spells on each block kept those waves that sloshed over the gunwales from dousing the salt and the crew, repelling the water back into the bay. And with a touch more of his magic, the salt was lifted up onto the deck without any awkward straining of ropes and nets and the fear of the solid but not impervious blocks shattering against the swaying hull.

Nor did it take long for him to enspell the hold where the salt would be kept, adding extra layers of protection on top of the spells laid on the blocks themselves. As soon as he was finished, Dominor climbed up the ladderway and emerged on the deck, letting the sailors start lowering the blocks to the cargo hold down below. Lord Aragol positively beamed at him.

"Our gratitude cannot be expressed enough! Come—I insist on giving you a drink in thanks for your aid, Lord Chancellor!" He clasped his arm around Dominor's taller, broader shoulders and steered him toward one of the aft upper cabins. "I have been saving in my cabin a bottle of the Western Marches' finest vintage—two hundred and seventy-three-year-old *glassip*, as smooth as a virgin's skin," he added, waxing eloquent with a slow, lascivious sweep of his hand. "I'll wager you haven't tasted the like in your life! It's in this cabin up here . . ."

The earl's sons were already in there ahead of them; the elder was finishing the pouring of four goblets of an amber liquid from a dusty, brown-glass bottle. "I opened the bottle to let the *glassip* breathe, Father, just as you said to—Lord Chancellor, we are indeed grateful for the trade of the salt; comsworg is a common oil-berry where we come from, but our climate is too cold to efficiently evaporate seawater in saltpan bays, save in the height of summer. We cannot rely on shipments from the desert lands to the north, with our sea-trade under threat from our enemies. Nor can we purchase the kind dug out of the ground to the east, for that is all Natallian land."

He held out a goblet to Dominor, then passed one to his father, nudged his brother with one, and took one himself.

"To prosperity and independence," Sir Kennal stated, raising his cup.

"To the acceptance of our apologies for our ill behavior," Sir Edour added, at a nudge from his brother.

"To the aid you represent," Lord Aragol added, lifting his own. "It is our custom, Lord Chancellor, to make a toast when drinking the first sip of *glassip*."

"Then to the peaceful exchanges our two peoples may have in the future," Dominor agreed, lifting his own. They all tipped their cups back together.

It *was* a smooth liquor, he discovered. With a dark mint aftertaste that didn't quite bite, but blended in smoothly. It wasn't until he had drunk several swallows more, chatting with the men and finding out that their sea voyage would likely take a full five weeks with good weather and steady winds to complete, that he realized the undertaste was indeed vaguely familiar.

Intrigued, Dominor drank a little more. Corvis lands had produced a liquor from a combination of berries, grain, and a certain herb that was a connoisseur's drink; he had managed to bring along a full case of the bottles in their exile, with the self-imposed vow to drink only one carafe a year. This liqueur was even better than the nostalgia-sweetened Corvis brandy he carefully hoarded. He drained the cup as the brothers teased each other about how seasick they had been at the beginning of their voyage, tasting the dregs where the minty flavor seemed a little stronger, a little more bitter, a little surer in its identity—

Falomel powder. His blue eyes snapped wide. It rendered mages unconscious, their powers useless for hours. Cursing, he tossed aside the cup and lunged for the door. Or tried to. He got one leg into place before the doctored drink caught up with the rest of him. Arms outstretched, he hit the floor ignominiously. Mouth struggling, throat flexing to call out his twin's name, to alert the others, he succumbed all too quickly to the cold and the dark cloaking him, struggling to berate himself for drinking the traitorous libation of their Disaster-borne foe.

On the shore, Evanor frowned. *Is that ship . . . yes, the sails are being unfurled . . .* He watched a little bit longer, waiting for a longboat to be lowered and his twin to come ashore. *The anchor's going up!* Standing up on the wagon, he shaded his eyes—the ship was moving! The sails, filling with the northerly breeze, were moving the Mandarite ship away from the shore!

"*Dominor!*" He focused his will, focused his voice, determined to reach his twin. "*Dominor, can you hear me?*"

Nothing. No reply. He could tell his twin was still alive, at least. There was a resonance between them, tied from the moment they had first shared their mother's womb, and sensitized by Evanor's affinity for all sorts of vibrations . . . but he could tell nothing more.

"*Dominor!*" Whirling when he still got no answer, he called out to the trees. "*Trevan! They're kidnapping Dominor!*"

Moments later, a golden eagle burst from the trees. It shrieked and beat hard after the ship, while Evanor waited impatiently on the sand. He watched the eagle soar closer, watched it dip down toward the ship when it got out there. Five seconds later, a gunshot echoed back to him, just as a shape wobbled over the rail and down, dropping into the water.

Evanor knew the view of what was happening traveled faster than its sounds, and realized what that sound and that sight meant. Heart in his throat, Evanor leaped out of the cart he was sitting on. Hitting the ground at a run, he raced toward the waterline. He splashed into the water, uncaring of the waves, trying to get close enough to do something, anything, to stop what was happening to his two brothers.

Agonizing minutes later, a shape bobbed toward him, a seal with reddish fur. Blood seeped from its back and shoulder. Evanor grabbed Trevan, supporting the gasping creature, even as it shifted with bared teeth and a barely caught-back moan of pain. He looked at the wound, as bloodied fur became bloodied cloth, and peered into Trevan's pain-glazed eyes . . . then looked up at the ship, as the wind caught its sails in full, carrying it away along with the still-receding tide.

Cursing, the fourth-born brother splashed back toward the shore, hauling his younger brother through the waist-high water. There was no telling how bad the wound was, or what kind of damage the gun-weapon could do—only their new sister, Kelly, could tell them what needed to be done to heal Trevan's injury.

It hurt with every heavily burdened step he took, abandoning his abducted twin.

Kelly! Trevan has been shot by a gun-thing!"

Kelly gasped and dropped the banner she had been taking down. It fluttered to the floor far below, causing Koranen to shout and cover his head, running under the balcony for protection as the wooden bar across the top of the long, color-shifting cloth sailed straight at him.

"Watch what you're *doing*!" he yelled up at her, even as the wooden rod clattered hard on the stone floor.

"Trevan's been *shot*!" she shouted back, abandoning the balcony railing in a sprint for the eastern courtyard. Of course, Evanor wasn't there yet, and she paced worriedly as the others gathered, summoned by Koranen.

Minutes later, Evanor and one of the carts rattled into the courtyard, sliding as he locked the wheels just long enough to stop. Jumping down, he grabbed Saber. "They took Dominor! They did something to him—they lured him onto their ship," Evanor restarted with a shake of his head as the others exclaimed. Kelly was already climbing into the bed of the wagon, as he told them what had happened. "They made a fuss about the salt getting contaminated by the algae in seawater, or by the tar in their ship hull and the bilgewater, so he went with them to secure their hold with his magic—and then they set sail with him! When I couldn't rouse him, Trevan gave chase, and they shot him with their gun-thing!"

Kelly, examining the wound in Trevan's chest, had to look away after only a moment. She blanched at the mess of the injury, the rhythmic spurting of the blood from a torn artery. Pressing her hand over the wound to apply pressure made her aware of the warmth of the blood seeping free. She had to lean over the side of the wagon cart, breathing hard, as Koranen took over for her. Injuries greater than scratches and scrapes always made her feel ill, and the feel of the blood trying to escape against her hand was not something she ever wanted to experience again. At least the strawberry-copper haired man was unconscious, so he wasn't suffering much at the moment.

Morganen caught her shoulder, shook her. "Kelly! Focus! You know what this weapon does—*how* do we treat it?"

She compressed her lips, drew in a deep breath, and pulled her wits together. Doyles didn't throw up at the sight of a little—okay, a *lot*—of blood. "I have to check to see if the bullet lodged in his body, or if it passed through." Bracing herself, she turned and carefully rolled Trevan over, just enough to look under the backside of his right chest and shoulder. He had lost a lot of blood, too, on that side. Sucking in a breath, she whirled away and leaned over the edge of the cart. "I am not going to be sick. I am *not* going to be sick . . ."

"Easy," Saber murmured, moving up and cradling her head against his chest. His own memories of battle were probably just as unpleasant. What he could see of the wound suggested it was even nastier than an arrow-made wound.

"I'll . . . I'll be all right. I'm certain it passed through . . . but it could have pierced his lung. I think it nicked a major vein; he's losing . . . a lot of blood." She pushed away from her husband, braced herself again, and pressed her fingers to that still, pale throat. The pulse wasn't overly strong . . . but neither was it so weak she couldn't find it right off; he hadn't lost that much blood. Yet. That thought steadied her nerves a little. "The back of his shoulder's a mess, but with the bullet gone, you can use whatever magic you would for a bad stab from a sword or a spear—"

"That's all we need to know, Sister," Morganen informed her, patting her shoulder. "Saber, get her out of the cart so we have some room to enspell."

The eldest of them did just that, lifting Kelly out of the bed and out of the way, as Morganen and Wolfer climbed in to take her place. Evanor, too agitated to help, clutched at the side rail of the cart bed; Koranen held his shoulders, giving the missing brother's twin some moral and physical support. Kelly clung to Saber as long, tense minutes passed, as the two brothers muttered and gestured and did things over their brother.

Finally, Wolfer sat back on his heels, and Morganen stood, bracing his arm against the back of the driver's bench. The youngest of them blotted sweat from his forehead. "He'll live, but he's lost a lot of blood."

As the others relaxed, the second eldest of them lifted something red and green and slimey on his fingertips. "I'd like to know how he got seaweed in the wound, myself . . ."

Kelly paled again at the unsettling combination of colors.

"He apparently transformed on the deck when he landed, was shot and fell overboard, then managed to transform into a seal to swim back to shore," Evanor explained. "I had to choose between saving him, and going after Dominor . . . It's my fault!"

His hands slammed in fists against the side of the wagon. The brother lying on the bed jerked and cracked his eyes open with a groan. "Dom . . ."

Guilty that she hadn't heeded her instincts when Dominor had been so proud of his trading agreement—the opportunity to lure him onto their ship—Kelly looked at the others. "Can't we go after him?"

"With what?" Koranen asked her bitterly. "We don't have a ship! Not even a *rowboat*. We are *exiled* here on this stinking rock!"

"And Trev is the only one of us with a *useful* flying form," Wolfer added. Kelly noticed that his cheeks were flushed slightly, his gaze averted. His fingers were also rubbing the braid of hair around his wrist. That hand was clenched in a white-knuckled fist.

Saber shook his head, forcing himself to think rationally. "Lord Aragol said his people have few male magicians among them. If they took Dominor, it is because they want his services as a mage. They will keep him alive for that. We have to believe that."

"It's my fault. First I come here, bringing the first Disaster of the Mandarites arriving here, and now this new Disaster," Kelly muttered, looking at the once again unconscious Trevan. "I thought there was something odd about the proposed trade. I should have stopped him! I should have listened to my instincts, that there was something fishy about this suddenly friendly trading deal . . ."

Saber turned her to face him and lifted her chin. "You are no more at fault than any of us. Destiny is Destiny, in this universe. We can only do our best, even if it is not enough. You are not a Seer, to know the future, or to read the intent in a man's mind. Not even Morganen can do that. And Evanor, you did the right thing. If you had not brought back Trevan, we would have lost *two* brothers . . . and one much more certainly to death than the other. They will keep Dominor alive for his powers," he repeated. "*If* he keeps his temper and arrogance in check and bides his time until he has a sure chance to escape . . . he will escape and return to us."

"He is smart enough to do that," Wolfer agreed, climbing down from the back of the wagon, sighing. "Koranen, help me find materials to make a stretcher. Trevan is too weak to be moved without one."

"It will be a difficult, uncertain recovery, with so much blood lost," Morganen agreed grimly.

"Well, I'm a type O; you could give him some of mine," Kelly offered. At the other's blank looks, she reminded herself there were plenty of differences still left between her old world and this new one. Patiently, she explained. "That means I'm a universal donor. If you give someone the wrong type of blood, it could cause an immune reaction. But type O doesn't. I just have to make sure I only *get* type O, because all other types will cause me to have a reaction and die." They eyed her a little oddly at her remarks, and she shook her head. "It's too complicated to explain in detail, but trust me, you could give him a pint of my blood, about a small mug's worth at most, and it won't hurt me. That should be enough to help him recover."

"There *is* a spell to do it, to transfer blood from one person to another," Morganen agreed thoughtfully, "but it doesn't always work; maybe this 'type' thing is the reason why."

"Technology's knowledge harmed him. Maybe technology's knowledge can help him," Kelly agreed, then looked up at Saber as the head of their family, and ultimately responsible for Trevan's well-being, when he wasn't in any shape to respond. "Can we at least try?"

He nodded, troubled with the worry over both brothers, but a little relieved she knew about and could do something to help at least one of them. "Do what you can for him."

"Then we'll take him to my workroom," Morganen stated. "Kelly, come ahead with me; we'll need to prepare for his arrival. As soon as the others bring him, I'll do the spell, then he can be carried straight to his chamber to recover. Evanor, fetch some juice. Both of them will need it when the transfer is over, according to what I have read about this spell in my books."

Nodding numbly, Evanor moved away in compliance. It was a good thing, giving the shock-numbed twin a task to complete; he looked like he needed distracting. Morganen and Kelly headed to his tower just a short distance away, while the others moved to help Wolfer and Koranen enchant a temporary stretcher to carry Trevan.

Kelly sat on a stool, drinking greedily at the mug of juice Evanor had brought. She felt a little dizzy and would have liked to lie down for a few minutes, but she had given blood before—if not in a chanted, no-needles kind of way—and at least knew what to expect afterward. Except it felt like she'd had *two* mugs' worth drained from her. The others had carried Trevan off, worried in that silent, supportive way men often had when one of their own was wounded. Only Morganen remained behind with her, putting jars of ingredients back in their places; ingredients for the blood-transfer spell, and ingredients for a scar-removing poultice he had packed onto both sides of his brother's magically sealed wound.

This was the same workroom she had arrived in, and the workroom she had been in the night before. The mirror Morganen had used both times as a Gate between universes still stood in its cheval stand. It wasn't reflecting the room, however, but a scene from her own world, the gun shop where they had "borrowed" the gun that was still tucked at her back. Setting the mug down on the worktable beside her, she removed the gun and its beltline holster. She had never actually owned one, and she didn't ever want to again. Not after seeing the mess a bullet had made of Trevan's chest.

Stupid, testosterone-riddled things . . . "Morganen?"

"Yes, Sister?"

"Can we put this back?" she asked, lifting the nylon-holstered gun.

"Certainly."

"Um—just let me remove the fingerprints, first," she added, taking the weapon out and removing its clip, and the bullet in the chamber. Morganen passed over a couple scraps of cloth from a shelf, and she rubbed the bullet, the clip, and the gun. Using the cloth, she pushed the spare bullet into the spring-loaded clip with a bit of effort, yanked out the wrinkle caught by the mechanism, and nodded at the two pieces, clip and gun. "Okay. Guns don't hurt people on their own, but I don't want the wrong kind of person getting their hands on this and hurting others with it, in this realm. It's bad enough the Mandarites have their own version, however crude."

"Give me a moment." Morganen muttered, finishing his tidying, then fetching out a pot of greenish powder he had mixed in bulk the previous night.

Kelly, warned by his performance of the night before, quickly stuck her fingers in her ears. As he cast the powder at the glass surface of the mirror, he shouted several mystical words that still made no sense to her, but which rolled like thunder. Only when he had cast the fourth handful of powdered whatsits at the glass and it had flashed did she take her fingers away from her ears.

"Put it there, on that back counter, while the clerk is still busy with a customer," she directed.

He stretched out his hand, snapped a command, and the gun

floated easily into the mirror, rippled through it, and, as Morganen strained, hand trembling, the gun eased quietly to the counter. He repeated the procedure, and the clip followed it through. He dropped his hand just a second after the clerk turned around, about a second before the gun shop worker noticed the gun on the back counter. Normally there wasn't sound in a scrying mirror unless it was specifically enspelled for it, but this was a partial doorway between the two worlds. They could hear, if a little muffled and faint, the man's exclamation; first that the gun was out there at all, then in recognition of it as the missing weapon, and then a third time that it had been fired, and that four bullets were missing.

Morganen blotted at the sides of his nose, where the headband on his brow didn't catch the sweat. "Your universe is *very* hard to work magic in. I can only be thankful I'm here, not there, where it would be even harder. Here, at least, I can draw on various sources to augment my power. Over there, it's like moving through . . . what did you call it last night? That gray, stone-like stuff your people use to build things?"

"Concrete?" Kelly offered.

"That's it. *Con creet.*" He shook his head, leaning back against the worktable beside her. After a moment of watching the clerk punching buttons on a device called a *fone*, some sort of audio communicating device like a scrying mirror for the ear, he glanced at her. "Is there any place or person you want to see, before I close the link?"

Kelly started to shake her head. Then changed her mind. "Yes, there is. You showed me what's left of my house, but we didn't run across anyone who actually knew me," she stated, thinking only briefly of the burned timbers and bits of metal appliances that had survived the inferno. "Hope. I want to see my friend Hope."

Morganen stiffened slightly as she spoke, so she explained why, worried he didn't think it was worth the effort to locate Hope. "She was my closest friend in the medieval society, there. All of my old friends back in the Northwest have pretty much forgotten me, and my distant kin and I were never all that close . . . I should have attended three events in the last month and a half, ones that she would have been at as well; I want to make sure she's all right."

"You'll have to direct me," he reminded her, moving away from the worktable and over to the frame of the mirror. He cast a different kind of powder at the mirror, and it stabilized, cutting off the sound but not the view.

"You remember how to get back to the highway from the gun shop?" Kelly asked, staying on the stool, since she still felt a little unsteady from the blood transfer and watching over his shoulder from her perch.

"Yes—this way?"

"No, no, to the left, not the right. To the right is City Hall. There it is, in the distance. Head north—the way you're pointing—and get off two rampways down the road."

It was odd, navigating by what was essentially a double-width, full-length, wooden-framed, crystal-clear video; at least, that was what it looked like to her as he brushed frame and surface to control the view, now that the surface was solid and he couldn't pass his hand through it. Kelly judged the time of day, the lack of afternoon rush-hour traffic, calculated the passage of the days . . . and realized what day it was back on the other side of the looking glass.

"Keep going north!" she ordered, as he started to veer the view to the right, following the ramp. "I just realized where Hope is; she's at the fairgrounds. There's a medieval faire going on, if today's the Saturday I think it is."

"Just tell me where to go," he agreed amiably, adjusting their heading. "I am at the service of my queen."

She wrinkled her nose. "There aren't any visitors to impress, anymore."

"Then I'm at the service of the first of hopefully many more sisters-in-law," he corrected himself, smiling.

It didn't take long to locate the fairgrounds. The tents on the civic playing field in the distance drew them. So did the line of vehicles heading that way and the people getting out of their cars when the image in the mirror arrived at the site. Not just the ones already out there, clad in medieval garb, from tunics and trews to elaborate Rennaissance wear, but also the ones dressed in T-shirts, and baseball caps, jeans and sunglasses.

It seemed like a lifetime ago, but she remembered those dark, bigoted scowls all too well. The citizens who had harassed her to the point of burning her in her bed were converging on her friends in the Society. Her breath caught in fear as she realized *why* the local bullies were there. "Good grief! *Three* Disasters!"

"What's wrong?" Morganen asked, unsure why people going to a fair would upset her, however oddly dressed half of them were.

"Those are some of the same people who harassed me just for being in the Medieval Society! The ones who thought I was a witch—oh, my god!" Kelly slipped off the stool, eyes wide, as she hurried to Morganen's side.

"*That* looks like a longish version of a gun-thing," he murmured, focusing the view on the man taking a long metal object out of his pickup truck.

"It's a rifle, and you bet your sweet backside it's a type of gun-thing!" Kelly shot back, staring at the scene displayed before them. "This is not good . . ."

"If they harassed you to the point of burning down your home around you, then they're not here to discuss the weather," he agreed tightly. "We should *do* something—"

"I'm going back." Even as she said it, Kelly knew she was crazy. "Get that mirror open again; I'll be right back—I have to go get something."

"Kelly?" he questioned as she headed for the door. When she looked back at him, he stared at her with troubled eyes the color of her own. "You're leaving us? You're leaving Saber?"

Surprised, Kelly stopped and blinked at him. *She knew.* It was a liberating feeling, a bit shocking, but wonderful enough that she smiled. In fact, she outright grinned. "Not on your life, Morg—be ready to pull me back through at my command, too. I'm *staying* in this realm, when I come back through."

Nodding, he let her go. With a little smile of his own, as soon as she was out of his workroom, he thought, *Just as I'd hoped she would decide. One down, six more to go, before it's my turn.*

I must remember to have her point out this friend of hers to me, too.

TWENTY-THREE

Trevan was going to be all right. Saber reminded himself over and over of that. Evanor, still guilt-ridden about the only choice he could have made, was tending his younger brother. Koranen was hovering, and Wolfer had gone to lope down to the eastern beach in wolf-form to fetch back the second cart. It was Saber's duty to wake Rydan and inform him of the second Disaster that had happened.

A streak of strawberry-topped aquamarine raced across the garden, as he walked along the ramparts. It was Kelly, in a hurry to get somewhere. To get back to Morganen's tower, he realized. *But there's no reason for her to be in such a hurry; there's nothing anyone can do for either Trevan or Dominor, since we don't know that ship well enough to scry into its interior . . .*

Unless his little brother was attempting to pull off a miracle. Informing Rydan could wait; the oddest of the eight of them was sometimes difficult to summon from whatever nook in his tower he hid in to sleep. Rydan was often also unpleasantly uncommunicative when he was summoned during daylight hours.

Hurrying back through Trevan's northeast tower—their injured brother slept like most of the rest of them did in the comforts of the donjon wings, with the only exception their night-loving brother—Saber made it to Morganen's tower and started down inside. He heard his brother calling out a powerful, unfamiliar spell, the words thundering up the stairs toward him, as he descended the last curving flight. The spell was beyond Saber's ability to cast, that was certain.

Only by the miracle of some very strong aether-shielding spells was whatever Morganen was doing *not* affecting the weather outside. It was that strong of a spell. In fact, Saber wouldn't have even *known* about the spell, had he not entered Morganen's heavily shielded tower . . . and had the door at the bottom of the stairs not been standing open. Reaching the partially open door, he winced back from a flash of light, then peered cautiously around the corner, too much of a mage to abruptly interrupt whatever his brother was do-ing, in case the enchanting was at a delicate stage.

It didn't appear to be, though. Morganen and Kelly stood in front of his main scrying mirror, the large one that never left this chamber. She had something bundled in her hands, and his brother was eyeing her warily.

"Are you sure you want to do this?" Morganen asked his sister-in-law.

"Very sure. Ready?" she asked, looking at him. Neither of them saw Saber at the door off to the side.

"Always. Step on through," the youngest of them said.

Saber realized the image in the mirror was *not* of a ship, interior or exterior. Was not, from the many odd items in view, of any place in his known realm. Which meant it had to be her realm.

Which meant she was leaving him.

Shock held him still, as his wife stepped through. With her burned pajamas bundled in her hands.

The mirror stopped rippling the moment she was completely through, releasing him from his immobility. "*No!*"

"Whoa!" Morganen caught him, as he lunged across the room, reaching for her, trying to catch her. "Saber—*Saber!*"

"You *bastard*!" Saber snarled, knocking his youngest brother away, as he stared at the enspelled mirror and the strawberry-haired woman on the other side. His fists shook with the need to do something, anything to get her back. "How could you let her go?"

Sprawled on the floor, Morganen laughed—laughed! Torn between needing to go after his wife and throttling his brother, Saber glanced anxiously at the former and glared furiously at the latter. His brother sat up and shook his light brown head, still chuckling. "Relax, Saber. She's coming back."

"What?" Saber looked between the two of them again, the image of his wife on the other side, shouting and raising her bundle, her words faint but audible, and his brother still half-sprawled on the floor. "She's coming *back*?"

"*Yes*. And if you don't mind, I have to be ready to pull her out." Sighing, glad of his matchmaking efforts, despite the rough way he was "thanked" for them, Morganen pushed back onto his feet, still grinning. "I'm also getting a little tired of being knocked around by you, but I'll forgive you this time. *Again*. Since you love her so much."

Kelly stumbled as she came through, emerging in the middle of the confrontation, between the two lines the Middle Ages Society members and bigoted townsfolk had made. So did the two groups, falling back on both sides with exclamations of shock as she literally came out of nowhere between the two groups. Dizzy once more from running so much right after giving blood, Kelly oriented herself. She spotted her friend Hope, the one she had been looking for . . . but now was not the time for a reunion, however brief a time she would be here. Whirling to face the other way, she lifted her ruined pajamas high in the air.

"*Murderers!*" she shouted, catching everyone's attention with that word. She glared at the townsfolk who had harassed her, summoning up her feelings about what had happened, feelings she had set aside in the challenge of dealing with a new world and its new, strange rules. "It wasn't *enough* for you, was it, to spread all those lies about me, driving away my customers with your baseless, superstitious, *petty* fears!

"Do you *see* these?" Kelly demanded, waving the bundled clothes in her hand. She shook out the top, displaying the seared mark that had burned her ribs, then tossed it down. "Do you see *this*?" she added, shaking out the pajama bottoms, which were much more thoroughly scorched from roughly the top of the knee down. "I was in my *bed*, you *murderers*! Fast asleep, until the roof collapsed in flames *on top of me*!"

Tossing down the second garment, she glared at them, hands on her hips.

"That's right—arson and murder, because you're so gods-be-damned *stupid* enough to believe in superstition, of all things! This is the twenty-first century, well into the Age of Reason, you dumbheads, not the twelfth century!"

She stomped her aquamarine-clad foot, pajamas tossed on the ground and hands planted on her hips. This particular tirade had been inside of her all along, locked down and set aside because there had been no reason to let it out. But with even more vigor than Pandora, she was yanking open the lid here and now, and hers was a box of trouble she was going to aim right at the unmentionables facing off against her medieval society friends.

"Paganism is a *religion*, you prejudiced bastards, and it's perfectly legal to be practiced. *Guaranteed by the Constitution*, you gun-toting morons! The same gods-be-damned Constitution that gives you the right to *carry* those guns—and *what* were you going to do with them, today?" she demanded, striding toward one of the three cradling a rifle in the front line. "Were you going to try to kill someone *else*, today? Huh? Murder is the only thing against the law that I have seen happening here. And you asinines not only *attempted* it on me, you came here today to try it again!"

She turned and paced down the line, as the man she had faced down had the grace to look ashamed, awkwardly shifting his rifle out of the way. Kelly wasn't done.

"These people are historians! You've got people recreating the Battle of the Bulge, and Gettysburg, and World War II—*these* people recreate battles like Agincourt, and the days of William the Conqueror, and the War of the Roses!

"Do you accuse a man in a re-created, gray Confederate uniform of owning slaves in this day and age?—*Do* you?" she demanded, far more imperiously than she had acted as a queen. Turning as she strode back, she pointed at some of the people she knew. "*He's* a computer programmer! *She's* a waitress! *That* one's a doctor! A *doctor*! He's a podiatrist, a specialist in *foot* injuries, for God's sake! There aren't any witches here—witches don't *exist* in this world!"

"Then how did *he* get here, and you, too, and how did you survive that fire, if not by witchcraft?" one of the other gun-carrying men demanded as the others gasped and stepped back again. He held his rifle in one hand and pointed with the other. She looked where his finger jabbed.

Saber stood there, between the two lines of people. Glaring at the row of townfolk and doing his best to ignore the oddities of his wife's world. He had appeared in his sleeveless aquamarine overtunic, the muscles of his arms bulged rather impressively where they were folded across his chest. Saber knew he looked impressive, because some of the men facing his wife and her friends flinched when he twitched those muscles. It was good, because he wanted these barbarians to know he was here to protect his wife.

His words were slow, hard-chosen against the sluggish aether around him, but he managed to make the Ultra-Tongue spell work well enough to be understood. "*She* is not a 'witch' . . . but *I* am. Someone among you tried to kill my wife," he added on a growl. "I think that someone is *here*." Unfolding his arms, he spread them, voice rising with each hard-changed word. "*Coshak medakh valsa crodeh, inswat meerdah tekla var-deh! Pensih comri Verita-meh, Veritagis, sumol des-reh!!*"

The very air crackled with the force of the energy he was shoving through it. His hand slashed out, and the people in front of him reflexively ducked—but they couldn't avoid it. Not when his brother was feeding him power from their own world to supplement his own. Sometimes it paid to be one of the Eight Brothers of Prophecy.

Three people started to glow, luminescent yellow. Two of the rifle-wielders and one more who had come with them. "*There!*" Saber shouted, pointing at the trio. "*There* are your fire-makers, your arsonists—your would-be *murderers!*"

One man had dropped his gun, he was so busy whirling around and around, brushing and scrubbing and slapping at the glow that radiated from his clothes and skin. The other two simply took off, so fast that one left his baseball cap behind, and the other discarded his rifle as surely as the first of them had. The others who had accompanied them in the mindless fervor of an impending riot quickly scattered as well. The first one to glow stopped trying to get rid of the light, ignored his van, and fled on foot. Hollering about the demons of hell, or something like that, as he ran off.

Saber bent over, bracing his hands on his knees as he breathed hard from the effort of casting magic in this world; it was a truly bizarre realm, in more ways than just the visible ones. Kelly hurried over to his side, pleasing him with the concern in her aquamarine eyes. "Saber! Are you all right?"

He nodded, waited a moment, then straightened again and wiped at his face. "It is not easy to cast even a simple truth-finding spell, in this world of yours."

"Well, I'll be glad to get back to *ours*," she agreed under her breath, glancing back at the other half. Most of the society members were still in shock from their very odd display. Some had backed off, and a few had even started running for the far side of the fairgrounds, just as the mob of prejudiced townsfolk had. Only one ran *to* them. Her friend Hope.

"Kelly! You're alive! You're all right!"

"Hope!" Kelly caught her dark-haired friend and they embraced hard. "I've been wanting to get ahold of you—"

Hope pulled back and thumped her in the arm, her brown eyes glistening with emotion. "Where have you *been* all this time? I couldn't even find you!"

Some of the others were coming forward now, exclaiming over the odd show. Kelly quickly drew Saber to her side and cobbled together an explanation she hoped would pass. "Everyone, this is Dr. Nightfall; he's a scientist working for the government. He's been helping me put together evidence against the arsonists who almost claimed my life, because of their highly misinformed prejudice against the society. We didn't get enough to take them to court, but we're pretty sure those three men did it—that whole light show was just a trick of pre-dusting them with a photoluminescent powder while they were mixed into the crowd. Exposure to enough oxygen over time makes it glow strongly like that."

"But, *how* did the two of you appear here, out of thin air?" the doctor she had pointed out, demanded.

"That's sort of classified," Kelly improvised with a quick grimace.

"Even Dr. Nightfall doesn't know how it works. I suggest the rest of you take the news of this little would-be riot to the papers—but leave our names out of it, please. We're not supposed to be using this stuff for personal reasons," she added cagily, lying for a very good cause. "I don't want to get the government pissed off at us. Now, if you'll excuse us, we have some things to discuss with my friend, here."

Catching Hope's arm, she hustled her and Saber off among the tents at the edge of the field, seeking out her friend's jewelry-selling stall. Pulling them into the back of the tent erected behind the stall, she embraced Hope once again. Hope returned the hug with equal fervor.

"I *know* you're lying," Kelly's friend whispered in her ear, as Saber eyed the cot and its zippered sleeping bag, the flashlight-lantern on a folding table, and the other odds and ends of Earth civilization that weren't quite like anything he had ever seen before. "But I don't mind." She pulled back enough to eye Saber with her weighing gaze, then whispered once more in Kelly's ear, grinning lasciviously. "Just tell me there's more of them where *he* comes from!"

Kelly laughed and hugged her friend. Hope had her own oddities, but she was a good woman, and Kelly had missed her. "*Eight* of them, actually, and seven still bachelors—but you wouldn't *believe* where you'd have to go to find them." She shook her head. "Hope, I can't stay, here. I belong with—oh! Where are my manners?" She smacked her forehead and gestured at him. "Saber, this is Hope O'Niell. Hope, this is Saber of Nightfall, my husband—yes, that's his real name, and yes, I really married him.

"Hope, here, was my first and best friend when I moved here from my old home three years ago," Kelly added, hugging the somewhat younger woman around the shoulders.

Saber and Hope exchanged polite nods.

"I really *do* have to be going. And I don't think I'll be coming back very often. I like you, and I like most of the people in the Middle Ages Society, but I don't like living in this town, and I don't belong anymore where I used to live, back up near Seattle. So I'm staying with Saber and his brothers . . . do you understand what I'm saying?" Kelly asked her friend.

The other woman narrowed her eyes slightly. "You're trying to say we'll probably never see each other again."

"Sort of," Kelly agreed reluctantly. "Probably; it's pretty tough to come back here for a visit, from where I'm living now."

Hope shook her head. "We'll see each other again." When her strawberry-haired friend opened her mouth, she shook her head again, holding up her hand. "No, we will. Trust me." She eyed Saber once more, then smiled slyly. "If he's a witch, then so am I."

"Hope, he really *is* a mage," Kelly returned firmly, trying to convince her friend though she knew it was fruitless.

Her friend grinned. "I *know*—get it?"

Saber frowned at her, this woman his wife was making her goodbyes to. "You . . . are a *Seer*?"

"Not all the time, and only in occasional, irritating flashes of insight, but yes, I am. Oh, don't look so surprised!" she ordered Kelly, who was staring at her in uncertainty. "I told you when we met that I knew we'd be great friends, didn't I?"

"Well, yeah . . . but anybody could have guessed that," Kelly pointed out, recovering from her shock. She shook her head after a moment, then shrugged philosophically.

It didn't surprise her, somehow, that her friend professed to have psychic powers. Then again, Kelly had just grown used to a whole world of magic, so it shouldn't surprise her that her birth-universe held a little "magic" of its own, in its own way. Morganen had implied as much, shortly after her arrival. Now, however, this world felt like the stranger one of the two to Kelly.

Reluctantly, she sighed. "We really do have to go. Morganen's waiting for us. Elsewhere."

"So that's why I couldn't find you, then. All this time, you've been . . . elsewhere." Hope eyed the man in the tent with them, then pulled her friend aside. "Do me a favor?"

"What's that?" Kelly asked, curious.

"Give me a couple of months to settle my affairs, then invite me over. *Elsewhere*," she added pointedly with another glance at Kelly's handsome husband. When Kelly started to speak, her friend cut her off. "I don't belong in this world either, Kel. If those guys with the guns knew *I* could sometimes sense things, *my* house would be next. And they'd make abso-damned-lutely sure I was in it, too, because I actually *have* 'witch' powers."

Kelly bit her lower lip. She couldn't speak for the others . . . but she knew a few things. One of them was that, while the eight men now in her life were good companions, and her husband was all she could hope a husband to be . . . she wanted female companionship in her life. "Okay. But only on one condition. Take a midwife course or something; buy books on childbirth, and books on other stuff. Lots of different subjects. Where we are, they don't exactly have any hospitals or libraries nearby, and I don't trust any of the brothers to 'know nothin' about birthin' no babies!', if you know what I mean. Mages or otherwise."

"Deal! How do I contact you?" Hope asked, clasping Kelly's hand.

"I'll have Morganen watch you once in a while. Don't worry, I've seen his scrying mirror, and it *does* blank out the improper bits—it's a long story," Kelly added as Hope arched a brow in confusion. "I could also have him scry your kitchen, so all you'd have to do is put a note on your refrigerator saying 'Kelly, I'm ready to go' in big letters, and we'll contact you. Or whatever else you need to say to us. If we need to get in touch with you, we'll do the same. I know there are

a few things *I'd* like to have on the other side, if you don't mind doing a little shopping for me?"

Hope grinned and hugged her enthusiastically. "You won't regret
this! Give me a list of anything you want me to bring over, and I'll
bring it. Though if you ask for a lot, it may take me a year to get it
all together."

Kelly laughed and hugged her back. "Given the fact that everything I owned burned down in the fire, that's one heck of a shopping
list, all right. We'll send you some things to sell to pay for it all, I
promise. Gold or gems or something."

"We must go now," Saber reminded his wife. "Morganen said
the way would not stay open for very long."

Kelly nodded and released her friend. She stepped back and
caught Saber's hand. "I promise, we'll see each other again, on the
other side . . ." She broke off and grinned as it hit her, what the
'other side' was made of. "On the other side of the looking-glass.
Literally!"

Saber pulled his wife against him, holding her close. They would
go back together, for he wasn't about to leave his wife behind. He
eyed the woman in front of them. She stood about an inch shorter
than his wife, with more curves—though his wife, with the benefit
of plenty of regular meals, was developing some really nice ones—
naturally tanned skin, and longer, dark brown hair. Clad in clothes
that were almost properly styled, a two-layered skirt hiked up
slightly on one side and a ribbon-trimmed blouse that slipped off
one shoulder at the neckline, she was attractive in her own way.

Of course, she wasn't as beautiful as his Kelly, but for other
men . . . a thought made his mouth curve up in humor. "I did hear
what you said to my wife, and I think it would be a *good* thing for you
to come and join us. There are seven more verses to fulfill after all,
in our Song of Destiny. You just might be one of them."

"And I think it's about time to leave here, before we spend all day trying to explain *that*," Kelly asserted. "Morganen!" she called out, looking up at Saber with a smile. "Take us home!"

The world swayed and rippled around them. Out of the tent and back into a workroom a whole universe away. As soon as her balance steadied, Kelly turned around, looking at the mirror. Hope stepped into the view, first a blot of darkness, then her gypsy-clad body. She peered around the tent, waved her arms through the air . . . then smiled and shook her head. Straining, Kelly could just make out her words.

"What an adventure she must be having, in the other world!"

"I'll close the link in a few moments."

Kelly looked over at the youngest of the brothers. He looked tired, but his gaze was on the woman in the view. Since she couldn't read Morganen's expression, which was normally quite amiable and open, Kelly censored most of the thought that flashed through her mind. Most of it; she let only a roundabout trickle come out. "I, um, invited her to come across and live with us, when she gets all her affairs in order. Which will probably be in less than a year—Saber said it was okay, in case you were wondering."

Morganen grinned at her. "So quick to pin the blame elsewhere, Sister? How many times do I have to *tell* all of you? I *like* women! Go on, get out of here. Saber, have you told Rydan, yet?"

"No—I got distracted," Saber admitted with a glance at his wife. He tightened his grip on her hand. "We will do that now. Thank you, Brother."

"Just don't ever hit me again." His smile fading, Morganen watched them leave, then glanced toward the mirror again. He had left the link active, in case anything else might be needed to deal with the foreigners, but it didn't look like it was needed.

The woman in the view was frowning softly, touching her fingers to the air—to the exact plane where the Gate intersected her world.

There was no way for her to come across, not from her almost mag-icless side, but she evidently still felt its location. That startled Mor-ganen.

As he watched, she caressed her tanned fingers through that plane with a little smile. She had a gamin face, warm with a generous mouth and laughing brown eyes, lighter in hue compared to the dark lashes fringing them. If she could find the intersection zone in that realm of so very little magic . . . if she was sensitive to things, like a Seer . . . she *was* powerful. As Morganen studied her, she spread her hand flat just in front of the mirror's point of view, per-haps in a good-bye gesture, perhaps for one last touch of something truly magical in her life.

Of pure instinct, of unconscious will alone, his own body moved forward. His hand came up, spread flat . . . and passed into the mirror.

On the other side, from her perspective, a hand came out of nowhere. It was strong, supple, and almost as stoutly muscled as the other man's hand had been. Palm met palm, fingers touched fingers, and she *felt* the warmth and strength that was that masculine hand. A warm that zinged through her whole body instantly.

Gasping, Hope snatched her hand back. The hand pulled back be-fore her heart finished pounding hard, just as she started to re-extend her own hand to touch it again. Lowering her fingers, she eyed the air in front of her for a long moment in wide-eyed thought. Then smiled just a little, narrowing her brown eyes speculatively before silently re-minding herself to return to her business.

There were many things that needed to be done before she could go "Elsewhere," too—*her* current home and belongings were still perfectly intact and needed to be taken care of somehow, after all. Yes, it would probably take Hope O'Niell up to a year to disentangle herself from this realm, and it was time for her to get started.

On his side of the mirror, Morganen pulled his hand free and touched his palm to his chest, watching her. Kelly's friend. *Hope*. He had heard the words being exchanged while his brother and sister-in-law were on the other side of the looking glass, translated through his own draught of the Ultra-Tongue spell. It would be good to have a Seer in the family.

I suppose she might do for one of my brothers . . .

He watched her straighten her clothes, followed her with a touch of the frame as she went back out to the front of her tent to attend to her customers. She had a natural swing to her hips that no man would ever ignore and enough soft curves to remind him his own body was filled with hard planes by contrast. Those curves were exactly what he liked to see on a woman's body. With that awareness came a single, whispered thought passing through his mind.

Or she might do very well for me. Your Destined wife's title is "Hope" after all. Why can't it also be her given name?

But there were a lot of things to do, first: a brother to heal, another brother to rescue . . . and six more wives to secure, before he could think about walking the eight altars with a woman of his own.

It was no use tormenting himself by watching her, by entertaining thoughts about her. It seemed destiny had blatantly named her as his hope, but he could not claim her. Not until his brothers were wed so that he could be, too, according to Prophecy. As much as Morganen wanted to continue watching her, this friend of his eldest brother's wife . . . he had work to do. Turning and picking up a handful of the red binding-powder that resolidified the border between their worlds, he cast it on the mirror, firming its surface. Then reluctantly murmured the words that dissolved the scrying link entirely.

Her image, smiling and cheerful as ever as she talked with the other people at the fairgrounds, dissolved slowly into his own, his own face thoughtful and somber as he stood in his workroom. A murmur, a stroke of the frame, and he refocused it on a place in his own world, far enough away that it would have taxed most other mages to reach. Morganen simply drew in more power from the world around him, tapping into energies that only Rydan, of all of the rest of them, could feed upon during the height of a storm. Most of his moments of exhaustion were simply an illusion, after all, a facade to reassure his brothers that he was only a little more powerful than the strongest of them . . . instead of vastly more powerful than all of them combined.

Sometimes a little white lie, carefully maintained, was a mage's most useful spell.

The first place he looked was empty, no one there. Murmuring, edging the view along cautiously with a protective spell to keep this scrying from being sensed, he went looking for his quarry through once-familiar halls. It was time, and more than time, to start phase two of their Destiny.

TWENTY-FOUR

I thought you were leaving me."

Kelly bit her lower lip at that rough admission. The knowledge that she had hurt him, however inadvertently, hurt her. Proof her discovery was an accurate one. She really did love him. Tugging him to a stop at the landing where they had first fought, where she had first seen magic with the closing of the door there on the landing beside them, she looked up at her husband. "Saber, I have something to say to you."

This was it, then. She had given him something last night she had not wanted to give to him, when he had pressed her for her true feelings. He had heard the hesitation, the uncertainty in her voice last night. Cupping her chin to tilt it up, Saber looked into her aquamarine eyes, then closed his own, accepting it. "If you truly want to go back to your home, I will not stop you. Perhaps . . . perhaps true love *can* be one-sided, sometimes . . ."

Kelly gaped at him as he released her, unable to believe he was . . . he was . . . he was *giving up* on her, that was what he was doing! Just when she thought he was shaping up into proper husband material, he pulled a stunt like this? Her outrage needed an outlet . . . and it found one as she snapped her hand up and did to him what she had done once before to his now missing brother:

The Granny Doyle maneuver.

"*Ow!*" Saber grimaced as those fingers pinched his ear ruthlessly. She yanked his head down over the half foot of difference separating them, until their foreheads almost touched.

"I *love* you, you big oaf!" Kelly half-roared at him nose-to-nose, mad he would give up on her so easily. "*That's* what I was going to tell you!" Releasing his ear, she grabbed a fistful of the tunic she had made for him and kept him down at her level, fierce and freckled, unleashing her virago side ruthlessly on the big lug. "And if you think I'm going to let you go, *you* are an idiot!"

He blinked, stunned.

"That's right, an *idiot*! *This* is my home now, Saber—and don't you forget it! *My* home," she growled, yanking him so close by his tunic, their noses bumped awkwardly. "*My* castle! *My* kingdom! *My* husband! *Mine!*"

He gaped at her.

She grabbed both of his ears and kissed him.

Her possessiveness penetrated his thick skull thoroughly. Wrapping his arms around her waist and lifting her off her feet, Saber swung both of them around, until he staggered back against the outer wall and leaned there, holding her up against him, kissing her back with equal fervor. This was *his* wife, all right—and he had to believe her, for she had yelled like a termagant. Or rather, like a redhead. *His* wife. Between kisses, he managed to gasp, "Kelly—*Jinga*, I love you so much!"

"Mmm—ditto—" she managed through the kisses that peppered his face. Then slowed her assault on his spell-shaven skin.

Saber pulled his head back, resting it against the stones behind him warily. "What's wrong?"

"We've got to tell Rydan what's happened." She sighed, grimacing as she stopped kissing him. "And I feel guilty about wanting to toss you to the floor and make love to you, when I more or less created this whole Disaster—Dominor, Trevan, the Mandarites . . ."

"Destiny is Destiny," he reminded her, giving in to the inevitability of fate; he held her against him a moment more, then finally lowered her to the floor. "It would have happened regardless." Taking her hand, he pulled her up the stairs. "We can hate it and resist it all we want, but it is our Destiny, when Prophesied by a true Seer. Come; we'll tell my brother together."

It didn't take long to cross from Morganen's tower in the east to Trevan's in the northeast, then to Rydan's in the north, where the northern of the two mountain ranges on the island reached up closest to the castle. Abandoning the ramparts for the interior, Saber led Kelly to the room that was level with the ramparts on the guard wall, the only one Rydan allowed his brothers—and now his sister-in-law—to enter in his tower domain.

Inside, the window embrasures were all covered with black velvet drapes at their windows. Only one set of curtains stood open, letting a narrow beam of light stream through an arrow-loop slit into the otherwise dimly lit chamber. There were a few unlit lightglobes in their stands, their milky-white spheres unlit, and a large disc of steel, a gong hanging from a black-painted stand in the center of the room. Kelly thought the black, black, and more black theme was a bit overdone, but it was Rydan.

Saber strode to the frame, picking up the leather-wrapped stick hanging from a cord on the frame.

"I'm over here, Brother."

Startled, both of them turned and faced that deep-recessed, southeast facing window. Rydan stood in it; with his black clothes and black hair blending in with the black curtains pushed to one side, neither had really noticed him. He stood on the side away from the shaft of sunlight slanting in from the north, looking out at the view of his brother's tower from the shadows.

"Rydan, Trevan is . . ." Kelly tried to say, petering out when she couldn't quite bring herself to inform this intimidating, brooding man what had happened. It was her fault, in a way, if one believed in Destiny.

"Do you think I would not know when my own twin was injured?" the light-avoiding mage murmured as they eyed him, both uncertain where to begin.

"Dominor was kidnapped by the Mandarites," Saber explained, dropping the wand and moving to join his younger brother. Kelly joined them, as he continued. "Trevan tried to get to Dom, and they shot him. Trev got himself back far enough through the water for Evanor to get him up here, though he was badly hurt. His injury is healing, and he will recover, thanks to some successfully transferred blood from my wife."

Kelly reached up and touched Rydan's arm briefly. That made him look at her in surprise, as if he were not used to physical contact anymore; given she'd never seen his brothers so much as hug him, Kelly guessed that was a distinct possibility. She thought it was sad in a way. "I'm so sorry, Rydan. I keep thinking there was something I should have known better, something I could have prevented. But I seem to be plagued by Disaster, ever at my heel."

Oddly, that caused the black-haired man to let out a laugh. Or maybe not so oddly—it was Rydan, after all. Not even his brothers really understood him, from the puzzled look on Saber's face. His smile was slight and rueful. "Perhaps, now that you have confessed it, no more need come at your heel . . . and the rest of us can move on and do our best to avoid our *own* Destinies."

"*Good luck*," Saber muttered, and got an elbow in the ribs from his wife.

Rydan shook his head, his black hair sliding over his shoulders. "I could send a storm after their ship . . . but that would run the risk of drowning Dominor. How is his twin taking this?"

"Badly," Kelly stated, remembering how awful Evanor had looked, pale with tension, guilt, and grief.

"He tends your twin; I think to ease the guilt in losing his own," Saber added to his night-loving brother.

Rydan nodded. "I will help Morganen and Evanor make a mirror, tuned especially to Dom . . . but it will take time, without him here to speed the making and attune it quickly to his presence directly, extending the range most mirrors can scry. It *will* find him, eventually, and Ev will be able to to sing to him between then and now, to let him know he is not alone." He turned to leave and glanced at his sister-in-law. "He will be relatively safe, in the meantime. The Song of the Sons of Destiny assures it, if nothing else."

"I'll take your word for it," Kelly agreed with one last shiver for her new life in a realm filled with magic. She looked up at her husband, and he gripped her hand, comforting her silently with his support.

Though he could be a little jealous of the attention his brothers gave her, Saber couldn't begrudge Rydan's responses to his wife. Something in Kelly drew his taciturn, withdrawn, brooding brother out of his self-imposed shell, just a little bit. That alone was worth the price of watching his brothers admire the only female among them.

In the act of leaving them, Rydan turned and studied his kin. "Little Sister—do not go beyond this Chamber. Ring the gong, if you should ever have need of me, and I will hear it and come. Or summon me through Evanor. But venture only this far. The realm beyond is not for anyone else to know."

"I'll respect your privacy," Kelly agreed. She flicked her free hand at the room around them, smiling slightly. "I left each of your towers alone in my cleaning frenzy, didn't I? Though by rights, since Saber isn't a bachelor anymore, *his* is open to my inspection, now."

"We will discuss *that* elsewhere," Saber informed her, tugging her away, back outside as his brother disappeared down the stairs across from the door.

It was a long climb to the chamber at the top of the dome. When Kelly reached the top, she went to the eastern windows, the ones she had once crawled out of, thinking she had been locked in by what had merely been a stuck door. Kneeling on the cushioned bench seat, she looked out across the distant sea.

The ship wasn't even on the horizon anymore. Dominor was truly gone, snatched by a group of men desperate for a magical advantage over their gender-gifted foe. Kelly shook her head. "Talk about your battle of the sexes . . ."

"What do you mean?" Saber asked, standing behind her where she knelt on the benchseat of the shallow embrasure, here at the top of the donjon.

"On my world, only in the past hundred years have men stopped behaving very badly toward women—that tirade I gave?" she added, glancing back at him. "That *was* my world . . . and still is, in many of its kingdoms. We women have had to fight hard to be given the recognition that is rightfully ours, equal to men . . . and I have to confess that it still doesn't quite happen that way all the time even in my home country, a partnering of equals in the eyes of everyone.

"It worried me at first, when I came here. I thought you'd be the same way most of the men in the medieval era of my world would act, the era similar to the way you and you brothers dress. Chauvinistic, condescending, and way too arrogant for your breeches."

Saber shook his head. "Men and women are equal. Different, as you said, but equal. Had I been born a woman, I would still be the heir to Corvis. Had I been born a woman, I would still have magic . . . or perhaps not," he murmured thoughtfully. "I do not think I could have been born anything else, the same as my brothers; we are the Eight Sons of Destiny, after all." He smiled at her. "Which makes us rather special, and deserving of special women in our lives."

Kelly planted her hands on her hips, looking back at him over her shoulder. But she was smiling as she did it. "Oh, do you, now?"

Pulling her backside against his hips, Saber smiled. "I will show you just how special you are to me, and how special I hope to forever be to you." His smile faded a little and was replaced by intensity in his gray eyes. His firm grip gentled and slid from her hips to her belly, cupping her tenderly in the curve of his arms. "Will you bear my children, Kelly? Will you make me happy?"

"Tirades, pinches, Disasters, and all?" Kelly asked, mulling it over for a moment. But only a moment. "If you can *survive* me, I suppose I can manage that."

He grinned and pulled her off of the bench, tugging her over to the bed. "I know something horrible you can do to me, if you do it in just the right way."

"And that would be . . . ?" she asked, intrigued and mystified by what he meant. She *hoped* he meant hot, passionate romping on their bed. That was one of her favorite parts of this whole marriage thing so far, though she was positive there were even better things waiting for them in the future. Weird as it was, she was getting used to this world.

His gray eyes gleamed like laughing, desire-hot steel, as he lowered her to the bed, grinning lasciviously as he braced himself on his elbows over her. "Make me 'eat pillow.'"

Laughter rang out from the top of the donjon.

His quarry was leaning over a pool of water, examining the creatures that swum below the surface. She was alone, her brow pinched in a tight, worried frown. Morganen tipped the viewpoint in his scrying mirror until it looked up from the surface, and connected the two with a brief, quiet chant.

"*Oh!*" The woman on the other side quickly looked around her, then down at him again, brushing her long curls out of the way where they had escaped her braid. Her whisper hissed across the distance between them. "Morganen. I didn't expect you to call . . ."

"I know. But it is time."

She paled slightly and brushed her hair away from her face again. "Now? This will *not* put him in a good mood, you know that. I'm . . . I'm afraid."

"But it *is* your Destiny. *Now*," he added firmly, as she hesitated a moment more. "As soon as you can safely get free—and do not delay. There is no telling what *he* might do, when you have put him off for so long. The odds of Fate are already stretched too thin."

Nodding, she twitched, listening to a sound too faint in the connected surfaces of mirror and reflective water for him to hear. Morganen quickly cut the connection. This was a dangerous game both of them played, one they had been playing for three and more years. So close to completion, discovery and failure was *not* a healthy option. He was patient, and watchful; she was braver than she knew, and very careful.

It would work. Hopefully.

And so it begins . . . again.

Song of the Sons of Destiny

The Eldest Son shall bear this
   weight:
If ever true love he should feel
Disaster shall come at her heel
And Katan will fail to aid
When Sword in sheath is claimed by
   Maid

The Second Son shall know this
   fate:
He who hunts is not alone
When claw would strike and cut to
   bone
A chain of Silk shall bind his hand
So Wolf is caught in marriage-band

The Third of Sons shall meet his
   match:
Strong of will and strong of mind
You seek she who is your kind
Set your trap and be your fate
When Lady is the Master's mate

The Fourth of Sons shall find his
   catch:
The purest note shall turn to sour
And weep in silence for the hour
But listen to the lonely Heart
And Song shall bind the two apart

The Fifth Son shall seek the sign:
Prowl the woods and through the
   trees
Before you in the woods she flees
Catch her quick and hold her fast
The Cat will find his Home at last

The Sixth Son shall draw the line:
Shun the day and rule the night
Your reign's end shall come at light
When Dawn steals into your hall
Bride of Storm shall be your fall

The Seventh Son shall he decree:
Burning bright and searing hot
You shall seek that which is not
Mastered by desire's name
Water shall control the Flame

The Eighth Son shall set them free:
Act in Hope and act in love
Draw down your powers from above
Set your Brothers to their call
When Mage has wed, you will be
   all

—THE SEER DRAGANNA